CRIME THROUGH TIME II

Sarah Smith shows us life behind the cabarets in fin-de-siècle Paris in "Fearful" . . . Investigators are hired to prevent the death of William the Conqueror in eleventh-century England in *Edward Marston*'s "Domesday Deferred" . . . *Dianne Day* takes us to late-Renaissance Venice in "Anna and the Mirror" . . . Hugo and Nebula Award winner *Nancy Kress* presents her first historical mystery, "A Scientific Education" . . . and many more amazing stories from throughout time—and throughout the world . . .

MORE MYSTERIES FROM THE
BERKLEY PUBLISHING GROUP...

SISTER FREVISSE MYSTERIES: Medieval mystery in the tradition of Ellis Peters...

by Margaret Frazer

THE NOVICE'S TALE	THE SERVANT'S TALE	THE BOY'S TALE
THE OUTLAW'S TALE	THE BISHOP'S TALE	THE MURDERER'S TALE
THE PRIORESS' TALE	THE MAIDEN'S TALE	

PENNYFOOT HOTEL MYSTERIES: In Edwardian England, death takes a seaside holiday...

by Kate Kingsbury

ROOM WITH A CLUE	DO NOT DISTURB	PAY THE PIPER
SERVICE FOR TWO	EAT, DRINK, AND BE BURIED	CHIVALRY IS DEAD
CHECK-OUT TIME	GROUNDS FOR MURDER	RING FOR TOMB SERVICE
DEATH WITH RESERVATIONS		

GLYNIS TRYON MYSTERIES: The highly acclaimed series set in the early days of the women's rights movement... ''Historically accurate and telling.''—Sara Paretsky

by Miriam Grace Monfredo

SENECA FALLS INHERITANCE	NORTH STAR CONSPIRACY	THE STALKING-HORSE
BLACKWATER SPIRITS	THROUGH A GOLD EAGLE	

MARK TWAIN MYSTERIES: ''Adventurous...Replete with genuine tall tales from the great man himself.''—*Mostly Murder*

by Peter J. Heck

DEATH ON THE MISSISSIPPI
A CONNECTICUT YANKEE IN CRIMINAL COURT
THE PRINCE AND THE PROSECUTOR

MAGGIE MAGUIRE MYSTERIES: A thrilling new series...

by Kate Bryan

MURDER AT BENT ELBOW   A RECORD OF DEATH

CRIME
THROUGH
TIME II

EDITED BY

Miriam Grace Monfredo

and

Sharan Newman

BERKLEY PRIME CRIME, NEW YORK

CRIME THROUGH TIME II

A Berkley Prime Crime Book / published by arrangement with the editors

PRINTING HISTORY
Berkley Prime Crime edition / August 1998

All rights reserved.
Copyright © 1998 by Miriam Grace Monfredo and Sharan Newman.
This book may not be reproduced in whole or in part,
by mimeograph or any other means, without permission.
For information address: The Berkley Publishing Group,
a member of Penguin Putnam Inc.,
200 Madison Avenue, New York, NY 10016.

The Penguin Putnam Inc. World Wide Web address is
http://www.penguinputnam.com

ISBN: 0-425-16410-1

Berkley Prime Crime Books are published
by The Berkley Publishing Group,
a member of Penguin Putnam Inc.,
200 Madison Avenue, New York, NY 10016.
The name BERKLEY PRIME CRIME and the BERKLEY PRIME CRIME
design are trademarks belonging to Berkley Publishing Corporation.

PRINTED IN THE UNITED STATES OF AMERICA

10 9 8 7 6 5 4 3 2 1

CONTENTS

Introduction

P.D. James gives her own account of her beginning as a crime-writer: she was the inquisitive child who wanted to know about Humpty Dumpty: did he fall or was he pushed? I, on the contrary, was from an equally early age fascinated by historical mysteries, as and when I came across them in my undirected, omnivorous historical reading in the Oxford (free) Public Library. Did Mary Queen of Scots actually have her husband Darnley set up to be killed by the Scottish nobles—or did Scottish nobles of the sixteenth century need no encouragement from a woman to do what came naturally? This is only one example; although it is one to which I eventually produced my own solution, thirty years after first reading the tragic (or murderous) Queen's story.

In one sense, of course, all writing of history is an attempt to solve the particular mystery of what happened when (and, if you like, whodunit). But there is another, inner mystery concealed there, which has always been of special interest to me: what were they like, our ancestors, so near and yet so far? Like us, with the same primitive emotions of love, hatred, jealousy, greed (all the passions that lead to murder)? Or utterly unlike us, their primitive emotions undergoing a sea change, thanks to very different societies and circumstances?

It is not a coincidence therefore that I have always enjoyed the use of history as a background to fictional mystery, ranging from Josephine Tey's classic *Daughter of Time*, to Agatha Christie's books with an Egyptian or archaeological background (among my favourite of her work; it seems to suit her talent to be distanced from her familiar cosy world of English murder). Josephine Tey, roughly speaking, goes for the strangeness of the past, where Agatha Christie preserves roughly the same types.

Reading *Crime Through Time* II with enormous pleasure (and not a little enlightenment), I was struck by the variety of responses by the nineteen authors to the problem of the past. Eric Hobsbawm, the Marxist historian, recently celebrated his eightieth birthday by declaring that "human beings stay much the same." This is certainly the line taken by a good many of the writers, giving us well-crafted stories with colourful backgrounds, which use the language of our own time as though to emphasize the sameness. Walter Satterthwait's cheerful exploration of the world of the hunters and gatherers is told in modern-speak: "You don't really know what cold is . . . until you wake up and look outside the cave and you see a big old glacier in the garden trampling the petunias . . ." Similarly J. M. Roberts suggests that the Romans "can seem like modern people dressed in togas"; although his story—quite a history lesson in its own right—uses the arrival of "barbarian" prisoners of war and the racism of the ancient world as part of his plot.

Ed Hoch, on the other hand, focuses on the experiences of Genghis Khan's slave, when his master was in mid-plunder of Russia, and far from employing contemporary language, plunges us into a world of yurts or tents ("The largest yurt of them all was reserved for Genghis Khan"), fermented mare's milk and catapulted fireballs. The adventures of L. J. Rowland's samurai detective in seventeenth-century Japan, actually depend on the particular society in which he finds himself: there is for example clever use of a broken netsuke, which could not be transported into a modern setting. Similarly, William Wu's Chinese who came to work in America in the late nineteenth century mixes Confucius with the setting of Death Valley, in a way that must be special to that time and place—and those imported labourers.

Certain writers have been inspired by true stories, notably Jan Burke, who nonetheless provides a very stylish story, in a way that the original was probably not. Elizabeth Foxwell writes a mystery round spiritualism and the *Titanic*—the latter is a perennial subject for fiction, but the spiritualism gives it a special twist. C. N. Douglas goes even further in introducing Holmes' femme fatale, Irene Adler, and Edward II as the Prince of Wales and Gilbert and Sullivan, and the telephone in its early form, and mesmerism . . . Lastly, I suppose as a British writer of the so-called "evacuee" generation, I was especially pleased that this extraordinary social experiment conducted in World War II, in theory to provide safety for British children from air raids, has been seen as fit for a historical mystery. May others follow!

In the meantime, the whole of the rest of history is waiting to welcome crime-writers. The mystery still remains to be solved: dying (and killing) just like us or totally different?

ANTONIA FRASER

Preface

The first *Crime Through Time* collection of stories grew out of the friendships we have with other writers of historical mysteries and our desire to allow the reading public to sample the wide variety within the field. We were extremely gratified both by the quality of the material we received and the enthusiasm of all concerned. It encouraged us to prepare another anthology of original historical mystery stories; thus, *Crime Through Time* II.

For this second collection we invited some of the first group of writers to join us again. Anne Perry, Gillian Linscott, Edward Marston, Edward Hoch and Maan Meyers have all given us new work. To our delight, other established historical writers, such as Robert Barnard, Walter Satterthwait, Carole Nelson Douglas and John Maddox Roberts, who were unable to contribute to the first collection found the time for this one.

Moreover, the interest in writing (and reading) historical mysteries has markedly increased in the past year; consequently we found a number of other authors we wanted to invite. Some have recently begun new series. Dianne Day, Sarah Smith and Laura Joh Rowland have all received a great deal of attention and praise for their very different, excellent mysteries. We are glad to welcome them to the ranks. Also, it is with great pleasure that we introduce Elizabeth Foxwell, with "Unsinkable," her first published story. We are sure it won't be her last.

The reader will also notice authors in *Crime Through Time* II who aren't associated with history, or even mystery, writing. Nancy Kress, Michael Coney and William Wu are well known to readers of fantasy and science fiction, but they are also secret historians who are using these pages to let the world know of their previously hidden interest. And Jan Burke, while content in her contemporary Irene Kelly series, has a degree in history and a library of research books crying to be consulted. We happily allowed these authors to share their interest here.

We are also grateful to Antonia Fraser for writing the introduction to this volume. Since she excels both in the field of mystery and in her more academic historical work such as *The Gunpowder Plot*, we felt she would be the perfect person to comment upon our blending of both.

Early twentieth-century author Amy Lowell said that books are "the very heart and core of ages past." Your editors trust that you, the readers, will enjoy these stories of ages past as much as we enjoyed collecting them for you.

SHARAN NEWMAN
MIRIAM GRACE MONFREDO
August 1998

CRIME
THROUGH
TIME II

*W*alter Satterthwait has lived on both sides of the United States and abroad in Africa, Thailand, Greece, and the Netherlands. He has worked at a variety of jobs, including that of encyclopedia salesman, which may account for the wide range of knowledge displayed in his writing.

Like many of our authors, Walter writes books set in the present as well as the past. *Accustomed to the Dark* is the most recent in his contemporary series featuring Santa Fe detectives Joshua Croft and Rita Mondragon. The first in the series, *Wall of Glass*, was nominated for a Shamus award.

His history mysteries feature some of the more colorful real-life characters of the nineteenth and early twentieth centuries, such as Lizzie Borden (*Miss Lizzie*), Oscar Wilde (*Wilde West*) and most recently *Escapade*, a new twist on the country house murder, at which Harry Houdini and Sir Arthur Conan Doyle must solve the crime. *Escapade* was nominated for an Agatha award; and in France it won the Prix du Roman d'Adventures.

Walter Satterthwait likes to alternate between writing the Croft books and his historical mysteries because he feels it keeps him on his toes, and that this is a good thing, "even if I sometimes get cramps."

For his contribution to this anthology, he must have cramped to his neck. It is the first-person account of the first detective, long, long before forensics, magnifying glasses or even a vocabulary to describe the crime.

MURDER ONE
A BERTHOLD THE MEADMASTER STORY

Walter Satterthwait

Nowadays, of course, murder is an everyday kind of thing. Lie in your bed, snoring peacefully in the privacy of your own home, and you'll likely get your lifeline severed by some sneak thief. Walk along the street, minding your own business, and you'll likely get it snipped by some itinerant psychopath.

What does this teach us? That things have basically gone to hell. And that itinerant psychopaths keep better hours than sneak thieves. I blame agriculture, myself. It wasn't like that back in the old days, back when we were mostly hunters and gatherers. Back then we'd never heard of murder. Didn't even have a word for it. Not that everything was peaches and cream. We had mastodons to deal with, and cave bears, and saber-tooth tigers. And we had the weather. You think it gets cold now, I suppose, when winter comes around and the snow starts to flake away from those low gray clouds. You don't really know what cold is, let me tell you, until you wake up and look outside the cave and you see a big old glacier in the garden, trampling the petunias under a couple hundred feet of dirty hissing ice and ragged groaning rocks. We moved around a lot, back then.

But you want to hear about the murder. The first murder. It would make for a better story, probably, if I could tell you that it happened on a dark and stormy night, with the rain hurtling down and the wind rattling through the trees. But it wasn't like that. That's the nature of nature, of course, and that's why we storytellers get paid so well to improve upon it.

Okay. Once upon a time. I was sitting on the cave floor, in the anteroom, pounding at the acorns, when my wife came sauntering in. This was my first wife, Ursula.

"Marta wants to see you," she said.

I lowered my mortar. "Marta?"

She nodded, a bit impatiently. She was like that, Ursula. Lovely, very lovely, with long brown hair down her back, and down her front, too; pretty much everywhere, in fact. She had a beautiful brow ridge, wide and steeply sloped, that she sometimes cracked walnuts on, absent-mindedly, late at night as we sat around the fire. These days you don't see very many brow ridges like hers; and I've got to confess that now and then, when I'm alone in bed watching the firelight flicker softly against the ceiling, I still dream about Ursula's.

She was lovely, yes, but she was also definitely impatient. She said, "Marta, yes."

"Wants to see *me*?"

She rolled her dark brown eyes. "That's what I said, isn't it?"

"But why?"

"How would I know? Klaus came and said she wanted you." Klaus was Marta's consort that year.

"But I haven't done anything," I told Ursula.

She smiled a sour smile. "I'll say." If it hadn't been for that brow ridge I would've run away, long before this.

I set down the mortar. "I guess I'd better go find out what she wants."

She snorted. "I guess you'd better."

I stood up, brushed the chips of acorn shell from my chest, turned to leave.

"Wait a minute," said Ursula. I turned back to her.

She frowned, impatient again. "You're not going like that?"

I looked down at myself. I was naked, but I was always naked then. All of us were.

I looked at her. "Like what?" I asked.

"You've got little bits of acorn all over your face." She moved closer, brushed at my beard—almost affectionately, I thought. I grinned and reached for her, and she stepped smartly away.

"Forget it," she said. "You haven't got time."

I grinned again, my best grin, the one that Ursula used to say made her legs go all wobbly. "How about later," I said, "when I get back?"

"I'll be at my sister's," she said. Ursula's legs hadn't wobbled for a long time, and neither had we. "I won't be back till late. Maybe tomorrow morning."

"Oh."

She flapped her hands at me, fingers loose. "Go, go. Marta's waiting."

I went. It was a beautiful spring morning, bright and warm and spectacularly sunny; no dark, no gloom at all. The blue sky was stretched taut over our narrow little valley, and the trees that draped the hillsides were blazing with green. Children were running along the footpaths that wound through the tall shiny grasses, giggling and hooting. Off in the distance, a dog yapped merrily. It should have cheered me, all of it; but the fact is, I was uneasy. A summons from Marta usually meant that something was seriously wrong somewhere, and during the walk to her cave I spent most of my time trying to figure out what it might be. Always a waste of time—trying to anticipate the Gods' little pranks.

Marta was in the ceremonial chamber, sitting on her ceremonial throne, wearing her ceremonial robe. This was the skin of a lioness, smudged with woodsmoke now, and slightly tattered. (It was supposed to provide Marta with wisdom. It hadn't done that for the lioness, obviously, or she'd still be wearing it; but religion, as history teaches us, isn't necessarily rational.)

Sitting in a desolate heap on the floor in front of Marta, her legs crossed, head lowered, shoulders hunched, long black hair streaming forward, was young Karla, Marta's niece. And sprawled back along a stone bench at one side of the chamber was Berthold the Meadmaster. His long legs were outstretched, and his hands were raised back behind his narrow head, both the hands and the head resting against the gray wall of rock. He was smiling faintly as he steadily gazed at me. Lying beside the bench was that infernal leather bag of his, large and bulging. My heart sank.

"Greetings, Doder, Son of Watt," Marta said to me. More ceremony.

"Greetings, Most Sage and Slender Queen," I said. I glanced at Berthold. Neither his gaze nor his faint smile wavered.

"We have a problem," Marta told me. As though the presence of Berthold hadn't already made that clear.

"Oh?" I said, pretending interest. "What might that be?"

"Gunter is dead."

"Ah," said I. Gunter was Karla's husband. I looked down at Karla, who still sat hunched forward, lost in grief. "Sorry about that, Karla." I looked back at Marta. "So what's the problem?"

I wasn't being callous. I'd actually been fairly fond of Gunter, a nice young man and a fine hunter. But back then, dying happened a lot more frequently than it does now—the mastodons, etc.; and also some very unpleasant diseases, all of them unattractive and most of them fatal—so we took it with a certain nonchalance.

Marta said, "We're not entirely sure how he died."

I frowned. "What do you mean?"

"We think he may have been—" As I said, there was

no word for it, and Marta hesitated before she came up with: "—destroyed."

I looked from her to Karla, whose shoulders suddenly shook—she was sobbing. I looked to Berthold. His smile had gone, but he was still watching.

I looked back to Marta. "Destroyed? By what?"

"By one of the Outlanders, we think."

I frowned. "But why would an Outlander, um, destroy Gunter?"

"We don't know."

"And what makes you think it was an Outlander who did it?"

"This," said Marta, and she held up a narrow strip of cloth, gray and frayed, and offered it to me.

I took it. The strip had been torn from a larger piece, and each end of it was crumpled, as though the two ends had been tied together. It was Outlandish, all right. At the time, we didn't have cloth. Didn't make it, didn't use it.

And it carried the smell of Outlander, a smell not unlike cumin, but a cumin that had gone somehow rank; a dense stench that burned the nostrils and clawed at the throat. It was faint on the cloth, but it was unmistakable.

"Where was this found?" I asked Marta.

"Wrapped around Gunter's neck. It was what destroyed him. He was strangled."

Somehow I stopped myself from hurling the filthy thing to the ground. We were nonchalant about dying, as I said; but not about the dead themselves. The dead we buried as soon as they hit the ground. Whatever it was that killed them, it might be catching.

"Ah," I said, and I nodded sagely, and handed the strip back to Marta with a casualness that was maybe a tiny bit brisk. Off to the side, I noticed, Berthold was smiling again.

"And what would you like me to do?" I asked Marta, although by then I already knew.

"We have instructed Berthold to investigate. He has requested your assistance."

"Ah," I said again. "Well, of course, Your Slenderness, he does me great honor. But surely there are other people in the clan who might provide—"

"Berthold has requested you. And, if you'll remember, you were of great help to him in the matter of The Missing Vat of Tasty Soup."

"Yes, but—"

"And also in the matter of The Disappearing Necklace of Pretty Blue Stones."

"Yes," I said, "but those were all simple thefts. This is much more complicated, Your Suppleness. I—"

Marta raised a hand. "The Great Mother wishes it."

Well, that was that, of course. This was before your Lightning Gods and your Cattle Gods and all the rest. Back then, the Great Mother wasn't just the Supreme Being, she was basically the only Being. If she—or Marta, her representative—wanted something done, it got done.

I sighed—silently—and nodded. "Of course," I said.

Marta returned the nod. "The Great Mother thanks you," she said, and she turned to the Meadmaster. "Berthold?"

Berthold lowered his hands to his lap and raised his eyebrows attentively. "If I might be permitted to ask a few questions of Karla?"

"Certainly. Karla?"

The young woman raised her head. I saw that her eyes were puffy, her face blotched. Her lower lip was caught between her teeth, as though she were trying to stop it from trembling. She sniffled once, nodded, and then turned toward Berthold. She seemed to me very vulnerable then, and even younger than her fourteen years.

Berthold swung his long legs off the bench of stone and sat forward, resting his arms on his thighs, clasping his hands together between his outspread knees.

"Now," he said. "Karla. Please tell me what happened this morning."

Karla glanced at Marta, who nodded. Karla looked

back to Berthold. "I was asleep," she said, "when suddenly I heard a sound. A cry. It woke me up. The fire had gone out, but dawn was coming and there was enough light for me to see. I looked around. The cave was empty. Gunter was gone."

She sniffled again. "And then, as I sat there, I heard the cry again—"

"This second cry," said Berthold. "Was it as loud as the first?"

Karla nodded. "Yes. Yes, I think so. I knew it was Gunter, and I rushed from the bed and out of the cave. At first, I saw no one. And then I saw Gunter. He was lying about thirty feet from the entrance. I thought that he'd slipped, fallen down and hurt himself. I ran to him."

She sniffled again, took a deep breath. "He was lying on his back, and *that*"—she nodded toward the strip of Outlander cloth, which Marta had draped along the arm of her throne—"*that* was wrapped around his neck."

"He was lying," said Berthold, "on his back?"

"Yes. His face was . . . blue, almost black, and his tongue was sticking out. It was *terrible*. I untied that *thing* and I ripped it from his neck. I—"

"The piece of fabric," said Berthold. "It was tied in the front?"

She frowned, puzzled. "Yes . . . Why do you ask?"

He smiled. "Simple curiosity. Please continue."

"Yes," she said. "It was tied in the front, below his chin. I ripped it off and I shook him, tried to awaken him. I tried and tried. But I couldn't." She lowered her head once again.

"And what then?" asked Berthold.

She looked up. "I ran to the cave of my sister, Heidi. She's ill, she's been with fever now for two days, but I needed help, I was desperate. Heidi was asleep, but Ulrich was awake, her husband, and he ran back with me to Gunter. He tried to revive him, too. But it was no use. Gunter was . . . dead."

"And then?" asked Berthold.

Karla glanced again at Marta, then back at Berthold. "And then we came running here, and we told Marta, and she sent for you, and"—Karla nodded toward me— "for Doder."

Berthold nodded. "And where is Ulrich now?"

Marta spoke. "I sent him back, to stand guard over the body, and stop people from trying to bury it."

"Excellent," said Berthold. He turned to me. "Well, my friend," he said, "time for us to get to work, eh?" He bent down, grabbed the rope that was looped around the top of the bulging leather bag. He stood up and held the bag out to me.

I took it. It was as heavy as I remembered it being. It was filled with crocks, and the crocks were filled with mead. Sighing again, I swung it up over my shoulder.

"Careful," Berthold told me. He turned to Marta. "My queen?"

"Yes?"

"May I take that piece of fabric? It may prove useful."

"Certainly," she said. She lifted it from the arm of the throne and handed it to him. Leaning toward me, he tucked it into the narrow opening of the bag. Then he clapped me merrily on the shoulder. The other shoulder. "Off we go," he said. It was, of course, to carry his mead that Berthold needed an "assistant." For some reason, several years ago, he'd taken a fancy to me. Not in any physical way—I don't think that Berthold had ever taken a physical fancy to anything, except mead. But he had decided that, during these investigations of his, he would have no one else haul his supply from place to place.

He had already cracked open his first crock by the time we arrived at our destination. Gunter and Karla's cave was one of the smaller ones, at the edge of the valley, on the other side of the mastodon tracks. As we approached along the dusty path, through the trembling fields of grass, we saw Ulrich standing alone. When we were nearer, we saw the body. It lay in the middle of the path, five or six feet away from where Ulrich stood.

"Greetings, Ulrich," said Berthold, almost cheerfully.

Ulrich was short, dark brown, thin and sleek. His face was grim as he nodded. "Greetings, Berthold," he said. "Greetings, Doder."

"Terrible thing, isn't it?" said Berthold. He took another swig of mead.

Ulrich nodded sadly. "Terrible. Why would they do such a thing?"

Smiling, Berthold raised a single eyebrow. "Whom do you mean?"

Ulrich looked at him, frowning. "But wasn't it the Outlanders? That strip of cloth . . . ?"

Berthold smiled again. "Ah yes. The Outlanders. Why indeed?" He shrugged. "Well, that's precisely the sort of thing we're here to learn." He turned to me. "Oh, stop puffing, Doder. You can set it down now."

With a grunt, I swung the bag from my shoulder, set it down on the ground. Crocks clinked and clanked within.

Looking down at the body, Berthold sipped thoughtfully at his crock, then said, "He certainly does look dead, doesn't he?"

That he did. Gunter's eyes were shut. His pale, stiffened tongue poked obscenely from his open mouth. The patches of skin that showed through his beard and hair were mottled a bluish-black, like an enormous bruise. Gunter was—had been—a small man, about the same size as Ulrich. He seemed even smaller now, somehow shriveled, as he lay there silent and naked against the brown dust. Berthold glanced left and right. "No good tracks," he said, and turned to Ulrich. "You and Karla did a fine job of disturbing the ground."

Ulrich frowned, as though wounded. "But we were trying to revive Gunter. We weren't thinking about tracks."

"Clearly not," said Berthold. He sighed. "Very well.

Suppose you tell me exactly what happened this morning.''

What Ulrich told him was more or less what Karla had said. He had been tending to his wife, Heidi, when Karla came running into the cave, hysterical. After a moment, he had understood that something had happened to Gunter. He had followed Karla back here, attempted to revive Gunter, then run with Karla to Marta's cave.

Berthold nodded. ''Your cave,'' he said, ''yours and Heidi's, is another hundred yards into the forest? In that direction?'' He nodded toward the south.

''Yes.''

''Did anything unusual occur this morning, before Karla arrived?''

''No.''

''You heard nothing, saw nothing?''

''No. I was inside the cave, Berthold. With Heidi.''

Once again, Berthold nodded. ''When you first came to the body with Karla, did you see anyone about?''

''No.''

Berthold sipped again at his mead. ''And after Marta sent you back here, was the body as you'd left it?''

''Yes.''

''And no one has interfered with it since?''

''Some people came by and wanted to bury it. But I told them that Marta wanted to wait.'' He glanced toward the south for a moment, toward his cave, then looked back to Berthold. ''May I go now? Marta asked me to return to her when you arrived. And I must find someone to stay with Heidi.''

Berthold was staring down at Gunter. He nodded. ''You run along.''

For a moment, Ulrich, too, looked down at the body. He said, ''He was a good man.'' He looked back up at Berthold. ''He'll get buried soon, won't he?''

Berthold smiled. ''Tell the queen that she can send the burial detail whenever she likes.''

Ulrich nodded, and then, with another sad glance at

the body, he shuffled off.

Berthold watched him for a moment, then turned to me. He sipped at his crock, then said, "Let's see what we have here."

He squatted down beside the body and silently studied it for a few moments. Finally he said, "He's very clean, wouldn't you say?"

I nodded. "Gunter always had excellent grooming skills."

He reached out, lifted one of Gunter's hands. "No marks on the hands," he said. "No marks anywhere, except around his neck." He looked up at me. "Help me turn him over, would you?"

"What for?" I asked.

"To get to the other side," he said, and he grinned, for this was the punch line to a very old joke. His sense of humor was one of the many reasons why Berthold spent so much time alone. "Please don't ask questions, Doder. Just help me turn him over."

Reluctantly, I did. Gunter's flesh was cold and slack. I stepped back, rubbing my hands on my thighs. My thighs didn't warm them; they chilled my thighs.

"Curious," said Berthold.

"What?"

"Here. This indentation in the skull." His slender finger dipped lightly into the injury, and my stomach dipped lightly into my knees.

Swallowing bile, I straightened up. "He hit his head when he fell?"

Berthold shook his head. "There are no rocks here, nothing that could make such an impression. No, he was struck with some sort of blunt instrument."

"A musical instrument?" I frowned. "A whistle?" At the time, the whistle was our only musical instrument. "How could a whistle do that?"

"Not a *musical* instrument."

"A great many whistles, maybe, dropped from a great height?"

"No, no," he said impatiently. "I mean a *thing*. A *blunt* thing."

"Ah." I nodded. I looked at him. "What blunt thing?"

His eyes narrowed. "When we discover this, perhaps we shall also discover who destroyed him."

He pulled himself upright and then stared off thoughtfully across the valley. Without looking at me, he handed me the empty crock.

I took it. "Another?" I asked.

He nodded, still looking off. I slipped the empty into the bag, pulled out a full crock, uncorked it.

Handing him the crock, I said, "Was it the Outlanders?"

He turned to me and smiled. "Let's ask them, shall we?"

The Outlanders lived to the south, a few miles beyond the cave of Ulrich and Heidi. We walked the distance in silence, Berthold sipping now and then at his mead. When we were still more than a few hundred yards away from the Outlander village, the dense, rank stench of them began to clot the air.

By then, Berthold had finished the second crock. He handed it to me and said, "Another, please."

I swung the bag from my shoulder, slipped in the empty, plucked out a fresh one. "You're going through those pretty quickly," I pointed out.

Taking the fresh crock, he nodded. "This is a three crock problem, my friend." He sipped at the crock. "Now, listen to me. When we're among the Outlanders, do me the kindness of keeping your thoughts, such as they are, to yourself."

"I—"

"Not a word."

"All right," I said. "Fine." His fine hand at diplomacy was another reason why Berthold spent a lot of time alone.

The smell got stronger and more suffocating as we approached. To my amazement, Berthold was well-known to the Outlanders. When we passed by the first of their frail wooden structures, some of them emerged from inside and waved merrily, calling out his name. The young of their breed ran toward us, laughing, cooing with pleasure, jabbering in their ridiculous Outlander language. The reek was so thick now that my eyes were watering.

They were a strange-looking race—they were all immensely tall, for one thing, and they all wore clothes, trousers of leather, blouses of cloth. They wore them, I guess, because they were mostly hairless, except for some thin, flimsy, yellowish stuff sprouting at the tops of their round little heads. All of them, young and adult alike, looked like infants who had somehow grown to a preposterous size. I was coughing badly, nearly gagging, when an Outlander male suddenly came toward us.

"Hey, Berthold," he cried. "Fantastic! You're looking great!" He spoke The Language surprising well. Grinning widely, he held out his enormous hand and snatched up Berthold's smaller one and pumped it furiously.

"Thank you, Bob," Berthold said. "This is my assistant, Doder."

"Hey!" said Bob. He held out his hand and a wave of stench blasted me. Swallowing, I took the hand and let it crush my own for a moment. "Fantastic!" said Bob. "Any friend of Berthold's is a friend of mine!" He released me finally, then turned to Berthold. "So what's happening? What brings you here?"

"Nothing good, I'm afraid," Berthold told him gravely. "One of our people has been destroyed."

"Oh, no," said Bob. He shook his head sadly. "Bad one."

Berthold said, "The piece of fabric, please, Doder."

I set down the bag, rummaged through the crocks inside, found the strip, handed it to Berthold.

"And this was found," he said, "wrapped around the

man's neck." He held the strip out to Bob, who took it and examined it for a moment.

"Hey," said Bob, and looked up. "This is ours!" He frowned. "Looks like some of Tammy's stuff." He glanced around at the crowd of wide-eyed Outlanders who now surrounded us, then called out, "Tammy?"

A female stepped forward. Bob jabbered at her for a moment, handed her the cloth, then jabbered some more.

The female nodded, jabbered back at Bob, then returned the strip.

Bob looked at Berthold. "She says it's part of a blouse she made. The blouse was stolen. It was hanging out on the line, and someone walked off with it."

"When was this?" asked Bertold.

"Last week."

Berthold nodded. "Tell me, Bob. Has anything else gone missing from your village lately?"

Bob cocked his round little head. "Funny you should ask," he said. "There *was* something."

"And what was that?"

"Some thorn apple seeds. Someone took them from Pete's house. That was about a week ago, too."

"Pete the Priest?" said Berthold.

"Right." Bob seemed concerned. "I've been pretty worried. I wouldn't want the wrong person to get his hands on those."

Berthold nodded, then took a sip of mead. "I suspect, Bob," he said, "that the wrong person already has."

Before nightfall, we were all back in Marta's cave—Marta, Karla, Ulrich, Berthold and me. We were sitting around on the stone benches, except for Marta, who sat on her ceremonial throne, and Berthold, who stood in the center of the room.

"Clearly," he said, "it was not an Outlander who destroyed Gunter." He upended his crock, took a swallow of mead.

"But what," said Marta, "of the strip of cloth?"

"Their leader, Bob, informed me that the strip came

from a blouse stolen last week from one of the Outlander women.''

Marta sat back, crossed her legs. ''And how do you know that this Bob''—her sarcasm curled around the strange-sounding syllable—''spoke the truth?''

''One has merely to smell the thing,'' said Berthold. ''It smells of Outlander, yes, but the smell is faint. Had an Outlander been in contact with it recently, it would fairly reek of their distinctive odor.''

He sipped again at his crock. ''And even assuming that some Outlander possessed a motive for killing Gunter—obviously an unwarranted assumption—why would this mythical Outlander bother to strangle him? Even the smallest of their women is larger and stronger than Gunter was. Any Outlander could have killed him with a simple blow to the head.''

''But there *was* a blow to the head,'' I said. ''You told me so yourself.''

''There was indeed. But could an Outlander, stinking as he would, approach close enough to strike Gunter without Gunter being aware of it?''

''The Outlander could've thrown a rock,'' I said.

He smiled. ''Perhaps. But the blow that struck Gunter was powerful enough to render him unconscious immediately. And yet—'' he swigged some mead, turned to Karla ''—Gunter's wife tells us that Gunter cried out *twice*.''

Karla blinked. ''But perhaps he saw the Outlander, and cried out. And then he turned and ran, and the Outlander, as Doder says, threw a rock. And he cried out again when he was hit.''

''Gunter would then have fallen forward. But there was no dust on his face or chest.''

Karla frowned. ''Maybe I made a mistake. About the second cry.''

''Oh, you made a mistake,'' said Berthold, and smiled cheerfully. He turned to Marta. ''Karla, of course, stole the blouse from the Outlander village. And she also stole some thorn apple seeds. Now, very few people know that the effects of these seeds, when eaten, is to mimic serious illness—fever, night sweats, prolonged sleep, and ultimately death. But Karla would have known. As your niece, she is of the royal line.''

Scorn flashed across Karla's face. ''Ridiculous! Why would I steal thorn apple seeds?''

Berthold smiled once more. ''To give them to Ulrich, of course. So he could feed them to his wife. So she would be quite unconscious while he helped you destroy Gunter.''

Ulrich was very quick. He leaped from the bench, dashed across the room, hurtled out the door. Only to be dragged back through it, an instant later, by two of Marta's guards, Wolfgang and Friedrich. Berthold had posted them there before the meeting. Two other guards, Leopold and Loeb, followed close behind.

For a moment, Ulrich squirmed against two pairs of strong hands. Then he turned to Berthold and shouted, ''It was her! It was her idea! I hit him, yes, with a rock, but it was she who strangled him!''

''Idiot!'' snarled Karla. ''*Coward!*''

Marta looked at Leopold and Loeb. ''Take her,'' she said.

And that's the true tale of the first murder. Karla and Ulrich confessed—not with any great eagerness, naturally; but we had ways of making them talk. They were in love, and poor Gunter and Heidi, Ulrich's wife, stood in their way—so they decided to remove them. Back then it was strange, unheard of; now, of course, it's an old story.

The funny thing is, even after they were stoned to death, and Gunter's relatives (and Heidi) had been appeased, the village was never quite the same. A kind of closeness was gone from among us. People began to eye each other warily. It was as though Karla and Ulrich had let loose some sort of demon. By doing what they'd done, by demonstrating a capacity for evil, they had also demonstrated that all of us, any of us, might share in it.

Some of the people actually left the clan, wandered off in pairs or on their own. Among them was Berthold. He just disappeared one day, vanished, six months later. It was said that he'd gone to join the Outlanders; but no one really knew.

As for me, after Berthold left I stayed with the clan for another few months. And then my wife, Ursula, took sick—a terrible fever, with night sweats and prolonged sleep—and at last the poor woman passed away. And I decided that it was time for me to move on, as well.

And so I came here, to this valley. And along the way . . .

But that's another story.

*J*ohn Maddox Roberts is the author of the SPQR series, the "memoirs" of Decius Caecilius Metellus, written when he is in his nineties, midway through the reign of Augustus. Metellus is the last man alive who remembers many of the people and events of the late Republic, so they are already historical writings when he sets them down.

The first SPQR book was nominated for an Edgar, and there are now nine in the series, the most recent being The Princess and the Pirate, *and a half-dozen short stories (including the following). Unfortunately, the later SPQR books are available only to readers of German.*

John also writes science fiction and contemporary mysteries, in English. His new mystery, Desperate Highways, *is now available from St. Martin's Press.*

He says of his work: "Rome in the late Republic is like the modern world reflected in a fun-house mirror. So many aspects are so similar to our own world and experience that the Romans can seem like modern people dressed in togas. Then they can do something so weird that they are like beings from another planet ... Sometimes history and mystery are the same thing."

THE ETRUSCAN HOUSE

John Maddox Roberts

Julia said, "You know the look on a bull's face when the flamen's assistant bashes it between the eyes with his hammer?"

"Of course. Why?"

"Because it's the look on your face right now."

It was a lovely day in late fall. Julia and I sat in the little courtyard of our house in the Subura, enjoying the good weather while it lasted. The sounds of our crammed, noisy neighborhood made their way in past the walls and through the trellises, muffled and no more unpleasant to our urban ears than the buzzing of insects in the country. For the first time in years there were no screams, sounds of riot, or fire alarms.

"It doesn't seem natural," I said. "Clodius is dead and I already miss the worthless scoundrel. Milo is in exile and I truly miss him. Caesar is off slaughtering Gauls, and Crassus is dead in Syria. I haven't seen the City this calm since—well, since before Cicero's consulship, anyway. That's been a dozen years or more."

"You just need something to do," she assured me. "For two years I've listened to you complain about how overworked you've been. Now it's over and you're bored.''

It was true. My aedileship had been prolonged for an extra year, an office so crammed with duties that one year was enough to kill most officeholders, not to mention the ruinous expense of it. But Julia was right. Two years of sleepless nights, responsibility for almost everything in the City, prosecuting corruption and malfeasance, listening to everybody's problems, all the while organizing and celebrating unbelievably lavish Games had left me temporarily unfit for leisure. I did not expect it to last. Leisure had always been among my specialties, but was one I was seldom permitted to enjoy for long.

The gods had been attending our conversation closely and brought our tranquillity to an end forthwith. Juba came bustling in, exuding the overweening satisfaction of an important slave bearing news of some difficulty.

''A message from Caesar!'' he announced. ''And a— a delivery!'' Juba was our steward, a Mauritanian transferred from Julia's former household. Since Julia was a Caesar, all of her slaves regarded the great Caius Julius as little less than a god, an assessment I did not share.

''What sort of delivery?'' I demanded.

''You really must see,'' he said, relishing my potential consternation. ''And the messenger will deliver the letter only into your own hand.''

''This sounds bad,'' I said.

''I am sure my uncle has his reasons,'' Julia admonished me.

''He always does,'' I muttered sourly, not quite loud enough for her to hear. We went out to the atrium, thence to the front gate.

''Oh, dear,'' Julia said. Gathered outside in the narrow street was a minor crowd, gawking at the twenty men chained neck to neck before my gateway.

''Senator Decius Caecilius Metellus the Younger?'' asked the man in charge of the coffle. He was a short, pug-faced Cretan in the garb of the professional slave-handler.

"Until the old man dies, that's who I am."

"Then this is for you." He handed me a bronze message-tube, sealed at one end with wax bearing Caesar's signet. I broke the seal and a small square of dingy papyrus fell out. It had been scraped and reused several times and was nearing the end of its useful existence.

" 'Decius Caecilius,' " I read aloud, " 'take care of these for me. They are to fight in my triumphal games.' " I handed the little papyrus to Julia. "He hasn't lost his touch with the pithy, laconic phrase."

"Caius Julius is very busy up there in Gaul," she said primly. "He has no time for polite formalities." She began to walk down the line of captives. "What are we to do with these?"

They were all enemy warriors captured in battle. That much could be seen in their appearance and bearing. Civilized soldiers are downcast and demoralized in captivity, but these were Gauls and Germans of a dozen tribes, aristocrats by their own reckoning, and capture only increased their arrogance.

Of late, Caesar had been parcelling out his prisoners among his supporters and anyone who owed him money. He couldn't concentrate them in one place because the Senate feared he was building a private army in Italy. I had to oblige him, because he was covering a large portion of my debts and I was doing everything I could to avoid further service in his army in Gaul.

"I'll lodge them in the Statilian School," I told Julia. "It could be worse. He might've sent his bears and wild bulls, and then where would we have put them?"

"I don't like them," she said. "They're ugly and smelly and savage and—Oh, my!" She had come to the last man in the coffle and stared up at him, enraptured.

He was worth a second look. Taller than the others by a head, he had glossy waist-length hair, and his face, although disfigured by the customary Gallic mustache, was as handsome as Apollo's, although somewhat sterner. The tattoos on his arms were of the highest quality. He had managed to keep himself and his clothing cleaner than the others. Unlike the bearded Germans, the highborn men of Gaul plucked every hair from their hides save the scalp and the upper lip. Arms folded, he gazed down at Julia, insouciant as a foreign ambassador, not at all humiliated or embarrassed by his neck-ring and chains.

"Can we keep this one?" she asked.

"Best stand back, m'lady," the head slave-handler warned. "That's a wild animal there."

"Oh, I think not," Julia said.

"Well, enough of this chitchat," I said. "Listen to me, you lot. Your troubles are over. You are in Rome now, the center of the world. I am going to take you to a place where you can wash up and get those chains off. Then you'll have nothing to do but gorge yourselves and practice with weapons all day long, and I know how you savages love to do both. You won't have to degrade yourselves by performing any sort of productive, useful labor. In the upcoming fights, many of you may survive, which would certainly not happen if you were to continue opposing Julius Caesar. Best of all, you are out of Gaul. I've been there, so I know what an awful place it is."

Then I repeated the message in Gallic and German, to the great admiration of my neighbors.

"I'll just trot these over to the school and have them all disposed of by noon, my dear."

"If you must," Julia said, gazing far too long at the tall barbarian.

Statilius was not happy with the new arrivals.

"Where am I going to put them?" he demanded. "In summer they'd be no problem, but December will be upon us soon and a dozen rich men are boarding their fighters here." December being the favored month for celebrating *munera*. "Besides, most of the men here are volunteers, or at least slaves and convicts who've taken the oath. They aren't going to like sharing the facilities with filthy barbarian prisoners. It's bad for morale."

"December means Saturnalia, too," I reminded him. "Is your wife's heart still set on that statue of Diana from Aphrodisias? The one in the import shop out by the Circus Flaminius?"

He scratched his chin. "I suppose I could make room for them in the stables. The *equites* have gone out to temporary quarters on the Vatican, where they have room to train."

I watched the smith strike the irons from the prisoners; then I went to the tall man, who was rubbing his neck, which had been reddened by the ring around it.

"You have the look of a man too proud to obey orders and inclined to try an escape. For your own good, try no such thing. You are in a place where nobody loves you and where many lust for the reward offered for returning a runaway. Just do your duty and in time you might earn your freedom."

He actually smiled. "I am where I want to be."

"That's an odd thing to say," I responded, taken somewhat aback.

"You were with Caesar back when the war started," he said, watching me with unnerving fixity.

"Have we met?"

"No. But I saw you at some of the conferences."

"Oh. Well, you barbarians look much alike to me. Were you allied at that time, or in arms against Rome?"

"Both."

Despite what I had told him, he did look vaguely familiar, although I could not quite place him. There had been many such conferences and every Gallic tribe had its own pack of chieftains to attend. I remembered only the most prominent of the allies and enemies.

He walked off to join the others, and my boy Hermes walked over to examine the new arrivals. He trained at the school most mornings, when I had no other use for him.

"Here's a pack right out of the trees," he observed.

"And I'm responsible for them, thanks to Caesar," I informed him. "I want you to keep an eye on that tall one. I don't think he's foolish enough to run, but the really proud ones are prone to suicide."

"I can't watch him all the time," Hermes protested.

"Just while you're here. You'll be able to tell if he's up to anything. Volunteer to be his training partner. You know how merry Gauls are when they fight. If he isn't smiling and laughing while you beat each other bloody, you'll know he's up to something."

"Why so much concern for this one?"

"Caesar must want him as a star performer in the triumphal games. Otherwise, he'd never let one as dangerous as this live. If I let one of Caesar's pets get away, he'll make me regret it for a long, long time."

The Senate meeting the next day followed a pattern that had become tediously familiar. The adherents of Caesar wanted more of everything for the glorious conqueror: more troops, more honors, more powers than he already had, which were unprecedented for a Roman proconsul. His enemies wanted the opposite. They wanted him stripped of his *imperium*, forbidden to celebrate a triumph, his monuments destroyed and Caesar himself recalled to Rome in disgrace to be tried for treason. Since the two sides were about equal in numbers, these debates went on forever. Since he is now a god, people no longer remember how precarious was Caesar's power base in those days.

The deciding factor was Pompey. The two still cooperated closely, and Pompey worked tirelessly to get Caesar what he needed to bring the Gallic war to a successful close. It was understood that, when Caesar came back in triumph to Rome, he would return the favor, giving Pompey the Eastern war that Crassus had bungled so fatally.

Pompey, I thought on that day, was looking old and tired. Once he had been compared to the young Alexander. Now nobody would compare him even to the old

Philip. His face and body sagged and a lifetime of soldiering and administrative duties had used up his once boundless energies. His veterans, upon whom his power was based, were getting no younger either. I was certain that, when he got his Eastern command, the result would be as disastrous as that of Crassus.

I took no pleasure in the prospect, even though I had spent my life hating the man. After a generation dominated by the three giants, I feared that Rome would be overrun by their second-rate epigones. I was right about that, but at the time I wasn't thinking so far ahead.

Toward the end of the session, Pompey, as one of the year's consuls, recognized a senator named Lucius Fabius Sanga, whom I had never seen before. His family, though ancient and illustrious, were rarely seen in Rome. For more than a century they had spent most of their time in the Provence, where their close ties to the Gallic nation of the Allobroges had given them great wealth and privilege. A Fabius had saved Rome from Hannibal, so he was guaranteed a respectful hearing until he should tread on too many sensitive toes, at which time he would become somebody's enemy.

After a lengthy self-introduction in which he recited the names and deeds of his glorious ancestors, he got down to business.

"Honored Conscript Fathers," he said, using Cicero's favorite formula, "I come before you today so that my family may once again render service to the Republic. Our efforts to bring an end to this bloody conflict between the people of Gaul and of Rome have been ceaseless. I have been empowered by the chieftains of northwestern Gaul, still unsubdued, who are now prepared to pledge eternal peace with Rome, the pact to be solemnized by the most terrible oaths and the surrender of hostages." This sent a buzz of consternation through the assembly. For the first time that day I began to take an interest in the proceedings.

Marcus Antonius, soon to join Caesar as quaestor, jumped to his feet. "He speaks of a pack of primitive tribes with no more political cohesion than a handful of rocks! The promises of disorganized savages are worthless unless Roman legions occupy their territory!" Peace with Gaul was the last thing Antonius wanted. Only total victory by Caesar was acceptable, and he wanted to be a part of the victorious army.

Caesar's faction cheered Antonius's words. They quieted when Cicero stood. Since returning from exile he had stayed in the political background, writing and lawyering. When he spoke publicly, it was usually in favor of abridging the power of the great men of the day. He feared that Caesar was poised to become Dictator.

"While the tribes of Gaul are famously independent in times of victory," he began, "yet terrible fear may make even Gauls unite to save themselves. And Caesar has given them cause to fear Rome. The gods themselves know how it pains my heart to deny so glorious a warrior as young Marcus Antonius a chance to win honor in combat with the barbarians—" He paused while his adherents chuckled. "After all, when the Mad Hercules appears on the scene, surely the rebellious Gauls must flee to the Ocean and swim to Britannia to seek refuge!"

At this the Senate roared and the face of Antonius flamed. At that time he was better known for his ludicrous eccentricities than for military accomplishments. The year before he had cultivated a full beard and gone about wearing a lion skin and carrying a huge club in imitation of Hercules.

"Nonetheless," Cicero said, "we must consider what is best for Rome, not what will provide the greatest renown for her most glorious, though least tried, hero." When Cicero got carried away with his own sarcasm he knew no moderation. He raised a good laugh, but the vicious hatred with which Antonius hounded Cicero to his death may have been born on that day.

"Just who," Cicero asked, "speaks for these northwestern chieftains?"

Sanga replied, "Gobannitio of the Arverni came to me as the head of a delegation that included great men of the Parisii, the Pictones, Aulerci and a dozen other tribes."

"Just a moment," I said, rising for the first time that day. "Is Gobannitio not the brother of Celtillus, who was executed by the Arverni for trying to make himself their king?" This had happened during my service in Gaul.

"And justly so," said Sanga. "Like ourselves, the Gauls despise monarchy and love republican institutions."

"You see, Conscript Fathers?" said Cicero. "It may be possible to civilize these people after all. I call upon you to empower Fabius Sanga to bring a deputation of these chieftains here, to negotiate directly with the Senate."

There were boos and hisses and many obscene noises from Caesar's party and a vociferous argument began. Caesar's men pointed out that, as proconsul of all the Gauls, Caesar could not be left out of affairs within his province. His enemies considered the affair to be proof that Caesar was waging a needless war at great expense to aggrandize himself. This last was not strictly true. While Caesar overlooked no opportunity to spread his own fame, he was making the war pay for itself, and had filled rather than emptied the treasury. But then, disputatious senators never allowed tedious facts to get in their way.

Antonius was in especially fine form that day, and he did not confine his activities on Caesar's behalf to the Senate chamber. By midafternoon he was out on the Rostra, haranguing the Forum crowd like an angry Tribune of the People. Caesar was a great favorite with the mob, and Antonius displayed considerable rhetorical gifts as he portrayed the Senate's plan as an act of treachery against Caesar. Cicero tried to plead his case but he was no match for Antonius when it came to rabble-rousing. Cicero was at his best when addressing his peers in the Senate, or arguing before a jury.

It looked as if Rome's brief season of peace and quiet was at an end.

The knock at my gate came entirely too early. Out of office, I had resumed my custom of staying in bed until the sun was well up in the morning. I have never understood the virtue in stumbling around blindly, bumping into things, half-asleep in the dark. It was still quite dark when the knock came.

"Get up," Julia ordered. She had been up for quite a while, being, as a Julian, full of patrician virtue.

"What for?" I asked, trying to bury my face in a pillow.

She snatched it away. "There's a lictor outside."

"So what? Give him some money and tell him to get lost and not to find me until a reasonable hour. Lictors always need money."

"Get up before I empty the chamber pot over you."

She meant it, so I got up, splashed some water on my face and lurched to the door. Hermes was already there, gossiping with the lictor, who leaned on his fasces.

"This had better be important," I grumbled.

"Senator Metellus, the consuls require your presence at once."

"Both of them?"

"That is correct. They await at the house of Pompey."

I threw on one of my older togas and followed the man through the dim gray light of earliest dawn, Hermes at my heels.

Pompey's house was not especially ostentatious. He wanted people to keep in mind that he was only in Rome temporarily, always ready to go out and rejoin his legions. I found him seated with his colleague, Metellus Scipio. Neither of them looked to be in a better mood than I was.

I looked around. "Where's the rest of the Senate?"

"We just wanted you, Decius," said Scipio, who was a kinsman of mine, by adoption.

"Fabius is dead," Pompey said with Caesarian brevity.

"Which one?" I asked, there being a number of Fabii in the Senate at that time.

"Lucinus Fabius Sanga, of course!" Pompey barked. "The one who caused such an uproar in the Senate yesterday."

I yawned. "Is that all? What's one dead senator more or less? We never see the Fabii Sanga in Rome anymore. They're practically Gauls by adoption."

"I couldn't agree more," Pompey said. "But this one acquired a sudden prominence and we have to look into the matter. We want you to find the killer for us. You have a reputation for this sort of thing."

"Gladly. Marcus Antonius did it. I'm going home now."

"Senator!" Pompey bellowed in his parade-ground voice. "You are going nowhere except to view the body of the late Quintus Fabius Sanga, after which you will report to us your findings."

"Oh, very well, if you insist. But Antonius did it. He practically killed the man in the Senate chamber yesterday, he was so angry. I rather like Antonius, but the Antonii are all hereditary criminals, everyone knows that."

"Nonetheless," Scipio said, "you must at least go through the motions of an investigation. And"—he cleared his throat; a bad sign—"it would be very convenient if Antonius were *not* to be the murderer after all."

"Eh?" my political fur began to bristle. "What's this?"

"Caesar wants Antonius to join him in Gaul immediately," Pompey explained. "He's taken a liking to the fool, don't ask me why. Just now relations between Caesar and the Senate may be described as delicate. I don't want the balance upset by an obscure senator like Fabius Sanga and an idiot like Marcus Antonius."

"Well, I'm afraid I may disappoint you. If the evidence points to Antonius I will not conceal it. You had better get a writ of exile ready for one of your tame tribunes to pass. That way, he can go join Caesar and maybe all this will have blown over by the time the war ends, and he can come back for the triumph.'' The sad fact was, murder wasn't considered a terribly serious crime at that time, so common had it become.

I described the interview to Hermes as we followed the same lictor to the final resting place of the late Fabius Sanga. ''I fear Pompey is not his old self,'' I told him. ''The old Pompey wouldn't have cared about upsetting Caesar, and he would have ordered me to conduct my investigation according to his instructions or face exile myself.''

''He was married to Caesar's daughter,'' Hermes reminded me. ''Everyone says he was devastated when she died last year.''

''Yes, there are few things more pathetic than an old man in love. It's always a bad sign when someone like Pompey experiences actual human feelings so late in life.''

We crossed the Sublician bridge into the Trans-Tiber district. It was devoted to the river traffic and to entertainment. Most of Rome's resident foreigners lived there. It was also the location of an institution called the Etruscan House and that was where the lictor led us.

The Etruscan House was only a year or two old, built by a wealthy freedman named Gorgias. He had an idea for a business that combined inn, whorehouse, baths and jakes under a single roof. He figured that, if his place provided for every demand, people would spend all their money there and not bother to go anywhere else. Unconfined by the City walls, land was relatively cheap in the Trans-Tiber, so he could build on a lavish scale. A recent fad for things Etruscan provided the name and the theme of the decor.

Gorgias received us at the door of his establishment, looking rather put out. Possibly he perceived the murder of a senator to be bad for business, although I am not sure why this should be.

"This way, Senator Metellus," he said. "Awful thing, this. Never had anything like it happen before, not in my inn."

"I suppose. Why was he staying here, rather than in the City?" Ordinarily, a man of Fabius's birth would have stayed in the house of a relative or friend rather than in an inn.

"Probably because of the rest of his party," Gorgias answered.

I saw what he meant when we entered the wing Fabius had taken for his entourage. He was travelling with about twenty Gauls, some of them decently Romanized, shaven and shorn and wearing togas. But the rest wore checked trousers and mustaches and twisted neck-rings. They looked angry, which is something Gauls can do with great flair.

"Where is the body?" I demanded.

"This is an insult beyond bearing!" shouted a fat, mustachioed old villain. "The Allobroges demand vengeance for our murdered patron!"

"Oh, quiet down," I ordered him. "Right now, our legions are all that stand between you and annihilation by your fellow Gauls and their German allies. We'll take care of this matter, never fear." Mention of the Germans sobered the Gauls.

We found the late Fabius Sanga lying abed, the sheets in some disorder around him, his head twisted at an odd angle, face a fine shade of royal purple, eyes bulging and tongue outthrust like a gorgon's. To all appearances, he had been efficiently throttled by a large and powerful pair of hands. I saw no stab wounds and it didn't look as if he had been clubbed, but blood had poured copiously from his mouth.

"Hermes," I said, "run along to your sword practice. When you get to the school, ask Asklepiodes to come here." The boy dashed off and I turned to the fat Gaul.

"How does it happen that you didn't notice your patron being messily done to death?"

"The murderer must have used witchcraft!" he said. "He cast a spell of sleep upon us." The other Gauls nodded and insisted that this was so.

"Spare me. You followed the Gaulish custom of going to bed thoroughly besotted. You'd have snored through the battle of the gods and the giants. Gorgias?"

"Yes, Senator?"

"I hate to seem foolish by asking something obvious, but was Marcus Antonius here last night, by any chance?"

"Yes, he is here most evenings when he is in Rome. Last night he and the unfortunate Fabius got into a terrible argument. Several times I had to ask them to desist, but the argument kept breaking out anew every few minutes."

"It was that great rogue Antonius!" said one of the Romanized Gauls. "He threatened our patron with death many times!"

"I intend to get the truth from him," I said. "In the meantime, none of you are to leave these premises. Don't think you have escaped suspicion. You Gauls are as treacherous as Greeks, as everybody knows." Actually, we Romans were not amateur practitioners of that art, but the Gauls were in my territory, so they had to put up with my insults.

"Ah, Senator," Gorgias said hesitantly, "Marcus Antonius is still here, if you wish to question him."

"Truly? That is brazen, even for him. Lead the way."

I followed the host to an extremely lavish suite of rooms, typical of the incredibly profligate Antonius. On campaign he could endure hardships fit to kill the toughest legionary, but in civilization he liked to affect the lifestyle of a king. When traveling, he had his golden drinking cups carried before him on a litter, like images of the gods in a religious procession.

I found Antonius, like Fabius, abed. Unlike Fabius, Antonius was snoring. I had to shake him for quite a while before he came around and opened his reddened eyes. He looked at me without comprehension, so I had a slave hold a basin of water handy while I thrust Antonius's head beneath the surface repeatedly. At last he shook his head, puffing and snorting, and seemed to be conscious.

"Antonius," I said, "you're a moron."

"Better men than you have told me that, Metellus. Why are you so angry? I never slept with your wife that I recall." Antonius had tremendous charm when he chose to display it, but he was far too hung-over to be charming that morning.

"You don't remember half of your life. Do you remember killing a man here last night?"

"Where am I?" He looked around. "Oh, the Etruscan House. No, I remember nothing much after addressing the crowd in the Forum yesterday afternoon." He rubbed his palms over his face. "Who did I kill?"

"Lucinus Fabius Sanga."

He looked up, alarmed. "No! I've never been so drunk I'd forget killing a senator! Besides, it was just a political wrangle over his foolish plan for a negotiated peace with the Gauls. I had nothing else against the man and that's not a killing matter."

"A lot of people won't see it that way. Cicero will have you before a special court and he won't just ask for exile."

"Oh, come now," he said. "Even Cicero can't have a citizen executed for murder, if it doesn't involve patricide or treason or poisoning." He paused. "He wasn't poisoned, was he?"

"Strangled."

"Well, then, you see?"

"He will have you forbidden fire and water. That means no military duty with Caesar. Not that it matters much, since you may have destroyed Caesar's chance of keeping his *imperium*. You know that his enemies will jump on an opportunity like this. They'll say that you murdered Fabius on Caesar's behalf."

"But I didn't kill him!" he bellowed, now thoroughly frightened. That was something you didn't often see in Antonius.

"Calm yourself," I advised. "I am going to investigate and if there is any way I can clear you, I will."

"Yes, do that! You are famous for this sort of work, Metellus, and you can count on me not to forget it!"

"I serve the Senate and People," I said solemnly. I didn't tell him that Pompey was urging me to clear him, even if I had to fake it. The gratitude of a man like Antonius was always a useful thing to have.

"Yes, yes, of course. What are you doing?"

"Examining your hands." I had taken both by the wrists and turned them to see from all sides. They were huge hands and immensely powerful, easily capable of snapping a human neck. His infatuation with Hercules was no minor fancy. The Antonii traced their lineage to a son of Hercules named Anton, and I could almost believe that it was true. Antonius had the physique you see on statues of that demigod. He was massive as a bull and about as intelligent.

"There is blood under your fingernails. Why is that?

He studied them as if he had never seen them before. "I have no idea."

"Do you usually wear so many rings?" Like others of his social set, he wore massive gold rings on every finger and even his thumbs. One was a signet, the others decorated with cameos, images of the gods or symbols to attract good fortune.

"When I'm not with the legions. They give extra force to a punch."

"So I noticed. There's blood on them, too."

"I'm sure there is a good explanation, if I could just remember."

"Do try," I said. "In the meantime, do not leave this place. I am going to leave my lictor here at your door. He's a consul's lictor, so you won't be arrested and hauled away, but expect to be besieged as soon as word of this reaches the Forum, which I am sure has happened by now.''

He scratched his stubbly chin. "Well, no sense going hungry." He began to bawl for food and wine. Shaking my head, I left him. My own reputation was not of the best, but seeing Antonius always made me feel like a boring old Stoic.

I summoned Gorgias again. "Describe the events of last night.''

"Well, it all started out quietly enough. Antonius and his friends caroused on one side of the courtyard. Fabius and his Gauls were on the other. I think there'd have been no trouble if the new dancers had arrived on time.''

"Dancers?''

"A troupe from Crete, wonderful performers and acrobats, guaranteed to keep everyone in a good mood. But they were delayed on the road from Brundisium by bad weather, so I sent to the *ludus* and had Statilius send me some wrestlers and boxers. He sent twenty-one of his best men, all very strong and skilled. Well, you know Antonius.''

"All too well. He had to challenge the winners, just to show that he's the strongest and bravest man in Rome.''

Gorgias sighed. "Indeed he did. And then some of Fabius's Gauls had to challenge *him*, lest their manhood be impugned. It got very disorderly and in no time Fabius and Antonius were bellowing at each other over some political matter I didn't understand. Antonius repeatedly had to be restrained by his friends from attacking Fabius with intent to maim.''

"He is an intemperate man," I agreed. If Antonius was brawling with the wrestlers and boxers, that could explain the blood on his hands. I could present it as an excuse, anyway.

I saw Asklepiodes coming down from the wing where Fabius and his party lodged. "A rather dull case this time, Decius," he reported. "An extremely commonplace strangulation accompanied by separation of the neck vertebrae. It took a very powerful man, but there are many such in Rome."

"Could you tell if the murderer was wearing a number of rings?"

He shook his head. "The finger marks are plain but rather diffuse. If a ring were turned inward so that it stamped its mark into the flesh it might leave postmortem evidence, but even that is doubtful. I can testify that the crime was performed with human hands rather than with any form of ligature, but beyond that I cannot say."

"I don't suppose you were here last night?"

"The Labyrinth is my favored venue for leisure hours," he said, naming the Trans-Tiber's most famous brothel. He ate and drank there for free by making his medical services available to the employees.

From outside came a great commotion. That, I knew, would be the Senate arriving in force. Things would begin happening fast now. I scanned the courtyard, assessing its possibilities. I was skilled in law, politics and rhetoric. My lengthy time as aedile had given me a good eye for spectacle-planning. Romans loved all four arts.

The Etruscan House was built on the plan of a common inn, but on a huge scale. Its four sides were three stories high, the balconied galleries facing inward onto the courtyard, which was about fifty paces on a side. At one end was a raised platform for entertainers. The tables had been removed for morning cleaning.

I clapped Asklepiodes on the shoulder. "Old friend, oblige me. Go back to the *ludus* and tell Statilius that I want him to bring all his men here for a review. I'll explain when they get here."

The Greek was mystified, but promised to do as asked.

Moments after he left, senators came boiling through the entrance like an invading army. Within seconds, they had separated like two packs of snarling dogs, with the pro-Caesarian faction on one side, the anti-Caesarian faction on the other. While they bawled at each other, a double line of lictors entered, fasces at their shoulders, and behind them came the year's two consuls. The noise quieted a little when the consuls entered. Pompey saw me, beckoned, and I walked to his side.

"I hope you've found your way to the bottom of this matter," he said.

"I believe I have, and I don't think you'll be disappointed."

Cicero strode to the center of the courtyard and raised an arm. "Conscript Fathers! I demand that the praetors arrest Marcus Antonius for the foul and cowardly murder of Lucinus Fabius Sanga!" Local citizens, drawn by the clamor, were beginning to scramble onto the galleries to enjoy the fun.

"I forbid it!" shouted a tribune who happened to be a friend of Antonius, as if this were a vote in the Senate.

"Quiet down, all of you!" Pompey bellowed. "I have appointed Senator Decius Caecilius Metellus the Younger to investigate this murder and we will take no action until we hear his report!" There came loud applause from the upper galleries. I was very popular with the commons at that time.

"I beg your pardon, Consul," Cicero said. "But appointing a special *iudex* is a praetorian power lost by the consuls more than a hundred years ago."

"Get hold of yourself, Cicero," Scipio admonished. "We have to determine whether there is sufficient matter to warrant a trial before the praetors come into it."

"If I may have your attention!" I called. "Senators and citizens, if you will allow me to take charge of this assembly, I believe that we can quickly set this matter to rest."

"Do so!" Pompey shouted before anyone else could protest.

"First we must have order," I said. "Gorgias, set up chairs on the platform and a bench before it. Here is how we shall proceed: The consuls, the praetors and their lictors will take their places on the platform. The tribunes of the plebs will take the bench in front. The rest of the senators will stand on the first gallery. Other citizens on the upper galleries. I need to have the court-yard before the platform clear.''

''Senators!'' shouted Cato, as I had expected he would. ''This place is a tavern and a brothel, the haunt of Rome's lowest rabble! It is unbefitting the dignity of the Senate to meet in such a place!''

''Why?'' yelled some wag from an upper tier. ''There are more whores and thieves in the Senate than in the Labyrinth!'' Uproarious laughter followed. In those days, citizens did not fear their elected officials.

Before long, the lictors had everyone herded into their proper places and then ranged themselves in a line be-hind the officials holding *imperium*. At my signal, Antonius was brought out to stand before the platform. He was proud and arrogant as always, but I could see the apprehension in his eyes. For all he knew, he really had killed Fabius. At another signal, slaves brought out the ghastly corpse of Fabius, still on his bed. The citizens set up a ritual mourning at this sight. They had never seen him, but the name of Fabius was revered, so he rated a certain amount of civic respect.

I strode into the courtyard and placed myself before the platform. ''Consuls and praetors, senators and citi-zens,'' I began, ''Marcus Antonius, quaestor by accla-mation, soon to join the legions of Caius Julius Caesar in Gaul, stands accused of the murder of Senator Quintus Fabius Maximus Allobrogicus. As special investigator of this crime, I now present you with my findings.'' Briefly I described the debate in the Senate, followed by the drunken entertainment and brawling between the two the previous night.

''And now,'' I said, ''allow me to present the staff of the *ludus* of Statilius Taurus.''

In through the portal came Statilius, and behind him marched his swordsmen. Within minutes, the trainers had some three hundred men ranged in ranks, crowding the courtyard, unarmed and dressed in their tunics. The trainers kept a sharp eye on them to maintain order, but they were not chained or otherwise confined. A few were

criminals condemned to the arena, but these considered
the chances of mortal combat greatly preferable to death
on the cross. Others were free volunteers, men who
craved excitement and battle, but had no stomach for the
discipline and austerities of the legions. Most were prisoners of war, barbarians from primitive warrior tribes
who considered death by the sword a fine thing, but were
terrified of work, which was strictly the province of
women and slaves in their societies. Spartacus had
taught us the folly of forcing unwilling men to be glad-
iators.

"Metellus," Cato cried, "have you some justification
for this ludicrous spectacle?" He didn't have much support. Even his fellow senators were already looking over
the men and laying bets on the next big games.

"Statilius Taurus," I said, "call out the men you sent
over here last night to entertain the patrons."

Statilius signalled a trainer and the man began calling
out names. Soon twenty men stood in front. They had
the long arms, scarred faces and deformed ears of men
who specialized in wrestling and boxing.

"Gorgias informed me that twenty-one men arrived
last night," I said.

"Boxers and wrestlers fight in pairs," Statilius said.
"Why would I send an odd number?"

"An excellent question," I shouted, "and one that
occurred to me the moment Gorgias spoke the number."
I looked out over the ranks of men and saw one tall
form in the back row, blond head lowered so that his
face was obscured. I pointed toward him. "Statilius,
have that tall one brought forward."

Instantly, he raised his head and began to push his
way forward, not waiting for the trainers. He stood before the consuls with folded arms, proud as any king. In
the upper galleries, the Gauls of Fabius's party set up
an enraged jabbering, pointing at the man and shouting
imprecations.

"I did not send this man!" Statilius protested. "He's

a swordsman completely unskilled in Greek-style combat!''

"No," I said, "you did not, but that wouldn't have stopped him. He slipped out of his quarters, joined the lot coming here to perform, and ducked into one of the side rooms so as not to be recognized by someone in Fabius's party. This one always acts on his own initiative.''

"So, Roman," said the Gaul, "you recognized me after all." He said this in excellent Latin, the sort taught to the sons of highborn foreigners.

"Not immediately," I told him, "but something Fabius said in the Senate yesterday jogged my memory."

I gestured grandly toward the platform and the galleries. "Consuls, senators, my fellow citizens, allow me to introduce Vercingetorix, prince of the Arverni, son of that Celtillus who was executed by his people for lusting after a crown, and nephew of Gobannitio, who was treating with Fabius Sanga for peace with Rome. He is a very resourceful man. To scuttle the peace talks he had to kill Sanga and to do that he had to get to Rome quickly. The only way he could get to Rome unnoticed was as a prisoner, so he attached himself to a train bound for Rome. Who would notice one more Gaul among so many?''

I addressed him. "You speak good Latin and you seem to know your way around Rome. I take it you have been here before?''

"As a boy I spent months at a time here on embassies with my father, chieftain and rightful king of the Arverni. Your great ant heap of a city is not as awe-inspiring as you think. As for killing Sanga, I am a prince of the Arverni and I make no apology for what I do on behalf of my people. He and my uncle would have set the Roman foot upon our necks and made us no better than those Allobrogian dogs up there." He pointed toward the party of Fabius. "Death for all of us before a dishonorable peace!''

This brought a good round of applause from the upper

galleries. He was one handsome, majestic Gaul and Romans have a great love for bold rogues. Senators, by contrast, are common and boring.

"Vercingetorix," Pompey said, "how did you hope to make your escape?" He had a high regard for this sort of enterprise, too.

"If your senator here had not recognized me, I would have bided my time at the school, then stolen a good horse at first opportunity. If stopped at a border, I might pass myself off as a Provincial. If not, I would cut my way free or die trying. That is how a nobleman of Gaul conducts himself." Another round of applause.

"And increased your standing among your countrymen no end," I said. "Gauls love foolhardy adventurers."

"Kill me or let me go," Vercingetorix said. "Just don't bore me to death." The upper galleries whooped and stamped. They loved that sort of gesture.

"Statilius," Cicero said, "have one of your trainers kill that man. He is just a rebellious slave."

"Just a moment!" said one of the praetors on the platform. "I am Praetor of the Foreigners, and this case belongs to my court! I demand that he be remanded to my custody!"

"Not so fast!" yelled Antonius, no longer a suspect and deliriously happy with the fact. "In the first place, Cicero, this man is neither a slave nor a prisoner, but a foreign prince here in Rome of his own free will. As for you"—he turned to the praetor—"the Praetor of the Foreigners has jurisdiction only over *resident* foreigners, and Vercingetorix has not applied for that status. He is a Gaul, and Fabius Sanga was a Provincial, although a citizen of an ancient name. This case belongs to Caesar, who is Proconsul of Gaul and Illyria!" It was a pretty good argument for a man as hung-over as Antonius, and it went over well with the commons.

Nobody was paying any attention to me anymore so I left for home. It had been a pretty good day's work even if it started so abominably early. I'd put both Pompey and Antonius in my debt, which came in handy in later years.

As all the world knows, we didn't execute Vercingetorix that year. After a deadlocked wrangle in the Senate, he accompanied Antonius to Gaul, where Caesar was too busy with other matters to bother about a murder in Rome. Vercingetorix was released and immediately raised a rebellion in which thousands perished and he met his own end in Rome, but seven years later.

Would all those lives have been saved if we had done away with him when we had the chance? I doubt it. The Gauls were doomed as a nation the minute Caesar decided to make his reputation by conquering them. At least he made Romans of them. Grandsons of Vercingetorix and his chieftains sit in the Senate today. Not that the Senate these days amounts to anything. Gauls and Romans were both better people back then.

These were the events of two days in the year 702 of the City of Rome, the consulship of Gnaeus Pompeius Magnus and Quintus Caecilius Metellus Pius Scipio Nasica.

*E*dward Marston currently writes radio drama, theatrical drama, contemporary mysteries, young adult novels, historical mysteries, golf mysteries, nonfiction, short stories and the occasional one-act skit for American and British mystery conventions. He swears he does not have an identical twin brother but we are suspicious.

He is well known for his Elizabethan series, featuring Nicholas Bracewell, book holder for and the one sane person in a London theater company. The seventh book in the series, The Roaring Boy, received an Edgar nomination in 1996. The most recent in that series is The Wanton Angel.

Edward Marston's other historical series is set in newly Norman England at the time of the Domesday Book, featuring Ralph Delchard and Gervase Bret, who travel throughout the kingdom uncovering malfeasance and administering justice. The sixth and latest in that series is The Stallions of Woodstock. In this short story, these eleventh-century investigators are called upon to prevent the murder of William the Conqueror, a difficult task, since even a large part of his own family wishes him dead.

DOMESDAY DEFERRED

Edward Marston

"Winchester is a city of eunuchs!" complained Ralph Delchard.

"You are being unjust to it."

"Look around you, Gervase."

"I do so. I live here."

"Churches down every street. Three monasteries—Old Minster, New Minster and Nunnaminster. The Bishop's Palace Wolvesey. It is such an eerie place for a virile man to be that I feel threatened. Religion has castrated the whole city."

Gervase Bret laughed tolerantly. His companion was a soldier, a restless man of action who was never happy in the presence of so much ecclesiastical power, attested to, as it was, by the massive towers which loomed above them and by the Benedictine monks who were hurrying past on their way back to the cathedral. Gervase and Ralph nudged their horses along the crowded High Street. When the bells for tierce rang out with deafening authority, Ralph had to shout above them to make himself heard.

"Why on earth did you do it, Gervase?"

"Do what?"

"Take the cowl."

"I did not," reminded the other. "I left the Order at the end of my novitiate."

"Yes," said Ralph, "but you were actually on the point of joining those tonsured virgins. How could you even consider it? Trading your manhood for a life of pointless meditation? It's unnatural!"

"Celibacy is a virtue!"

"Then I willingly embrace vice!"

Gervase laughed again. His youthful flirtation with the monastic life was something on which he looked back with a mixture of affection and relief, nursing fond memories of his time within the enclave, yet grateful that he had renounced it. Life as a Chancery clerk was much more to his taste, and his betrothal to the lovely Alys had banished any wistfulness about his departure from the Benedictine Order. His rejection of the cowl had another important benefit. It enabled him to meet and to work alongside Ralph Delchard.

"Why have we been summoned?" yelled Ralph.

"The King must have more work for us."

"We have done our share, Gervase. I am tired of riding around the shires of England to decide who owns which land and how much they should be taxed. I want to stay at home. I want to rest. Is that unreasonable?"

"No, Ralph."

"Is it too much to ask?"

"I think not."

"Then I will demand that the King release me!"

Gervase raised a mocking eyebrow. Ralph chuckled.

"Well," he said on reflection, "I will *mention* it to him in passing. Only a fool would try to demand anything of William. He has Norman blood in his veins. Hot, red, surging, angry blood. Defy him and you may suddenly lose all interest in life."

"It is rumoured that he is unwell."

"Even more reason to obey him, Gervase. When a bear is sick or wounded, it is the worst time to upset him." The bells chimed relentlessly on. "Dear God!"

howled Ralph. "Why must Christianity be so earsplit-
ting?"

As soon as they entered the royal palace, they sensed
that something was amiss. The guards had been doubled,
gates and doors habitually kept open were now locked,
and the newcomers, though familiar visitors, were challenged at each stage of the way to identify themselves
and to declare what business had brought them there.
After leaving their horses at the stables, it took them
several minutes to reach the antechamber next to the
hall. Armed guards in helm and hauberk once again
blocked their way and asked who they were. Gervase
carried no weapon but they eyed Ralph's dagger with
cold suspicion. The visitors were ordered to wait. Their
brusque manner did not endear the guards to Ralph.

"What is going on here?" he challenged.

"You will be told in good time," said one of them.

"I wish to be told *now*."

"Be patient, my lord."

"How can I be patient when some numbskull like you
is asking me who I am every time I come to a door?"
He drew himself up to his full height. "My name is
Ralph Delchard and I have done the King good service.
So has Gervase Bret here. We are royal commissioners,
engaged in the great survey which the King has initiated,
come to answer his summons. Tell him that we are
here."

"He knows, my lord."

"How?"

"Your approach was noted and reported."

"Note and report it again, you idiot!"

"I do not answer to you, my lord."

"His summons was urgent."

"We have our orders."

Hands on the hilts of their swords, the guards stood
shoulder to shoulder in front of the door. There was no
way past them. Ralph was smouldering. Gervase took

him by the elbow and led him to the other side of the room.

"All we can do is to wait," he advised quietly.

"I've a mind to bang their stupid heads together!"

"Where will that get us?"

"It will relieve my irritation," said Ralph, throwing a resentful glance at the two men. "I'll not be treated like this. We are wont to be shown directly into the King's presence. Why do these oafs bar our way? And why is the whole palace crawling with armed guards?"

"They are protecting the King."

"From *us*? We are his loyal subjects, Gervase."

"Everything will be explained in due course."

Ralph was only partially mollified. He retreated into a sullen silence. Gervase, by contrast, remained alert and inquisitive. He crossed to the window to look out into the courtyard, studying the disposition of the guards and trying to draw some conclusions from the impressive show of security outside. When more visitors arrived at the palace, they were closely questioned before they were even allowed to dismount.

Drifting across to his friend, Ralph peered over his shoulder to take a desultory interest in the activity outside. He was in time to see two ladies riding into the courtyard with their train. Even they were subjected to a ritual interrogation.

Ralph suffered a rare lapse into a biblical mood.

"It is easier for a camel to go through the eye of a needle than for innocent visitors to enter the royal palace in Winchester."

Gervase grinned. "I did not know that you were so well-versed in the Gospel According to Matthew," he said, turning to his friend. "We will convert you to the Faith yet."

"I put my faith in my sword arm."

"That, I suspect, is why you were sent for, Ralph."

"What do you mean?"

"You will see."

Raised voices came from the hall. The two men

caught only a few of the words before the door burst open and a short, slim, nervous figure in episcopal garb stormed out with a monk at his heels. The two of them went off down the corridor with more speed than dignity. Gervase recognized the bishop at once.

"Maurice of London," he observed.

"Our late chancellor."

"What brings him to Winchester?"

"I do not know," said Ralph. "Nor why he has been sent home again in such haste. But I like this stern treatment of the Church. It augurs well."

"The Church would disagree."

"It always does."

"I meant that it would disagree most strongly with your choice of Bishop Maurice to represent it." Gervase smiled discreetly. "He is hardly a typical prelate."

Ralph went off into an irreverent peal of laughter.

A third guard appeared in the open doorway and beckoned the visitors over. Gervase and Ralph composed themselves before going into the hall.

William the Conqueror, King of England and Duke of Normandy, was huddled in a high-backed chair at the far end of the room. There was no air of conquest about him now. He seemed more like a victim than a victor. Wrapped in a fur-trimmed cloak, he looked old, tired and pale. Long and unrelenting years of soldiering had taken their toll. A big man, with unusually long arms and legs, he had somehow shrunk in size and power. The face retained its character but the glint of invincibility had faded from the eyes. Nothing could actually frighten him, but he appeared at last to have discovered a need for caution.

He was not alone. Standing behind him was a tall, thin, angular monk in his late twenties, massaging the royal temples with supple fingers and whispering words of comfort to the King. As the pain was slowly coaxed out from his pounding head, William began to sigh with gratitude, almost like a lover yielding to the amorous caresses of his mistress.

Ralph and Gervase bowed and stood before their King. He studied each of them in turn for a moment before lowering his lids to surrender to the seductive touch of the healing hands. With a benign smile, the monk worked gently on, probing the forehead and scalp with his fingertips. Ralph, who had ridden in battle many times behind the military genius known as the Conqueror, was astonished to see his revered general in such a depleted condition. He shot Gervase a look of disbelief.

In an instant, the picture before them changed.

"Enough, Brother Godfrey!" said the patient, sitting up and waving a dismissive hand. "Away!"

Brother Godfrey took a step back, bowed to the King, gave a nod of acknowledgment to the visitors, then shuffled out of the hall. The guard followed him and closed the door after them. Ralph and Gervase were alone with their King.

William appraised them again and shrugged an apology.

"I am not at my best," he said wearily. "My head aches and my body is fatigued. No remedy has been found for my ailments. That monk is the only physician who can bring relief. His hands have almost as much magic as Brother Osmund's."

"Brother Osmund?" said Ralph.

"From New Minster," explained Gervase. "I have met him. A clever doctor. A skillful man in the fight against pain."

"Quite so," added William. "But, alas, Brother Osmund is himself unwell and was unable to attend to me. He sent this pupil in his stead. Brother Godfrey has stilled my demons."

"We are pleased to hear it, my liege," said Ralph.

"Maurice was to blame."

"We saw the bishop leave."

"He would insist on arguing with me," said William

testily. "The moment he did that, warfare broke out inside my head once again. I need peace and quiet. I crave isolation."

There was a long pause. The King gathered his strength.

"You are wondering why I sent for you," he said.

Gervase was deferential. "We are at your command."

"Yes," said Ralph, with gruff politeness. "Dispatch us where you will, my liege, and we are on our way. Which part of the kingdom must we visit this time?"

"Winchester," said William.

"But we are already here."

"This is where I wish you to stay."

"To look into the returns for Hampshire?"

"No, Ralph," said the other. "This is nothing to do with the great survey—the Domesday Book, as it has come to be called. The Final Judgement. The task I have for you concerns my own Domesday." He gave a defiant smile. "I am not yet ready to be called to account."

Ralph was puzzled, but Gervase understood very clearly.

"There is no question of that," he reassured. "Your reign will continue for many years yet. The health and strength for which you are rightly famed will soon return."

"Not if the assassin has his way, Gervase."

Ralph tensed. "Assassin?"

"Did you not see all the guards?"

"Saw them and suffered them, my liege."

"I am a prisoner in my own palace," complained the King. "That was what Maurice and I were arguing about. He wanted me to move to the castle and cower behind its fortifications. I'll not be driven out of here by anyone. Least of all by the bishop of London." A harsh laugh. "Maurice only wants me to vacate the palace so that he will have free rein among the ladies here. There is a rampant stallion under that mitre of his. The man burns with holy lust. When Archbishop Lanfranc reproved him for his lechery, do you know what Maurice told him?''

''What, my liege?''

''That his exploits in the bedchamber were essential to his health. Lechery was his medicine. When he heard that wondrous excuse, Lanfranc blushed for a week.''

''You talked of an assassin,'' said Ralph anxiously. ''Has any attempt been made upon your life?''

''Several, over the years. Kings are never popular.''

''No monarch in Europe is more secure upon his throne.''

''That only makes me an irresistible target.''

''To whom?'' asked Gervase.

''To anyone and everyone,'' said William with an expansive gesture of his arm. ''Conquest produces enemies. Some have waited many years for the chance to kill me. Saxons, Danes, Welsh, Scots, and the King of France would happily dance on my grave. And I do not need to look as far afield as that.'

''In what sense, my liege?'' said Ralph.

''I have a mutinous family,'' sighed the King. ''Odo, my half-brother, bishop of Bayeux and earl of Kent, a man I have loved and garlanded with honours, now languishes in a dungeon in Normandy. Hand him the dagger and he would cheerfully plunge it into my heart. Then there is my eldest son, Robert.'' A shudder went through the King. ''He has betrayed me and turned my old age into an ordeal. And there are others besides those two. Many others. Too many.''

''You have lived with such threats for years.'' noted Ralph. ''What makes you think that one of your enemies will strike now?''

''There have been signs.''

''Of what nature?''

''The kind I cannot ignore,'' said the King. ''I have been spied on at prayer in the cathedral. Someone tried to force his way into my bedchamber at night. At a banquet earlier this week, my wine was poisoned and the man who tasted it for me lies grievous sick. How many more signs do I need?''

"None," agreed Ralph. "Let me be your body-guard."

"I have enough of those."

"Then how may we help?" said Gervase.

"By looking where others are unable to look. By staying here at the palace as my guests. This mouse is guileful. It will take a cunning pair of cats to catch him." The King hauled himself upright. "I know your merit. You have a nose for crime and corruption. I can fill the palace with guards but they would never find an assassin. He would see them coming. Only you can pick up his scent and move with the requisite stealth."

Ralph pondered. "I hate to agree with a bishop," he said at length, "but Maurice of London is right. You would be far safer in the castle. Move there at once, my liege."

"I do not run from danger, Ralph!"

"This is a strategic withdrawal."

"I will never be safe while this man still lives," said the King with bitterness. "Hide away and I simply prolong my existence a little. Stay here and I tempt him out into the open. It is the only way."

"But it involves such a risk," said Gervase.

"That is why I sent for you. Find him."

"Where?" asked Ralph.

"Wherever he is."

The rest of the day was spent in familiarizing themselves with the geography of the palace and with its daily round of activities. Assigned an apartment, the two friends were also given an immunity from the prying attentions of the guards. Ralph and Gervase could move at will around the building. To attract less attention and to cover more ground, they separated and pursued individual lines of inquiry.

Ralph Delchard began with the captain of the guard. "How long have you been at the palace?" he asked.

"Five years, my lord."

"Then you should know your duties by now."

"Has there been some complaint?"

"None that I have heard."

The captain relaxed. He was a big, broad-shouldered man with a white tunic over his hauberk. Dark blue eyes glistened either side of the iron nasal of his helm. They were standing in the courtyard. Ralph noticed that guards were stopping the latest arrivals to question them.

"How many men have you lost?" he asked.

"Lost, my lord?"

"In the time you have been here. How many have been dismissed from royal service?"

The captain shrugged. "Two or three."

"What was their offence?"

"Laziness and insubordination," said the other.

"Would they harbour grudges?"

"Probably."

"When were they dismissed?"

"A long time ago, my lord."

"Do they still reside in the city?"

"No," said the captain. "They left Winchester as fast as they could. I gave them the sharp edge of my tongue. They did not linger for a second dose." A thought struck him. "Except for Huegon, that is."

"Huegon?"

"He has been seen here recently. That surprised me."

"Why?"

"Huegon was thrown out of the palace in disgrace and warned never to come near it again. He was caught taking bribes to allow certain women into the palace at night."

"Prostitutes?"

"Yes, my lord," said the captain with a grim chuckle. "Most paid him in coin but some rewarded him with favours. Huegon was found bare-arsed in the straw with one of the women, rutting like a stag."

"What was his punishment?"

"He was left to rot in a dungeon and repent of his

wrongdoing. Then he was upbraided in front of his fellows. When he was dismissed, Huegon was very bitter."

"What did you say to him?"

"Nothing. He was ejected by the King himself."

"Indeed?"

"Huegon has good reason to feel vengeful towards him."

"Why?"

"The King hates corruption among his knights," said the captain with an approving smirk. "He made an example of him in a way that Huegon will never forget."

"An example?"

"His ears were cut off."

Gervase Bret moved among the other denizens of the palace. He spoke with servants, cooks, ostlers, a chaplain, two minstrels, and anyone else in the royal service who could provide a morsel of information. By the time he had finished, he knew everything of consequence about the daily routine of King William. His footsteps then took him on impulse in the direction of New Minster, the monastery which stood at the heart of the city, adjacent to the palace itself.

He found Brother Osmund in the infirmary.

"You will not remember me," he said.

"I remember you well, Gervase Bret," returned the old monk. "You once discussed the virtues of Augustine of Hippo with me. You had actually studied *De Civitate Dei*."

"Not as closely as you, Brother Osmund. You exposed my ignorance but did so with such gentleness that I did not feel in any way humiliated. I thank you for that."

"And I thank you for coming here, Gervase."

"I heard that you were ailing."

"Yes," said the other, grimacing as a sudden pain hit him. "I have been here in the infirmary for days. It is a poor doctor who himself is in need of doctoring. Illness will damage my reputation as a physician."

"Nothing could do that, Brother Osmund."

The old man was plainly in great discomfort. He lay hunched up on his mattress under a rough woollen blanket. All the colour had been chased out of his wrinkled face and there was a quiet panic in his eyes. It seemed cruel to engage him in conversation, but Brother Osmund knew things about the King which could be of help to Gervase.

"The King misses you sorely," said Gervase.

"I despise myself for letting him down."

"Is he often indisposed?"

"Headaches descend on him from time to time. They match his black moods. I thank God that my fingers have been able to relieve his pain. The King has come to rely on me."

"When did you last visit him?"

Brother Osmund went off into a fit of coughing and it was minutes before he was able to answer the question. Gervase knelt beside him and listened with care to the frail voice. Brother Osmund was fiercely loyal to the King, divulging nothing of a confidential nature, yet giving Gervase enough insights into the royal malady to make his journey to New Minster worthwhile. When another spasm of pain shot through the patient, Gervase put out a consoling hand.

"Say no more, Brother Osmund. I have troubled you enough."

"It was kind of you to come."

"I wanted to pay my respects."

"You have medicined my mind."

"Good," said Gervase. "When you have recovered, we will talk again about Augustine of Hippo."

"Perhaps."

Osmund smiled sadly. He brightened when he saw someone coming towards them. Brother Godfrey was carrying a wooden bowl in his hands. He gave a nod of greeting to Gervase before turning to the patient with concern.

"How do you feel now, Brother Osmund?" he asked.

"The pain still torments me."

"Here is something to banish it," said Godfrey, holding up the bowl. "I have mixed the potion in accordance with your instructions. Drink it down."

The newcomer lifted the old man's head up with one hand so that Osmund could more easily sip from the bowl. Gervase was struck by Brother Godfrey's tenderness and affection. It was almost like watching a devoted son attending to his father.

"Godfrey is my salvation," said Osmund. "Without him to look after me, I believe that I should have perished already."

"The Lord still has work for you at New Minster."

"I may survive to do it. Your skill has given me hope."

"You taught me all I know," said Godfrey with pride.

"Use that knowledge to heal me."

"I will, Brother Osmund. I will."

The potion seemed to have a calming effect. Pain ebbed away and the old monk lay back with a look of contentment. His eyes glazed over. Brother Godfrey whispered to Gervase.

"Let him sleep, I beseech you. He needs rest."

"Of course."

They stole quietly out of the infirmary. Gervase threw a glance over his shoulder.

"What ails him?"

"A disease is eating at his entrails," sighed Godfrey. "It is hideous to watch him suffer so. I can arrest the pain but a cure still eludes me."

"He fears the worst," said Gervase.

"I know."

"Is he like to die?"

Brother Godfrey's face puckered with alarm.

"Osmund must not die," he said. "I love him."

Ralph managed a brief exchange with Maurice of London. Still exasperated, the bishop was mounting his horse for departure. A dozen knights were in the saddle to escort their master out of Winchester. Maurice was flanked by two monks. Ralph bore down on him with a purposeful stride.

"I crave a word, Your Grace!" he called.

"Do not delay me," said Maurice. "I am eager to quit the palace and return to a city where my advice is respected."

"You argued with the King, I believe?"

"That is no concern of yours."

"I was outside the hall when you swept out."

"I do not like eavesdroppers."

The bishop tried to ride off, but Ralph took the reins of his horse to detain him. Maurice's ire swelled. Veins stood out on his forehead and words hissed out of him like steam.

"Stand aside!"

"I wish to speak with you, Your Grace."

"How dare you obstruct my path. Who are you, sir?"

He glared down at Ralph, but the latter held his ground. Maurice peered at him more closely, then nodded resignedly.

"Ralph Delchard!"

"I wondered when you would recognize me."

"This is not the first time you have got in my way," said the bishop. "I seem to recall tripping over you when I was chancellor here. You have a talent for obstruction."

Ralph beamed. "It has often been admired."

"Not by me."

Ralph looked up into the pinched face of the bishop. It was difficult to believe that such an unprepossessing man was such a successful libertine. His consecration had not been allowed to interfere with his pleasures. Maurice had found a way to reconcile his episcopal duties with his lecherous promptings.

"I am trying to serve my King," continued Ralph, "and I can best do that if I know the substance of your quarrel with him." He led the horse away a short distance so that their conversation had a token privacy.

"We both know that he is in danger, Your Grace. What is its source?"

"His own folly."

"I have never heard King William called a fool before."

"He is too stubborn for his own good," snapped Maurice. "Why ask for my counsel if he discards it? I would have put a ring of steel around him that only an army could pierce."

"And where would that army hail from?"

"Come, my lord. I am sure that you have heard the reports from our intelligencers. The Vikings have been making preparations for several months."

"They would never reach Winchester."

"Not in numbers, perhaps. But they do not need to."

"What do you mean?"

"One would be enough to kill a king."

Gervase spent an improving hour with the steward, an arrogant man with a crushing self-importance but one whose knowledge of the household was invaluable. Gervase gleaned an immense amount of information about every aspect of the royal palace. To achieve that, it was well worth enduring the steward's supercilious manner.

When Ralph went back to the apartment, he found Gervase poring over a sheet of parchment with a stylus in his hand.

"Writing a letter to Alys?" he teased.

"No," said Gervase. "I have turned artist."

"Let me see."

Ralph studied the diagram that his friend had drawn. It was a plan of the royal palace, crude but identifiable, replete with a series of tiny crosses.

"What do these represent?" asked Ralph, pointing.

"Guards."

"Are there really as many as that?"

"I counted them."

"What else did you do?"

Gervase gave his friend a concise account of his

movements since they parted and Ralph was fascinated.
He responded with the details of his own investigations,
and it was Gervase's turn to have his curiosity aroused
to the point where the questions bubbled out of him.
Pooling their evidence, they began to sift it with care.
Ralph was the first to reach a verdict.

"Huegon may be our man," he decided.

"He has a motive certainly," agreed Gervase, "but
hardly the means. Look at my drawing. Guards everywhere. How would this Huegon slip past them?"

"In the most obvious way. By looking like one of
them. Only another soldier could deceive all those soldiers. He knows every room and corridor in the palace,
Gervase. Huegon knows where to hide."

"The King has a guard beside him at all times."

"One man can murder two if he takes them una-
wares," said Ralph, thinking it through. "Besides, the
bodyguard is not always in attendance. The King dismissed him when he spoke to us."

"That is true."

"Huegon is the villain here. I feel it in my bones."

"Acting on his own behalf?"

"Or in the pay of foreigners. A man who can be led
astray by prostitutes would be easy prey for the bribes
of enemy spies. Bitterness breeds traitors."

"Huegon has enough bitterness. That is clear. But I
am still not convinced that he is our man, Ralph." Gervase indicated the parchment. "Study the drawing."

"Why?"

"It holds the answer we are seeking."

"One of those crosses is Huegon."

Gervase grew pensive. "Perhaps we should be looking at a cross of another kind," he said. "Bishop Maurice."

"He is no assassin. For all his bluster, Maurice is as
loyal as anyone in the kingdom. He was a shrewd chancellor until his consecration. No, Gervase," Ralph said
firmly, "the bishop is too busy fornicating to have time

for betrayal. Why do you even mention Maurice?''

"I remembered what the King said about him.''

Huddled under his cloak, William the Conqueror sat in the pool of light from the flickering candles. Food and wine lay untouched on the table before him. When the door opened at the far end of the hall, he did not even look up. Two figures were conjured out of the gloom. Brother Godfrey and the guard waited until the King became aware of their presence. A nod dismissed the guard and the man vanished into the darkness. They heard the door close behind him.

"I am sorry to call you so late," said William with evident strain, "but my head is bursting apart. Work your magic, Brother Godfrey. Bring me some rest."

"I will," promised the other.

The monk stepped behind the chair and began to massage the patient's temples, gently at first, then with more pressure. After a few minutes, a sigh of relief escaped the King. His eyes closed, his tension seemed to ease. The fingers worked tirelessly on, exploring the whole scalp for pain, and drawing it slowly out. William began to doze.

"Sleep," whispered Brother Godfrey. "That is what you need. Sleep, sleep. Surrender yourself to sleep and you will soon be restored. Your mind and body want rest. Sleep, sleep."

The massage continued until the head eventually lolled to one side. Hands which had eased the King into his slumber now took on a different role. Brother Godfrey untied the rope at his waist to slip around the neck of the sleeping man. It was as far as he got. Ralph Delchard leapt out of the shadows to fell the monk with one blow of his forearm, and the King was suddenly awake, standing over his would-be assassin with a sword held at the monk's throat. Gervase Bret emerged from a dark corner to look down at the villain.

"*Why*?" demanded the King. "Who paid you to kill me?"

"A voice from Heaven bid me do it," said Godfrey.

"Did it also bid you to poison Brother Osmund so that you could take his place as my physician?"

The monk's eyes moistened with regret. "It was the only way to reach you," he explained. "I had to inflict pain on someone I love in order to kill someone I hate. You have done too much damage to the Church," he accused, pointing a finger at William. "You have killed and looted your way through England like a barbarous heathen. You betrayed your God. He instructed me to call you to account."

The King bawled a command and a dozen armed men burst into the hall. Ralph hauled the monk up from the floor. Brother Godfrey was dragged unceremoniously out by the guards.

William sheathed his sword and gave a broad grin.

"It seems as if my Domesday has been deferred."

"We have Gervase to thank for that, my liege," said Ralph.

"It was that remark about Maurice of London, my liege," recalled Gervase. "You said that lechery was his medicine. The bishop's health depended on it. Yours depended on the skills of Brother Osmund. Yet he was indisposed when you needed him most. I visited him in New Minster. I wondered why such a noted physician could not heal himself. My suspicion fell on Brother Godfrey. He was biding his time to strike. All we had to do was to contrive the opportunity for him."

"Yes," said Ralph ruefully. "I was searching for an assassin among the soldiers when, all the time, he was lurking inside the cowl of a Benedictine monk."

"I am deeply grateful to you both," said the King.

After he had showered them with praise, the friends left the hall together. Gervase could not resist a teasing nudge.

"Do you still call Winchester a city of eunuchs?"

"No," conceded Ralph. "Not while it has men like Brother Godfrey in its midst. I loathe what he tried to do, but I admire the wild courage which drove him on to do it. Who would have thought the Church had so much pulsing manhood in it?" He gave a ripe chuckle. "No wonder they elevated Maurice to a bishopric!"

Edward D. Hoch is undoubtedly the preeminent mystery short-story writer today. His work has earned him an Edgar award and many other commendations. He has published over 700 short stories, 200 articles and reviews, 5 novels, and 9 collections of short mystery fiction. In addition he has edited 20 annual Year's Best Mystery and Suspense Stories *and 25 anthologies.*

Many of his stories have historical themes. One of his recurring characters is late 1800's cowboy detective Ben Snow, and another is Dr. Sam Hawthorne, who practices medicine and detection in the 1920's and 1930's.

With such a variety of interests, it shouldn't have surprised us to receive this story from Ed. But it did. Who could have known that Genghis Khan, in the midst of his plunder of Russia, would need the services of a slave to investigate a murder?

THE MOVABLE CITY

Edward D. Hoch

N ow, in the year 1222 as the Mongol armies of the
great Genghis Khan pressed forward into Russia,
plundering the land between the Volga and Dnepr
Rivers, there was one named Bazin who rode with them
though he was not himself a Mongol. Taken as a slave,
Bazin now worked with other slaves in the armory, making and repairing the bows, arrows, spears and swords
the Mongol hordes used in combat.

It was an arduous life, even for a young man in his
twenties, traveling with the nomadic Mongols across the
countryside. Victory for the Khan's armies on the bat-
tlefield often meant packing up everything in the movable city for a journey of hundreds of miles to a place
where the city could take root again, if only for a few
weeks or months. The Mongol armory occupied a large
tent or yurt, a cylindrical structure of latticework poles
covered by felt. A conical roof of poles had an aperture
at the top for the escape of smoke from the stone hearth
below. In varying sizes the yurt served as living quarters,
battle tents, hospital and even slave quarters for a city
that often contained as many as a hundred thousand warriors. The largest yurt of them all was reserved for Gen-

ghis Khan, with lion and leopard skins on the outside
and ermine and sable within.

Bazin shared his yurt with several other slaves who
worked in the armory, and it was one of these, Shabani
by name, who brought him word that the Mongol city
would be on the move once more. Bazin was just fin-
ishing work on a bow of stiff wood, the army's principal
weapon, when the young man with the mottled skin told
him, "Great Khan has scored a victory at the Volga.
The city is moving north."

With the Mongol warriors in the field it fell to the
women and children, along with working slaves like Bazin and Shabani, to prepare for the move. Each yurt had
to be mounted on a cart drawn by a dozen or more oxen,
and much of this work was done by the women. It was
toward dusk on that day when a strong mist moved in-
land from the river, obscuring many of the surrounding
yurts. Bazin moved helplessly, gathering up supplies
from the armory, finally lighting torches to guide his
way through the mist.

"Bazin!" a woman's voice called out. "Is that you?"

In the flickering torchlight he recognized Vasca, the
comely daughter of the treasury guardian, Juchi. "Here,
Vasca!" he called out, waving the torch. "This way!"

She came at him out of the mist and he saw at once
that she was alarmed. "Have you seen my father? I
though I heard him cry out, but I can see nothing in this
river fog."

"Come with me," Bazin urged, taking her arm. "He
should be in the treasury preparing for our departure."

The treasury yurt was smaller than the armory, and
the dying fire at its center was enough to cast its glow
over the entire interior. Bazin saw the leather and brass
chests full of gold coins and looted jewelry. He saw the
tables at which the soldiers of Genghis Khan lined up
to receive their meager pay. And then he saw something
else.

"Stay back, Vasca," he cautioned, holding the torch
higher as he moved forward.

But she had already seen enough to know. "It is my father!" she said with a gasp of terror, running forward toward the crumpled figure amidst the chests.

Juchi lay on the ground, all life gone from his body. He had been strangled with a silken bowstring.

When the guards were summoned, Bazin and the other slaves found themselves rounded up, chained and imprisoned in one of the smaller yurts, already loaded onto a cart for transport to the city's new location. Bazin tried to sleep, to empty his mind of thoughts of what the next day could bring. Slaves meant nothing to a great conqueror like Khan. If a crime had been done and one of them was suspected, he would order them all killed, perhaps even dismembered in the Chinese fashion as a lesson to others.

"Will they kill us?" Bazin's fellow slave Shabani whispered from his side in the darkness.

"We will know soon enough."

They traveled through the night, bumping over the rutted road toward an unknown destination, an entire city of several thousand tents, with warriors in their chain-mail shirts, slaves, herdsmen, saddle-makers, physicians, mapmakers, shamans, musicians, women and children, all on the move. There were falconers with hooded birds ready to seek out prey, wheeled catapults brought all the way from China, entire herds of horses, cattle, sheep and camels. And riding at the front with his personal bodyguard was the great Genghis Khan, the most powerful man on earth.

Bazin wondered what would happen to Vasca now that her father had been slain. He had come to know her in a general way during the ten months since his capture by the Mongol hordes in southern Asia. He knew that her mother was dead and her only relative was an uncle named Tyer, Juchi's brother. Thinking such thoughts, he drifted in and out of sleep until the cart finally came to a jolting stop.

"We are here," Shabani told him. "Wake up!"

"I have barely slept."

Mongol guards prodded them with spears, forcing them from the yurt. Their commander shouted instructions, and after waiting in the chill dawn air they were led forward. Bazin saw at once that the great tent of the Khan, the largest of the yurts, was already standing at the center of the new city and it was toward this yurt they were marched. Everywhere families were removing their tents from the wagons, or in a few cases building new ones. The openings of the tents always faced south in keeping with the sacred rule, the exact direction determined by the compasses they'd brought from China. Shamans moved among the people giving their blessing.

Only once before had Bazin seen the great Genghis Khan, on the day he was taken captive and doomed to a life of slavery. A hundred other prisoners had been put to death, but the great Khan rode past the remaining captives, pointing out young women for his officers and strong young men for the slave quarters. Bazin still remembered the sight of him, a stocky Oriental on horseback, stringy black beard hanging from the edge of his jaw, eyes cold as the tundra. One motion of the hand, and Bazin had lived. This time, perhaps, the decision would be death.

There were twenty of them herded like animals into the great Khan's yurt of linen and gold, forced to crawl on their hands and knees. Bazin quickly realized that all were slaves who worked in the armory. Genghis Khan, a man in his mid-fifties, sat unmoving atop a small throne. The yurt's fire blazed in front of him, casting a glow over all. As the slaves remained in a line on their knees, one of Khan's regimental commanders, General Noyon, stepped forward to speak.

"Our esteemed warrior and brave brother Juchi, keeper of the treasury, was brutally slain, strangled by a silken bowstring in the bloodless manner of death befitting his noble birth. This happened under cover of fog, as we were about to move from our old encampment. The motive for the crime is clear, since a leathern chest of gold coins was stolen from the treasury tent at the same time. Our brother Juchi was strangled by the thief. This silken bowstring was woven in the armory tent.'' He held it aloft. ''One of you slaves is the killer and thief.''

All was silence for a moment and then the great Khan spoke. ''If the guilty slave does not reveal himself and return the treasure, all twenty of you will be beheaded, starting at the eastern end of the line. As the Mongol tide has swept across Asia from east to west, so too your heads will fly until the truth is known.''

A tall swordsman with powerful arms took his place behind the first kneeling man, raising his sharpened scimitar. ''Wait!'' Bazin shouted, leaping to his feet. ''Wait, my great Khan. I beg permission to speak.''

The commander pointed a finger at him. ''Cut out that man's tongue!''

But Genghis Khan spoke. ''Let us hear him first. He may keep his tongue for a few more minutes.''

''Mighty Khan, if you kill these innocent men you still will not recover the missing treasure. What do humble slaves know of silken bowstrings? Would any of us slay Juchi in a bloodless manner because of his noble birth? Or would we run him through with a sword or arrow and be done with it?''

There was silence again as the Khan seemed to ponder Bazin's words. The tall swordsman was moving down the line toward him. Then the Mongol conqueror spoke. ''Your words carry a certain wisdom, slave. Can you also tell me the killer's name?''

''Not yet, mighty Khan. But give me my freedom for a day and I will find the one you seek.'' It was a rash proposal, but the alternative was instant death.

Once more Genghis Khan was silent. Then he spoke. ''What is this slave's name?'' he asked General Noyon.

''He is Bazin, taken in the southern campaign some ten months back.''

''Hear me, Bazin,'' the great Khan spoke. ''At this time tomorrow you will tell me the name of the thief and murderer, and the location of my plundered treasures, or your head will be stricken from your body. Do you understand?''

"Yes, my lord."

"Away with you now! Your fellow slaves in the armory will remain at work, under close guard. If you attempt to escape, they will join you in eternity."

Freed for the moment, Bazin quickly left the Khan's yurt and found Vasca waiting for him among the trees. "Have they freed you?" she asked.

"Only until tomorrow. Then I must reveal the killer or die myself. And I must find the missing treasure chest. General Noyon is certain the silken bowstring used to kill your father came from the armory."

"Anyone could have gotten in there to steal it," she told him. "I have been in there myself with my father and uncle. All the commanders like General Noyon come to replenish their weapons, and even individual warriors might come to replace a broken bowstring."

He agreed it was true. "But they will not blame one of their own. Not with slaves as easy scapegoats."

Vasca headed away from the main encampment toward the river and when they had reached it she pointed and said, "Across this water is freedom for you. Swim it and be gone to safety."

But Bazin shook his head. "My fellow slaves would be killed if I fled. I must stay and do what I can."

"Even if it means your own life?"

"Perhaps I can discover the real killer."

They came to a yurt set among the trees by the river, some distance away from the others. A few head of cattle and a horse grazed nearby. "This is my uncle's," she told Bazin. "I will be staying here with him."

Tyer appeared from among the trees, followed by a woman Bazin did not know. Both were carrying wood for the yurt fire. Vasca's uncle was taller than most Mongol warriors, with a stringy beard somewhat like the Khan's own. His deep dark eyes went from his niece to Bazin. "What is this slave doing here?" he asked.

"He has been granted a day's freedom by the Khan to find my father's killer, or else he will be put to death."

Tyer's face softened, as if in sorrow at Bazin's approaching doom. "Find Juchi's killer and I will reward you personally," he promised. "Come, Vasca, it is nearly time for the funeral service."

She entered the tent to procure some amulet, treading through an opening already worn bare by the passage of feet. Bazin wondered what she must feel with her father dead, forced to live with an uncle and his woman until some Mongol warrior claimed her for a bride. The woman, not much older than Vasca, had attractive Mongol features and skin that was darker than most. As Bazin stood by awkwardly, knowing he would not be among the funeral-goers, she finally introduced herself. "I am Cathay, Tyer's woman. Where were you taken captive?"

"In the south, nearly a year ago."

"Your family?"

"All killed by the Khan."

She eyed him up and down. "Vasca likes you. I can tell. If you are not killed tomorrow she could even become your woman."

"How—how is that possible?"

"They always need fighting men. Haven't you noticed that everyone over fourteen rides out these nights into battle? Even slaves are given arms if they have proven their loyalty."

He helped her get a fire going and then wandered out of the yurt. Mongol warriors were usually buried with honors, and the undertaker was one of the busiest men in the movable city. When Vasca and her uncle returned from the funeral he saw at once that she had been crying. "Come walk with me," he said.

"I can't, Bazin. The cows are late for their milking. I must work to earn my keep at my uncle's tent."

He wandered alone along the river, seeking out something that might be different from their last campsite. In many yurts he could see warriors sleeping after the long night's journey, and he knew that meant they would be riding into battle again with the coming of darkness. It was the missing leather chest that he sought as much as the killer, but he saw them everywhere he looked. Virtually every family had one for transporting their goods, often carpets looted from some caravan or women's silk garments bartered from an Arab trader.

His journey around the city of tents finally brought him to the treasury and he attempted to enter. It was General Noyon himself who blocked the doorway. "No slaves admitted here!" The odor of his breath told Bazin he had been drinking *ayrag*, the fermented mare's milk which was the Mongols' favorite beverage to instill courage before battle.

"Surely you remember me, great General! The Khan himself gave me one day to recover the stolen treasure and find the killer of brave Juchi."

The Mongol glared at him. "Better you look in the slave quarters than in the treasury."

"I only wish to become familiar with the layout of this yurt, which is strange to me. Simply accompany me as I walk around, that is all I ask."

Noyon grumbled but did as Bazin suggested. As with the other yurts, the interior of the treasury tent was laid out in a circle around the fire that burned beneath the roof opening. As he had seen the previous night, there was a long table used for dispersing stipends to the troops. Locked chests of leather and brass stood behind this table, and more were positioned near the opposite wall. One was even open, and men were counting out coins at a second table.

Bazin tested the walls of the yurt. "Perhaps the missing chest might have been removed through an opening in the wall."

The Mongol general shook his head. "See how tightly the latticework is woven. There is no break or opening."

"How can we be sure this is the same tent that served as the treasury at the previous campsite?"

"You know the larger ones are unique, slave! Did you not notice the cloth of gold woven to the exterior? And if the chest was stolen in that manner, there would have been no need for killing Juchi."

His words made sense. Bazin studied the men working in the treasury, none of whom he knew. Most were older, except for one who had lost an arm in battle and was unable to fight. "Do slaves ever work here?" he asked the general.

"Of course not! They tend the herds and work like you in the armory. Some are carpenters and craftsmen of various sorts. Like yourself, they were taken after battle, their lives spared because their skills were needed."

Bazin gave a final look at the treasury. "Could the chest have been buried and the coins dispersed among the other chests?"

"Impossible! The coins and gold pieces were counted after discovery of the theft. And any fresh digging in the camp was uncovered and examined. The thief planned well. He knew that the confusion of moving camp would prevent a thorough search of the yurts. He waited until just the proper moment for his crime."

They went outside together. "I see the catapults are moving up," Bazin said. "You will attack the enemy tonight."

"Slaves have lost their tongues for saying less than that. If you value yours, keep it silent." General Noyon turned and strode away.

Given the freedom of the city for a day, Bazin chose to follow the catapults as they trundled toward the front lines. They were massive wooden machines on wheels, developed by the Chinese, capable of hurling heavy stones or flaming objects great distances over walls and moats. The Khan's armies had three in service this day, and he knew others were being built. He tried to envision a thief using one of these machines to catapult the stolen chest out of the camp, but to what avail? The treasure would be lost, perhaps scattered among enemy soldiers. Besides that, it took more than one man to wind the catapult's ropes and launch its cargo.

The hours of late afternoon were filled with activity as the troops emerged from their tents to prepare for battle. There were horses to be saddled and weapons to be checked. Bazin watched it all for a time, and then began to wonder where he would spend the night. He was reluctant to return to the slave quarters behind its guarded fence on his last night of freedom, perhaps his last night of life. Presently, as dusk settled over the valley, he returned to Tyer's yurt because he knew Vasca would be there.

"She is giving the cows their evening milking," Cathay told him, explaining Vasca's absence. Busy at the hearth, she was preparing the evening meal before Tyer rode off into battle. Bazin saw that their leather chest was open, and he could not help peering inside. But there was no missing gold, only a Persian rug, some inlaid silver and clothing.

"Did you unload this tent by yourself?" he asked, knowing that some women did.

"No, no. Tyer had it off the cart and in position before I arrived. I traveled with Vasca to comfort her. He works hard. This has been a difficult day for him, burying a brother this morning and riding into battle tonight."

Tyer came up from the river where he had been washing himself. "What luck, Bazin?" he asked.

"None, I fear. There is not a clue to what happened."

Tyer shook his head sadly. "I will go with you in the morning to the great Khan's tent, to plead for more time."

Bazin watched as he dressed for battle, adjusting the chain-mail shirt and donning the leather-and-brass helmet. Then Tyer checked his horse, its neck, chest and flanks covered with leather because he would be in the first lines of attack. At last he picked up his lacquered leather shield and mounted the horse. "I will be back," he said, and the words were meant for Cathay.

• • •

When darkness had fallen, Bazin led Vasca up over the next hill, following the route of the Mongol army. From there they could see the attack on the city that lay in the distance, the catapulted fireballs lighting the sky as they streaked across the face of the moon toward their target.

"God, it's beautiful!" Vasca said, lying in the grass by his side.

"But men are dying there, perhaps even your uncle."

"Don't say that! I have buried a father this day."

As the Mongol cavalry drew nearer the city walls, a barrage of flaming arrows was launched by the horsemen. If there was any response it could not be seen in the darkness. "All this for the treasury of Genghis Khan," Bazin said. "Another city looted, thousands of people slaughtered, more slaves like me taken captive. Is it any wonder that I will die in the morning unnoticed? All of us might die, our places taken by a new crop of slaves."

"Do not speak that way. My uncle is of noble birth. He has influence with the Khan."

They were starting back toward their city of tents when suddenly a mottled face appeared before them, lit only by the moonlight. It was his fellow slave, Shabani. "What are you doing here?" Bazin asked.

"I have escaped from the slave quarters! No one saw me. Come flee with me, Bazin, or surely we will die in the morning."

"If we flee, eighteen others will be put to death. You must return before the midnight bed-check."

He shook his head. "I will never return."

"Shabani!"

But the man with the mottled face vanished into the darkness, making for the river. "What will you do now?" Vasca asked Bazin.

"Nothing. Pretend I never saw him. I only hope he makes it."

They returned to her uncle's yurt, where they could still hear the distant sounds of battle. Cathay pretended to sleep but they knew she was awake, anxious for Tyer's return. That did not come until after midnight, when the whinny of a horse alerted Bazin to his arrival. He moved his hand away from Vasca and sat up on his straw mat.

"How went the battle?" Cathay asked her man.

Tyer looked around at them, exhausted but unhurt. "We will need another night or two to topple the city's walls. For now we sleep."

"Were many killed?" Vasca wanted to know.

"Many, on both sides. The Khan ordered a retreat to regroup our forces."

"Will they attack us?"

Tyer shook his head. "No one would challenge the forces of Genghis Khan." He shed his chain-mail and dropped onto the mat by Cathay's side. In a moment he was asleep.

Bazin was awakened at dawn by the first rays of the rising sun coming through the yurt's entrance and striking him full in the face. He rolled over and tried to block them out, but then realized that Vasca was already up and preparing food.

"Did you sleep well?" she asked, seeing that he was awake. Her voice was low, so as not to disturb the others.

"Well enough, for what might be my last night."

Her breath caught at his words. "My uncle will go with you. No harm will—"

But as she spoke a shadow fell across the entrance. Two Mongol warriors from the personal bodyguard of General Noyon had come to bring him before Genghis Khan. Suddenly Bazin saw the answer, saw what he must do.

He grabbed up one of Tyer's arrows and plunged it into the earth at the yurt's entrance. "This far and no further!" he yelled at them. "You will not enter this tent! I will come out to join you."

"Come quickly," one of the men said gruffly. "No one keeps the great Khan waiting."

Bazin bent to kiss Vasca goodbye. "I will be back," he promised. Tyer had awakened by then and dressed quickly, accompanying Bazin in silence.

They passed through the wooded area to the main sections of the tent city, where rows of yurts stretched as far as Bazin could see. "This is a bad day," he told Tyer. "I feel it in my bones."

"Be brave," the Mongol said. "I will speak on your behalf."

Bazin glanced around at the guards and saw that Vasca and Cathay were coming too, hurrying along in the rear. As they passed near the slave quarters, he had another surprise. Shabani had been recaptured and was in line with the other armory workers. They were being marched toward the big center tent to face the judgment of Khan.

Once again Bazin entered the tent on his knees and faced the Mongol ruler's throne. General Noyon came forward and spoke. "Great Khan, you have given this lowly slave Bazin one day to find your missing treasure and reveal the killer of brave Juchi. He has not done so."

Tyer started to step forward in his defense, but Bazin himself stood up, inviting the wrath of Khan as he had on the previous day. "I have had no chance to speak until now," he said. "I am prepared to recover the treasure and reveal Juchi's killer."

"Impossible!" General Noyon snorted.

"The killer is in this yurt right now."

Genghis Khan leaned forward on his throne. "Speak now, slave, but be prepared to prove your accusations or you will die a thousand deaths!"

Bazin took a deep breath. "I have already shown you yesterday how this would not be the crime of a slave. Strangulation with a silken bowstring, so as not to spill noble blood, meant that the killer and thief was probably a noble himself, of equal or higher rank. Furthermore, he—or she—was someone known to Juchi, whom he admitted to the treasury after hours and without question. I admit I had no clue to the killer's identity or the location of the stolen chest until I awakened in Tyer's yurt this morning with the sun in my eyes.''

"You saw the rising sun as an omen?'' the general asked.

"I did, because it rose on the eastern horizon as it always does. Yet the rising sun came through the yurt's entrance to strike my face. The entrance was facing east, not south, and that told me Tyer had slain his brother.''

Vasca screamed as her uncle pulled a dagger from his belt and lunged at Bazin. But General Noyon gave a quick signal and his guards wrestled Tyer to the ground. Bazin looked back at Vasca to be certain she was all right and then resumed his explanation.

"Cathay told me Tyer had unloaded and positioned the tent himself. I believe he chose a spot away from the others so no one would notice his additional activities. This morning, when I realized it, I asked myself why this wrong direction was necessary. The answer came when I remembered how the earth was flattened and worn at the entrance. The yurt had been there only an hour or so, too recent for the passage of feet to have worn the entrance to the bare earth. A hole had been dug and then refilled, with the earth tamped down until it looked worn. Something had been secretly buried there and the yurt positioned so the bare ground would seem like the passage of feet at the entrance. What else but the stolen chest? After burying it, Tyer must have realized the surrounding trees made it impossible to position the tent facing south as it should have been. Luckily for him it was away from the main group of tents, so he thought no one would notice the wrong direction.''

"Is the treasure chest there?'' Genghis Khan demanded.

"I believe it is, great Khan,'' Bazin assured him. "When the general's guards came for me this morning

I pretended to block their path by plunging an arrow into the earth at the entrance to the yurt. It struck something only a few inches down.''

Khan raised his hand to General Noyon. ''Take your men and bring me what you find there.''

Tyer had collapsed onto his knees. ''Great Khan, I was maddened by the wealth I saw there whenever I visited my brother at the treasury. Please forgive me. Forgive me for my sins against you and against my brother!''

Genghis Khan was silent until the general's men returned carrying the leather chest. Noyon himself opened it, tipping it until the gold coins cascaded at Khan's feet.

A swordsman moved into position behind the kneeling Tyer. Bazin looked back at the line of slaves where his friend Shabani stood. ''Wait, great Khan! In return for recovering this treasure I ask two favors. Lift the punishment from all the slaves and allow them to return to work at the armory. And spare the life of Tyer so he may fight again for the glory of your name!''

Genghis Khan was silent for a moment and then he spoke. ''The slaves may return to work as you request. And you will be freed to join us as a warrior. Tyer will ride at the head of our legions this night, to victory or to death.''

Bazin spent the night with Vasca and Cathay. It was after midnight when they brought back Tyer's body, tied to the back of his horse. He had charged up to the city's walls alone and been cut down by the defenders' arrows.

It was Cathay who gave them the horse. ''Across the river is freedom,'' she said. ''The Khan will not pursue you or punish the slaves now that he has his treasure back. Go! And be happy!''

Bazin rode all night with Vasca clinging to his waist. They settled finally far to the west, beyond the Goryn River. Five years later, when their daughter was two, word came that Genghis Khan had died, and the Mongol empire was split among his three sons. Soon the greatest conquering army in history, with its movable cities and hordes of a hundred thousand men, was no more.

Anne Perry's first book, The Cater Street Hangman, *takes place in 1881 and introduces Charlotte Ellison, a young woman of good family whose sister is murdered. When Charlotte marries Thomas Pitt, the investigating policeman, the scandal is almost as great as the murder itself. Both the series and the marriage endured, however, and Thomas and Charlotte have appeared in more than fifteen books to great acclaim and numerous award nominations, including the Edgar, Anthony, and Agatha.*

Not content with chronicling the lives of the Pitts, in 1990, Anne began a new series, set in the early Victorian period just after the Crimean War. The Face of a Stranger *features William Monk, a man who, because of amnesia, must rediscover himself, and Hester Latterly, a Crimean nurse, who must readapt to a society that she has moved beyond. These books have proved as popular as the Charlotte and Thomas Pitt series.* Weighed in the Balance *is the seventh Monk and Latterly mystery.*

The following tale is set in Spain during the later years of the Inquisition. It marks a departure in time and place for Anne while still reflecting the deep concern for justice that infuses all her work. And, for this medievalist, at least, it is refreshing to see those involved in the Inquisition treated as the various and complex individuals they were.

THE CASE OF THE SANTO NIÑO

Anne Perry

Frey José leaned a little further forward. His ear was almost to the floorboards as he listened at the crack which gave onto the room below. Beside him in the dark, Frey Domingo was breathing heavily in his excitement. José could feel the rough texture of his black Dominican robe, he was so close; and smell the warmth of his body. He had blown out the candle in case its faint light should shine through and warn the men below that they were overhead. At all costs they must not know that. No heretic would betray himself if he knew the inquisitors were only feet away, listening and remembering every word.

Personally José thought it was a waste of time. And he was also extremely uncomfortable. It was a ridiculous position, crouched here with his face on the floor and his knees buckled under him. But Frey Domingo was certain it would be profitable, and it was all in the service of God and the Holy Inquisition. The enemies of the Faith must be rooted out and if possible, by persuasion, their heresies turned and their souls saved. Frey

Domingo was always sure about everything. He was years older than José, thin, ascetic. In his youth he had been a fine scholar. José had been told that he actually wore a hair shirt under his robes, like the great Torquemada, Inquisitor General of all Spain. He had not known whether that was true or not. If it were, it might account for his temper!

Frey Domingo hissed between his teeth and poked José sharply in the ribs. Obediently José returned his attention to the room below.

"So what was it he said?" the voice came gently, curious, interested. It was Felipe, a familiar of the Inquisition who practised as an agent provocateur, pretending to be a fellow accused and drawing out damning confessions. José disliked his smooth, deceitful face and his elegant clothes. He knew people sometimes bragged of offences they had not really committed, or said things in anger which were only partly true.

Frey Domingo had pointed out that honest sons and daughters of the Church would hate heresy as much as anyone, and never, however frightened or angry, admit to such a dishonest thing. Perhaps he was right. He ought to listen to what was being said.

"That we had made a mockery of the Mass," the other voice replied. That must be Esteban Gomez, accused of just that heinous crime.

"Oh?" Felipe's voice was raised in interest. "How?"

"By conducting our own, with everything backwards, of course," Esteban answered. "And dancing about and laughing."

"Not so serious," Felipe said soothingly.

Next to José, Frey Domingo clicked his teeth in irritation.

José smiled. Good thing the candle was out and Domingo could not see him.

"Those miserable brothers of the Holy Office think so!" Esteban said angrily.

"It isn't, not without a proper Wafer of the Host." Felipe sounded pleased. "Pretty futile really. Just a few drunken men making fools of themselves. Who else was there?"

Frey Domingo let out a little grunt. Felipe was being too precipitate.

"Just friends," Esteban answered, his voice more careful now, and also perhaps angry, offended by something.

"Hardly matters," Felipe said quietly, as if he had turned away, no longer interested.

"Why?" Esteban demanded. "What are they charging you with?"

"Stealing a Wafer of the Host," Felipe replied with a ring of pride. "A real one of course. We put a knife to it, and it ran blood!"

There was a hesitation.

José felt Frey Domingo's fingers dig into his arm till he was sure he must have left bruises.

"Did it?" Esteban's voice was high with surprise. "Ours didn't!"

Again there was the hesitation; then Felipe's response came, sharp with victory.

"Are you sure it was a real one?"

"Of course!"

"From a church? Consecrated?"

"Naturally. What use would it be otherwise?"

José groaned with the pressure of Domingo's grip. It was stifling up here, and he had no room to move, let alone escape.

"Sorry," Domingo whispered and let go. "We've got him! I told you he was guilty!"

José had no argument.

The next move was obvious. Esteban would be put in a cell with his co-conspirator, Rodrigo Sanchez, and Domingo and José would listen to what they would say to each other while they imagined they were alone.

After the midday meal—which had been particularly sparse—José had found himself in an argument with Domingo over nothing in particular. He had tried to agree, for the sake of peace and because Domingo was his superior. But Domingo would not be agreed with. It must have been the hair shirt. José would have been happy for him to wear silk, if it would improve his temper. What was the advantage to wearing something that scratched and tickled all the time, if it made you unbearable to be with?

"Anyone can be pleasant when they have all they wish," his confessor had once told him sincerely. "The art lies in being pleasant when you yourself are in discomfort, or even pain."

José would have bought Domingo silk, with pleasure, if he had had the nerve. Only, of course, being a Dominican friar, he owned no money with which to purchase anything.

Once again they were crouched on the floor of a lightless room, listening to a conversation in the cell below.

"Well, what did you tell him?" It was not Esteban's voice, but a deeper, harsher one. That must be Rodrigo Sanchez. He sounded angry, and perhaps a little frightened.

"Nothing!" Esteban denied it urgently. "Nothing he didn't know already!"

"What?"

"He said he took a Wafer of the Host, and when he pricked it . . . it bled! Ours didn't bleed! He's in much worse trouble than we are!"

"He said that?" The harsher voice was high with disbelief.

"Yes! I swear!" Esteban assured him.

"Did you tell him yours didn't?"

"Yes . . ." Now there was doubt in Esteban's voice, uncertainty and a quiver of fear.

Silence.

Domingo pushed José aside and pressed his ear to the crack in the floorboards.

Still silence.

José was jammed up against the wall. It was hot and extremely uncomfortable. If Domingo really did wear a hair shirt, his armpits must be raw!

Suddenly Rodrigo's voice came through quite clearly.

"Did you say anything about Alvaro Lopez?"

"Alvaro Lopez?"

"Yes—don't repeat everything I say like a fool. Did you?"

"No! What would I say?" Esteban was indignant. José could picture his face with its sharp nose and wide, round eyes.

"About the child!" Rodrigo grated. "What do you think I meant?"

"What child?" Esteban sounded totally confused.

"Well, where do you think the blood came from?" Rodrigo demanded crossly.

"What blood? There wasn't any blood! Wafers don't bleed!"

"Of course they don't bleed, you fool! What did you think you were drinking? Wine?"

There was a moment's silence below.

José could hear Domingo breathing.

"Holy God!" Esteban cried desperately. "What are you saying? I thought it was chicken's blood!"

Domingo was shaking. José could feel the room chill around him; a new kind of fear altogether gripped his mind. For the first time he could ever remember, he was glad Domingo was there so close beside him he could feel the heat of his body in the airless room.

"Did you!" Rodrigo's voice was icy.

There was a sob from Esteban.

"Control yourself!" Rodrigo snapped. "Admit nothing! They can't prove it."

"What about Alvaro? They'll burn us!"

"If they burn Alvaro, that's his problem. Just you keep quiet. Say you know nothing but a bit of stupidity, and you'll get nothing worse than paraded through the streets in the sanbenito."

"I don't want to get paraded through the streets in a canvas shirt with flames and devils on it, for everyone to laugh at and throw stones at!" Esteban squeaked. "And anyway, they never do just that! They'll try to confiscate my house and my shop! I'll have nothing!''

"You'll have your life!'' Rodrigo said grimly. "That is, if you do as you're told!''

"I will! I will!'' Esteban protested. "I don't know anything about a child. I don't even know what child!''

"Some boy from the village of Los Piños.'' Rodrigo sounded almost off-hand.

"How d'you get him?''

"Took him, of course! What d'you think?''

"He'll tell!'' Esteban was panicking.

José was so cramped crouching motionless, his muscles were crying out to move. Domingo, so close beside with his voluminous black and white robes, seemed almost to suffocate him. He could smell the sharpness of sweat.

"He's dead, you idiot!'' Rodrigo said with disgust. "It was heart's blood you drank. Ask Alvaro!''

"Oh, yes,'' Frey Matteo said earnestly when they were gathered just outside the chapel after early evening prayers. Like any other Order, they kept the prayer offices of the day except when other duties prevented them. "I've heard whispers about it. They say the Holy Child was beaten with more than a hundred lashes before he died.'' He leaned a little closer, confidentially. "And he never cried out . . . not once.''

"Nobody could be beaten a hundred times and live through it!'' José protested. "Not even fifty! How old was he?''

"About ten,'' Matteo answered, moving aside to let two novices pass. "Of course no normal person could, but he wasn't normal. He was a holy child . . . a martyr. Have you arrested Alvaro Lopez yet?''

"Of course we have!'' Domingo assured him. "He denies it . . . as you would expect.''

"What does he say?'' Matteo's long, sad face was puzzled.

"That he doesn't know anything about it,'' Domingo said derisively, beginning to back towards the refectory.

"He's lying, but even he would hardly admit it, would he? He knows he'll burn for that. What sort of a man kidnaps a child and murders him for his heart's blood?"

"A heretic!" José answered with a shudder, keeping up with him. "Someone who has sold all decency to the devil." He crossed himself. He tried to visualize the child, terrified, snatched by insane, masked men and carried away out on some hillside, to be beaten and killed so they could cut out his heart for the blood. What kind of belief, except that of the devil, could inspire such a thing? Usually Frey Domingo's convictions annoyed him. He was so certain of everything, so dogmatic and humourless, no one could shake him into ordinary, human doubt. Somehow today that was comforting. Men could go mad and daylight could see monstrous acts of depravity not thought of in nightmares, but still Frey Domingo would be there, the same as always. There was more to be said for that than José could have believed, even a couple of days ago.

"Miracles, of course," Frey Matteo was going on, waving his hands as he spoke, and looking earnestly at Domingo. "Catalina Hernandez said that praying to him had cured him of the bleeding."

"Praying to whom?" José asked. He had not been listening.

"The Santo Niño, of course!" Matteo replied. "The Holy Child! It just shows how God will create something divinely good out of the worst wickedness imaginable, doesn't it?" He made the sign of the cross.

Alvaro Lopez continued to deny taking or harming any child, so naturally he was put to the torture. He was taken to the lower room designed for that purpose and filled with engines of one sort or another, racks and benches and pulleys. He was tied to the board, head downwards, the rag was stuffed down his throat and the water dripped on it until he choked, but he was stubborn as a mule. He was removed from there and helped to his feet. His hands were tied behind his back and then he was lifted by them until his shoulders were wrenched out of their sockets, but still he refused to confess.

He was a big man, built like a blacksmith. Torturing him was hard work.

Eventually, covered in sweat, he was taken down again, and laid on a different bench, a level one this time. They could always try the rack, but before that, Domingo would use persuasion again. Reason was always better than force. Repentance was to be desired above all else.

The torches on the walls were flickering and making the shadows dance. It was surprisingly hot down here. It must be the lack of air.

"Why do you keep on lying?" Domingo said quietly, bending close to Alvaro. "We know that you were involved. The others who were there with you have admitted it! You are only causing yourself more pain by persisting in denial."

Alvaro had been staring at the flaming torches sending yellow light against the stone walls. Now he turned with a grunt of pain to look at Domingo. He had a broad, sensuous face and bold eyes.

"So someone told you I was there, did they?" he said hoarsely, his throat swollen from the rags.

"Yes," Domingo said with certainty. He smiled very slightly.

"Who?" Alvaro demanded, and then coughed and choked.

José fetched him a tin cup with a little water and held it for him to drink. It was a practical measure. Alvaro could not tell them anything if he could not speak. He had pointed this out to Frey Domingo before.

"You know I can't tell you that!" Domingo said indignantly. No one ever betrayed informers to the Holy Office. If they did, no one would dare inform.

There was one leniency allowed, though, in all justice.

"Have you any enemies that you know of?" José intervened.

Alvaro gave a harsh, jerking laugh. "A dozen!" He

cried out involuntarily as the slight movement caught his agonized muscles. "Where do you want me to begin?"

"With the most likely to do you wrong," Domingo replied, as if the answer was obvious.

"How about Julio Borges?" Alvaro asked curiously. "He owes me money."

"That is of no concern to me," Domingo replied implacably. "Anyone else?"

"Rodrigo Sanchez." Alvaro leered a little. "I never touched his wife, but not for want of her offering, and he knows it!"

Domingo's face must have registered his knowledge, because Alvaro saw it immediately. "That's it!" he said triumphantly. "It's that fat pig Sanchez! He's blaming me because of Manuela! He's the one you should string up by the arms! Pig!"

Manuela Sanchez was duly interrogated, not in the torture chamber but in one of the ordinary rooms with table and chairs. She agreed that her husband disliked Alvaro Lopez, but she said it was for better reason than he knew. Far from not desiring her, Alvaro had very much desired her, and had taken advantage of Rodrigo's absence to force his attentions upon her on a number of occasions.

"Could your husband know this?" Domingo pressed, his brows drawn together in bitter disapproval.

"Oh no!" she denied quickly. She was a handsome woman, buxom, shining-haired. It would not be difficult to imagine two men coming to blows over her, or to lies and betrayals.

"No? Why not?" Domingo put his head a little to one side. It was very hot in the interrogation room with its walls bare except for the great wooden crucifix and the torch brackets. There seemed to be no air today and the sun outside was merciless. "Surely you told him, so he could protect you from this man's assault upon your virtue?"

José rolled his eyes and held his tongue with difficulty. Sometimes Frey Domingo did not seem to be part of reality. Had he been born in holy orders? You did not have to be very wise to perceive which a lusty woman would prefer between the muscular Alvaro, or the bitter Rodrigo with his careful, cunning nature and his finicky manners.

Manuela looked straight at Domingo, meeting his eyes without a flicker. "Because I was afraid they would fight each other, and Rodrigo would get the worst of it," she answered demurely. "He is not nearly as big as Alvaro, or as strong." Her eyes were bright, belying her folded hands. "The only way he could win would be with a knife, and that would be murder. I wouldn't have that on his soul, Father Inquisitor."

Domingo was stumped. He nodded sagely, and let her go, after warning her about the dangers of unchastity. But heresy was the crime he was set apart to pursue, not lust, or even marital infidelity.

"Alvaro lied!" he said to José the moment she was gone and they were alone again.

"So did Rodrigo!" José argued.

"No he didn't!" Domingo looked annoyed. He hated being caught out, however slightly. "He didn't tell us he had a personal acquaintance with Alvaro, because we didn't ask him!" He remembered that with satisfaction.

"I did," José said with a greater satisfaction.

Domingo froze, his eyes hard. "What?"

"I asked him," José repeated, wondering if he was being very wise. He swallowed. "Just to conform with the legalities," he added, which was true . . . more or less.

"And he didn't say anything about Alvaro and his wife." Domingo's lips closed in a thin line. "Of course he didn't! He didn't know! She told us that."

"Wouldn't you know, if she were your wife . . . with a man like Alvaro?" Jose asked.

"No, I wouldn't. Not if I were a trusting man, with a pure heart." Domingo lifted his chin a little.

"I suppose you wouldn't," José agreed, thinking to himself, Not if you were an idiot with both eyes closed.

"I don't know what you mean!" Domingo retorted, aware of the inflexion and not understanding it.

"I know you don't," José agreed. "What are you going to do with them?"

"Imprison them until trial and the auto-da-fé," Domingo answered him. "They are all guilty, either by fact or by association. Alvaro kidnapped the boy and killed him. Rodrigo and Esteban knew of it, and therefore are accomplices. They consented to it."

"Esteban didn't know of it!" José protested.

"He does now . . . and hasn't told us," Domingo pointed out, rising to his feet. "That means he is defending them. Although that is an idea, Frey José, quite a good one. Perhaps if he confesses, he can save his soul, and he need not burn. A penitent sinner is far better than one going to his death with guilt still in his heart."

"But Alvaro says he's not guilty, and we haven't proved that he is!" José objected, standing up also.

Domingo stared at him, his eyes level and angry. "Why are you defending him, Frey José? He has defiled another man's wife, and lied about it, to her discredit. Rodrigo knew nothing about it, so he is a credible witness. Alvaro is guilty. Now I have business to attend to in the town; then I am going to ride out to Los Piños, the village where this abomination happened, and assure the good people there that we have the heretics who murdered their child, and they will surely burn." He moved towards the door. "It may be some small modicum of comfort to them to know that God prevails, and that the Holy Office serves His justice to the saving of souls." He made the sign of the cross. "Now I am sure you have duties to perform. You had better be about them."

Domingo's business in the town kept him longer than he had expected. It was fully five hours before he returned and found a situation which was almost beyond belief. Frey Matteo told him, perfectly seriously, that Alvaro Lopez had been released.

Domingo was dumbfounded.

"What?" he shouted, startling the elderly friar hurrying by with a basket of bread. "Released? Re-arrest him!" he commanded. "Who did it? Find him for me, and I'll put him on a month's bread and water myself!"

"Frey José," Matteo said nervously, shifting from one foot to the other. "He said there was no evidence, something about a quarrel between Alvaro Lopez and Rodrigo Sanchez, and it made the only evidence untrustworthy."

"Untrustworthy! I'll give him untrustworthy!" Domingo heard his own voice rising out of control. How could anyone be so gullible? "He's worse than a fool ... he's an arrogant, disobedient fool! Arrest him."

"We don't know where he is, Father Inquisitor!" Matteo apologized unhappily. He wrung his bony hands together. "As soon as we let him go, he fled!"

"Not Alvaro, you fool—José! Arrest José. I'll deal with him when I come back."

"Back, Father Inquisitor?"

"I'm going to where this fearful thing happened, to comfort the family of the Santo Niño. If I don't go now, I'll not get back before dark. It's nearly noon already."

"Oh yes ..." Matteo crossed himself. "Blessed be his name. Maria Benedetta says she has been cured of the lumbago by lighting a candle to him."

"Good. Now go and put José in a cell, and give him nothing but water, until I get back."

"Yes, Father Inquisitor."

Domingo had his mule saddled—Dominicans, like other friars, did not aspire to ride horses—and began his journey. It was hot and his hair shirt was even more than ordinarily uncomfortable. It would be indulgent to dream about silk, even sinful, but he did think about cotton. It was extremely hot, and the road rough and dusty winding through the fields and olive groves. Everyone knew about the vanity and excesses of bishops, but it would be nice to ride a horse sometimes, so much less bumpy! Mules seemed to resent being ridden and it was apparent every step of the way.

It seemed an interminable journey through the heat of the day before he reached Los Piños, where the miracles had happened. Only the prospect of meeting the parents of such a sublime child sustained Domingo's strength. At least he would be able to tell them that the Holy Inquisition had found the perpetrators of the crime, and they would be suitably punished. If they wished, they could come to the auto-da-fé and see it for themselves.

When at last he arrived in the village square he stopped by the well and asked two women there about the child and his parents.

They drew him water shyly, their faces full of awe. After all, he was the Holy Father Inquisitor, with the power not only of life and death, but of heaven and hell in the eternities. He could send a soul to damnation. Once, he used to find their fear almost exhilarating. Now it touched him with discomfort; one might even call it something not unlike guilt.

"The Santo Niño," he repeated after he had thanked them.

They crossed themselves and blessed his name.

"His parents?" he said again patiently. "I need to speak to his mother and father, to tell them we have found the men who took him. Where are they?"

A small crowd was gathering, old men, women and children.

They looked blank. "We don't know, Father Inquisitor."

"But this is Los Piños! You must know them!" he insisted.

"No, Holy Father!"

"Well, how many small boys are missing?"

"None, Holy Father. No children are missing here."

He was losing patience. "There must be! Please think. There is no need to be afraid. I have come to bless his house, and to bring some solace to his family. Now, where are they?''

But no one could tell him. He scoured the village, and the next village, and the next, until he was so hot his skin was red and raw under his hair shirt and his head pounded like a blacksmith's anvil, but no child was missing anywhere. Every single boy, and girl for that matter, between the ages of four years and eighteen was accounted for. Certainly a few *conversos*, Jews who had taken the Christian faith, had had a drunken party, and behaved badly, saying a few blasphemous things they regretted when sober, but that was all. Maybe a Holy Wafer had been stolen, maybe not. It was impossible to say. But there was no Santo Niño. That was a certainty. There was only hatred, fear, and superstition grown monstrous.

At sundown they offered him hospitality, but he refused with thanks. No matter his hunger, thirst, aching body and pounding head, he must ride back. There was a wrong to be put right, before it was too late and the fires of the auto-da-fé claimed lives unjustifiably. And he must speak to Frey José, and let him go. He would give him a severe warning, of course. He had behaved completely irresponsibly.

The one good thing about it was that the mule was exhausted too. He could not ride the poor beast all night. He would have to borrow a horse. Tomorrow José could ride back to fetch the mule. It would be a good penance for him.

On the other hand, perhaps he might do it himself. Maybe he deserved the penance more, and a little time alone to think more deeply about his judgement.

The physical discomfort of a mule ride in the sun would be small enough, compared with the trouble on his mind as he considered his conscience. He had been saved from a terrible wrong by grace, not by his own actions or charity.

It must not happen again.

𝒟*ianne Day, author of the Fremont Jones series, set in early twentieth-century San Francisco, only began to write seriously some ten years ago. Although born in the Mississippi Delta, she moved to the Bay area as a child and went to schools in Sunnyvale and San Jose before attending Stanford. She has two graduate degrees and worked as a psychologist, psychotherapist, and health services administrator before starting to write—after which she worked at whatever it took to support herself and her writing habit.*

Dianne now happily writes full time. The first Fremont Jones book, The Strange Files of Fremont Jones, *won the Macavity award as best first mystery of 1994. The second,* Fire and Fog, *was equally well received. It opens with the 1906 earthquake, which is only the start of the excitement. The third in the series,* The Bohemian Murders, *is now available, and the fourth,* Emperor Norton's Ghost, *will be out in 1998.*

Taking advantage of the chance to do something different, Dianne has given us a beautiful, chilling tale from late-Renaissance Venice, ''Anna and the Mirror.''

ANNA AND THE MIRROR

Dianne Day

🜚

My father is the Master of all mirror makers. In Venice it is said, not openly, but whispered behind fans and gloved hands, around corners, beyond closed doors, that in his youth, Umberto Castiglione sold his soul to the Devil in exchange for the deepest secrets of quicksilver and glass.

I, Anna, daughter of Umberto, believe this may be true. Certainly there is no one else in the world who can make a mirror the equal of his. My papa's mirrors hang in the glittering palace of the French King at Versailles; they hang in the holy halls of the Vatican, reflecting the gold and white robes of the Pope, the purple silks of bishops and monsignors, and the searing scarlet of the cardinals, those princes of the Church; here in Venice hangs Papa's greatest mirror, a luminous marvel that adorns the Doge's palace. And in our tall house on the Grand Canal, the Ca' Castiglione, the mirrors of my papa are everywhere.

Yet before Umberto, through all the centuries when Castigliones established their fortune in the making of glass on the island of Murano, they never made a mirror. Papa alone has the skill to cast and to handle, without breaking, the vast sheets of glass. He learned it before I was born, before my mother died, and the sisters I never knew, and the brother I can barely remember. So sometimes I do wonder how this came to be. . . .

Making a mirror is a mystical process, says Papa. He does not allow anyone other than himself and one apprentice into the long, dark, shed-like rooms in his factory near the Arsenal during that crucial time when the quicksilver grows and cleaves to the glass. I picture the mirrors growing themselves in darkness, perhaps to incantations, perhaps in silence, certainly in some secret alchemical kind of energy where alien substances are bonded together immutably, forever. Magic, Papa says: "You do not make a mirror, you grow it, by your own hand, out of the power of your mind. . . ."

Yet I have observed that it is not all so mystical, no matter what Papa may say. For example the mirror factory is near the Arsenal, where sailing ships are built and serviced, and not on that part of the island of Murano the Castigliones still own, because the less distance they are moved, the less likely those vast sheets of glass are to break. Much of being Maestro is about control . . . and who would have more control than a man reputed to have been given it by the Devil himself? The priests? I do not think so. I may be young, but I am bright for a female, I have been well-schooled, and now for the past three years that I have been left alone with him, Umberto Castiglione has been my main subject of study. The visions in his mirrors may be clear, but Papa is not. I know for a fact: Quite often he lies.

On the Eve of All Hallows in 1750, that is to say, on the last day of October in the seventeenth year of my life, late in the afternoon I opened the casement doors of my bedchamber and stepped out onto the balcony. I felt as if some restless spirit, perhaps my mother, perhaps those sisters I had never known, were calling me. Yet it was not a spirit, but rather Nature herself who called. The very air was charged, heavy with the tang of sea salt, replete with moisture that left droplets on my skin and in my hair. Far away from across the roofs of all the houses I heard a continuous booming roar, which was the pounding of the Mediterranean's waves on the fragile sands of the Lido, at the entrance to the lagoon. Soon the wind would pick up, stale remnants of late summer blowing out of Africa, blowing trouble across the sea. The wind would beat the tide back into the protected waters, no matter whether that tide be coming in or out; tomorrow there would be the *acqua alta*, the high water that would spill over the Riva Degli Schiavoni to fill first the Piazzetta and then the Piazza San Marco, finally reaching its liquid tendrils up the low-lying streets, farther and farther ... until eventually the sun would come out, and all of Venice would bask in her own reflection. A mirror unto herself.

Umberto Castiglione would not like that. I stood on my balcony and smiled. Suddenly, nothing would do but that I should go out into the teeth of it and greet this coming storm.

I closed the casement doors and locked them, quite deliberately, as if my hands were not trembling with the keenest anticipation I could ever recall. I flung across my shoulders the voluminous black cape we women of Venice must wear to hide our clothes and our jewels, to comply with the ancient sumptuary laws. Many complain, but I do not, for I have learned these capes can hide other things, as well.

The Ca' Castiglione is an old house, dark and dank, as musty as most of Venice. It was built in the thirteenth century, before the days of grand center stairways, and so the stairs are mean and narrow, clinging to an inside wall as they zig and zag their way down four floors. The top is the nursery floor, unoccupied. The second level, where I had been, was all sleeping chambers. The first floor, the *piano nòbile* with its grand salon, had been my mother's territory and would be mine someday. Someday ...

The ground floor would likely remain forever empty now. Like so many of the old houses along the Grand

Canal, the Ca' Castiglione was once a place of commerce. Glass was bought and sold, bargains for goods and materials struck, in the many-columned main hall only steps up from the waters. But Umberto would never stoop so low as to do business in his home, not he, not since he has bought his way into the Book of Gold. Venetian aristocracy is ruled not by birth but by money. Controlling the secrets of the mirrors has made Umberto the next thing to a prince. If he wants to keep me at home with him forever, if as he says he loves me too much to let me go, who is there to say No to such a man?

I ran down the stairs like a hushed shadow in my soft shoes of morocco leather. Past the echoing silence of the grand salon, down to the empty hall and through its deserted forest of naked columns, leafless trees reaching their branches into the vaulted heavens of peeling frescoed vegetation. Out the rear door and into the garden I ran, with the black cloak billowing out behind me, ignoring the voice of my old nurse who called down to ask where I was going, called out: "Donna Anna, your papa will be home soon!" Across the garden I ran, and through the gate into the narrow, brick-paved *calle*. Alone.

The *calles* of Venice are twisting and secretive; they narrow down without reason and open up into sudden *campi* with no warning. Even when you are sure you know where you are going, there are times when you don't know where you are. What is required is simply to keep moving on. My pulse was pounding, my breathing shallow; there was a stitch in my side and I thought I might be going insane. But still I ran, driven by I could not say what. Until at last I broke around the last turn and into the Piazza San Marco. Shopkeepers were closing doors and windows against the storm; restauranteurs were bringing in table and chairs; one waiter chased a white tablecloth snatched up by the errant wind.

My cloak filled with the same wind and buffeted me about like a rudderless boat under full sail, but the lure of the lagoon drew me down, down, relentlessly down to the *fondamenta*. And there, on a set of broad, shallow steps flooded with choppy water, I looked down and saw beneath the waves what I had come for, what the storm had brought, now winking up at me: a mirror of my very own. A small mirror from someplace far away, perhaps worked loose by wind and rain from the sands of Egypt. A mirror Umberto Castiglione had never touched, did not know existed, and so had never infected with his magic spells.

The waters of an *acqua alta* in its early stages are pale green, like strained spring apples or thin pea soup. I reached down into this green water and closed my fingers over the hard, shiny oval that promised me so much. My gift from sea and storm.

My mirror fits in the palm of my hand. Its glass is scratched from time spent on its journey to me; its copper rim and back are dulled and dented; nevertheless this mirror has been loved. By its maker, for example: You can tell that by the way the copper has been chased about the rim. By its former owner or owners: You can tell that by its age. And now this mirror is oh so cherished by me. I know I can rely on its reflection. . . . Or so I thought, until today. Today I cannot quite believe my eyes.

For a little more than a month I have carried my mirror with me, in purse or sleeve or a pocket that ties about my waist. I do not use it to look only at myself, but also to check the mirror's vision of my surroundings with what my own eyes tell me. Particularly at home I do this; for what else have I to use as a check for reality? How can I see through another's eyes? How can I know that what I see through my own eyes is the same as what another sees, particularly when I know that I live in a house where every mirror may lie? I grew up in that house, it is the only reality I have ever known intimately. To ponder much on this is to court madness, yet I do ponder upon it anyway: If my eyes see the same as the mirror on the walls, and the mirrors were made by Umberto, and we know Umberto lies . . . then what is the truth?

My own mirror would tell me. Or so I believed. And so one morning early in December, when I took the mirror from my pocket and cupped it in the palm of my hand, I had a nasty surprise. The face that stared back at me was not mine. Not Anna.

Oh, she looked like me. The same red-gold hair, the same creamy skin with its faint scattering of tiny freckles that will not yield even to daily drenching with the juice of costly lemons. The same mouth with bowed upper lip and the lower one a little too full, so that I may seem pouty or petulant when actually I am not. But the eyes . . .

They were the same color as mine, golden-brown rays shooting from the pupil through an iris of muted green, like rays of late sun sinking through a murky forest. But those eyes were not mine. They looked like mine, and so I cannot say how I knew they were not, but I did know. I put the mirror away, back in the pocket. The hand in which I'd held it felt icy cold.

All through the day I kept checking; and all through the day those eyes, like mine but not mine, stared back at me. And that night my papa was more tender than usual. He placed his blunt index finger on my lower lip and said: "Anna, what is troubling you?"

I blinked, and shivered. Presuming me cold, he drew me closer, until the thick hair of his chest swarmed over my naked breasts and I wanted to fight free of it— wanted to scream and beat it away like spider webs.

He asked me again: "Anna?" And this time he pushed at my lip until the soft flesh grew painful against my teeth and I knew I had to answer.

I said the first thing, other than the truth, that came into my head. "It is nothing, Umberto." He does not allow me to call him Papa anymore, though that cannot stop my thinking of him as Papa . . . because, after all, he is still my father.

"Tell me," he insisted, as I had known he would.

"You won't like it," I said, my own increasingly devious mind now catching scent of an opportunity.

"Nevertheless, you will tell me."

I sighed, as if with the greatest reluctance he were drawing forth this information from me. "I want to go out to the *casini* as other women do. And at night I want to go masked to the *ridotti,* not to gamble, but for amusement, for frivolity. I am too much alone, Umberto. My friends, the girls I grew up with, and went to school with, all are married now. I want to go where they go, do as they do."

"Anna," he said sternly, in a Papa sort of voice, "you are not married."

His face, with its elegant, sharp nose, was only inches from mine. I stared into his eyes, which are as blue as the sea on a sunny day. "Am I not, Umberto?" I asked. And on his name, Umberto, my voice broke and my chin quivered.

That was how I got some degree of freedom, and my companion, my *cicisbeo* Giovanni, whom I call in the Venetian manner, Zan. Zan will never be my lover or even a true friend; he fears Umberto too much for that; but at least now there is one other person who knows the truth of why the Ca' Castiglione is no longer a house where people are welcome: my father is afraid that at any social occasion he will betray himself with a look, a touch. . . .

I was getting used to those eyes not mine in my mirror. The morning Zan came to be my companion, before he arrived, I took the mirror out. I gazed into it for a long and searching while, and said: "Thank you."

She said, "You are welcome." Her voice was very much like mine.

She smiled. My free hand, the one not holding the mirror, went to the corner of my mouth. I was not smiling. Nor in the mirror image did a hand move. In rapid succession I felt a cold wave of fear and then a warm rush of gratitude; this was the first clear evidence that I was not, after all, insane for thinking that was not me in this mirror.

"Who are you?" I whispered.

But she had turned her face in profile to me, and would say no more.

I burned with desire to know her name, but she had fled. She no longer lived in my little mirror. Time and time again I checked, a thousand times a day or more, only to find her gone. Her sudden absence made me a little frantic. Where had she gone?

For distraction, I amused myself with Zan. He was not young, yet younger than Umberto, and still handsome, especially about the calf and thigh. The pantaloons of Venetian men can be quite revealing, and Zan responded well to teasing. He introduced me to the Contessa Alissa Garibaldi, and I subscribed to her *casini*. Afternoons were gay now; I began to look in the contessa's mirrors for the woman who looked like me but was not I. Thus went my days at fast and faster pace.

My nights changed too. "Teach me," I said boldly to Umberto. "Do not be gentle with me. I'm not a little girl anymore. I want to know what other women know."

He taught me. I am sure he taught me well; at least I know he taught me thoroughly, with his long fingers and his wet tongue and that club between his legs. The more reckless, the more wanton I became, the more he loved me. The more I hated him.

I took to watching us, myself and Umberto, in the bedroom mirrors . . . and one night, I was astounded to find her there, looking back at me. She saw me see her in the first mirror, on the wall to the left; and in the second, on the wall opposite the foot of the bed; and in the third mirror, on the wall to the right. Each time my eyes brushed hers, her chin rose higher. I smiled at her over Umberto's shoulder; as I smiled, I squeezed harder with those secret muscles I had learned about from the other women at the contessa's, and my papa grunted with pleasure. She smiled back at me, and in her smile was a promise. I knew I would find her again.

The next day, I did. But not for a long time. I had looked in every mirror in every room of the house without result, I was almost in despair when I recalled a small mirror on the top floor, in the nursery. Up the stairs I went, eagerly, forgetting to hold up my skirts, tripping a bit on the hems and stirring up old dust that made me sneeze. I pushed through the door with its handle at shoulder height, which had once seemed to me so impossible to open but now was so easy that I did it without thought . . . and it occurred to me that there might be other things I could do that had once seemed impossible. . . .

There! There was the mirror I remembered, a rectangle barely a foot wide and and two feet long, on the wall at the foot of the bed I'd slept in as a child. Near this mirror sat the chair in which my nurse had rocked me many a time to sleep. Impatiently I pushed the chair out of the way and stepped up to the mirror. And there she was.

"Who are you?" I demanded in a harsh voice, without preamble.

"I am Anna," she replied.

"You cannot be," I challenged her, "for I am Anna, and you are not me."

"Oh," she said, raising her chin and turning her head slightly so that she regarded me slyly from the corners of her eyes, "my name is the same as yours, but I spell it differently. You're right, we are not quite the same, you and I."

"How do you mean, you spell it differently? There is only one way to spell a name."

"No, you are wrong. I live in the mirror, and so I spell it backwards. A-N-N-A."

"But that is how I spell it, A-N-N-A!"

"Nevertheless, it is not quite the same, is it?"

"Why not?"

"Because I live on the other side of your reality," she said, with a tantalizing little smile . . . and then she vanished. The mirror was empty, no reflection at all. And that was frightening.

"Don't leave me!" I cried, pressing my palms to the cool, empty glass. "Oh don't, please don't leave me."

Very faintly, from far, far away, I heard a false little laugh, such as has come out of me some nights of late. So she, the Other Anna, was still here somewhere. I would find her again.

Day by day by day I looked, in every mirror in the house. My own old copper mirror I hid in a drawer because she never visited it now—I sensed she had in some way grown too large to be contained by it. Anna now preferred the biggest mirrors, where I could see her from head to toe. Anna was the woman I wished to be, or so I thought; she had taken the lessons Umberto offered and profited by them, whereas I . . .

I looked forward to Carnival, when I could go masked every night. Because increasingly, although I carried on my wanton charade with my papa, and thus he said he would allow me and Zan to attend the *ridotti* during Carnival, I wanted only to hide in shame. I loved my papa still, and yet I hated him, so I was breaking, breaking in two.

Carnival in Venice begins on Saint Stephen's Day, the day after Christmas, and lasts until Ash Wednesday. Here we do our celebrations both well and long, with light and colors and music. Music of every kind, all day and all night. The music alone is enough to make one mad.

I bought a special mask for myself and the Other Anna. A mask with two faces, one on the front, and one on the back, one that smiles and one that frowns, attached to a black tricorne hat with a flowing black veil to each side. In my long black domino, with this instead of the usual half-mask, if I stand still it is impossible to tell if I am coming or going. If I am smiling or frowning. Indeed, it is impossible to tell much of anything about me at all.

Umberto Castiglione, who has not gone out at night, not even for Carnival, in the three years since he began training me to take my mother's place in his bed, saw how anonymous I had become in my costume. It excited him as nothing else had ever excited him before. He dismissed my Zan, with whom I had grown comfortable, and announced that he would take me to the *ridotti* himself. . . .

"Ma Donna Misteriosa," that was the name he gave me to all who called out their question: "Eh Umberto, who is this lady so well-disguised, who brings you out of your mourning at last?"

Inside the mask I could not breathe. Nor could I see well through the mesh that made its eyes look blank, like the eyes of a statue. Sounds were muffled as well. And all this was a great blessing, for Carnival can overwhelm almost anyone at any time; and whereas I had been prepared for an adventure with Zan, I was not prepared for the change that came over Papa. He drank too much wine. He sang too loudly. And even in our own gondola, with a servant who knew, who must have known who I was, Papa could not keep his hands off me.

I did not speak. The woman in the double mask was silent, even when Papa opened my cloak and unlaced the front of my dress until my breasts spilled out, even to the pink half-circles of aureola at the tops of my nipples. "Like that!" he said with satisfaction, trailing his thick fingers across my burning skin, "Let them see, let all of Venice see how beautiful you are, and that you belong to me!"

I could not remember whether I wore the smiling or the frowning side of the mask to the front. When I reached up to find out by touch, I could not tell—the feeling all seemed to have fled from my fingertips.

The night went on, unseasonably warm, which only added to the general air of licentiousness. Beneath the mask my ears rang, and the beat of the drums, which could be heard everywhere, got into my blood. Toward dawn Umberto Castiglione, Master of Mirrors, whose name is written in the Book of Gold, pushed his daughter Anna into a corner at the Ca' Mosca. He sucked her breasts one by one in full view of any who would look, and did not cover them after; he parted her cloak all the way to the hem, raised her skirts, and pushed himself inside her with her back to the wall. She helped him when he fumbled . . . and beneath her mask she cried.

When he was done I said, without thinking, with the mask in its eerie way deepening and magnifying my voice: "Papa, take me home."

She was in the mirror in my bedroom. The sky outside was blood-red with dawn, a sunrise that screamed in the sky the way I was screaming in my soul.

"Come, Anna," said the Other Anna in the mirror, "come with me. We will be together now, you and I."

I had already thrown down the mask. I dropped the cloak, tore off my ruined dress and stepped out of my shift, entirely naked. The red light fell through the windows and made the hair of my crotch blaze like a burning bush. Anna reached through the mirror . . . the glass broke . . . I took her hand . . . and went with her into her world.

Umberto Castiglione is dead. My papa died long before this, and I am glad Umberto is now also gone. I cut my hand but it does not matter, cut it on the long, sharp shard of mirror with which I pierced Umberto's heart. Or perhaps I cut it later, when with another piece of broken mirror-glass I slit his throat just to be sure he cannot come back and hurt us anymore. There is blood on my breasts and on my belly, and running down my thighs. In the mirror she has blood on her too.

Yes, she is there: Anna. She and I are one and the same.

Laura Joh Rowland is a second-generation Chinese-Korean American. She has a BS in microbiology and a Master of Public Health from the University of Michigan. She has worked in the sciences, and as an artist and writing teacher.

Her first novel, Shinjū *(Random House, 1994),* a mystery set in seventeenth-century Japan, was a finalist for the Hammet and Anthony awards, and the Barnes and Noble *"Discover Great New Writers"* competition. The next two books in the series are Bundori *(Villard, 1996)* and The Way of the Traitor *(Villard, 1997).* All three feature the samurai detective Sano Ichirō.

Laura says she started this series because *"I wanted to explore a place and a time I'd never seen in any novel before. Seventeenth-century Japan was my choice because it provided fascinating real characters and backgrounds to inspire my imagination. Also, as a member of America's ethnic minority population, I wanted to experience an all-Asian culture.... To me, the past, which is largely unknown territory, seems fresher and more exciting than the things we see on TV every day."*

For this anthology, Laura has written a story, *"Mizu-age,"* that is firmly grounded in the society of Tokugawa Japan and still as immediate and comprehensible as any contemporary drama.

MIZU-AGE

Laura Joh Rowland

Edo, Genroku Period, Year 2, Month 5
(Tokyo, June 1689)

Temple bells tolled midnight, and all of Edo slumbered—except Yoshiwara, the walled pleasure quarter where revelry lasted until all hours. At the Hanakiya, Edo's most exclusive brothel, the festivities marked a special occasion: a young girl's *mizu-age*, her sexual initiation into the life of a courtesan.

In the parlor, lanterns glowed; musicians played a lively song on flute, drum, and samisen. Maids served refreshments while pretty courtesans flirted with the fifty samurai guests seated on the tatami floor. Among these were Sano Ichirō, the shogun's *sōsakan-sama*—Most Honorable Investigator of Events, Situations, and People—and his chief retainer, Hirata.

Following polite custom, Sano poured sake for his host, Ishida Genzan. "A splendid party," he said. "Many thanks for inviting me." In the Tokugawa *bakufu*, Japan's military dictatorship, socializing comprised an integral part of business. Political alliances were forged at such events as this. A new official like Sano needed every opportunity to know his colleagues—even if he didn't care for a particular type of entertainment.

114

Ishida, member of the Judicial Council, was an important contact.

"The pleasure is mine." Ishida returned the favor. Near Sano's own age of thirty, he was tall and muscular, with bold eyes and a ready smile in a strong, handsome face. He wore a gaudy maroon and gold kimono of the latest fashion, and his knotted black hair gleamed with wintergreen oil. Tipping the servants extravagantly, he told Sano, "Drink up. Everyone must help me celebrate my victory!"

A month ago, the Hanakiya had announced the upcoming debut of a new courtesan. Tales of her beauty and charm had swept through Edo. An auction had been held, offering to the highest bidder the privilege of being her first client. Ishida, a frequent Yoshiwara visitor and profligate gambler, had won, paying a large chunk of his family fortune for the *mizu-age* and the accompanying gala.

"This is a vulgar disgrace," muttered the plainly dressed samurai seated next to Ishida. "A warrior should practice self-discipline, not self-indulgence."

Ishida performed the introductions: "*Sōsakan* Sano-*san*, meet my honorable younger brother, Monemon."

He was an inferior version of Ishida: not so tall or handsome, with a pronounced stoop to his shoulders. Sano knew that he occupied a lesser post in the government, serving under his brother and dependent on Ishida's goodwill. He refused Sano's offer of sake, and a foul mood surrounded him like a cloud.

"Please excuse Monemon's rudeness," Ishida said. Frowning at his brother, he ordered, "Behave yourself!"

Then the door opened. The music halted. A group of maids entered the room, escorting a beautiful, piquant-faced young girl about thirteen years old. "Presenting Miss Chidori," they chorused.

Chidori wore a red kimono embroidered with sandpipers—her namesake. Lustrous black hair flowed to her knees. Wide, somber eyes surveyed the assembly; her mouth trembled.

"She's afraid," Sano said, deploring the practice of forcing children into prostitution.

Other guests applauded, congratulating Ishida on his coup. The music resumed, while the maids paraded Chidori around the room. Behind her walked an older woman dressed in gray—the *yarite*, chaperone and teacher of courtesans. She had a haggard face that might have once been pretty, and eyes that looked sad even as she smiled.

Hirata had come equipped with a printed guide to Yoshiwara culture. Now he pulled the small book from under his sash and consulted its brightly illustrated pages. These described various attractions of the pleasure quarter and related local gossip. " 'Chidori came from Totomi Province at age seven,' " he read. " 'Her father died in an earthquake, and her mother couldn't support her, so she sold Chidori to a procurer for the Hanakiya.' "

"Perhaps she's better off here; at least she has food, clothing, shelter, and a chance to earn her freedom," said Sano, although the conventional argument failed to convince him. As a detective, he'd seen the dark side of glamorous Yoshiwara. He knew about the disgrace of women sentenced to prostitution as punishment for petty crimes, their abuse by cruel proprietors and clients, futile escape attempts, and occasional suicides. To him the party seemed less a celebration of happiness than of greedy lust.

"That must be Kachō," Hirata said, indicating an elegant courtesan, dressed in a lavish black kimono printed with plum blossoms, who stood by the door. "Ishida was her patron. He promised to pay off her debt to the Hanakiya." Before a courtesan could leave Yoshiwara, someone had to reimburse the brothel for her purchase price, as well as the cost of her room and board over the years. "He planned to marry her. But then he became attracted to Chidori, forsaking Kachō."

Bitterness shadowed the courtesan's lovely eyes.

When Ishida lifted his cup and beckoned to her, she came reluctantly to pour his sake.

"Here's to past good times," Ishida said, laughing as he toasted her. "But the old season must yield to the new, eh?"

Kachō's face crumpled, and she fled the room, sobbing. Pitying her, Sano said to Hirata, "How awful to have the prospect of freedom come so close, and then lose it." She appeared about twenty-seven, the age when most courtesans retired—sometimes to work as brothel managers or servants, but more commonly as street prostitutes. Early death by disease, starvation, or violence often followed.

"It's especially hard for her because Chidori was her *kamuro*," Hirata said.

The prettiest of the girls bought by brothels became *kamuro*—child attendants—to high-ranking courtesans like Kachō. What began as a loving sisterly relationship could deteriorate into jealous rivalry when a girl grew up and stole her elder's clients, as Chidori had done.

The procession reached Ishida. Face flushed with liquor, he fondled Chidori's hand, while she demurely lowered her gaze. "I'm the luckiest man on the plain tonight!" Ishida exclaimed, alluding to the popular euphemism—*lucky plain*—for the pleasure quarter. "Don't you agree, Younger Brother?"

Monemon gazed with undisguised longing at Chidori; she smiled shyly back at him. Rising, he bowed and said, "Excuse me," in a frostily polite tone, then stalked out the door.

"The book says he's in love with her and wanted to be her first patron," Hirata said, "but he was forced to yield to Ishida's wishes."

"What a cheerful party," Sano remarked. The procession continued, and he watched the *yarite* caressing Chidori's hair, glowing with fond pride as she accepted the guests' compliments on the beauty of her protégée. "At least one person seems to be getting some enjoyment out of this."

"That's O-ume," Hirata said. "A former prostitute with a mysterious past. The book gives no details—I bet the writer made that up just for something interesting to say."

Soon Ishida announced, "Enough of the preliminaries. I'm ready for business!" Amid cheers, the maids and *yarite* led Chidori away to the bedchamber. Ishida called after them, "I'll just step outside a moment, and then I'll come up." Unsteadily he walked toward the back door and the privies in the alley. "Good night, everyone!"

The party continued, but Sano kept remembering Chidori's fear. He didn't want to stay while the ritual took place, even to curry political favor. "Let's go," he said to Hirata.

They'd finished their drinks and made their farewells, when loud screams disrupted the party. Ishida burst into the room.

"*Sōsakan-sama!*" he cried, beckoning to Sano. "Come upstairs quickly. Chidori has been murdered!"

In a lamplit chamber furnished with bamboo blinds, a painted screen, and fine lacquer cabinets and tables, Chidori lay sprawled on the futon. A green cotton sash with a red poppy design circled her throat. Her sightless eyes stared in terror; a bloated tongue protruded from her lips.

Sano spoke to the guests and servants who had followed him upstairs: "Stay outside, please." He noticed Monemon and Kachō among them. Monemon's ashen face was taut with suppressed emotion. Kachō watched in avid excitement, eyes agleam. Sano turned to Ishida. "You found her like this?"

"Yes." Ishida wore the stricken expression of a drunken man shocked into sobriety. "I opened the door, and there she was. Some evil person must have sneaked into the house and killed her."

"Weren't you in the next room?" Sano asked O-ume, who knelt beside Chidori's corpse, weeping.

She nodded: It was the custom for the *yarite* to wait

nearby during a *mizu-age*, in case trouble arose. "I didn't see anything. I didn't hear anything except the music from downstairs—until Ishida-*san* yelled." Grief contorted the *yarite's* haggard face, while sobs racked her body. Her anguish dispelled Sano's initial suspicion of her. "Oh, my poor darling. Dead in the flower of her youth!"

Pushing through the excited crowd, Hirata entered, saying, "The back door is unlocked, but there's no one in the alley. If the killer got in that way, he's gone now."

"This is not only a shocking incident, but an outrageous offense against myself," Ishida said, recovering his bravado. "I paid dearly for her; she was mine. *Sōsakan* Sano, you must catch the killer."

Sano hesitated. Crimes in the pleasure quarter came under the jurisdiction of the Yoshiwara police, and he took orders from the shogun, not Ishida. However, he had a certain amount of discretion in choosing his cases. Ishida was a powerful man whose future cooperation might prove valuable. And Sano wanted justice for the frightened child who had died on the night of her initiation into a life of disgrace.

"I'll do my best," he said.

After ordering everyone to wait downstairs, he and Hirata examined the crime scene. "No signs of a struggle, nothing seems out of place," Sano observed. He noted the quilt that covered Chidori's legs. "It looks like she was sitting up in bed, waiting for Ishida, when the killer attacked." Carefully he removed the sash from her throat. "This may be the only clue."

"There's something in her mouth," Hirata said.

He extracted a wet, crumpled piece of blank paper.

"I've heard that young courtesans hide paper in their mouths before *mizu-age*, so they can moisten themselves with saliva before the client enters," Sano said. "To reduce the pain."

Gently he closed Chidori's eyelids. As he laid her arms by her sides, he felt a small, hard lump in her sleeve. Curious, he folded back the hem and pulled out a *netsuke* figurine, finely carved from pinkish jade. It represented a woman dressed in the voluminous kimono of centuries past. Her left arm was broken off at the wrist.

"That might have been valuable, before the damage," Hirata said. "What do you think it means?"

"We'll find out." Sano placed the *netsuke* in the drawstring pouch at his waist. "For now, you determine whether anyone was seen entering or leaving through the back door, or behaving oddly around the quarter. Maybe the killer is a stranger, as Ishida says." Recalling the tense atmosphere at the party, Sano suspected otherwise. "I'll interview the people in the house. It's possible that we'll find the killer among them."

The interviews revealed that almost all the party guests had stayed in the parlor between the time of Chidori's departure and the discovery of her body, with either Sano or Hirata to verify their statements. The proprietor, maids, and courtesans had been there also, and the other staff in the kitchen. Courtesans not attending the party were entertaining clients in private rooms, or sitting in the Hanakiya's display window in full view of the doorman and pedestrians. No one had seen or heard anything suspicious. The only two people not satisfactorily accounted for were Monemon, Ishida's jealous brother, and Kachō, his spurned lover. They were also the only ones with any apparent motive for murder.

After dismissing the other guests and asking Monemon to wait in the parlor, Sano found Kachō in the bathchamber of the courtesans' living quarters. "Where did you go when you left the party?" he asked from the doorway.

Kachō reclined in a tub of steaming, perfumed water, surrounded by attendants. One combed her long black tresses; others filed her fingernails, shaved her armpits, and plucked hairs from her brows. "I went to my room."

"Did anyone see you? Speak to you?"

Annoyance darkened Kachō's face. "Must we talk about this now? I'm busy."

"A young girl is dead," Sano said, noting her obvious lack of grief. "Murder investigations take precedence over grooming. Answer the question, please."

"Oh, all right." Kachō winced as a maid pulled a particularly stubborn hair. "I was by myself the whole time, with the door shut, and even if anyone had spoken to me, I wouldn't have answered. I wanted to be alone."

Then awareness flashed into her eyes as she realized the dangerous position in which her statement had put her. "Look, you've probably heard that I was angry with Chidori because she stole Ishida from me. But I didn't kill her—I could never hurt a girl I considered my little sister. Still, I won't pretend to be sorry she's dead. Now that Chidori is gone, Ishida has asked me to entertain him tonight. He wants me again."

Kachō's face shone with happiness. "He's waiting in the guest chamber."

Where she hoped to persuade him to make good on his promise to marry her, Sano guessed. Despite her denials, she'd had motive for murder—and opportunity. Her room was just a short walk around the corridor from the chamber where Chidori had died. And Ishida hadn't wasted any time mourning the death of his prize, even though he'd urged Sano to capture her killer.

"Is this yours?" Sano asked, holding up the flowered sash that had been used to strangle Chidori.

"Certainly not. I wouldn't wear such a tawdry thing." Kachō grimaced. "I've never seen it before."

None of the Hanakiya's other courtesans, guests, or staff had admitted owning or ever having seen the sash, either. Did this mean that a stranger had brought it and killed Chidori?

Sano displayed the *netsuke* figure. "What about this?"

Kachō gave the figure an indifferent glance and said, "Oh, that's Chidori's good-luck charm. She brought it with her when she came to the Hanakiya. She said it was a family heirloom.'' Kachō sniffed. ''Worthless piece of junk, in my opinion. When I offered to help her glue the broken piece back on, she said she didn't have it. It must have gotten lost ages ago.''

''Yes.'' Sano examined the *netsuke's* truncated wrist, whose edges had been worn smooth. Chidori must have handled the figure often, treasuring the memories it symbolized. But what, if any, relevance did it have to her death?

''If you don't mind, I have to get dressed now,'' Kachō said. ''Ishida will be getting impatient.'' She rose from the tub. The attendants draped her with a large cloth. ''And I can't wait to see the last of this place!''

It was dawn by the time Sano and Hirata reconvened in the empty parlor. The Hanakiya's staff had gone to bed, and the guests had left—including Monemon, against Sano's orders. Such evasiveness, combined with his unexplained absence from the party, didn't exactly indicate innocence.

''If he's going back to Edo, we'll catch up with him,'' Sano said.

He and Hirata hurried through the pleasure quarter, its brothels and teahouses shuttered and streets deserted in the pale early morning light. Outside the Yoshiwara gate, the road led through green rice fields where farmers toiled, and marshes full of twittering birds and buzzing insects. The sun rose golden in the cloudless summer sky. As they walked, Hirata reported the results of his inquiries.

''Chidori seems to have been the favorite child of Yoshiwara. I couldn't find anyone with reason to kill her. The people in the streets and nearby houses didn't notice anyone entering or leaving the Hanakiya at the time of the murder. But there were sightings of a suspicious character in the area: a tall man hiding his face under a wicker hat.''

''That could be important, or not,'' Sano said. Many

men came to Yoshiwara in disguise, whether in observance of the seldom-enforced law forbidding samurai to
visit the pleasure quarter, or to preserve privacy. Such
furtive behavior didn't necessarily mean that someone
had committed a crime. "We'll follow up on the reports
when we get back to town."

They descended the embankment to the Sumida River.
Its rippling waters sparkled in the brightening sunlight.
Mist cloaked the eastern marshes; gulls soared and
shrieked. A canopied ferry with two oarsmen in the stern
drew up to the dock. Passengers waited to board for the
trip to Edo. Among them Sano spied Monemon. He was
pale and wan, his shoulders stooping even lower.

"I need to ask you some questions," Sano called.
"We'll ride with you."

Looking extremely displeased, Monemon nodded.
Sano and Hirata climbed into the ferry, sitting opposite
him. As they glided over the shimmering water past
barges and fishing boats, Sano said, "Your departure
from the Hanakiya coincided rather neatly with Chidori's murder. Where were you?"

"Walking outside." Monemon hunched forward on
the edge of his seat, as if to make the boat move faster.

"Can anyone confirm that?" Sano asked.

"I doubt it. I purposely stayed in the alley to avoid
meeting anyone I knew."

"Because you didn't want them to wonder why you
were sneaking in or out the back door of the Hanakiya?"
Hirata said in an accusing tone.

"No. Because I needed to think." Monemon cast a
pleading glance at Sano.

"That's understandable, considering your feelings toward Chidori," Sano said sympathetically. "The occasion can't have been pleasant for you."

Monemon didn't deny it, or pretend to misunderstand.
"She was so beautiful and sweet and innocent," he said.
Memory unfocused his eyes, which were fixed on the
rice warehouses that lined the shore. "I used to pay a
fortune for the privilege of hanging around the Hanakiya

just so I could talk to her at parties. The other men laughed at me and asked why I didn't choose an older woman who could satisfy my needs. But I didn't care." Pain roughened his voice. "I dreamed of taking her away from Yoshiwara before she became tainted by the pleasure trade."

"Maybe you did take her away," Hirata suggested.

"You think I killed Chidori?" Monemon's face creased with confusion. "Why would I do that, when I loved her with all my spirit?"

"Because you didn't want anyone else to have her—least of all, your brother," Hirata said.

"That's a lie!"

Rising, Monemon lunged at Hirata. The ferry rocked; the boatmen and other passengers shouted for him to sit down. Sano and Hirata forced him back into his seat.

"I didn't kill Chidori," Monemon declared with fierce conviction. "If you want to know who did, let me give you a hint: Ask my brother where he was when she died."

"He said he went to the privy," Sano said.

Monemon gave a disdainful laugh. "I was in the alley, and no one used the privy there. I didn't see my brother at all."

Sano and Hirata exchanged uneasy glances. Was Monemon lying to incriminate Ishida and protect himself? Or had Ishida killed Chidori, pretended to discover her body, then asked Sano to investigate the case as a way of deflecting suspicion? While the usual penalty for murder was execution, under Tokugawa law a samurai could kill a commoner and get off with a reprimand—unless the murder was particularly cruel, disgusting, or scandalous. For this crime, Monemon or Ishida could receive a sentence of demotion, exile, or compulsory suicide if convicted.

And Sano could make a powerful enemy by wrongfully accusing Ishida.

"Why would your brother want Chidori dead?" Sano asked.

Monemon turned away: Either he didn't want to violate the samurai code of family loyalty any further, or he, too, feared Ishida's wrath. "Draw your own conclusions," he said, then maintained a brooding silence for the rest of the trip.

The ferry docked at Nihonbashi, Edo's merchant quarter, where vendors hawked goods from open storefronts along narrow, crowded streets. As Sano and Hirata finished a quick meal at a noodle stall, Hirata said, "Why would Ishida kill Chidori, after winning the *mizu-age* and hosting a party?"

"I have an idea," Sano said.

He led the way to a street of moneylenders' shops and entered the largest one. Customers argued with clerks who weighed gold and clicked abacus beads. The proprietor, a stout, smiling bald man, came forward.

"Greetings, *sōsakan-sama*. Matsui Minoru at your service."

Matsui was one of the nation's principal bankers and moneychangers, owner of many businesses, and one of the richest merchants in Japan. He was also Sano's prime source of information on the finances of prominent citizens.

"Tell me what you know about Ishida Genzan," Sano said.

"He owes money to every banker in town except me. Yesterday he asked me for an emergency loan, but I refused him." The merchant's smile creased his eyes into slits. "Old Matsui is too smart to fund such a reckless spender. I'll be very surprised if Ishida honors his debts."

"Did he say why he needed the loan?" Sano asked.

"To buy a night of pleasure in Yoshiwara. Not a very sound investment, but typical of Ishida."

Sano thanked Matsui. Outside, he said to Hirata, "If Ishida won the auction for Chidori's *mizu-age* and then couldn't pay, he might have killed her rather than renege on his bargain.'' A proud samurai would do anything to avoid losing face.

"I bet Kachō did it," Hirata said. "She benefits the most from Chidori's death. And the murder weapon was a woman's sash.''

"Which nobody at the Hanakiya admits to having seen before," Sano reminded him. "With so little privacy, could a courtesan buy a new item of clothing, then keep it hidden from the other residents?''

"They're protecting her," Hirata suggested, then shook his head in frustration. "We haven't any proof against Kachō or the other suspects, and no one seems about to confess. Maybe the killer really was a stranger.''

"Chidori didn't try to run away when the killer entered the room," Sano said. "She didn't call the *yarite*, who was next door. Therefore, it's likely that she knew her killer. But we do need to consider the possibility that there's a roving strangler loose in Edo.''

Police headquarters was located in the administrative district near Edo Castle. Sano had once worked behind its high stone walls as a *yoriki*—senior police commander. Outside the gate, he and Hirata encountered a samurai dressed in full armor. The samurai lifted his helmet, and Sano recognized a former colleague, *Yoriki* Hayashi.

"How nice to see you again, Sano-*san*. What brings you here?" Hayashi spoke in a cold, courteous tone; a sneer curled his thin lips.

"I'm investigating a murder." Sano explained the circumstances of the case, then said, "Have there been any similar crimes lately?''

Hayashi pondered the question, taking his time about answering. The *voriki* resented Sano's promotion, but couldn't refuse to help a man who now outranked him. "There was one last month," he said at last. "A fisherman strangled his wife. But he's been executed, so he can't be the killer you seek.''

"I want to see the records anyway," Sano said.

"Suit yourself." Hayashi stalked through the gate in a huff.

Sano and Hirata followed. As they passed through a courtyard lined with police barracks, Hirata said, "What do you hope to find?"

"I'm not sure," Sano admitted. His samurai's extra sense told him that the *netsuke*, symbol of Chidori's history and identity, was the key to the case. Even from his limited detective experience, he knew better than to overlook what appeared to be minor parties in a murder investigation, or the victim's less important relationships. Hence, he'd begun considering another possible suspect, seeking motive to match opportunity. And the police records were a good place to start. "I'll know when I see it."

In the archives room of the rambling wooden police building, Sano and Hirata spent hours poring over scrolls describing crimes in and around Edo. Finally Sano found what he was looking for. "Here," he said, passing the scroll to Hirata.

"Citizen of Totomi Province; arrested for theft along the highway," Hirata read. "Claimed that the money was earned honestly, to pay an old family debt." Noting the criminal's name, the date, and the sentence imposed by the magistrate, he raised his eyebrows in surprise. "So you think this is the killer?"

"There's something I need to check first," Sano said. "Come on. We're going back to Yoshiwara."

Under a sky aglow with the pink and gold of sunset, the pleasure quarter awakened to nocturnal life. Music and lantern light spilled from crowded teahouses. The warm night already reeked of perfume, liquor, and frying food. From caged windows, courtesans flirted with potential clients. A drunken samurai, dressed in a garish orange kimono, staggered past Sano and Hirata, singing; his two swords clanked at his waist.

At the Hanakiya, Sano spoke to the proprietor, who

took them upstairs. The house was filled with the lively bustle of courtesans and servants preparing for the evening festivities. After a successful search, Sano and Hirata waited in the proprietor's office for the suspect. They now believed they knew who had killed Chidori, and needed only a final confirmation. Yet sadness overshadowed Sano's anticipation: If his theory was correct, then this murder was a tragedy for both victim and killer.

Yarite O-ume entered. Her eyes were swollen from weeping, her face bruised by fatigue. But she faced Sano with dignity, hands folded in the sleeves of her black kimono.

"Did Chidori know you were her mother when you killed her?" Sano asked quietly.

Shock blanched O-ume's complexion and rounded her eyes. "How . . . how did you . . ."

"We found this in your room." Sano held out his open palm. Upon it rested the pink jade figure of a little girl. Her tiny fingers clutched a larger hand broken off at the wrist. "This is the missing half of Chidori's family heirloom. When you sold your daughter in Totomi Province, did you give her one of the pieces with the promise that they—as well as the two of you—would someday be reunited?"

The *yarite* dropped to her knees, covering her face with her hands. Sano continued, "You were alone in the room next door to the guest chamber. Before Ishida came upstairs, you went to Chidori, bringing a sash you'd never worn in Yoshiwara. She didn't realize you meant her any harm until you twisted the sash around her neck. You obviously loved her very much. Why did you strangle her? Did the reason have something to do with your mysterious past—or your arrest?"

"I never stole that money!" O-ume gasped between sobs. "I earned it, *zeni* by *zeni*, working as a prostitute for six long years, to buy back my daughter. But when I finally saved enough and came to Edo six months ago, the highway guards searched me and found my money. They accused me of robbing travelers. The magistrate didn't believe me when I explained. He took the money away and sentenced me to work here, in the same house as Chidori. I recognized her. She remembered me right away. And she still loved me."

O-ume looked up, and the joy of their reunion shone through her tears. "We kept our relationship a secret. I promised Chidori that I would get her out of this place, and we would live together. I prayed that somehow I could pay off her debt and free her before the *mizu-age*." Then the *yarite* bowed her head in desolation. "But I hadn't any way of earning money here. The time for Chidori's initiation came, and there was no hope left. So I did the only thing that would spare her the pain and degradation that I've suffered. I killed my darling little girl."

Sano saw his own dismay reflected on Hirata's face. Had Chidori lived, perhaps she might have been one of the few lucky courtesans who escaped Yoshiwara through marriage. But O-ume's act of mercy had more likely saved her from the harsh fate of the majority. Still, the law required observance.

"I'm sorry, but I must arrest you for murder," Sano said. "You'll have to come with us."

Nodding in resignation, the *yarite* stood. "There's no need to tie my hands," she said sadly. "I won't try to escape. Now that Chidori is dead, I've no reason to live. But I have a favor to ask. May I please have my *net-suke*?"

Filled with pity, Sano handed over both broken pieces, reflecting that murder didn't always result only from anger, jealousy, or pride. The motives of Mone-mon, Kachō, and Ishida paled beside O-ume's. In this case, love was the more destructive emotion. Then Sano and Hirata led O-ume out of the house. In the street, the crowd had grown; laughter and music filled the night. Ahead, near the gate, the drunken samurai in the orange kimono danced and reeled, still singing. Suddenly O-ume broke into a run.

"Stop!" Sano cried.

Dodging pedestrians, he and Hirata chased the prisoner. But instead of fleeing out the gate, O-ume accosted the drunken samurai. She grabbed the short sword at his waist, yanking it from the scabbard. With an anguished cry, she plunged the blade into her throat. Blood spewed as she collapsed to the ground.

The cheerful crowd noises turned to screams. Sano pushed past horrified spectators and knelt beside the *yarite*. Eyes and mouth agape with agony, she writhed, then went still.

"We should have tied her hands," Hirata said regretfully. "We should have guessed she would do this, and prevented it."

Rising, Sano shook his head. "She's paid for her crime. Justice has been served. And she and Chidori are together again."

In the spreading pool of blood lay the broken *netsuke*. The two figures had fallen from O-ume's hand, miraculously landing side by side, mother and little girl.

Nancy Kress is a Nebula- and Hugo-award-winning science fiction author, the fiction columnist for Writers Digest *magazine, author of nine books and numerous short stories. Her newest releases are* Oaths and Miracles, *a bio-thriller,* Beggars Ride, *the last volume of a critically acclaimed trilogy, and* Maximum Light. *She is considered to be one of the leading authors in the field of fantasy and science fiction today. The following story, however, is her first historical mystery.*

A SCIENTIFIC
EDUCATION

Nancy Kress

"I am not partial to dogs," Lady Jamison said sweetly, "although, of course, tastes differ."

Mrs. Cox smiled fixedly. Her two pugs, who had accompanied her on a morning call, lay heavily asleep on the hearthrug. Thirteen-year-old Charlotte Jamison glanced at her older sister. Lydia smiled before again bending her head over her needlework.

"It's not," Lady Jamison went on in her gentle voice, "that I entertain the slightest objection to animals in their proper place. The stables, the hunting party, a cat in the pantry. Cook always keeps a cat in the pantry, does she not, Lydia? But not in the drawing room. But, then, in these sad times, so few people know what belongs in what place, do you not agree, Mrs. Cox?"

Mrs. Cox, newly arrived in the neighborhood from, as Mama put it, "Heaven knows where," continued to smile brilliantly. It would take more than that sort of snub to upset Mrs. Cox, Charlotte thought, or to stop her from making morning calls on Mama. How far *could* Mama go before Mrs. Cox would take offense? It was an interesting question. You could even consider it a scientific experiment, if it wasn't so stupid.

"Well, *I* like dogs!" Charlotte said. She plopped herself off her chair, full-length on the hearthrug, and tickled the closer pug. It opened one sleepy eye and glared at her.

"Charlotte, do sit quietly," Mama said. "You must remember, my dear, that in three more years you will be out."

"Then I have three more years to tickle dogs," Charlotte said. Outrageous, of course, and she'd hear about it later, but anything to end this boring conversation. Why were ladies so tiresome? If they didn't like each other, Mrs. Cox should stay home, or Mama should have Firth say *she* wasn't at home. Or, if they wished to quarrel, they should just do it, and not go mealy-mouthing each other while Lydia sewed demurely away like the saint she wasn't.

"Such a high-spirited young lady," Mrs. Cox murmured, watching Charlotte, and now it was Mama's smile that glittered dangerously. "And so pretty."

Charlotte scowled. She wasn't pretty, and she knew it. Her hair was sparse and lank and wouldn't curl, no matter what Miss Frost did to it. Her figure was flat, even for thirteen. She would never look like Lydia, who was beautiful, or like Mama, who had been a great beauty in her day and who still had cicisbeos trailing after her. "Cluttering up the place," Papa used to say, when he was alive.

"Charlotte hasn't yet come into her best looks, of course," Mama murmured. "I noticed just the other day how much more advanced in beauty our dairymaids are at my daughter's age. So buxom, with such pretty plump arms. Very rustic."

Mrs. Cox smiled harder. Her own daughter, Miss Jane Cox, constantly fought plumpness. Charlotte again tickled the pug. It opened the other eye and bared its teeth.

"Quite," Mrs. Cox said, and stood. "Well, I mustn't keep you, dear Lady Jamison. I merely wished to pay my respects after hearing of your slight indisposition yesterday. I wouldn't dream of neglecting such an esteemed neighbor as yourself, you know.''

"Oh, I know you wouldn't,'' Mama said, too sweetly. "Lydia dear, ring for Firth to show Mrs. Cox out.''

When she had gone, the pugs trailing behind her, Lydia said, ''Really, Mama, that was too bad of you. You always see visitors to the door yourself.''

"I doubt she noticed,'' Mama said, ''unaccustomed to good manners as she must be. Charlotte, open the window, please. I can smell the shop lingering in the room.''

"Such a mushroom,'' Lydia said. ''Of course, she wanted you to invite her and the odious Jane to dine when Sir Frederick is here.''

"Over the ashes of Farnham,'' Mama said acidly. "Not that I think Miss Cox can hold a candle to you, dearest. Although if you *could* manage to stay out of the sun, it would help. Miss Cox has such a white skin.''

Lydia flushed. Mama twitted her often about her complexion, which would never be as white as Mama's. Somehow, Charlotte had noticed, Mama found a way to mention this at least once a day.

"Yes,'' Mama went on in her pretty voice, ''Miss Cox carries too much flesh, but she *is* pretty, in a vulgar sort of way. *Perhaps* we had better ensure that Sir Frederick doesn't meet her while he's visiting Brother.''

"Perhaps,'' Lydia said colorlessly. Her needle trembled.

"I mean,'' Mama went on, ''it's not as if you'd had any other offers, Lydia. And you are nearly twenty-three. Why, at your age, I'd already been married for three years and a mother for one! Of course, I was accounted a great beauty. My mother was completely satisfied with me. Did you say something, dearest?''

"No,'' Lydia muttered. Charlotte watched her muddle her needlework.

"Yes, perhaps Sir Frederick should not meet Miss Cox.''

"Or meet Charlotte, either!'' Lydia suddenly burst

out, as Charlotte had known she naturally would. Lydia never could contain herself when Mama became unbearable. "Charlotte, what possessed you to behave like that while that upstart was here? You quite disgraced yourself, you know, you little snip. And why are you hiding your hand behind your back?"

"I'm not hiding anything, Lydia! And I don't care if I don't see Sir Frederick or if you don't get him to offer for you or if he likes Miss Cox better! The whole thing is stupid."

Lydia rolled her eyes. Mama smiled sadly, as if Charlotte were the greatest cross in the world to bear, but of course Mama would bear it. Charlotte flounced out of the room, moving her hand from behind her back to a fold of her dress to hide it.

The pug she'd tickled had bit her.

When Sir Frederick alit from his curricle, he had a dog with him.

Charlotte, watching from a third-story window, didn't think much of the baronet, who was short and skinny. But the dog was pretty, a white-and-liver spaniel with long silky ears. A pity Brother couldn't have had only the dog to visit. Although if it chased the poultry, Mama would have a fit.

Charlotte turned back to her table, set up in a corner of the unused nursery. No one else ever came here. It was the one place in Farnham that was truly hers, and she could keep the table covered with as many vases, tins, and substances purchased at the village apothecary as she chose—at least, as long as she paid a shilling of every allowance to Betsey, the chambermaid, to not tell Mama. Charlotte considered it money well spent.

Carefully she lowered a piece of kindling into a glass candy bowl. From the coal scuttle, normally unused in summer, she took a hot coal with a pair of kitchen tongs, and laid it on top of the kindling. Gently she blew downward. The coal brightened; the wood flared and caught fire. Instantly Charlotte clapped the top onto the candy bowl. The fire burned a few moments more, then sputtered and went out.

With fire tongs she lifted the candy bowl and placed it on the right pan of a small scale. An unburnt piece of wood in an identical candy bowl already weighed down the left pan. Charlotte held her breath.

The pans wobbled, then the left dipped slightly.

Charlotte blew out her cheeks in disappointment. Faughhh! Why wouldn't it work for her? Doggedly, she went through the entire sequence again. And then again. Nothing. Why not? This experiment had worked for that French chemist, Monsieur Lavoisier! When he had burned wood, he had combined the "oxygen" in the air with something that emanated from the burning wood, and so proved that the weight in one vessel exactly equaled the other. No matter had been destroyed by the burning. But she had tried and tried, and no matter how carefully she worked—

"Charlotte! Where are you, you stupid girl? I've been calling and calling!"

Lydia! She mustn't see! If Mama found out what Charlotte did here . . .

Charlotte rushed to the door. She caught her older sister at the threshold and deliberately ran into her. Both of them tumbled to the floor in a tangle of muslin, long sashes, and Lydia's hairpins.

"Charlotte! You . . . you . . ."

"Don't cry, Lydia! Are you hurt? I'm so sorry!"

"I'm not crying!" said Lydia, who was. "You damnable gypsy! Look what you've done!"

Really, Lydia's language could be worse than Betsey's, if Lydia was angry enough. Charlotte supposed she picked it up from Brother. And that ugly look in her eyes . . .

"Get down to the drawing room," Lydia ordered, picking herself up. "Mother wants you. Sir Frederick is here. What were you doing in the nursery, anyway?"

"Is Mama mad at you, or just me?" Charlotte said, to divert her. A snooping Lydia was dangerous.

"Why should she be mad at me?" Lydia cried. "I do every last particular she asks of me, always!"

This was true, Charlotte suddenly realized. It didn't make Charlotte like Lydia any better.

"Oh, do come downstairs," Lydia said, dragging Charlotte roughly toward the stairs. Her nails bit into Charlotte's arm.

But outside the drawing room, Lydia stopped and arranged her face. Her eyelashes fell, her lips unclenched. She let go of Charlotte and folded her hands sweetly together. But Charlotte saw her tremble.

Stupid husband-hunter.

"Ah, there you both are," Mama said sweetly. "Sir Frederick, may I present my younger daughter, Miss Charlotte Jamison."

Charlotte curtsied. Sir Frederick rose and bowed. He wasn't any better-looking close up, but of course he was very rich.

Suddenly she noticed that her fingers were black with coal dust. Oh, lord, if Mama should see . . . Swiftly Charlotte knelt by Sir Frederick's dog. Fondling its ears, she wiped her fingers in the long, silky hair.

"My daughter is dotingly fond of dogs," Mama said. "Sir Frederick, yours appears to be quite a remarkable animal."

"On what are you basing your assessment, Lady Jamison?" Sir Frederick said. "You have not seen Boil do anything as of yet."

"And that is what I base my assessment on. He has as yet performed no tricks, made no overtures, in no way distinguished himself, and yet he impresses."

Sir Frederick smiled. "I thank you. But I'm sorry to disappoint you by saying that Boil, alas, will never be able to entertain you with tricks. He is just a dog—"

"And quite correct you are!" Lydia cried warmly. "A mere animal shouldn't be treated like a human being!"

"—and my valued companion and friend. I perceive you do not care for dogs, Miss Jamison?"

". . . no, we . . . yes, I do," Lydia said, looking help-lessly at her mother.

Lady Jamison said smoothly, "Lydia is so docile, she frequently depends on all of us to instruct her on what to think. A charming quality in a young woman, don't you think?"

Sir Frederick merely smiled.

"Or in a dog," Mama added.

Even Charlotte looked up sharply from petting Boil. So that's the way it was, again. Lydia's eyes filled with tears. She rose shakily. "Excuse me, please, I . . . feel unwell."

Immediately Mama was all solicitude. "Oh, my dear, here take my vinaigrette . . . Charlotte, ring for Miss Frost . . . my dear Lydia, take my arm. Please excuse us, Sir Frederick. My daughter is unfortunately delicate."

"I am not!" Lydia said. "I know, Sir Frederick, you said you admired robust women, please don't think . . ."

"Hush, my dear. It's all right. I'm sure Sir Frederick rates other qualities higher in womanhood than strength of constitution. Do you not, Sir Frederick?"

"Indeed," he said colorlessly.

"I knew it must be so. Compassion, for instance. Come, my dear child, I will help you to your room."

"I'm compassionate!" Lydia cried. "You know I am!"

"Of course you are," Mama said soothingly. "Oh, Miss Frost, will you be good enough to help me with Miss Lydia, she's had another of her unfortunate attacks."

"I don't have . . . mean, I don't normally . . ." poor Lydia cried. Mama smiled compassionately and, with Miss Frost's help, led her elder daughter from the room.

Charlotte and Sir Frederick were left alone, staring at each other.

Charlotte said somberly, "Now you've done it."

"Done what?"

But Charlotte wasn't going to be the one to tell him. She just shrugged and turned back to Boil. The spaniel regarded her from deep brown eyes, with depths like soft ash.

Sir Frederick said quietly, "You mean that what I've done is send your sister into hysterics. Is she always like this?"

"Only when Mama flirts with yet another of Lydia's prospects!" Charlotte said, and clamped her hand over her mouth. Oh, lord, what had she just said? "No, Sir Frederick, I didn't mean that, please don't mention it to Mama . . ."

"Are you all so afraid of your mother, then?" he said, not ungently. "I never saw that Peter was."

"Brother is a man! But I'm not afraid of Mama, either!"

Sir Frederick studied her. "No, I don't believe you are."

"I just hate her," Charlotte said daringly, to prove she wasn't afraid, and went back to fondling Boil's long, silky, coal-smeared ears.

Boil was with her when Sir Frederick tracked her down in the old nursery.

But Sir Frederick wasn't supposed to be in the house! He and Brother had gone to Newmarket for the day, to the races. Lydia was crying in her room, Mama was with Firth going over accounts . . . Charlotte had been so careful! Before she even allowed Boil to come with her to the nursery, she'd been sure no one else would bother them. It was pleasant to have the dog lie at her feet while she studied or experimented, and she'd always been so careful to return downstairs before there was any chance of either of them being looked for. And now here was this stupid baronet . . .

"Hello," Sir Frederick said. "What's all this?"

"Nothing!" Charlotte said, standing in front of the table to shield it. But it was no use. Another fire was burning in the candy bowl, and she had to turn to attend to it.

"I'm sorry to intrude," Sir Frederick said, "but I was looking for Miss Jamison."

"Here?" Charlotte said scornfully, and Sir Frederick's face darkened. He said stiffly, "I assure you, only because I'd been told it's an emergency—"

"Told by who?" Charlotte demanded. "Lydia? If she'd 'told' you, you wouldn't have to look for her, would you?"

He didn't answer.

"Oh, she didn't tell you, she sent you a *note* . . ."

"I was told there was an emergency."

This was serious. Even Charlotte knew a young lady shouldn't send notes to an unmarried gentleman. She thought the rule was stupid, but she *knew* it. Suddenly she was worried about Lydia. "Please stay here, Sir Frederick. I'll be back as soon as I can."

Charlotte rushed upstairs. Lydia must have told him to go to the schoolroom, and he thought it was on the third floor, as in so many country houses, rather than the fourth . . . Mama had never wanted to be bothered by the noise of their music lessons.

She found Lydia in the empty schoolroom, distractedly fingering discarded ornaments that, not considered fine enough for the drawing room, had ended up here. Lydia clutched a decorative globe filled with quicksilver as if it were a vinaigrette. Or a lifeline. She looked as pale as even Mama could have desired. "Lydia . . ."

"What are you doing here, brat? Where's Sir Frederick?"

"What is the emergency?"

"Where is Sir Frederick? Out with Jane Cox?"

"Jane Cox?" Charlotte said in astonishment. "What's she got to do with anything?"

"Only that she's been throwing herself at him ever since he arrived! Not that you noticed, you stupid goose, but he danced with her twice last night, and not at all with me, and Mama told me he said . . . I'll kill her, I will!"

"Lydia, don't get hysterical—"

"I will! I will!" Lydia's voice rose to a shriek. "He's mine! He's my last chance! What will become of me if he doesn't offer for me! Even Mama says—''

"If Mama said a lot less, you'd stand a better chance," Charlotte said. Lord, she hated this. "Don't you realize yet that it's Mama, not Jane Cox, who's keeping Sir Frederick for herself?"

"You're a liar!" Lydia said. "Liar, liar, liar . . ." She put her hands over her ears and burst into hysterical sobs.

Charlotte stared at her for a long moment. She couldn't bring herself to touch Lydia. Instead, she went to find Miss Frost to send to her distraught sister.

Back in the old nursery, Sir Frederick had made himself at home.

"Lavoisier," he said, holding up Charlotte's book. "*The Treatise on Chemical Elements*. John Dalton. Henry Cavendish. When did these become part of a young lady's schoolroom education?"

"Give me those!" Charlotte said angrily. "Were you not taught not to snoop among other people's things? Besides, the books are quite unexceptional!"

"And quite remarkable," Sir Frederick said. "Have you been trying here, Miss Charlotte, to duplicate Lavoisier's experiment proving the absence of phlogiston in burning material?"

Charlotte stopped short. "You have studied M'sieu Lavoisier's experiments?"

"Indeed I have."

"I don't believe you!"

Sir Frederick's lips twitched. "But it's true. Boil and I are ardent scientific amateurs. He's named for the great chemist, you know."

"Oh! 'Boyle'!"

"Quite. But look, Miss Charlotte, this candy dish won't work to duplicate Lavoisier's experiment. It is not airtight."

"I feared that," Charlotte said, despite herself. "But it's the best I could manage."

"I'm afraid that to prove that oxygen combines with

burning material, you require better equipment: a proper glass retort with sealable beak, and a more accurate weighing device.''

"There is no chance of getting those,'' Charlotte said. So she couldn't duplicate the experiment after all. To hide her disappointment, she knelt and buried her face in Boyle's fur. He wagged his tail and licked her.

"I will procure for you the necessary equipment,'' Sir Frederick's voice said from above her. "Discreetly, if you think it will upset your mother.''

Charlotte peered sharply upwards. "Why would you do that? For me?''

"You are a fellow appreciator of science, are you not? Surely that is reason enough.''

Charlotte got to her feet. She stared steadily at him. All at once she was very conscious of her drab gown, her lank hair. She put a hand to her lips.

"My dear Miss Charlotte,'' Sir Frederick said, "are you really so unaccustomed in this house to simple kindness?''

"Yes,'' Charlotte said, and looked down at her feet because she found she could say no more.

"But your father has not been dead for very long . . . that is, Peter told me . . . .''

"My father!''

"Yes, am I mistaken? Peter told me that he was a most affectionate—''

"We do not speak of my father in this house, Sir Frederick.''

Sir Frederick bowed and turned to go. Before he reached the door, Charlotte, still staring at the floor with all her senses heightened by what had just passed, heard the rustle of a silk dress in the passage.

Sir Frederick stayed with Brother another fortnight. Charlotte avoided him, waiting to see if he would keep his word about the scientific equipment. She doubted he would. Meanwhile, she stayed away from the house as much as possible, eluding Miss Frost and romping in the park with Boyle, who did indeed have an unfortunate tendency to chase chickens, angering the poultryman and dairymaids. But Boyle was always there when she wanted him, always reliable, always glad to be with her. Her skin grew brown from the sun. She saw almost nothing of Lydia or Mama, busy with fresh rounds of gaieties in honor of Sir Frederick.

Mrs. Cox and Jane visited three times, always when Sir Frederick and Brother were present.

At an impromptu dance after a rout party, Charlotte watched from the hallway. Sir Frederick danced twice with Jane Cox, not at all with Lydia. Miss Cox's dark eyes sparkled, and her pretty plump arms shone pearly in the candlelight. Lydia went to bed in tears—Charlotte heard her weeping, through the wall between their rooms—while Mama smiled sweetly and flirted with another friend of Brother's, who seemed quite taken with her.

The next day, the doctor had to be sent for to attend Lydia, who refused to eat. "I'm afraid my daughter is high-strung," Mama sighed in the breakfast room, wearing a becoming lace cap on her curls. She sat with her back to the strong summer sunlight streaming in the window, and her white skin shone soft and young as Jane Cox's. "Poor Lydia has always been excitable."

"I am sorry to hear it," Sir Frederick said. Brother merely turned the pages of his newspaper.

"It has been a sad trial to us all," Mama said. Her eyes brimmed with pretty regret.

"Indeed," Sir Frederick said, and at his tone even Brother looked up—for a moment—in vague puzzlement. But then something in the paper caught his eye. "By Jove, look at this! Frederick, didn't you say your cousin is lieutenant aboard His Majesty's ship *Triumph*?"

"No, Peter. He had been on the *Triumph*, but transferred some months ago to the *Dauntless*."

"And a fortunate thing for him! Listen to this: 'It has been learned that His Majesty's ship *Triumph*, of seventy-four guns, last month salvaged 130 tons of mercury from a Spanish wreck off Cádiz. Unfortunately the parchment bags confining the mercury within wooden barrels rotted, owing to sodden conditions and the unusual heat of the weather. The heated mercury then diffused a noxious gas throughout the ship, which induced such debilities as excess salivation, partial paralysis, and loss of teeth. Several men perished, and the ship's livestock, consisting of sheep, pigs, goats, and poultry, shared their fate. Only the midshipmen enjoyed a partial escape, perhaps because these Gentlemen spent so much time on the open deck.' Gods!''

"It is most distressing," Lady Jamison said, chewing toast placidly.

Charlotte said, "Mercury will turn to gas at quite low temperatures, I believe. Little more than body temperature is required."

"Really, my dear," Mama said, with more feeling than had been evoked by the sailors' deaths, "if you *must* study such unladylike subjects, at least spare us at breakfast."

"But, Mama, it is quite remarkable that—"

"Do you and Brother ride this morning?" Mama said to Sir Frederick, and Charlotte fell silent.

In the great hall, however, she stopped to stare at the barometer her dead father had affixed to the wall. It was one of the few memories she had of him, shut up as he had been since she reached the age of six and Papa had . . . But she didn't want to think of that. Better to stare at the barometer, with its shining column of mercury, and try to imagine it diffusing unseen through the air of the *Triumph* . . . just how hot must the weather have been to cause the mercury to sublime?

An interesting question. She went upstairs to her secret books. Perhaps Lavoisier had written on this. Or Boyle, or Mr. Dalton . . . or perhaps she could devise an experiment to find out for herself! Was that possible?

She took the rest of the stairs two at a time.

• • •

A week later a huge box arrived for Sir Frederick, which he had the carter carry to his own room and did not mention at table. When Charlotte went up to the nursery, she found unpacked on her table such wealth as she had never imagined.

Glass retorts, with and without beaks. Laboratory lamps. Crucibles. An alembic. Vials of chemical substances, boxes and boxes of them. Books and pamphlets. An exquisite, delicately calibrated scale.

She sank onto the window seat and stared hungrily. Then, slowly, she gathered her sun-lightened hair at the back of her head and twisted it high. She looked at herself in the dusty mirror on the nursery wall. Then she looked again at the books, the glassware, the chemicals, the lamps, the kindness.

She had never been so happy.

That afternoon, Sir Frederick called on the Coxes, without Brother.

That evening, Lydia won a smile from Sir Frederick by petting and cosseting Boyle as the spaniel lay at his master's feet.

After a game of whist, in which Charlotte had to make a fourth because Lydia was sewing so compassionately on clothes for the poor, Mama laid her hand on Sir Frederick's arm and prettily begged him to take a last turn with her in the shrubbery, since "the night is so fine, and I am a great devotee of stargazing, and indeed of all scientific endeavors."

Brother announced that he had persuaded Sir Frederick to extend his visit to the end of the month.

In the middle of the night, Charlotte woke to hear footsteps in the corridor outside her room. Probably Firth, she thought, summoned to help Brother to bed. Many nights Brother sat drinking port until quite late, even when there were no guests at Farnham. Although if it was Firth, odd that a silken gown rustled . . . Charlotte went back to sleep.

The next day, Boyle went missing. After an extensive

search, the stableboy found him in a small shed, unused in summer. With him was a smoldering coal scuttle. The spaniel was dead.

"Who could have done such a thing?" Lady Jamison cried. "Poisoned! We have never had such a terrible cruelty at Farnham!"

"By God, whoever it was shall pay for it!" Brother said. "Fred, I am so sorry!"

Sir Frederick did not answer. He knelt beside Boyle's body, which the shaken stableboy had carried onto Farnham's front steps and then, confused about what to do next, had laid the dog down there. Sir Frederick bent far forward, and his face was hidden.

Lydia came rushing out the door. "Firth just informed me . . . oh, my dear Sir Frederick! How shocking for you, who loved him so much!" Impulsively, Lydia dropped to her knees beside him and put a hand on his arm. Charlotte saw genuine tears in Lydia's eyes.

She herself didn't know how to react. Boyle lay so stiff on the marble steps, his cold muzzle slimed with saliva and vomit, his limbs paralyzed at grotesque angles. *We have never had such cruelty at Farnham . . .*

"Papa," Charlotte said aloud, but her voice was so strangled that no one heard.

Brother said, "I myself shall question the poultryman and dairymaids. If any of them *dared . . .*" He strode off.

"Come into the house, Sir Frederick," Lydia said gently. "Or I will bring you a glass of whisky here, if you prefer."

"Thank you," Sir Frederick said, head still bent, and Lydia rose and pushed past Mama to go inside, not looking at any of them.

"*Never* anything like this," Mama said. "Betsey, fetch my shawl. The wind is picking up."

Charlotte's legs felt wobbly. But she made herself walk to the shed where Boyle had died.

The smoldering coal scuttle still heated the air. Charlotte sniffed: no odor. Holding her breath, she searched the shed. When she found nothing, she began on the surrounding grounds, working methodically in spiraling circles. Under a flowering gorse she found a warming pan filled with more heated coals. She knelt beside it and yanked on the chain around her neck until her locket broke free. Slowly she rubbed the locket across the warming pan, through the sticky ooze that still filmed it. The locket turned reddish.

Very few elements, according to M'sieu Lavoisier, would combine with gold.

One that did was mercury.

Slowly Charlotte returned to the house. In the great hall she glanced at Papa's barometer. But the glass was unbroken, the mercury inside intact. She walked up the stairs, toward Mama's sitting room, and then past it. Charlotte kept on climbing. In the old schoolroom she looked for the decorative globe filled with quicksilver. It was gone.

"You did it," Charlotte said. She struggled to keep her voice even. "You poisoned Boyle."

"I did not!" Lydia cried.

"You did it to show Sir Frederick how much womanly compassion you could feel. So he would feel rotten and you would be able to make him feel better . . . you, and not Jane Cox."

"Charlotte! How *dare* you make such an accusation to me!"

"I do make it," Charlotte said. She couldn't stop trembling. Her own *sister* . . . "You read in the paper about the mercury poisoning aboard the *Triumph*. Or Brother told you about it. And you . . . you went and . . ."

"If you presume to repeat any of this evil nonsense to Sir Frederick, you'll regret it the rest of your life!" Lydia cried. "You wicked, wicked child, to think I could do such a thing!"

"May you rot in hell, Lydia."

Lydia burst into tears. Charlotte walked on trembling legs from the room. She had not known she could feel this much anger. She could imagine Lydia dead, dying, poisoned as poor Boyle had been poisoned. Charlotte could imagine it with pleasure. The pleasure frightened her. Lydia was right, Charlotte was wicked, wicked . . . but not as wicked as a person who could murder a defenseless dog.

Shakily, Charlotte made her way to the deserted nursery. Her scientific books were there. Solace, stimulation, unfailing escape. But not this time. She could not open them for a long time. She sat staring at them, her mind numb, and when Miss Frost called for her, Charlotte didn't answer.

They buried Boyle in the shrubbery. Sir Frederick himself dug the hole, Lydia beside him. From her window Charlotte could see him talking and talking, although she couldn't hear the words. Evidently Sir Frederick was the kind whose grief was eased by words. Charlotte could see Lydia listening, nodding. From time to time she put a comforting hand on Sir Frederick's shoulder.

Charlotte went to find Mama.

She stammered out her story while Mama held her sewing motionless in her lap and fastened large blue eyes on Charlotte's face. ". . . and I looked everywhere for the quicksilver globe, Mama. It's *gone*."

"Gone."

"Yes. I think that Lydia . . . oh, it's too horrible!"

"It is horrible, yes," Mama said. She seemed to remember her sewing. Thoughtfully she bit off the end of the thread.

Charlotte blurted, "You don't seem very surprised!"

"Well, my dear, to tell you the truth, I'm not. I've known for a long time that Lydia was unbalanced. Ever since your poor Papa died so horribly . . ."

Charlotte was startled. Mama never mentioned Papa. Nor would she permit anyone else to discuss him.

"And then, to remain unmarried at her age . . . it disorders the brain, you know. Her fretting diverts too much blood to the bodily nerves, leaving less for the brain, and that nourishes animal propensities. If only Lydia had had the offers I had! But what can't be cured, must be endured. Pray ask Sir Frederick to come to me.''

''Sir . . . Sir Frederick? Not Lydia?''

''Sir Frederick,'' Mama said firmly. ''Lydia, I will deal with later.''

But Charlotte couldn't do it. Go out there, where Sir Frederick was burying his beloved pet and Lydia so pleased beside him, so happy to be needed . . . Charlotte couldn't face them. She sent a footman to tell Sir Frederick that Lady Jamison wished to see him.

Then Charlotte rushed to the nursery and immersed herself in her scientific books.

But there was no escape. She could not concentrate on the fascinating experiments of Monsieur Lavoisier with combustion, or Mr. Dalton's new theory of matter, or even on Mr. Henry Cavendish's exciting researches into the density and composition of water.

Shadows lay long when the sound of carriage wheels drifted through the open window. Charlotte jumped up. Sir Frederick's curricle, with his luggage strapped on, his tiger perched behind, and Sir Frederick himself at the reins, was just starting to move down the long, curving, shadow-barred avenue away from Farnham.

She had never run so fast in her life. Down the stairs, across the park, a shortcut through the trees. The hem of her gown tore; her hair shook loose of its ribbon. She caught him just where Farnham Lane joined the main road.

''Sir Frederick! Oh, please—Sir Frederick!''

''Miss Charlotte!'' He pulled up short, his matched greys dancing. ''What on earth—''

''You mustn't . . . go! I have . . . something . . . to tell you!'' She couldn't catch her breath.

He gazed down at her from the height of the curricle, his face suddenly somber. ''I don't think, Miss Charlotte, that you can have anything to the point to tell me.''

"But I . . . do! I know . . . who killed Boyle! And you, surely . . . have . . . a right to know.''

"I already know.''

Charlotte gaped at him.

"I know, but it suddenly occurs to me that you may not.''

"I . . . the mercury . . . a quicksilver globe in the schoolroom . . .''

Slowly Sir Frederick climbed down from his carriage. He put a hand on her arm, and Charlotte saw again Lydia making the same gesture, to him. Charlotte pulled away.

"There was . . . a quicksilver globe . . . I saw Lydia clutching at it, the day she sent you the note. It's gone. Lydia took it, and broke it to get the mercury out, and—''

Charlotte stopped. Sir Frederick pulled from his pocket the quicksilver globe. "Do you mean this?''

"But . . . but I found—there was mercury set to sublime on a hot warming pan beside Boyle—''

"You found mercury, yes. Lady Jamison told me all that you told her. Undoubtedly she did not wish me to hear it from *you*. But the mercury you found was not from this globe. Lydia gave it to me three days ago. It was her papa's, she said. Evidently your father liked inventions. The barometer, too, was his, your mother says.''

"But if you have the globe, then where did Lydia get the mercury to poison Boyle?''

Sir Frederick said, as gently as ever Mama herself could have done, "Lydia did not.''

"But—''

"I think I've said enough, Miss Charlotte. Or maybe too much.''

None of it made any sense. But suddenly Charlotte's head pounded, and she felt faint. "If not Lydia . . . it *must* have been Lydia!''

Sir Frederick looked as if he wished profoundly to be elsewhere. "I'm sorry to be the one to enlighten you.

Sorry that anyone must. But when your mother told me of your . . . investigative work, she also told me she had found the remains of the glass quicksilver globe among refuse in Lydia's room. She didn't know that Lydia had given it to me. And I did not tell her.''

"No!" Charlotte cried. "Don't say it!"

"I wish I didn't have to," Sir Frederick said. "You must be strong, my dear. I think you can be."

"Mama . . . Mama wouldn't have any other mercury . . .''

Sir Frederick's eyes were sad. "My dear child . . . but you couldn't be expected to know about all the medical uses of chemicals, no matter how precocious your scientific studies. Do you even know what ailment killed your father?''

Charlotte stared mutely.

"Yes, I know; Peter told me. There was a good reason you were kept away from him near the end, Miss Charlotte. You are only a child, and to see him like that . . . but what you don't know is that the French disease— syphilis—is often treated with a preparation of mercury, fats, and liquorice root. The three are kept separate until made into a poultice. When your father . . . died, there were ample supplies of each left over."

No, you must not go into Papa's room, my dear . . . not even the servants are permitted to nurse him . . . I alone can care for your dear Papa.

"But Mama . . . Lydia . . . Mama had no reason to kill poor Boyle!"

Sir Frederick looked away, down the empty road. He colored.

Footsteps in the corridor outside Charlotte's room, in the middle of the night. The swish of a silken gown. Mama smiling seductively over the breakfast cups. *I'm sorry to be the one to enlighten you, sorry that anyone must . . .*

"I do not wish to grow up!" The words burst out of her. Unbidden, unwanted . . . Charlotte was shaking. If this is what women were, did, must be, to attract and hold men . . . she would not do it. She would not!

Sir Frederick said quietly, "You are different, Miss Charlotte. And you will grow up differently."

For a moment Charlotte felt a wild surge of hope. "Yes! I will! And when I do . . . you've been so kind . . . you too care nothing for stupid rules of society . . . you are so interested in my scientific studies . . ."

Alarm appeared on Sir Frederick's face. Hastily he stepped backward, toward his curricle.

Charlotte said slowly, "You are going to marry Jane Cox."

"How did you know? I have offered for the lady, yes."

Jane Cox. Not a poisoner of dogs, not a desperate aging spinster, not a middle-aged flirt—but still, a woman. Pretty. Vivacious. Dressed in ribbons and lace. Uninterested in scientific advances, or in anything else of the mind.

Charlotte said dully, "I wish you happiness, Sir Frederick."

"Thank you." Hastily he climbed back into his curricle. From the safety of its high perch, he smiled down at her, flicking his reins, eager for escape. The horses started forward. Over his shoulder he called back to her, "And I wish you success with your scientific studies, Miss Charlotte."

Her studies. It was a choice, then. Watching Sir Frederick flee Farnham, Charlotte had never seen so clearly that it was a choice. Balanced on the scales, both samples more than a little charred. In the one pan, ribbons and white skin and offers of marriage and murderous desperation when they did not come, or had been outlived. In the other pan, Boyle and Lavoisier and the composition of oxygen and the density of atoms.

And Sir Frederick himself had given her the best, the most expensive, of weighing devices.

Charlotte made her way back to the house. On the portico, she passed Firth. She told him, in a tone that made the butler look up sharply, to send Tom-carpenter to her. She wished a bolt to be installed on the door of the old nursery, one that could be drawn from the inside while the room was occupied and locked from the outside when it was not.

"But, miss—" Firth began.

"Do it," Charlotte said, and continued upstairs to her laboratory.

The mysteries of Miriam Grace Monfredo center on the neglected history of women in nineteenth-century America. Her series featuring librarian Glynis Tryon takes place for the most part in western New York State. The first novel, Seneca Falls Inheritance, *is set in the 1848 village where the struggle for women's property rights and suffrage began. The next four Glynis Tryon mysteries involve other social movements such as temperance and the abolition of slavery that found among women their strongest supporters. Her fifth and most recent mystery,* The Stalking-Horse, *begins to explore the lives of Southern women during the Civil War. Monfredo's short fiction has appeared in periodicals and various anthologies that include two "Year's Best" collections. Her following story features an altogether different breed of western New Yorker.*

A MULE NAMED SAL

Miriam Grace Monfredo

I've got a mule and her name is Sal,
Fifteen miles on the Erie Canal,
She's a good ol' worker and a good ol' pal,
Fifteen miles on the Erie Canal.
— THOMAS S. ALLEN

Autumn sunlight shimmering across a broad ribbon of water held no aesthetic charm whatsoever for Peregrine Jeremy Peel the Fourth. Not while the toes of his boots were scrabbling for purchase at the edge of a graveled towpath, and his heels hung precariously over the concrete wall of the newly constructed Erie Canal. Directly beneath his heels, water lapped with the erratic rhythm of strong undercurrents. The young man could not swim, not a stroke. One step backward would thus end a long and for the most part honorable line of Peels, the ignominious exceptions to this being so few in number they did not bear thinking about; at least not now, Peel decided, when at any moment he might become one of them.

He was not altogether clear as to how he'd managed

to find himself in this position. To his immediate left crouched a growling dog the size of a Shetland pony; to his right were more than a half-dozen children, all of whom seemed afflicted with St. Vitus's dance and hence darted like fruit flies around a tall woman, nearly as tall as Peel himself, who had planted herself in his path. Beside the woman stood a draft mule that just might have been the most astute-looking of the lot. The mule, however, was not the one Peel had been assigned to question.

"What'd you say your name was?" This from the woman, a Mrs. Raffin, whose wild chestnut hair closely resembled a burning bush. She'd just lifted the mule's left front foot and was examining its shoe. Evidently no repair was needed, as the woman slipped the square-headed claw hammer she held into a loop in her belt. She then lowered the mule's foot to the ground and regarded Peel with skepticism. His plight she pointedly ignored.

Before answering her, Peel rocked on his feet and thereby managed to inch his heels forward on the towpath. The dog's growl at once deepened.

"It's Peel. Peregrine Peel." He didn't add "the Fourth." He didn't think Mrs. Raffin would be interested; Peel himself didn't consider it particularly interesting.

"Pee . . . Pear . . . *what*?" Mrs. Raffin struggled. "That name's a mouthful. Too many *P*'s!"

"I agree. It wasn't my idea. And you're welcome to call me . . . Just 'Peel' will be fine."

One of the youngsters, a boy in clean but tattered clothing and in need of possibly his first haircut, commented, "Maybe we could call you Pee-pee."

Peel's years in boarding school had deafened him to this gibe; still, he was distracted by the gleeful response of the boy's siblings and didn't immediately register the slight nip at the back of his arm. When he felt its sting, he turned to look into the flat brown eyes of the mule. Now that it had shuffled closer, Peel realized the bay-colored animal was far larger than it had seemed from a safer distance. It stood probably close to seventeen hands high—not including the long, pointed ears—and well over a thousand, muscled pounds. The mule tossed its head, ruffling its short brushy mane; then it pulled back its lips to display sizable teeth which were clearly the source of the nip. Since the facial cast of mules was foreign to Peel, it occurred to him that the animal might be grinning, while contemplating a more substantial bite. Peel almost took a fatal step backward, caught himself in time and edged sideways, rubbing his arm.

"Oh, don't mind her," the woman said, a husky laugh rising from deep in her chest. "Ol' Sal, she has a mighty re-fined sense of humor."

"Sal?"

"Sal. That's her *name*!" Mrs. Raffin looked at Peel as if he lacked something essential. Brains.

But weren't mules without gender—incapable of re-production? Peel couldn't recall exactly where he had gathered this fragment of wisdom.

"She's a beaut, Sal is," Mrs. Raffin pronounced firmly as if expecting argument.

The mule rolled her eyes at Peel, who said quickly, "Oh, indeed, a thing of beauty." And yes, he remem-bered now, "thing" *should* be the operative word here.

Peel, however, would be the first to admit he knew little else that was useful; he'd recently graduated from Harvard College but only by the skin of his teeth, as he'd very nearly failed every course he'd taken. Which had not sat well with Peregrine Jeremy Peel the Third, Esquire. Which explained why he, the Fourth—also Es-quire, though only just—now resided not in the worldly city of Boston, but in a small frontier town in western New York State. And why he now stood teetering over the Erie Canal. When the Canal had been opened by New York Governor De Witt Clinton the previous week, with a pageantry usually reserved for the coronation of European monarchs—something the young American nation had just rid itself of—it had been declared a world-class wonder of innovative engineering. Or, from Peel's current perspective, a world-class deathtrap.

And here he was, wobbling just above its slavering craw. Which would have come as no surprise to his father, who, on their last meeting, had declared gravely, "Peregrine, you are a great disappointment to me. You seem to care for nothing and for no one." Here, Peel recalled, he had looked around at the immense, but unfamiliar family mansion, the scrupulously tended grounds fronting Charles Street at the foot of Beacon Hill, and decided his father could be right. Peel had spent most of his years in schools elsewhere, while his mother's three-year Grand Tours of Europe had made her presence equally elsewhere. The one nanny he'd liked had been sent packing after nipping once too often his father's forbidden, imported Scotch whisky. Peel still wondered if Nanny's reckless defiance had been the reason he'd liked the woman.

"Peregrine, stop daydreaming and pay attention!" his father had demanded on that last day. "Your singular lack of purpose, your want of respect for the position of this family, force me to prevent your doing lasting damage to the good name of Peel."

To this end Peregrine had been foisted onto one of his mother's cousins, whose name was evidently not considered to be at risk. It was here, at a far reach from Boston society, that Peel *might*, in his father's words, "Learn something useful, unlikely as that may appear."

So who was he, Peel thought again, to question the sexual identity of mules? Sal, she would be.

He'd been forewarned that those living along the Canal—"canawlers" and their kin—were a breed apart, most of them drifters or squatters with a ready distrust of the law. And he saw that the woman continued to watch him guardedly.

"Just what is it you want here, Mr. P.?"

That seemed a reasonable enough question, in spite of the youngsters' unrestrained snickering.

"As you know, Mrs. Raffin . . ."

"Beryl. Call me Beryl!"

"Yes. Well, as you know, Mrs . . . Beryl, the local constabulary was notified that your husband has been missing for some days now." With this, Peel boldly attempted to step forward, away from the verge of drowning, but the dog apparently thought the verge exactly where he belonged, as the growl sharpened to a snarl.

Beryl, her voice lacking the urgency Peel would have preferred, said, "Quiet down, Killer." And while the dog complied instantly, he continued to eye Peel as only a large carnivore with the name of Killer could do.

"Course I *know* Pete's gone missin'," Beryl added, "but there's nothin' new 'bout that. He's gone missin' a lot. So what stirred up the dust this time?"

"Constable Stuart's dust, you mean?" Peel asked, while, with the dog checked, he gained some ground on the towpath. "Well, mainly he's . . . He's concerned about your husband." This *"your husband"* was not precisely the phrase his cousin, Constable Jamie Stuart, had used, but since there were children present, *"rotten bastard"* seemed inappropriate.

"Concerned!" Beryl responded with passion. "Nobody's been concerned about that rotten bastard's doin's for some time now. Else he'd a gone missin' long ago."

"Are you saying you think your husband might have met with foul play?"

"Foul play? What the hell's that mean? If it means somebody did him in . . . Well, maybe the bastard finally got his just deserts."

"I see." Peel said. Although he didn't. That Pete Raffin was a bad one from the constable's viewpoint didn't explain Beryl Raffin's like point of view. In Peel's limited experience, decent women were often attracted to scoundrels and would continue to defend them in spite of being ill-used by them. But Beryl obviously did not fit this category. Peel, who had been too distracted by his peril to do so before, now studied the woman more closely.

Beryl Raffin, tall and full-bodied, would be described

even by exacting Bostonians as statuesque, possessing a certain Rubenesque voluptuousness. Her face would undoubtedly be considered handsome were it not for the jagged scar that ran from temple to jaw, although the scar became visible only when the woman flung back her thick mane of hair. Peel also now noticed the purplish tinge of bruising to the skin around one moss-green eye. And while Beryl Raffin's language was saltier than would be approved by the bluebloods of Boston's Back Bay, those moss eyes held an intelligence Peel had not noticed before this more thorough scrutiny.

Now, breaking into his musing, Peel heard an unaccountable snuffing noise, and felt something poking at the bottom of his trousers. He looked down in time to see the dog remove its nose and raise its rear leg beside Peel's own.

"No!" Peel yelled. Suddenly recalling the animal's name, he added, "Please do not do that."

Beryl Raffin stepped forward, grabbed the dog's furry ruff and dragged it backward. "Stop that, Killer," she said with a casualness Peel thought unequal to the occasion. To Peel, she said, "Killer must like you."

The dog had admittedly stopped snarling, but Peel was forced to wonder if Killer's gesture of affection was an improvement. "Is there a possibility," Peel asked, "of striking some middle ground with Killer?"

"I doubt it. He either likes you or he don't." And Peel thought he saw a small upward tilt at the corner of Beryl's mouth that was not unattractive.

He thought he might begin to understand what earlier had seemed to be incomprehensible. Constable Jamie Stuart had sent Peel to make inquiries that might lead to the whereabouts of the missing man; or, as Jamie had phrased it, "to find out if Beryl could be involved in some permanent solution to the shenanigans of Pete Raffin."

According to the constable, it wasn't that Raffin didn't have his other detractors—to the contrary, he had plenty—but in Stuart's opinion, "Beryl's the only one in town with the guts to do anything about him. And while most hereabouts will say 'good riddance,' we've still got the obligation to make sure Beryl Raffin isn't involved in murder. Can't have *that* kind of thing going on. But if she is involved, then she needs proper counsel.''

This concern on the part of his cousin for the woman's welfare had bewildered Peel. Until Jamie explained that the numerous youngsters surrounding Beryl were not, in fact, her children, but the consequence of Pete Raffin's favored pastime. ''Still and all, Beryl takes care of them as best she can,'' Jamie had said. ''Which seems a damn nasty quirk of fate, since the local gossip—you know how women talk—is that Beryl herself . . .'' The constable broke off momentarily, then continued, ''Let's just say that Beryl is a fulsome flower unable to set fruit.''

Peel thought this poetic rendering to be characteristic of Jamie Stuart, a gentle though lugubrious man, convinced the world was going to hell, while fervently hoping he'd made a mistake. And Beryl Raffin might seem proof of some error in his apocalyptic reckoning.

But since, in the arcane language of the law, there was no *corpus delicti*, at least not yet, Peel failed to see what problem existed. Pete Raffin could simply be peddling his dubious wiles somewhere other than this particular town.

''I don't think so,'' had been Jamie's reply. ''No, I'd stake anything on it. Raffin has things too good here to leave voluntarily. Besides, he's got no money other than what Beryl brings in driving her mule—*honest* money, that is.''

''Beryl Raffin is a mule driver?'' Peel had then asked with a fair amount of incredulity.

Jamie Stuart had grinned. ''Yeah, Beryl's a hoggee, city boy.''

Beryl said now, ''I got no idea where that rat is, and what's more, I don't give a damn. Does Constable Stuart think I know?''

"No, that's not precisely what he thinks."

The throaty laugh rose again. "He thinks I killed him off? Listen here, I was gonna do that, I'd a' done it long ago." Beryl Raffin's laughter stopped abruptly. "Just what d'you think would happen to these here kids if I was to swing at the end of a rope? I'd like to have killed him, and I'll be no grievin' widow if somebody else did, but I didn't do it."

At that, Beryl Raffin turned on her heel and walked toward a dilapidated shack dwarfed by ancient oaks at the edge of the towpath. The mule Sal plodded along beside her. And now Peel saw that the mule's strongly muscled rump bore lacerations, some of the welts scarred over, some only recently begun to heal. But, given the pocketknife the tattered boy had been fingering, Peel wondered if Sal would escape further abuse.

Killer, to Peel's relief, loped after his mistress. Peel stood in thought, watching after them for a time. Beryl Raffin might or might not have murdered her husband, and Peel found himself hoping that she hadn't, but he now agreed with Jamie Stuart that *someone* had likely killed Pete Raffin. There *were* candidates. The constable had given Peel the names of two possible suspects, each having an undeniable motive: revenge.

Yet there should be a body. So where was it?

Birch leaves as bright as gold buttons cascaded around Peel while he walked back along the towpath to Jamie Stuart's closet-size cubicle located in the rear of the village firehouse. Peel, glancing at the water rippling beside him, decided the Erie Canal deserved some study. Happily this could be conducted from the protection of metaphysical distance, as it seemed fairly safe to assume that Raffin's body could not be lying on the Canal bottom. Preventing that would be the strong undertow. Nonetheless, a fruitful line of inquiry might be to find out if Pete Raffin had ever learned to swim.

And, Peel mused, he might also inquire as to when the thick concrete wall had been poured.

• • •

"What'd you mean, can we pull the wall down?" the brawny construction foreman yelped, while gesturing at the nearby Canal. "We just put it up!"

"I didn't mean pull it *down*, exactly," said Peel, wishing the man would not walk so close to what Peel had begun to view not as the popularized Clinton's Ditch, but as a monument to mankind's risky meddling with the natural order, or, in this case, the flow of things. Since this reminded him of his father's moldering opinions, he shrugged to cast off ancestry and resolved to think more progressive thoughts.

"Yeah, so what *did* you mean?" The thick-bearded foreman looked Peel over with narrowed eyes of mistrust as if confronted with borderline stability.

"Tell me," Peel asked, deciding on a different tack, "how quickly does the cement dry once it's poured?"

The foreman seemed to relax since this was, as Peel had intended, not only a reasonable question but one that had an answer.

The glance the foreman gave the Canal wall was of unabashed pride. "This cement dries quick," he explained, "so fast we call it White's Rapid-Rock. That's for Canvas White who invented the stuff. You hear tell of him? Went all the way to Europe, young White did, to see the waterproof cement they used in their canals. Too expensive to ship the stuff here though. So, one night after tossing back a few at Carey's Chittenango Bar, he threw together some pulverized local limestone and sand, rolled it up and dumped it into a pail of water. Next morning: Eureka! He finds a ball of stone. Stone! Waterproof hydraulic cement is what it's called. It dries real fast."

"Any other type of material used in the Canal construction?"

"Yeah, there's the grayish-blue clay we use to line the bed so there's not much seepage. Diggers named it Blue Mud of the Meadows. Listen, mister, just what're you gettin' at here?"

How much could the truth hurt? Peel wondered, other

than making him the laughingstock of western New York. Thus, with confidence, he asked, "Could something large be concealed in the concrete before it dried? Dried solid?"

"Something large like *what*? A tool, you mean—maybe a hand tool like a trowel?"

"No, I mean larger than that. About as large as, say, a man's body?"

The foreman's mouth opened but little sound emerged. It closed, the mouth, then opened again. This sequence occurred several times, reminding Peel of a fuse quietly spluttering on and off before the explosion. When at last it came, the foreman's burst of laughter must have carried throughout the entire county.

"A *body*! You asking if some *body* could . . . could just sort of lay down and"—the foreman was now choking on his own hilarity—"and get troweled over by the crew before the cement dried? Oh, sure! Happens all the time. That's why"—the laughter had begun to grate on Peel's nerves—"why the wall's so *lumpy*. C'mon! What *are* you, fella, some kind of lunatic or something?

Peel had miscalculated: there were things worse than being made a laughingstock. But, resolving to be at least a self-respecting lunatic, he drew himself up and said, "Then you are prepared, my man, to state unequivocally that the concealment of a body in your concrete would be impossible?"

The laughter stopped. "Say again," the foreman said.

Peel repeated the question.

"Yeah," came his answer. "I can state that uneqee . . . There's no way in hell it could happen. And a word to the wise, young fella—you might consider laying off the drink. Taking the pledge, you know?"

Peel sighed, thinking that, in fact, what he needed most right now was Constable Jamie Stuart's smooth Scotch whisky. He gave the foreman what he believed was a sobering nod, and left the man chortling into his beard. Peel supposed it too much to hope that the story of the drunk city-boy's questions wouldn't get overly embellished as it traveled the length of New York State.

All was not lost, though. Thought of the constable made Peel remember Jamie's comment about Pete Raffin's widely known affair with the wife of Eubie Strange. A motive for murder if ever there was one.

As Peel walked along the towpath, making sure he kept to its far edge, clumps of goldenrod swept his sleeve, leaving streaks of pollen like soft yellow broom strokes. He slowed to brush off the pollen and nearly stumbled over a raised section of seven or eight abutting planks, laid side by side, crossing the width of the gravel towpath like a five-foot segment of corduroy road. For a moment Peel was baffled, then remembered he'd been told by the foreman about escape holes cut into the Canal wall. It seemed that mules and horses occasionally fell into the water, then found themselves trapped, unable to scale the wall. The escape holes allowed an animal to swim to the opening, then climb up a ramp which brought it back to the towpath. Just one of the creative innovations of this engineering marvel, the Erie Canal.

A quarter-mile down the towpath, then a short distance on a dirt road, brought Peel to the home of Eubie Strange. And shortly, the aptness of the man's name put Peel in mind of the old conundrum of which came first, chicken or egg. The gaunt, loose-limbed Eubie was chopping wood behind what looked to be a thatched roofed cottage, a cottage which seemed quite ordinary until one realized that the entire roof was slowly undulating. Peel, after taking a second look, and before quickly stepping backward, decided a more suitable word for the roof might be *writhing*. What had first appeared as the roof's thatching was, in fact, a vast cover of snakes sunning themselves, coiled and twisted around one another in an intricate network. Undoubtedly the roof might have held a certain fascination for some. Peel was not one of them.

"Hullo." This came from Eubie, who leaned his ax against a nearby tree. The ax was immediately appropriated by a slim, bright green viper that slid up its handle. "Hey, get off a'there, Pip," Eubie said with great good nature, flipping the snake off the handle and onto the nearby woodpile. "Li'l Pip, he gets in the way sometimes," Eubie explained to Peel, picking up the snake and stroking it. Then he grinned, and said, "S'pect he just likes attention."

"I expect you're right," Peel said. What else could one say? After introducing himself, Peel asked by way of idle chat, "Tell me, Mr. Strange, do you name all your snakes?"

"Oh, they're not my snakes. They just live here."

"I see," Peel said, as this much was clear. "But they do have names?" Why on earth was he asking *that*? When what he should be asking was if Eubie had recently been released, mistakenly, from the Asylum for the Insane.

"Wal, of course they have names," Eubie stated with the puzzled tone of a man who'd been asked the glaringly obvious. "Can't have them livin' here with no names."

Peel suddenly felt a peculiar sensation, as if his ankle were being wound in a tight bandage. He looked down with extreme reluctance. And guessed that Eubie Strange might consider him unmanly if he were to scream at the long black snake winding itself around his calf.

"Now you take that there feller," Eubie said, pointing to Peel's leg. "He's called Stretch."

Peel struggled to keep down his bile. Vomiting on the snake might alarm the creature, and he was sure it would offend Eubie. "This fellow, Stretch," Peel said, attempting to strike an offhand attitude as the snake continued to wrap his thigh. "Is he—is he venomous?"

Eubie looked slightly hurt. "He's a black racer, don't ya know that? See his yeller belly?"

"No, actually, I can't see his belly. Is yellow a good sign?"

"Black racers ain't got poison, and Stretch he don't bite, anyhow. He's a real gentle critter—neighborly you might say. S'pect you can see that."

But Peel had studiously been avoiding eye contact with Stretch. ''Ah,'' he said, ''then that probably explains why he's so friendly—flicking his tongue and all.''

''It's cause you're warm, that's why he likes you.''

Peel was forced to wonder, for the second time that day, if the price of popularity wasn't just too damn high.

''Mr. Strange, I don't suppose you could make Stretch allow my leg its standard blood flow?''

''You don't like Stretch?'' Now Eubie looked as if he'd been cut to the quick.

Peel silently berated himself for a lack of sensitivity. ''I like him very much, Mr. Strange. So much, in fact, that I'd really prefer to have a better look at him—especially that yellow belly of his. Which is difficult from such a close perspective. He certainly seems a very handsome—handsome and *large*—specimen.''

Eubie stared at Peel as if he were babbling incoherently. Perhaps he was.

Peel tried again, determinedly, as by now Stretch had reached his groin. ''I wonder if you might just let me see him from more of a distance? *Right now!*''

Looking somewhat dismayed at Peel's demand, Eubie Strange stepped forward and gently unwound a surprisingly cooperative Stretch from Peel's benumbed limb. The man stood quietly while the snake's smooth length ran through his hands, since Stretch had begun to make a serpentine corkscrew around the man's upper torso. Curiously, however, the snake's head continued to thrust in jabbing motions toward Peel.

In the event that Eubie had been in error about a yellow belly, which Peel could not satisfactorily see, he started to take a step backward.

''Watch it!'' Eubie shouted. Peel froze.

From the corner of his eye he saw the sidewinding motion of a red-banded snake, one he had nearly stepped on before it slithered under the woodpile.

''That there's a milk snake,'' Eubie said with obvious

affection. "You can call her Red if you like. She's a shy one, though."

"I wonder if it would be possible, Mr. Strange," proposed Peel, "for us to just step into the road back there while we talk?" He took several steps himself in that direction.

"Talk about what?" Eubie asked, not budging while Stretch continued to corkscrew.

Peel considered the snakes on the roof again, and determined that a conversation in raised voices could do the job. He stepped, carefully, to the road's edge.

"Constable Stuart tells me that you . . . that you were acquainted with Pete Raffin," Peel shouted. "Or, to be more precise, that your wife was?"

"How's that?"

Peel, resolute about not venturing one inch back into viperland, repeated his question in a bellow.

Eubie again looked hurt, but moved toward Peel with his dark, undulating vest. "I ain't deaf, you know."

Peel apologized as he stepped back. "You *did* know Pete Raffin?" he prompted.

"Oh, yeah." And to Peel's astonishment, Eubie broke into a wide smile. "Old Pete, he done me a favor."

Misappropriating the man's wife was a *favor*? Peel wondered if the snake could have cut off the blood to Eubie's brain.

"Yeah, well, it's like this, Mr. Peel. See, Rosalie— that was my wife—she just hated snakes. I reckon that's hard to believe." Eubie patted Stretch and eyed Peel as if to test his faith.

Peel shook his head, then decided that might not be the desired response, so he nodded in disbelief. "Not really!"

"Yeah." The man now looked close to tears. "I can't hardly bring myself to tell this, Mr. Peel, but Rosalie . . . Rosalie, she tried to kill them snakes, she did . . . if you can imagine such a thing." Eubie clearly had trouble imagining it himself. "That Rosalie, she just took a shotgun, and she blasted away at the roof. Made me

mighty upset, that did. Upset the snakes, too, no end. So
yeah, I owe Pete Raffin a big favor. And you can tell
him I said so.''

What could produce a greater motive for revenge than
stealing a man's sweat-of-the-brow, creative efforts?
Peel asked himself while climbing the front porch steps
of Ludwig Honniker.

"Just call me Honk, everybody does." The man
grinned warmly at Peel and sat forward in his rocking
chair to offer a jug of powerful smelling whiskey. "Best
blackstrap this side of the Ohio," the barrel-shaped man
assured Peel. Honk jawed the wad in his cheek and casually expelled a long stream of brown juice that missed
Peel's boot by inches. A gray kitten, just emerging from
under the cabin, bounced over to investigate the tobacco
juice. Peel, with some vague recollection that nicotine
was poisonous, leapt forward; but before the kitten could
extend the tip of its tongue, a female cat soared through
the air and, even as she was landing, batted her offspring
halfway across the yard. Then she padded on without a
backward glance.

Appearing pleased with this timely maternal rescue,
Honk grinned and hoisted the jug over his shoulder, took
a long swallow, then swung it down and waved it at
Peel again. Peel's eyes were on Honk's enormous hands,
wondering if Pete Raffin had ever met with them. "No
thank you," said Peel to the whiskey, "but I appreciate
the offer . . . Honk."

"Suit yerself. Now let's see . . . You wanted to know
if I hold a grudge a'gin Pete Raffin—that your question?'' Honk expectorated before he chuckled. "Well,
no sir, I don't. Fact of the matter is, I owe Pete a hog-
trough full of thanks." Honk chuckled again.

"*Thanks*? After he managed to steal a substantial
amount of your own good whiskey?''

"You heard about that, did you? Well, maybe you
didn't get the whole story, Mr. Peel, on account of we
don't spread word—the word bein' *whiskey*—of that

around. Got lots of Temperance ladies in this here town, and they got ears and noses like bloodhounds. Truth of it is''—Honk began to laugh—''my old lady, she took The Pledge herself, see. Got all fired up about 'demon rum.' Never mind I don't make rum. Anyhow, last spring, couple days after I finished a new batch of the brew, I go to my shed back there. And I find all my jugs gone. So I heads on over to Raffin's place, 'cause I knew that rotter Pete, he'd always wanted to get his hands on my mash so's he could figure out how I make it. Since I make the best,'' Honk added.

He grinned, spit again, and rocked forward in his chair to give Peel a long look, his eyes twinkling. ''I find my jugs all right—Raffin's got 'em stashed under his porch. But one of 'em is broke, and the whiskey done spilled out. And layin' right in the middle of that puddle of mash is one big ol' dead rat. Rat's dead as a doornail. Now we never said a word 'bout that to each other, me and Pete. But he knew, and I knew. That whiskey he went to so much trouble to steal—well, it never got drunk. See the wife told me later''—by now Honk was nearly choking with laughter—''that she'd—Ha-ha!— that she'd poured lye into all them jugs. Yes, sir, Pete Raffin, he done me a service. 'Course he didn't do the rat no good.''

Honk was now laughing so hard he lurched from his chair and lay thumping his fists on the porch floor.

And so it went. Over the next few days, every person questioned had some similar anecdote regarding Pete Raffin's thievery, be it wives or whiskey. Peel concluded, as he walked back toward the firehouse, that Raffin was so inept a brute that half the town was indebted to him for entertainment. And no one had a plausible motive to murder him. No one except Beryl.

As he told Jamie Stuart when he arrived at the firehouse.

Jamie shook his head sadly. ''Afraid you're right, son. I got some bad news today.''

''Bad news? Raffin's body's been found?''

"No, but it might as well have. And we've got to bring Beryl in, Peregrine."

"Why? You aren't thinking of arresting her?"

"That's what I'm thinking."

"You shouldn't be."

"Now, Perry, I know you've taken a shine to Beryl, just like we all have, but we can't have women doing away with their husbands just because they're getting roughed up by them."

"No, the town cemetery would fill up pretty fast."

Jamie Stuart grimaced. "Look, Peregrine, your father sent you here to—how did he put it?—to develop some character, get some backbone. And I tell you, Beryl has to be arrested. Word has it she's been spending money— a lot of money. More than she could make in just a short time with that mule. Everybody knows Pete stashed all Beryl's money somewhere out back of that shack. Nearly blew a tramp's head off once for wandering drunk around the yard. Beryl would *never* dare take that money and spend it unless she knew Pete wouldn't be coming back. Ever."

Peel, in light of his investigation, found this disturbing. Eubie Strange took care of needy snakes that chose to squat—so to speak—on his property, feral cats looked after their kittens, and Beryl looked after other women's children. But who looked after Beryl?

"There's still no body," Peel persisted, surprised at his stubbornness.

"Doesn't have to be," Jamie said, sighing with an effort at patience. "If there is sufficient evidence to believe a crime has been committed, then we have to make an arrest."

"No."

"No, what?"

"No, I'm not arresting that woman. Absolutely not. No!"

Jamie Stuart studied Peel a moment before saying, "You know, city boy, you picked a mighty inconvenient time to develop backbone."

• • •

Peel reluctantly followed Jamie Stuart along the towpath to Beryl's. No matter how inadequate, he *was* an attorney, and now he racked his brain to find an excuse to keep Jamie Stuart from arresting Beryl. But as they neared the Raffin place his heart sank.

The shack had a new coat of paint. The roof no longer sagged. The dancing children all had new clothes and new boots and new haircuts. Killer, barking with joy, sported a new leather collar, which at least allowed Peel to grab and hold at bay the dog's hazardous affection.

When Beryl emerged from the shack, she moved with slow grace down porch steps that were newly bricked.

"Afternoon, Constable," she said, running her fingers through her wild hair. Peel noted with forlorn satisfaction that Beryl had clearly not spent any money on herself.

"I think you know why we're here, Beryl," said Jamie Stuart, his voice far from happy.

"No, I don't!" Beryl answered. Killer had begun to growl, and she tied him securely to a nearby birch trunk. While the dog snarled in impotence at Jamie Stuart, Beryl said archly, "Lessen you've decided I done away with that scoundrel."

"Where'd the money come from, Beryl?"

"Constable, you know damn well where it come from. From me and Sal, that's where. Earned it, we did. Nobody can say otherwise."

"But Pete never let you keep it. He took it and kept it himself. Everybody in town knows that, Beryl."

The woman shrugged. "So? Pete's not here."

"And that's the point. Now Beryl, why don't you make this easy on yourself. Tell us what you did with him. Mr. Peel, here, I know will do all he can to defend you. And if there were extenuating circumstances . . . In any case, I have to arrest you, Beryl."

Killer lunged at the end of his rope, nearly decapitating himself. Beryl Raffin just stood there staring at Jamie Stuart. And Peel, aware of inexplicably intense emotion, just stood there staring at Beryl. He barely noted the slight pinch, like the bite of a mosquito, at the back of his arm. Without thought, his mind fixed on the scene before him, he raised his hand to swat the insect and suddenly found his fingers caught in a wet vise. Pivoting, he confronted the brown eyes of Sal. He hadn't even heard the mule come up behind him. But there she stood, stock-still, gripping his hand gently between her very large teeth.

"Sal, let go," Peel said quietly.

Sal's grip loosened slightly, but with Peel's fingers still between her teeth, she tossed her head.

"What the devil's the matter with you?" Peel said more firmly, and cautiously attempted to withdraw his hand. To his relief, Sal let him go, then took a few quick steps along the towpath. Peel returned his attention to the constable and Beryl, and to the now stricken-faced youngsters.

One boy, the wit with previously tattered clothes and the pocketknife, was shouting, "You leave Beryl alone, Constable. She didn't do nothin' wrong." His voice cracked and his eyes glittered with tears. Peel saw that, contrary to his earlier suspicion, this boy was not the tormentor of Sal, because the one who *had* been was now obvious. During the past days the mule's lacerated rump had completely healed.

Several of the other children had begun to cry, and Beryl quickly gathered them into her skirts. As Peel watched this, growing more and more disturbed, he was unprepared for another, more substantial bite on his forearm. "Sal, what the devil are you doing?"

He'd said this loudly enough to draw some attention, so he repeated in a more restrained tone, "What's wrong with you, you crazy mule?"

Sal, giving a good imitation of a young filly, jumped back and then pranced along the Canal towpath, and away from the shack. The thing that held Peel's attention was the way the mule repeatedly looked at him over her shoulder. She would take a few steps, then stop, look back, take a few more steps, stop, look back . . .

Finally, Sal stood gazing at Peel with a stubborn persistence, and he, by now feeling he had little choice, followed her down the towpath.

Behind him the children wailed, Killer snarled, and the regretful voice of Jamie Stuart tried to coax Beryl into confession. The sounds faded as Peel followed Sal farther along the Canal. They met no one else on the towpath. Traffic had ceased several days earlier when the Erie Canal Board directed that draining for the winter should begin. During its first season, the Board estimated that 13,110 boats had used the Canal, but now, with the exception of a few red squirrels, the towpath was deserted.

Peel watched the mule ahead, and saw her hesitate just before the road to Eubie Strange's cottage with its writhing roof. Then she trotted on. A short distance farther, she slowed again, in front of the cabin of Ludwig Honniker. Honk, seated in his rocking chair on the front porch with several kittens sprawled on his lap, waved a brown jug at Peel and grinned happily.

"Sal, just what is it you have in mind?" Peel muttered after putting Honk's cabin safely out of earshot.

Sal tossed her head and fixed her flat brown eyes on Peel. "I'm still here," Peel assured her, feeling a fool but unwilling to give up hope that the mule had some intent other than a companionable stroll down an abandoned towpath.

And then Sal stopped. Dead in her tracks. She stood in the middle of the path with her nose pointed straight ahead. At absolutely nothing. Peel felt a frustrating disappointment. He *was* a fool.

"Thanks, Sal, old girl—or whatever you are. You've just confirmed my father's opinion of me—"

He broke off as the mule took several quick steps forward. And then Peel noticed that a few yards ahead was the plank covering of the Canal escape hole. He walked to the first plank, and as he bent down to lift it, the smell hit him. He reared back, then gritted his teeth and lifted the escape hole cover.

"He couldn't swim," said Jamie Stuart. "Damn fool must have fell in the Canal—likely as not drunk as a skunk—and he couldn't even swim!"

On a sagging canvas stretcher the remains of Pete Raffin were lugged away by two men with handkerchiefs tied over their faces. Beryl stood nearby with Sal beside her, her face as impassive as that of the mule. For a moment her moss-green eyes met Peel's; he shook his head very slightly and motioned for her to leave. When Beryl turned to walk away, calling, "C'mon Sal," her voice held an uncharacteristic anxiety.

Peel, however, didn't think anyone cared to arrest a mule. And who else could be arrested?

There was general agreement that the burial of Pete Raffin should take place as rapidly as possible, and none expressed a desire to examine the body too closely; still, the U-shaped depressions in the skull could hardly go unnoticed. Everyone assumed they were made by a horseshoe. And everyone knew that mules were notorious for kicking, and for doing so with no good reason.

It was the deep teeth-shaped cavities which Peel had seen in the thighbone, but quickly covered with his frockcoat before the others arrived, that suggested to him a somewhat different possibility. Pete Raffin, or Pete Raffin's body, looked to have been clamped and dragged . . . dragged into the Canal to drown? Or into the escape hole to conceal—*after* his death?

Jamie Stuart was now expressing satisfaction that the mystery of Raffin's disappearance had been, as he said, "so conclusively resolved." Although he gave Beryl a number of doubtful glances, he obviously did not intend to pursue the matter further. Nor did he need to: the death certificate would read "accidental drowning." Nasty Pete Raffin had, true to form, bungled his way to his own end. Who, or what, was to say otherwise?

Peregrine Peel considered, briefly, what Peel the Third

would think if his outcast son remained silent. But Peel now discovered it no longer mattered to him what his father thought. Thus he quietly stood there as the tall woman walked down the towpath with the mule plodding at her side. Beryl slung her arm over Sal's broad, scarred back and nuzzled the brushy mane, almost as if she were whispering into the mule's ear.

Then both woman and mule turned their heads to give Peel a long, enigmatic look.

*R*obert Barnard was born in Essex and educated at the Colchester Royal Grammar School and at Balliol College, Oxford. He then went on to lecture at universities in Australia and Norway. The wickedly funny mysteries he wrote about these experiences make us wonder if he has since been denied entry into these countries. He started writing in the late 1960s, has published nearly thirty novels and been nominated for the Edgar award six times.

He recently began an historical mystery series under the name of Bernard Bastable, the most recent being Too Many Notes Mr. Mozart, *perhaps the first alternate history mystery, in which the aged (?) Mozart is hired to give young Princess Victoria piano lessons. But the* nom de plume *could not disguise Robert Barnard's noted perception and wry assessment of society, which he displays in the following story, one Jane Austen might have written if only she'd had the nerve.*

SENSE AND SENSUALITY

Robert Barnard

"Mama is indisposed," said Mary Buchanan, as she unfastened the ribbons of her bonnet and raised it carefully, so as not to disturb her neat curls. She handed it to the Mertons' maid, who curtseyed and turned to take the bonnet of Eliza, the younger Buchanan sister, whose hair curled more naturally but less neatly.

"It has been an unhealthy autumn," commented Jane Merton, as she led them through into the parlour of Wilbye Manor. "So much mist and damp."

"Autumn is the time of mists," her brother James put in. "This year has been no different from any other."

"And Mama's illness is not feverish," said Eliza. "It is more . . . on the stomach."

The stomach was not something that could be more than mentioned in mixed, or indeed any, company, so they changed the subject.

"At least autumn is the season of balls and parties," said Mary Buchanan, who, like Jane Merton, was the sensible one of her family, but not overly so. "The ball at Greylands promises much."

"The ball at Greylands promises precisely what balls at Greylands have promised and provided for the last

180

twenty years or more,'' disagreed James. "The Chamberses are good enough folk, but they are not likely to change their habits or enlarge their views at their time of life, even for a daughter of marriageable age.''

"Charlotte has been of marriageable age these four years,'' commented Eliza Buchanan with a touch of relish in her voice. "Perhaps the Chamberses should have been more energetic in inviting eligible men to their balls.''

She smiled brilliantly at James, who registered that he had been smiled brilliantly at.

"And the ball here at Wilbye this year?—'' asked Mary.

"Will be as large as we can persuade Papa to make it, and as brilliant as the neighbourhood allows,'' said Jane Merton.

"Papa is very persuadable in such matters,'' said James, with a touch of bitterness in his voice. "He is extremely generous with Mama's money.''

"So penurious and grasping at sixteen!'' commented Mary Buchanan, with the satirical quality in her voice that overwise young people always risk provoking. "And why should your father not spend the money that came with his marriage? I'm sure your mama is fully in agreement with him on the proper hospitality that Wilbye Manor should afford the neighbourhood.''

"If he bothered to ask her,'' said James.

"Well, to us,'' said Mary Buchanan, "Mr. and Mrs. Merton are an ideally happy married couple, and no insidious hints will persuade us otherwise. Your papa consults your mama's opinion on everything, and always treats her with great respect.''

"When there are people by,'' said James, his soon-to-be-handsome face darkened over. "It is her fortune that he treats with greatest respect.''

His bitter tone risked a serious disturbance to the pleasant atmosphere of a morning visit.

"Pay no attention to my sulky brother,'' said Jane. "Papa and Mama are as happy as most married couples.

Naturally Papa, as a younger son of a Yorkshire bishop of limited private means, is conscious of his good fortune—the considerable fortune that Mama brought with her. It would certainly not be becoming if he hoarded it, and neglected the duties of a country gentleman.''

The duties of a country gentleman, especially with regard to balls, parties, excursions and picnics, were something they all had at heart.

"And your mother doubtless supports him in that," repeated Mary.

"Mama is as anxious as anybody to fulfill the obligations of a county family of consequence," said Jane, with a touch of self-righteousness. "And she has always greatly enjoyed balls and picnics."

"Dancing was once her passion," conceded James. "She has herself taught us both and an excellent teacher she has been too."

"Our papa is also a notably lively dancer," said Mary Buchanan. Her words seemed to have a significance beyond themselves.

"Perhaps that is what brought them together," said James, after a pause.

"More to the point would be what wrenched them apart," countered Eliza.

"Our father!" said Jane, with a bright smile. "The poor son of a poorish bishop! Terribly handsome, and dashing, and commanding, and someone to sweep a susceptible young lady off her feet."

"True," agreed Eliza, but with caution in her tone. "I'm sure that is what happened . . . Still, Mr. Merton is hardly more commanding than our papa habitually is. Papa is a man who almost always gets what he wants."

"What man doesn't?" said Jane, and it could be that the brightness of her voice contained also a note of bitterness. "In this case there were two men who both wanted the same thing, and so one had to lose."

"I can imagine your papa withdrawing entirely the moment our mama showed interest in another," said

James satirically. "It would be a blow to his *amour propre*."

"Not a frequent occurrence," said Mary Buchanan.

"And not one, I imagine," said Jane, "that is ever allowed to inflict real damage on its victim."

"Men!" said Eliza Buchanan.

"Never happy with us, never happy without us," said James.

"Leaving aside, my dear brother, the question of whether you may yet be considered a man," said Jane, "the habit of worldly-wise generalizations in a schoolboy is one that invites ridicule."

James shrugged, confidence undented.

"I am to be at our ball in January."

"Really!" said Eliza, ogling him, but mainly for practice.

"So, having sardonically commented on balls in general, and the Chamberses' balls in particular, you will actually find yourself attending one!" said Mary.

"I can comment on the Chamberses' balls because I have heard these last five years the comments of you and my sister, not to mention those of my mother and father, the morning after the ball. The comments are always the same, so I conclude that the balls are likewise. If I go, this year or next year, it will be like a first visit to the Scottish border country, already overfamiliar from the novels of Sir Walter."

"You will be insufferable when you *do* go to balls," said his sister. "You will stand at the outer edges of the assembly with a superior expression on your face, uttering the occasional sardonic comment to another sprig of like mind."

"Trying to give the impression that there is not a woman in the room sufficiently handsome to tempt *you*," said Mary.

"Until you are taken with the bright eyes of some young woman in the neighbourhood," said her sister.

"Or, more likely, until some young woman in the neighbourhood is taken by your good looks," said Mary

Buchanan. "Because it is flattering attention entraps a man into marriage as often as brilliant beauty." She did not look at her sister when she said this.

"Truly men are sad creatures," commented James. "Was it by flattering attention that your mama netted your father?"

"I think not," said Eliza confidentially. "The talk in the servants' hall—"

"Which you have eavesdropped on—?"

"Exactly so. Or to be more precise, the talk of our old cook, Joan, while picking red currants with a new kitchenmaid, with me silent as a mouse a hedge away— the talk is that she was the most brilliant beauty in the neighbourhood—"

"I have heard that too," said Jane.

"—and that he wooed her to prove that he could win a much greater prize than your mama."

There was silence while they all thought how difficult it was to imagine Mrs. Buchanan as the brilliant beauty of the neighbourhood. Some inklings of the evanescence of merely physical attributes, and of the vanity of human wishes, were intermingled in their meditations.

"Marriage is a sad business," said James. "I shall undertake it only to continue the Merton line—and then only late in life, when I can reasonably expect to be spared the worst of the disillusionment. Disgust in marriage must be the most insupportable of all emotions."

"Tea," said Jane firmly, as Bridget brought in the second-best service. Silence did not always reign when one of the Wilbye servants was in the room, but it did now. James's remarks seemed both disturbing yet brutally realistic.

"So-o-o, your papa married your mama as a sort of revenge on our mama for looking at another man," said Jane when they were alone again. "It seems a doubtful basis for marriage."

"Perhaps there was love too," said Eliza.

"Or perhaps he imagined himself in love, convinced

himself that he was," amended her sister Mary. "It must be said that Papa is not a foolish man."

"But there is no man or woman on earth, however sensible, who may not do a foolish thing at times," said Jane.

"And that foolish thing is generally a matrimonial folly," said her brother.

"The terms on which your parents live seem . . . amicable enough," said Jane. The two sisters thought. All four young people in the parlour knew it was not a marriage that could be described as happy.

"Mama is always anxious to placate Papa, and earn his good opinion," said Eliza.

"And Papa is always polite to Mama," said Mary.

"In front of you," said James.

"In front of us, and in front of the servants."

"And in private?" he pursued.

"In private, who can say?"

"An eavesdropper might know something," said James, looking at Eliza. She dropped her eyes demurely.

"I have overheard—walking past the sitting room or the study, quiet as can be so as to disturb nobody—wounding remarks, sarcasms, peremptory commands. I have never heard anything so vulgar as a quarrel."

"And the subject of these sarcasms?"

"Mama's loss of personal attractions, her lack of energy—lethargy one might almost call it."

"Everything you tell us seems to describe the end of love," said James. "And even of personal regard."

"Mama feels the loss of her beauty keenly," said Mary, "as others might mourn the loss of money, property, influence. When she was younger she tried to hide it, improve on nature, but nothing she could do had any effect, and she gave that up years ago."

"The lethargy is the effect of the loss of beauty," said Eliza. "She does not wish to be seen, now she can no longer attract, so she has no inclination to go about the neighbourhood, attend balls. She sits, she sews, she reads light literature. . . ."

The emptiness of the life described needed no underlining.

"No doubt Mama and she are having a good gossip now, while the men are hunting," said Jane, trying to produce a more cheerful note. "If anyone can rouse her up to take an interest in the neighbourhood, Mama can. They have remained friends, at any rate."

"All have remained friends in the Merton and the Buchanan families," said James. "It is a remarkable fact."

"Once having taught your mother the lesson that he could marry the toast of Hampshire if he put his mind to it, Papa seems to have determined to be agreeable," said Eliza.

"Yes . . ." said Jane slowly. "Your papa *determines* to be agreeable, rather than is so by nature, or through feelings of general benevolence."

"I think that is true," said Mary. "But perhaps we should give him some credit: he saw that the best thing was to be on excellent terms with his nearest neighbours."

"And perhaps," added Eliza, "if we were *not* giving him so much credit, it was agreeable to him to be constantly in the company of your mama, showing her how much the better man he is."

This was plain speaking indeed, but they were now too deeply in to draw back.

"You think that he *is*?" asked Jane.

"Frankly I do. Better informed, more decisive, an excellent landowner, an exemplary magistrate. Whatever Papa does, he does well. Whereas your papa is more . . . is more. . . ."

"Showy," said Jane. "He lacks application. What he does he does with dash, but too much noise. You are right. But in the case of our respective mothers—

"There the situation is reversed," Jane asserted. "Mama has kept her looks, has run the house admirably, presides at balls and assemblies with a grace and dignity that are universally remarked on. The perfect country gentleman's wife.''

"And perhaps it is not unpleasant for her," said Eliza, "being so much in the company of her neighbours, that the comparison is always being made, and always to her advantage."

Again there were a few moments of silence before Mary said, apparently out of the blue, "How wonderfully our father and your mother danced at the Waddingtons' ball in May. Do you remember, Jane?"

"I do. So lithe, so perfectly matched, so vigorous, each body responding so perfectly to the other."

"It was as if they were both thoroughly alive, for the first time in ages."

"Nobody mentioned *that* the morning after the ball," said James, a touch of resentment in his voice.

"Perhaps you should learn that as much is *not* told in these accounts as is told," said Eliza. "How could one describe your Mama's flush of pleasure, Papa's air of—I don't know what—"

"Pride," said Jane.

"Yes, that was it, pride."

"Perhaps those are things that *should* not, rather than could not, be described," said Jane thoughtfully.

"It sounds as if they will have been commented on in many households in the neighbourhood, if not in the two most concerned," said James. "And Papa—he looked on unconcernedly, no doubt?"

"Papa, as I remember, was much concerned with old Lady Waddington, fetching her cold collation, and sitting with her and making conversation while she ate it."

"Lady Waddington, the social arbiter of the county. It is odd that twenty-three years after his marriage Papa seems still to want to propitiate her, to gain her good opinion," said James.

"Without managing to do so, I would guess," said Mary. "To Lady Waddington marriage should be the joining of estates and fortunes. Anything else is a fever of the blood, and much to be disapproved of.''

"There is much to be said," James put in, "for marriages that join two moderate estates to make one fine one. Mama's choice was in every way a mistake.''

"Such talk is idle," said Jane, getting up and standing with her cup by the window. "What is done is done—and long done at that. We are the result of its doing. If our mama and your papa have moments of regret—well, I'm sure there are many couples who now and then entertain similar emotions. . . . How odd. That looks like one of your stablemen.''

"One of ours?" said Eliza, rising.

"What could be lacking at the hunt that Wilbye Manor could supply—your papa being so completely the hunting man? . . . He is not going to the stables, but to the kitchen . . . As I say, there may be moments of regret, but Papa and Mama are happy in their manner, they keep the 'noiseless tenor of their way,' and I'm sure they would wish no other fate—''

But she was interrupted by a great cry from the depths of the house. Silence fell on the little parlour. Jane looked around it, as if wondering whether her sheltered world there was coming to an end. They heard the clock ticking, but no one could move a limb to find out the cause of the disturbance. Within a minute they heard sobbing, coming closer, and talk. Then it stopped, as if the griever were composing herself. Then there was a soft tap on the door, and it opened.

"Oh, Miss Jane, Mr. James. Dreadful news. I can hardly bear to tell you.''

"Tell us, Cook," said Jane, going up and taking her hands. "This is worse than hearing.''

"There's been a dreadful accident. In the course of the hunt. It's your poor father. Baines here was there. He'll tell you.''

She thrust forward a short, thickset man, the one Jane had recognized, smelling of stables.

"It was in the thick of things, ladies, sir, when they'd got the scent and were all bunched up. Your father's saddle went—went clean astray. I know that saddle was properly secured, miss, I know it. I saddled the horse myself, and I saw your father, Miss Mary, checking it just before they rode off. I could swear to you—''

''Baines, we don't care whose fault it is,'' cried Mary. ''Mr. Merton, these young people's father—''

''Dead, miss. Under the hooves of the other horses. Dead when we got to him. They're bringing him home now.''

They turned horrified to the window. Across a stile leading to a field on the horizon a stretcher was being manoeuvred by stalwart servants, and behind them came an incongruously colourful collection of huntsmen, walking awkwardly, as if scared of emotion and embarrassed by death. Jane began weeping uncontrollably as Cook and Baines backed out of the parlour.

''And Mama is indisposed,'' said Mary quietly.

$\mathcal{M}$aan Meyers is the acronymic pseudonym of Martin and Annette Meyers. Annette writes the modern Smith and Wetzen mysteries, the most recent of which is The Groaning Board. She is also a past president of Sisters in Crime. Martin Meyers is the author of the Patrick Hardy series. As Maan Meyers they have written historical mysteries set at various eras in the past of New York City. The first, The Dutchman, begins when New York was still New Amsterdam. The next, The Kingsbridge Plot, is set at the time of the American Revolution. The Meyerses have carried the series into the nineteenth century with four more books, the most recent being The House on Mulberry Street and The Lucifer Contract.

For this story Maan Meyers returns to the New York of the third book in the series, The High Constable. The Rochester Rappers really existed. The Meyerses write, "A week after the conclusion to our story, Jacob Hays died. The Rochester Rappers returned to the City of New York shortly thereafter and remained to practice spiritualism until their deaths."

THE HIGH CONSTABLE AND THE ROCHESTER RAPPERS

Maan Meyers
(Martin Meyers and Annette Meyers)

🐝

The familiar purple brougham was waiting in front of the house when Jacob Hays, High Constable of the City of New York, and Chief Peter Tonneman made the turn on to Lispenard Street, their brisk walk having been cut short by the sudden downpour. Shifting his unlit cheroot from one side of his mouth to the other, Hays growled.

"It's Mr. Greeley," Sally Devlin announced. She took their top hats, giving them a good shake, hung them on the rack, then collected their drenched coats and provided Jake with a dry one. "He's in the parlor having tea." She eyed Peter Tonneman with his long torso, his lanky arms and legs. The short, bull-chested High Constable did not have a coat to fit his aide, but Sally would take care of that.

"And so to Greeley," Peter Tonneman said, with a twinkle in his eye, for Jake preferred the society of even-natured men and had little patience for the eccentricities of the publisher.

Still Horace and Mary Greeley had suffered a terrible loss the year before: their adored son Arthur, nicknamed Pickie, had died of cholera at the age of five.

On their entrance, Horace Greeley threw down the *Tribune* and jumped to his feet. "The d-d-dead," he sputtered, spraying wet biscuit crumbs. He began a shuffling pace about the room, so agitated, his hands shook.

"Good God, man. What's happened?" Peter Tonneman knelt at the hearth and stirred the logs to fire once more.

The publisher of the *Tribune* stopped his circumnavigation abruptly. "Pickie has sent word through the girls that great harm is going to befall someone I am close to."

"What girls?" Tonneman asked, although he was quite sure he knew the answer.

"Where have you been, Peter?" Greeley asked in disgust. "The utterly astounding Fox girls, Maggie and Kate."

"The Rochester Rappers." Old Hays raised one of his bushy eyebrows at Tonneman. "Close the window, will you, Peter? Before we're flooded out." To Horace Greeley, he said, "And who did *the girls* tell you was going to come to harm?"

"They didn't say." Greeley returned to his pacing, then stopped to remove his spectacles from the top of his bald pate. He ran his restless fingers through non-existent hair and started shuffling again, hands clasped behind his back, eyes on the floor. "But it will happen before another week passes. And most likely before midnight tomorrow." Greeley's black silk cravat was, as usual, askew, his collar nearly obscured by long, graying brown hair which grew to ear height and no higher, and his beard which sprouted like shrubbery from under his chin.

"I'm surprised at you, Horace. You've had the wool pulled over your eyes by a pair of pretty charlatans."

Peter Tonneman smiled. Old Hays was in the fine fettle. If there was anything Jake Hays had little use for, it was humbugs. The two young girls had arrived with their mother from Rochester only ten days before and taken the City by storm with their tales and demonstrations of contact with the spirit world through rapping. Hence, the appellation, the Rochester Rappers.

Peter closed the window. Outside, great sheets of rain, swept by the wind, hit the old house mercilessly, shaking window glass in the weathered frames. Greeley's carriage fairly danced with its battering. The poor harnessed beast remained stoic. "Your driver, Andy, is in my kitchen, Mr. Greeley, drying himself off." Sally set the tray down on the tea table.

"Thank you, Sally," Hays said. "We'll do the honors."

"Mr. Tonneman, sir." From under her arm, Sally produced a fresh, dry coat for Peter and helped him on with it.

"Why, this is my own coat, Sally. Dry as a bone. However did you do it?"

"Sent Andy next door and Bridget herself gave him this one." Sally curtsied and left. Peter poured and offered the plate of shortbread.

With a piece of shortbread wedged in his saucer, Jake took his tea and sat comfortably in the gold damask wing chair, crossing one leg over the other.

"I've read in your paper," Tonneman said to Greeley, "that these girls have had continued success talking with the dead."

Hays set down his cup of tea in disgust. "Not you too, Peter."

"You cannot blame me for being curious, Jake."

Greeley snatched a piece of shortbread, nibbling it

greedily like a hungry mouse. "You see," he mumbled through the thick butter cookie, "I'm not alone, Jake. What do you say now?"

Jake Hays maneuvered his cheroot, left to right, then up and down, as he studied Horace Greeley.

"Say something, damn it," Greeley finally exploded.

Hays's comment was short and to the point. "Poppycock." He squinted at Tonneman. "Peter—" What he had started to say was lost in a paroxysm of coughing.

Peter hid his concern for Jake Hays, smiling at Greeley. "Actually, I'm intrigued. I'd like to have a look at them. See what all the talk is about."

"Excellent." Greeley was delighted. "I've opened my home to them for these few weeks before Mary and I move to Nineteenth Street." The publisher made haste to leave. "I'll set a meeting at the farm. You won't be sorry. And Jake, you'll attend as well?"

"Poppycock." Hays walked to the window. His cough was getting worse. Well, if Saint Peter or Old Nick wanted him, they'd have a fight on their hands. "I've had enough of this rain."

As if by supreme command the rain ceased, the wet skies cleared, and timid rays of sunshine began to soften the gray.

Tonneman saw Greeley out.

"A contrary day for June," Hays mused aloud. He watched Greeley's driver help the publisher into his brougham. Then he grunted. He'd go along with this charade. He was certain he could prove these girls were charlatans. He just needed a plan.

"The bigwigs are falling over themselves to meet the Rappers," Peter said when he returned. "William Cullen Bryant, I hear tell, has been singing their praises. As have Bayard Taylor and Fenimore Cooper."

"I'm surprised at Fenimore," Hays said. "People with imagination often let their imagination lead them astray. These duplicitous girls and their mother are taking advantage of that, enticing people into sitting still for fancied-up demonstrations, while they translate what they claim are messages from the dead.''

"I understand their fee for a séance is one dollar per person and for that they put on quite a spectacle.''

"Then they should appear in Barnum's Museum and not in people's homes.''

"Well said. Their behavior is outlandish, I agree, but not illegal.''

"Would be if I was still running things.''

"But you're not.''

"More's the pity.'' Jake chewed on his segar for a moment. "They say the spirits communicate to them by rapping on tables and walls and such.''

"They have been searched and inspected by a committee of ladies. Ditto their surroundings, searched and carefully scrutinized.''

Jake puffed away on his cheroot. "Proving nothing.''

"Greeley just told me he's offered to finance the eleven-year-old's education in a private school.''

"And I'll venture a guess that they've turned him down. It would cut into their earnings if one of them had to spend several hours a day in a classroom.'' Jake tossed the remnants of his segar into the fire, chose a fresh one, and lit it. He smoked and stared into the flame of the snapping logs.

"I daresay, considering all the notoriety,'' Peter said, "that we'll find the demonstration edifying.''

All he received in reply was a grunt.

Peter Tonneman arrived home a short time later expecting to take comfort and tea with Charity, his wife of forty-two years.

"She's not returned yet, sir,'' Bridget, the little Irish maid, told him. "You remember she was taking the young ones to Mr. Barnum's Museum.''

Of course, he'd forgotten entirely. Charity claimed their grandchildren were her boon companions and the best tonic against aging.

"Will you wait your tea, sir?''

"No, not at all. I'll be in the sitting room."

He went upstairs, changed into dry trousers, and settled himself in his easy chair, his slippered feet on a footstool. He was sixty-one years old, tall and broad-shouldered as a young man, though he was father of three, grandfather of two. The years had flown by, and with Charity at his side he'd hardly noticed.

If he were to die tomorrow, he would have no regrets, for he had lived a life of honor. Having started as a constable in 1808, he'd retired in 1848, a captain in the Night and Day Police, the Star Police. New York had been the first American city to employ a full-time, professional police force, dubbed the Star Police because of the star-shaped badges they wore.

His city in 1850 was now over half a million souls, and growing daily with the influx of Irish immigrants.

"Husband . . ." Soft lips touched his cheek.

He reached up and captured Charity, pulled her plump, pliant body down on his lap. "See here, wife, do you think of me as an old man?" he demanded.

"Not right at this moment, my dear." She was laughing, not entirely hiding the fragment of a shadow that crossed her eyes.

He sensed something was wrong. "The children?"

"All well. The dear ones dragged me and their poor mama through the entire museum. The Chinese Collection was truly remarkable."

"And you?"

"Tired." She avoided his eyes and was saved from further queries by Bridget's knock and her arrival with the tea tray and the *Herald*. There was just time enough for Charity to get to her feet and adjust her clothing. "Dignity, Peter, dignity."

Peter laughed. "As my mother used to advise. Did I ever tell you why we say that in my family?"

She shook her head, barely listening.

"I was a wild young man, before you and I met, of course."

"Of course."

He'd hoped to see the corners of her sweet mouth turn up at his jest, but they didn't. "On this particular morning, I was suffering with a hangover and broke the chamber pot. When I told my mother, she looked at me sternly and said, "Dignity.""

"As well she should."

Peter stood and took the tea tray, dismissing the giggling Bridget with a smile. Something was not right with Charity and he wanted to know what it was.

"Dear me," Charity said, as she poured the tea. "To be caught in a compromising position with one's own husband."

"Some husbands and wives keep secrets from one another," he said, taking the cup from her.

Charity's eyes sparkled. "All husbands and wives keep secrets from one another." Peter loved her eyes. They were deep blue under her dark lashes and as brilliantly alive as they'd been when he'd first met her during that terrible blizzard in 1808. Now with her rich red-brown hair streaked with white, she was even more beautiful.

"And what secret, may I ask, are you keeping from me?"

She sat down in her chair and sipped her tea. "Why don't you tell me what you and Cousin Jacob were plotting today?"

He grinned at her. "We've decided to participate in a demonstration by the Rochester Rappers."

At this Charity went deathly pale, trembling so that her tea splashed over the lip of the cup into the saucer.

"Charity!" Peter took the cup from her and set it on the table. He wiped the tea from her hands with his napkin. "My dear, what is it? Did the tea burn you?"

"I'm fine." Her tone belied her words.

"Something is wrong. Tell me."

Charity drew a deep breath. "I've spoken to Philip."

"Yes? Is he all right?" Their son Philip was a man of forty-two years.

"No. My husband Philip."

"I'm your husband."

"You don't understand, Peter. I've spoken to Philip Boenning."

Philip Boenning. What was she saying? Philip Boenning was dead almost forty-three years. Charity had been widowed and with child when Peter first met her. He put his arm around her. "You are not well."

"I'm quite well. But I have a confession to make." The color was returning to her cheeks, and Peter breathed a sigh of relief.

"Aha! You've taken a lover."

"Oh, you are a dreadful man. Be serious. I've spoken to Philip Boenning and he blessed our union."

"I'm grateful." It began to dawn on Chief Peter Tonneman what Charity's confession would be. He was, he hoped, after all these years an observant man, and at least as good as a green copper, who would have concluded it immediately. "You've been to see the Rochester Rappers."

She paled again, and confessed, "I have."

"And you believe two young girls and drumming on tables?"

"There were four of us in attendance, and the sisters had messages for three from loved ones beyond."

"And the fourth, I daresay, was a last minute addition to your party?"

"Oh, Peter, you have become as cynical as Cousin Jacob."

"We shall see."

"I'll go with you."

"No. It will just be Greeley, Jake and me. Greeley's rapture with them is enough. The spirits have communicated with him; we'll see what they have to say to us."

Jake Hays smoked his cheroot and watched as Sally cleared away the tea service.

"Shall I open the window, sir?" she asked. "The rain has stopped for good, I think." Her employer didn't hear her. He was a trifle deaf. She raised her voice and started to repeat her question.

Jacob Hays pounded the arm of his chair; then fist into hand, he was on his feet. "Sally," Jake said, "send for Sam. I have work for him." The High Constable walked with her into the front hallway, took his hat from the rack, and set it squarely on his head.

"You're going out, sir?"

"I'm going next door to speak to Mr. Tonneman. If Sam gets here before I come back, give him a piece of your apple pie and have him wait."

Not long after, when Jake Hays and Peter Tonneman stepped outside, they saw coming toward them along Lispenard Street a cloaked figure driving a cart filled to capacity. As the cart came closer, the figure proved to be a spare, pockmarked lad with sharp black eyes and a pronounced hunch. Sleeping next to him on the seat was a yellow mongrel dog. The cart held four more roughly dressed boys, one, a large negro lad. Another, so small for his fourteen years, no one remembered his real name, if he ever had one; he was known simply as Tiny Tim. The boys sat smoking and, two by two, playing a hand-slapping game.

"Good day to you, Sam."

"And to you, High Constable." Sam tipped his cap, exposing an unruly mass of black hair. "And to you, Mr. Tonneman."

"Sam," Tonneman said.

"I have need of your services." Jake eyed Sam's companions who, still puffing away furiously, laid aside their slapping game to listen.

"That's why I'm here."

"Boys," the High Constable said.

"Good day to you, sir," they answered respectfully, doffing their hats, Tiny Tim's voice overriding the others.

Jake smiled. This was always the case when Tim spoke, for he had a barrel voice that was deep as he was small. "Good day to you, boys. I'm delighted that you will be joining us."

"A great honor, sir," Sam said.

"You are a solace in my old age, Sam."

Sam rubbed his nose with his sleeve. "I endeavor, Mr. High Constable, sir. Now, how can I assist the law today?"

"Not the law, me."

"Same thing, sir."

Horace Greeley's residence stood on a rocky bluff just north of Turtle Bay. It faced the East River on the path that would be Forty-eighth Street. The rambling old house was one of two on the estate of Susannah Skinner, the granddaughter of Sir Peter Warren, who'd bought Turtle Bay Farm in 1749.

The air was warm and moist, and heavy clouds hung overhead, threatening more rain. As Jake Hays and Peter Tonneman drove along the Eastern Post Road early the following afternoon, Jake continued his castigations. "I can't believe how frauds think nothing about devouring my City, as these girls have. More, I can't believe their absurd army of disciples. How many dollars have they collected in the ten days they've been here?" The High Constable held up his hand. "Don't answer that."

When he could get a word in, Peter said, "Charity has been to see the Rappers."

"Ye gods!"

"She believes she's received a message from Philip Boenning through them." Peter turned to his old friend and sighed. "After four decades he's given our marriage his blessing."

Jake was aghast. "I've always thought my cousin to be the most reasonable of creatures." He glared at his friend. "And what the deuce has happened to you, to allow her such irrational nonsense."

Peter said nothing.

Jake had barely stopped for a breath. Shaking his finger at Peter, he said, "What's come over you, Peter? And Charity? Can't you see that these girls are petty swindlers?"

The rest of the way was traveled in silence, with Old Hays fuming, and Peter Tonneman, if not smarting, certainly abashed.

Tonneman was jolted from his fitful doze by their carriage's sudden careering all over the road.

"Absalom," Jake called. "What the devil is going on?"

"Sorry, Mr. Jake," the driver called. "Venus took it into her head to go crazy on me, near pulled us into a ditch."

Tonneman put his head out of the carriage. Today's sky was no better than yesterday's. The dark clouds overhead promised rain and who knew what other grim events. Tonneman shivered, it was that sort of a day. He didn't blame the mare for being frightened.

With the animal tranquil again, their brougham turned off the Eastern Post Road onto the private lane leading to Greeley's house. Absalom stepped down and walked Venus and the carriage the last hundred feet to the hulking wooden structure. Two other carriages stood side by side in front of the broad, covered porch.

The farmhouse was badly in need of repair. Because of Pickie's death and the sad state of Greeley's relations with his wife—as everyone knew, she had refused to have Pickie vaccinated against cholera—the domicile at Turtle Bay had become known among Greeley's friends as Castle Doleful.

"Welcome, dear friends, welcome!" Greeley elbowed past the Negro maid and burst onto the porch, his collar askew, coat twisted behind him, pant leg half in his boot.

Jake raised a bushy brow at Peter as they came across the porch toward Greeley. Greeley was still greeting them effusively while the stout maid took their hats.

A rolled carpet atop stacked packing crates crowded the hallway.

"How are you today, Jemmy?" Jake asked. "How's that youngster of yours?"

"He makes his mama proud, Mr. Jake."

"Enter, my friends." Face flushed, eyes moist with excitement, Greeley led them into the musty parlor. "Are you ready for the marvel of our lifetime?" He motioned for them to sit and bustled about lighting more lanterns.

"Quite," Jake said. He rolled his eyes at Peter. Settling himself in a high-backed chair, breathing heavily, painfully, through a hacking cough, he asked, "And where are the charming young ladies?"

Greeley responded solemnly. "They are in my study, preparing themselves to commune with the spirits, Jake."

The room was filled haphazardly with carved, ponderous rosewood furniture, lushly upholstered. Ornate framed mirrors caught the light and spread it, displaying the Currier and Ives prints of New York scenes. Mrs. Greeley, a careless housekeeper at best, was a woman with exaggerated tastes.

A thump followed by the sound of a chair scraping the floor came from nearby. The men looked at each other. "Have they started without us?" Peter asked, amused.

"Not at all," Greeley replied, somewhat nervously.

"Will Mrs. Greeley be joining us?" Peter looked over at Jake. His color was bad and his cough was not getting better.

Greeley spoke over another curious thump. "Mother and little Ida are in town, seeing to our new home. She sends her regrets."

"Mr. Greeley, sir." The maid appeared in the doorway, holding an oil lamp. The light from the lamp shivered in her unsteady hand. With her other hand she held tight to the heavy cross which hung round her neck from a leather thong. "They ready for you."

"Now, Jemmy," Greeley said, standing, "don't you worry about anything." He patted the woman's arm, but she would not be consoled. Taking the lamp from her, Greeley led his visitors into his study. Their shoes echoed on the hardwood floor.

The room was stuffy, the draperies drawn. The fire in the hearth to dry the dampness from the air also brought out a faint lavender musk.

Sitting in the center of the room was a round mahogany library table, which Tonneman knew to be a fine example of American Empire. It was now, however, covered almost entirely by a Persian rug, its folds falling in layers to the floor. Candles offered dim illumination from sconces on either side of the hearth, barely betraying the forms of the others in the room.

Greeley set the oil lamp down on the table. At once the room was alive with shadows.

"Dear Mr. Greeley, we are ready." The voice was that of a very young girl, but the words were spoken with a powerful assurance.

"My dear Kate, Maggie, Mrs. Fox, these are my friends, Jacob Hays and Peter Tonneman."

As the two girls stood, Mrs. Fox, a small woman of considerable girth, stepped forward, dipped her head respectfully. She then withdrew into a dark corner.

The taller of the two girls stepped forward.

"This is Margaret," Greeley said. "Maggie everyone calls her."

The remaining girl, Kate, remained near the fire, hands clasped in front of her.

It was the barest breath, still Peter was certain he'd caught a whiff of alcoholic spirits from Maggie. A passing thought, because the sight of young Kate had rather unnerved him. The fire caught her huge feverish eyes, giving them a catlike glow. They seemed disembodied, hanging in space.

Maggie, at seventeen, was tall and slim with a high forehead, well-pronounced nose, and square chin. Her dark hair was parted in the center and swept back into a loose roll. She wore a dark green dress of ribbed silk with a lace collar.

"Kind gentlemen." The girl made a small curtsy. "We are happy to meet you, are we not, Kate?"

Maggie motioned to her sister, who now advanced to them, her eyes losing the odd glow as she came closer.

"She's but a child," Jake Hays said.

"A very gifted child," Greeley said.

Kate Fox's curtsy was deeper than her sister's; she was, if anything, more self-possessed. The child was small, very slight, with what seemed like an oversized head, but perhaps, Peter thought, it was the mass of sausage curls that surrounded her piquant face. Kate wore a dress similar to her sister's, but the skirt stopped above her ankles and revealed white hose and black boots.

Jake gave a hacking cough. He looked old and tired in the half-light.

"Jemmy," Maggie called.

"Yes, miss?"

"Brandy for the High Constable."

"Horace," Jake said, ritualistically starting the old joke they shared. "Shall we have a glass of brandy and water?"

"Yes," Horace replied, with humor. "You take the brandy and I'll take the water." Greeley was strongly against alcohol, but as a good host, kept such available for his guests.

Jemmy brought a decanter and took a glass from the sideboard. She set it on a table, poured, and left quickly. Jake did not refuse; he drank the brandy and refilled his glass. In the meantime Maggie took another glass from the sideboard and poured herself a portion of brandy.

"Maggie, dear." Kate's soft voice had an undertone of pure steel.

Chastened, Maggie set the glass back on the sideboard. "Perhaps we should all take our seats," she said, fixing Jake with an intense stare. "We must allow a certain quiet and repose to open ourselves to receiving word from our spirits."

The modest assembly took its place around the table as Kate indicated from where she stood behind her chair. Maggie was to sit opposite, Greeley to Maggie's left, Peter to her right. The High Constable was to Kate's right, next to Greeley and across from Peter. Hays set his glass and the decanter close to him on the table.

Mrs. Fox took her post at the door like a sentinel.

"I'm sorry, dear Mr. Hays, but the table must be clean of any items," Kate said. "Jemmy!"

"The covering as well?" Jake asked, preparing to pull the carpet from the table.

"Not at all," Kate said quickly. "The spirits prefer the cover."

Jemmy's re-entry, while instant, was with such reluctance that it seemed as if her feet were weighed.

"Please take the decanter and Mr. Hays's glass." Kate looked pointedly at her sister. "The other glass at the sideboard, too. Then you may leave."

Hays drained his glass; the maid did as she'd been told and fled, closing the door behind her.

Peter was amazed to see that the child Kate had quite taken charge of the proceedings with such assurance that she could give orders to Greeley's own maid, not to mention Jacob Hays. He looked over at Jake, but in the darkness Jake's face was not easily read.

Kate drew a deep breath. "We will now . . ." The girl shuddered. "There's a strange aura about you, High Constable. A beacon of pure light. You seem in a limbo somewhere between this world and the next."

Jake stared at the girl. "And what does that mean?"

She sighed. "Let us join hands. We must be a perfect chain, presented to the spirits as a pure tablet."

When Jake grasped the young girl's hand, another shiver went through her, but she didn't comment. Neither did he.

Peter felt himself the fool. He held the tiny, cool hand of Kate Fox with one hand and with his other hand clasped Maggie's.

"Lower the lights," Kate said in her sweet voice. "Then we may begin."

Greeley jumped to his feet. "Allow me."

"No, Mr. Greeley. Please, you know this, you must not break the chain. Mother always attends to the lights."

Mother Fox snuffed out the lights in the sconces and the oil lamp. Maggie murmured a singsong. The room was in complete darkness.

"Are we ready?" Kate whispered.

"We are ready, sister," Maggie answered.

An oppressive silence fell over the room. Peter could hear breathing, his own perhaps, but no other sound. His eyelids grew heavy.

Kate whispered, "Are you with us, spirits?"

Rap, rap. Peter jerked himself awake. The sound came from beneath the very table they sat around. In addition, he sensed a strange heat coming from the same place, and in the air was the stench of brimstone. He was sweating profusely. The child's hand was limp in his.

Jake held Kate's other hand. The girl would be hard put to get something by the two of them. He too had noticed the heat and sensed the new odor. Not brimstone, phosphorous.

Kate uttered a small sigh.

Rap, rap.

There was a tug at Jake's trousers. His lips twitched.

"They are with us. Do not break the chain," came Maggie's singsong.

A flurry of rapping responded.

"Tell us who you are," Kate said. She was answered with extended and forceful rapping.

Then an eerie silence fell upon them.

"Well, who is it?" came Jake's impatient voice.

"They will tell us in due time, Mr. Hays," Maggie said. "You must not rush them."

"The spirit has spoken to me," Kate said. "He wishes to prove his force."

"And how will he do that?" Jake asked.

"Do you have my right hand, High Constable?"

"Yes."

"Do you have my left hand, Chief Tonneman?"

"Yes."

"A magic penny, one of the two left on the dead man's eyes, floats in the air between our worlds. Would you like him to toss it to you?"

"Blast," Jake said. "Do it and get it over with."

"The coin is in the air. Where shall it land?"

"In front of Mr. Tonneman," Jake stated impatiently.

In the next instant Peter heard the clunk of a coin hitting the table.

"We'll leave the coin for the moment," Kate said.

"At last," Jake sighed. "Who is the spirit?"

"He is David Hays."

"Pshaw!" Hays exclaimed. "You're telling me my father is making those foolish rappings? You don't know my father."

"Quiet, please, Hays," Greeley said. "Have some respect for those who have passed on to the other world."

Peter could hear Hays's low growl and couldn't help smiling, though of course the whole business was making him uneasy. How were these girls managing this when he and Jake were holding the sister's hands at the table? The only answer would be that Maggie was doing the rapping with Greeley's help. But that was unthinkable.

"Tell us what you want, spirit of David Hays," Kate intoned. A fury of rapping followed. "Your father refers to the year 1782 when you and he trudged through snow to feed the starving soldiers of the Revolution. He says that though you were mere boy, you behaved better than most full-grown men. He regrets never telling you how proud he was of you."

"Father," Jake said, hoarsely. "This means the world

to me—'' He coughed violently. There came a dull thump and a deep sigh.

"I knew it," Kate cried. "He's dead. The spirits told me he was due. His aura foretold it."

"Jake!" Peter cried. "No." He broke the chain. "A light. Quickly."

"God in Heaven," Greeley shouted. "The prophecy." The publisher rushed to the mantel, returning quickly with the lamp. He struck a match. Bizarre shadows played over the High Constable's face where it lay motionless on the table, eyes wide open, staring. Blood dribbled from his mouth onto the Persian carpet. "Jemmy!"

Peter felt for a pulse. "He's gone." Peter closed his friend's eyes. Composing himself, he said, "Jacob Hays was a good man and he was my friend. He shall be sorely missed."

"Jemmy," Greeley shouted again.

The door opened and a large negro lad entered.

"Who the devil are you?" Greeley demanded.

"I'm Ned, Jemmy's nephew. She went to church. She sent me here to take her place." The lad looked down at Jake. "Oh, Lord protect us. Is he dead?"

"Yes," Peter said. "Would you be good enough to take him to another room, and have the High Constable's driver, Absalom, fetch the police."

"Police?" Maggie cried, panic in her voice. "Why police?"

Peter said, "I doubt if the brandy was poisoned, but we must follow regulations."

"My girls were in no way responsible for this," Mother Fox said. "It's God's will."

Ned lifted Jake Hays as if he were a sack of oats. "I'll place him in Mr. Greeley's bed."

"You'll do no such thing," Greeley said, his voice loud and unhappy. He turned his attention to Peter. "What in tarnation are you talking about? Regulations?"

"Horace, if you don't mind," Peter said, "this is now

an official investigation.'' He cast his eyes about the room. ''Who was near the brandy?''

''It's obvious,'' Maggie said. ''Jemmy did it. She brought it in.''

''And you poured yourself a glass,'' Peter said. ''Either one of you could have done the deed.''

''But why should anyone want to kill Jacob Hays?'' Kate asked. ''He was an old man. His time had come.''

''Either of you might,'' Peter said. ''Or perhaps your mother.''

Mrs. Fox gasped. ''Now look what you've done,'' she said to Maggie.

Peter looked young Kate in the eye. ''You were facing the loss of your family's livelihood. It was no secret that Jacob Hays was going to expose you for the charlatans you are.''

''How dare you, sir?'' Kate said, imperious as a queen.

Maggie sat heavily in her chair.

''Get going, Ned,'' Peter ordered, louder than seemed necessary.

Ned started for the door with Hays's limp body in his arms.

''Not my bed,'' Greeley shouted. ''The Rose Room.''

At that moment the door to the chamber crashed open, the windows flew up, and an angry wind swirled through, extinguishing the lamp. The room was pitch-black once more.

Before anyone could speak, there rose a tremendous racket, as if from all the tin pans of Hell. This was followed by a high-pitched voice. ''Who dares to mock the spirits of the other world?''

''They've come to punish us for blasphemy,'' Maggie whimpered.

The voice spoke again. ''Who called this séance? Speak, lest our wrath be mighty.''

''I am Kate Fox.''

''Kate Fox! Why do you ridicule us with your false

proceedings?'' Now the voice squeaked in what sounded to Peter like the calling in of the pigs.

"Kate Fox!" This new voice was deep and resounding, and it seemed to come from the table itself. "Why do you rap your toes on the hard wood floor and pretend it comes from our domain?"

"Kate, they know," Maggie shrieked.

"Be quiet, Maggie."

"But we are undone."

"Only by your loose whiskey mouth."

"You thought you could escape me, didn't you?" the high-pitched voice demanded.

"Jake," said Peter. "Is that you?"

"Yes. I may be dead but I'm still High Constable."

"Oh, dear God," Kate said.

"You'd better pray, Kate Fox. For I will not rest until my work on earth is done. Kate and Maggie Fox, you are unmasked in your duplicity. How dare you mock the spirits of the other world?"

"I mock no one," Kate said, gaining strength each time she spoke.

All was going more than well until Tiny Tim sneezed.

Once more Greeley restored the light in the oil lamp, revealing to all, Jacob Hays alive and well. "Hays! What the . . . ?"

The edge of the Persian carpet covering the table lifted and Tiny Tim crawled out from under, holding an expired candle. "I seen them toes beating on the floor, Mr. Hays. They was no spirits here."

"Thank you, Tim." The High Constable grunted. "Peter, I'm touched by your reaction to my death, but it was a bit much, don't you think?"

Mother Fox was outraged. "This is not the behavior of a gentleman, sir."

Hays ignored her. To her girls he said, "My father died a Christian, but he was born a Jew. He specifically asked that no pennies be placed on his eyes. His wish was respected. If I were not retired, you'd go to jail."

"Oh, no," Mother Fox cried. "They're mere children."

"But Pickie was here two days ago, Hays," Greeley said. "That's the truth. I felt his hand on my shoulder."

"Perhaps only because you wanted to feel his hand on your shoulder."

"I think we might let them go with a stern reprimand," Peter said. "If they were willing to leave town immediately and not return."

"I think not," Maggie said slyly. "You'd only disappoint your wife, Charity. She's coming to see us tomorrow to commune with her first husband."

"How dare you?" Tonneman shouted. "She'll do no such thing, you'll do no such thing." His voice grew even louder and his eyes took on a wild gleam. "Of all the unmitigated . . ."

Jacob Hays was suddenly weary of it all. "You will leave the City. Henceforth, you will have no more to do with Charity Tonneman."

"Why should we do that?" Maggie sneered.

"Because it's the right thing to do," Kate said. "We will do as you say, sir."

"And furthermore—" Peter Tonneman, beside himself, was screaming now. "You will never—"

Without warning, like repeated rifle shots, the rapping sounded again.

"No more of this nonsense," the High Constable said. "Desist."

While the knocking continued, the girls held up their hands, Kate gestured toward her feet. "We're not doing a thing," Maggie said. Their smiles were beatific.

"I suppose this new rapping means something too?" Peter demanded, his outrage near explosion.

"You must be the judge of that, Mr. Tonneman," said Kate. She cocked her head, listening. "The message is for you, sir . . . from Mary Ann . . ." More rapping ensued. The girl listened, eyes closed. When she spoke again, it was in another, different tone. "No, not Mary Ann . . . Mariana, your mother. Her message is, 'Dignity, Peter, always dignity.' "

Although Gillian Linscott now writes full-time, she has been a parliamentary reporter for the BBC, a civil servant, market gardener, and playwright. Six of her twelve mystery novels have featured amateur detective Nell Bray in a highly acclaimed historical series set during the struggle to obtain voting rights for British women. Gillian introduced her suffragette sleuth in Sisters Beneath the Sheet, *published in 1991. Nell's most recent adventures can be found in* Dance on Blood, *1998 from St. Martin's Press.*

   "The Ballad of Gentleman Jem" is a delightful excursion somewhat farther back, to 1858 and a problem often faced by crime writers; what happens when the criminal is more fun than the detective?

THE BALLAD OF GENTLEMAN JEM

Gillian Linscott

B

The alleyway was at right angles to the riverbank, in a part of the town where there weren't many pedestrians after dark. Half a mile away, the tower of the cathedral soared above bare lime trees in the close. Half a mile on the other side of the river, damp sheep grazed in the water meadows. But this alleyway had very little to do with the countryside and still less with the cathedral. The upper storeys of the houses almost touched, blocking off all but a narrow strip of the night sky. Mist was rising from the river, so that at nine o'clock on a November night most of the alley was as dark as a ditch, with only lantern light from one window throwing a narrow swath of light. At the end nearer the river, the darkness clotted into a mass that moved rapidly up the space between the buildings. As it came close to the strip of light the clotted darkness resolved itself into three human figures, treading so lightly, so nearly in unison, that they made hardly enough sound for one on the damp cobbles. Just short of the light they stopped. Then one of them, the smallest, took a noiseless step towards the window.

A fire was burning in a narrow grate but the room was still cold enough for the man inside to need to wear his overcoat. A cap of folded paper the shape of a strawberry punnet covered his head. The bare ends of his fingers, black-stained, poked out from woollen gloves that stopped at the first set of knuckles. In his hand was a wooden mallet. He was a small man, his face round and pink, his eyes fixed on something flat on the slate-topped table in front of him. He raised the mallet, hesitated a moment, brought it smartly down. As one, the three men moved towards the door.

When the door opened suddenly, the small man jumped back from what he was doing, mouth open, mallet in hand. Three men stood between him and the door, shoulder to shoulder. They came in three sizes, small, medium and extravagantly large, with an air of purpose that fused them into one. After an appalled stare, the man in the paper cap closed his mouth, then opened it again uncertainly.

"D . . . did you want some printing done, gentlemen?"

"We do not want some printing done. In fact, you might say that what we want is some printing not done."

The voice of the trio came from the medium-sized man in the middle. Now that the printer was able to separate their collective blackness into individuals, he could tell that he was the most gentlemanly looking of the three. He wore a stovepipe hat, sleek and new enough for the damp to cling to it like the bloom on a damson, trousers and overcoat of good black material, a port-coloured necktie with a gold pin. His voice was pleasant and so well articulated that it might have been an actor's. He had too an actor's ability to hold a pause. His words hung in the air.

"P . . . printing not done? But I'm . . ."

The man sat down on the room's one chair, a plain wooden one stained with ink, his hat on his knees. The other two took up their places, standing on either side of him.

"You are Nathaniel Bark, a printer."

"Yes sir. Advertising bills, orders of service, visiting . . ."

The man's black eyebrows came together. He clicked his fingers and his smaller attendant rummaged in a pocket and put into his hand a large piece of paper, folded in four. He unfolded it fastidiously, frowning when a smear of ink got onto his pale kid glove.

"This is your work?"

The printer nodded, hangdog.

"A gallows ballad, that's what it is."

"If you like, sir."

"That's just it, I don't like." He read, his actorlike voice echoing around the room. "*The barbarous killing of Mary-Anne Smith and the murderer's repentance and death on the scaffold on the eighteenth of November 1858.* George Trumper, topped last Thursday, that was."

"Yes, sir."

"You printed this and you wrote it too. No use denying it."

"I'm not denying it, sir." Just a touch of pride in the printer's voice, along with the fear. He added: "And if I may say so, sir, it's selling very nicely too."

"It's a cock."

"No it isn't. It's the truth. He strangled the poor girl. Strangled her and left her lying in—"

The kid glove rose in warning.

"I know that. It's not the murder we're concerned with. It's what you have him saying before he's turned off. Regret, repentance. Everybody taking a warning from his sad example. Did Trumper say any of that?"

"Well, in a manner of speaking . . ."

"He didn't and you know it. Trumper died cursing the judge and the hangman and the parson, so hot and strong they had to turn him off sharpish before the ladies got scandalized. Not a word about repentance or sad examples.''

''You couldn't expect me to print what he really said. It wasn't poetical. It wouldn't sell. The public expects the sufferer to say some improving words.''

By now, the printer's fear had been overcome by concern for his profession. He was standing up to the man, hands gesturing, round eyes glowing under the rim of the paper cap. The black eyebrows drew together again.

''I'm not concerned about Trumper. The man was a common sneak thief that did away with his dollymop. He had no reputation to keep up. You can tell as many lies as you can print about him and his like.''

The printer looked, *Well, then*? but said nothing. There was a few seconds' silence. In those seconds, the temporary courage went out of him and his face went as white as his paper cap.

''Do you know who I am?''

The printer's eyes went from the man's face to his companions' and back again. No help.

''You . . . you're the man they call Gentleman Jem.''

''I am Gentleman Jem. What do you know about me?''

''You're . . .'' He swallowed. ''You're a housebreaker. A very good one, they say.''

''I'm the best cracksman this place has ever seen or is ever likely to see. They talk about me in London, you know that? They talk about Gentleman Jem as they talk about Dick Turpin or Jack Sheppard. And they'll go on talking about me long after I'm underground.''

''I'm sure they will, sir.''

''And that is why you're not going to do to me what you did to Trumper.''

Suddenly Gentleman Jem was on his feet, screwing up the printed sheet, holding it in the fire with the toe of his boot until it smouldered into sullen fire. When it was ash he walked slowly back to his chair.

''Mr. Bark, in my line luck is everything. When a man

is as skilled in his calling as I am, and when his luck's in, all the crushers and all the judges in England are powerless against him. But what about when his luck's out?''

His voice had sunk to a whisper, but a whisper as audible as water running into a zinc bucket on a frosty morning. Distantly, the cathedral clock chimed the quarter. A curl of ash fell out of the fire and stirred in the draught from under the door. The printer didn't reply.

''I'll tell you. One day—it may be years or it may be tomorrow—my luck will be out like any common man's. And when it does run out, it won't be oakum picking or Van Diemen's Land for me. I'll be cutting my last fling on the air, Mr. Bark, with nobody for a partner.''

''Let's hope it won't come to that, sir.''

''It will come to that. I make no complaint about it now, and I'll make no complaint about it then. Depend on it there won't be any snivelling for mercy from me— no dodger's stuff about repentance or examples or leading a better life. I'll go out as I lived, in a gentlemanly way.''

For the first time since they'd walked in, the expressions of his two companions changed. They radiated a quiet pride in him and watched the printer to see that he was properly impressed.

''And I'm not having you doing the dodger for me. The idea that when people tell my story in years to come it will be spoiled at the end by some death-hunter's snivelling that you've invented to cadge pennies from greasy-fingered errand boys drives me mad, Mr. Bark. It drives me quite mad.''

His voice had become a shout and the expressions of the companions had changed to match. They were now a combined black glare.

''I hope . . . I can assure you, if you don't wish it . . . there'll be nothing of the kind.''

''There won't be, because I have friends, devoted friends, who'll take care of my reputation when I'm out of the world. Friends who are Roland to my Oliver, Jonathan to my Saul. On my left"—he gestured towards the small man—"my friend Dandy. On my right, Huggy Joe."

"Er . . . pleased to meet you, gentlemen."

They didn't return the greeting.

"You might wonder how they came by their names. Before he became my assistant, Huggy Joe was a fairground wrestler. His hug was famous. The man who came out of it with nothing worse than ribs caved in and a little rearrangement of the collar bones could call himself fortunate."

The big man beamed like a happy beagle. Gentleman Jem turned to the man on his other side. He was small, middle-aged and nondescript. He wore a dark cloth coat with baggy pockets over old corduroy trousers, a stained tartan cap, a red- and white-spotted muffler at his throat.

"Dandy. Short for Dandelion. Why Dandelion? The fact is, Dandy's such a shot with a pistol that if you were to hold out a dandelion on the end of its stem, he could shoot the head off it without as much as grazing your fingers. I don't suppose you have such a thing as a dandelion about you?"

The printer shook his head.

"Well, we must improvise." He looked above the printer's head at a row of proof pages skewered on nails against the wall. "The spectacles, I think, Dandy. Left side."

A crack, a smell, a yelp. An advertising bill for a local optician was swaying gently on its nail, a scorched hole drilled through the left side of the printed spectacles. By the time Nathaniel Bark had opened his eyes, before the echo of his yelp had died away, the pistol was back in Dandy's pocket, with no sign on his face that it had ever been otherwise. Bark groaned with fear and staggered back against his printing slab. Gentleman Jem stood up, smiling.

"So—may I take it there'll be no ballad for me when the time comes?"

"N . . . no, sir. No ballad."

"Good." Gentleman Jem put his hat on his head and moved towards the door, affable as a prince on a state visit. He paused by the printing slab.

"What are you doing here?"

Unwillingly, Bark's eyes went to the proof page nearest the door. Jem read.

"But that's Cloggy. They haven't even topped him yet. He's not due until the day after tomorrow."

"No, sir. But, you see, it takes time with the old gear I've got, and people do like to buy them on the same day. If I wait until . . ."

His scared eyes went to Dandy's coat pocket, but after a moment of silence, Gentleman Jem laughed and went on reading.

" 'Dismal fate' doesn't rhyme with 'intemperate.' "

"It's not far off.'

"Well, it will do for Cloggy. But none of this for me, understood?"

"Understood."

And as suddenly as they'd come, they were gone, leaving only a smell of powder in the air.

Long before Nathaniel Bark had stopped shaking, another set of footsteps came along the alleyway, this time from the direction of the main street. There was only one man and he walked softly, but not as softly as Gentleman Jem and his assistants. He wore a black overcoat and hat and carried a furled umbrella. When he got to the printer's door he gave one sharp rap on it with the handle of his umbrella and slipped inside as soon as it was opened.

"Good evening, Bark." He sniffed. "Why have you got the window open? And what in the world have you been putting on that fire?"

Bark murmured something about bad coal and moved the chair so the new visitor would have his back to the row of proofs.

"Shall I take your coat, Mr. Hudson?"

The visitor said he'd keep it on, but undid the top two buttons, revealing the high collar and white stock of a clergyman. His hair was dark, streaked with grey, his side-whiskers carefully trimmed. His expression was both greedy and nervous, like a boy scrumping apples.

"Have you done the honours by Clogger?"

"Nearly, sir. I'd done the corrections and I was just going to pull a final proof when you got here."

"You should have done it by now. You know I can't stay long."

"I'm sorry, sir. I . . . I got delayed."

From where the printer was standing, the singed hole glared at him through the spectacles. He scuttled across the room and picked up his ink roller. Trying to make the movement look casual, he grabbed the proof and wiped the roller with it. Mr. Hudson noticed nothing and Bark breathed again, but his hand was still unsteady and the proof he drew was blotchy from over-inking.

"Hold it for me," Hudson said.

He held it while Mr. Hudson read, making little clicking sounds with his tongue.

"It will do well enough."

"You think the rhymes are all right, sir?"

One of the incidental miseries of the visit from Gentleman Jem was that it had introduced self-criticism into his art.

"If a rhyme can bring a sliding foot to the path of repentance or confirm the virtuous man in his ways, it serves its purpose."

Bark thought, as he had often thought before, *You old hypocrite. Two bob a gross you take, no work and no overheads. Plus eight bob a week rent for this hole.* He knew what was coming next.

"Now, Bark, we'll look at the accounts, shall we?"

Some minutes later he said: "I make that four pounds twelve shillings and sixpence you owe me, including the two weeks' rent overdue."

Sadly, Bark climbed the steep ladder to his loft above

the printing shop and came down with a handful of silver.

"One pound five's the best I can make, sir. I'd pay more if I could, but with the boy to pay and the advertisement work not coming in as it should . . ."

Hudson's face went hard.

"I've a valuable resource tied up here, Bark. If you can't pay your rent, there's plenty of men ready to take on a good print shop."

Bark said, miserably bold: "Sir, if you could see your way to invest in a better press, I'd get more advertising work; then we wouldn't have to rely on the ballads the way we do."

"You're dissatisfied with our agreement, Bark?"

"No, sir."

"I shall expect a more satisfactory return next time."

He paused at the door, as Gentleman Jem had paused.

"I suppose after Clogger's paid the penalty there'll be no more hangings for some time."

"No, sir, not until after the spring assizes."

Hudson didn't say that was a pity, but the expression on his face left no doubt what he was thinking.

It was a hard winter. By the time of the spring assizes, Nathaniel Bark's debt to his landlord stood at eight pounds seven shillings and three pence and the luck of Gentleman Jem had run out at last. He'd broken into a house near the cathedral. The police must have had warning of his plans, because they were lying in wait for him. There was a chase across rooftops in which a constable fell to his death. The jury were unimpressed by Jem's claim that he had not pushed the constable or in any way caused him to fall and the judge pronounced the death sentence with the relish of a man who'd been waiting to do it for a long time. Nathaniel Bark was almost distracted. As far as he could he kept to his printing shop and the loft above it, sending the apprentice out to buy essential supplies. When business demanded that he should go out, he avoided back streets or empty squares. Several times he thought he saw Huggy Joe or Dandy. One black day, soon after sentence had been pronounced, he thought he saw them both together, coming in his direction, and scurried off in such a panic that he fell over the basket of a baker's boy and had to pay for the tumbled baps. More of his small stock of money went on a big new bolt for the inside of the door. It wasn't that he had any intention of disobeying the order he'd been given. What went scuttling through his dreams and snaking through his days was the fear that Huggy Joe or Dandy might find it necessary to reinforce that order with, say, a cracked rib or two or a singed ear lobe.

On the evening just thirty-six hours away from the date set for Gentleman Jem's execution Bark was in the printing shop with the apprentice, checking an advertisement for a sale of farm machinery. It was early April, still light at eight o'clock, and a scent of new grass was blowing across the river from the water meadows. But the window of the printer's shop was shut, the blind down, and the smell inside was of cheap lamp oil and ink. When a knock came on the door, Nathaniel Bark flinched.

"Who is it?"

Another rap. He signed to the apprentice to open the door a crack and stood ready for flight up the ladder.

"It is I, Bark."

At the familiar voice, the apprentice opened the door wide and Mr. Hudson walked in, annoyed.

"Is it ready? There's no time to waste."

"What?"

"The ballad on the hanging of the man Jem. We should print twice as many as usual. It's arousing interest quite out of the common."

The printer's jaw dropped.

"B . . . ballad on Jem?"

"Of course. You've got it set, I hope."

Bark's eyes went miserably from Hudson's face to the printing stone.

"I . . . I was thinking of not doing one for Jem."

"Not doing! The man's the biggest sinner this country has known in a generation. People will come thirty miles to see him hanged. We've never had a better opportunity."

"It will take time, and I . . ."

"Bark, how much do you owe me? I'll tell you. Counting this week's rent, it's almost nine pounds. Unless you want to be out on the street, you'll work day and night and have that ballad ready this time tomorrow."

After more on the same topic, Hudson went, leaving Bark with his mouth hanging open and his legs as weak as daisy stems.

"If you want *me* to work all night, that'll be five bob extra."

The apprentice, showing a precocious grasp of his trade. Bark, without seeming to register what he'd said, told him to go home, bolted the door behind him, then sank down on the chair, head in his hands.

The day fixed by law to be the last one on earth for Gentleman Jem wasn't much brighter for Nathaniel Bark. Going out onto the streets—already more crowded than usual in expectation of next morning's execution—meant that his skin crawled with fear of Huggy Joe and Dandy. Staying at home would expose him to another visit from his shareholder and landlord and the revelation that he had not done, and had no intention of doing, the work that might pay off his debt. That, beyond a doubt, would mean the loss of his room and printing shop. For a printer past his youth and unskilled in modern equipment, that was a long step down the slippery road to the workhouse. But he had no doubt about his course of action—or rather, inaction. Workhouse life was misery, but even in the workhouse they had to leave a man a rib cage to breathe with and a whole skull to keep his brains in. If he did as Mr. Hudson wanted, he could be guaranteed neither. So, unable to walk the streets or to stay at home, he broke the habit of an abstemious lifetime and spent the day in public houses, making pints of beer last a very long time. By early evening he'd gravitated to an unsavoury place near the outskirts of the city, the haunt of butchers from the abbatoir. As he sat in the corner nursing his beer he became aware of an urchin going from table to table with an armful of printed sheets. At a table near him a man took one of the sheets, laughed and pretended to cuff the urchin on the ear.

" 'E don't know what day it is."

More laughter from the whole table. The urchin, disconcerted, ran for the back door. As he passed, Bark grabbed one of the sheets from the top of the pile and, sure as hanging, found himself looking at exactly what he feared. Top line, 60 point, THE EXECUTION OF "GENTLEMAN" JEM. Under it, in letters only slightly smaller, "And his speech of repentance from the gallows." Then a woodcut of a hanging man and close-crammed stanzas of verse all the way to the foot of the page.

A moment's hope that some other print shop had perpetrated the thing died at first glance. He knew every chip and scratch in the capital letters, knew the woodcut. As he read, shaking and sweating, he realized that he knew every line of verse as well. What they'd done was to take stanzas from his earlier productions and splice them into a more or less appropriate whole, changing only the name of the condemned man. Who they were, he had not a shadow of doubt. Mr. Hudson, finding his tenant flown, must have pressed the apprentice into service. Between them they'd cobbled up this thing, then— horror of horrors—through error or greed, unleashed it on the world a day early, while Jem was still eating his last dinner only a few hundred yards away.

Bark shot out of the back entrance of the public house

with the faint hope of overtaking the urchin and snatching his stock from him, but there was no sign of the boy. In the dusk, empty crates and barrels seemed to take on the shape of Huggy Joe, every click of a starling's beak from the pub roof was Dandy cocking his pistol. He started running. He had some faint plan of catching a train for London, for anywhere, but in the dim light the road to the railway station was a lonely chasm between terraces of houses, with a dozen chances for an assassin. While he was trying to decide what to do he found himself outside a pawn shop of the most dejected kind. He went inside and, for one pound and his battered pocket watch, acquired an antiquated pistol, ready loaded, and a powder flask. He did it like a man in a dream, hardly recognizing his own voice. Darkness came and he scuttled fearfully between circles of lamplight, the pistol in his pocket feeling like a growth on his hip. He was cold and hungry, but his overcoat was back at home and the pistol had taken the last of his money. He found himself walking along a narrow road with a high stone wall on his right and recognized it as the wall of the prison. Then the bell started.

It came from inside the prison. At first he thought he'd panicked the night away, that it was morning already with the bell tolling Gentleman Jem to execution. But it was no heavy funeral toll. It rang quickly, urgently. Then there was shouting and running feet, just round the corner, coming towards him. He shrank back as a group of men in uniform carrying bull's-eye lanterns pounded up to him. The leader grabbed him roughly by the arm, peered into his face. Then, to the others:

"It's not him." To Bark: "Has a man come past?"

Bark shook his head. A whistle shrilled and the men went running back the way they'd come. He managed to get a question out to the slowest of them.

"What's happening?"

"He's escaped."

"Who?"

"Gentleman Jem."

Then they were gone, leaving him leaning against the wall as if they'd punched him in the stomach. Against reason, he knew the motive for Jem's escape. Somehow he'd got wind of the ballad and, not even trusting his best friends for his revenge, had broken out with one purpose—to settle his account with Nathaniel Bark, printer.

The only comfort was the number of men out looking for Jem. Once Bark had recovered enough to leave the comfort of the prison wall, he found the streets as busy as a market day. Constables and warders were milling around, helped and hindered by customers pouring out of pubs, shouting questions, seeing phantom prisoners in every doorway. It seemed to Bark only a matter of time before they caught their man and he had no wish to be there when it happened. His idea now was to make for home. If he climbed his ladder and barricaded the doorway to the loft, he could stay there until Jem was safely back in the condemned cell. He edged his way through the crowds to the top of his alleyway, took a deep breath, ran, threw himself into the safety of his printing shop and bolted the door.

A draught from the window blew cold on his neck. A voice from the darkness said, "Bark?" He could sense a shape looming somewhere between him and the cold fireplace. He screamed and backed towards the door, scrabbled for the bolt but couldn't find it. The figure by the fireplace was motionless, but there was scuffling in the loft. He was certain that the figure was Jem, with Huggy Joe and Dandy up above.

"Bark, what's happening?"

The voice was shrill, scared—but he was so full of his own fear that he didn't recognize it.

"Mr. Jem? Is that you, Mr. Jem?"

The pistol was in his hand. He cocked it, hand trembling, pointed it towards the figure by the fireplace. His sweating fingers bunched round the trigger. The whole world became a flash, a noise, powder fumes drawn into his lungs on his first shivering intake of breath, doubling him up with coughing. Then a voice from the loft ladder. From the coughing and the echoing in his ears he couldn't make out what it was saying. The pistol slipped out of his fingers and clattered to the floor. When he knelt to try to pick it up, his hand touched something cloth-covered and yielding. He groaned with terror and misery.

"Be quiet."

There were steps coming down the ladder, bringing a broadening circle of light as they came. It illuminated, first, boots on the ladder rungs and an overcoat, oddly familiar, then a pair of gleaming eyes under black brows.

Bark groaned again, in fear of man or ghost. Gentleman Jem stepped away from the ladder and walked towards him, carrying a stub of candle in a holder, wearing the printer's own peaked cap and overcoat, unmistakably flesh and blood. Bark, still kneeling, began to babble that it wasn't his fault.

"Who's that?"

When the candlelight fell on the thing beside him on the floor, Bark's babble turned to a breathless whooping then: "It's Mr. Hudson. Oh, I've shot him. I've shot a clergyman."

"He was confoundedly in the way. There I was, presuming on your hospitality and wardrobe, when I heard someone walk in. It wasn't convenient at the time to come down and meet him."

"I shot him. I thought he was you. I shot him."

Bark's voice was keening, half-mad. Coolly, Gentleman Jem stepped over him and looked down at the body. He whistled.

"By God, it's Holy Henry. The nark. The cove who told the crushers where to find me the night they nabbed me. He's no more a clergyman than I am. But what's he to you?"

"He's my landlord. I think he'd come about the rent."

Gentleman Jem whistled again, this time admiringly.

"When it comes to bilking your landlord, you really do the thing properly."

By now, it had entered even Bark's panic-struck brain that it wasn't tactful to go on insisting that he'd meant to shoot Jem. But he had to make him understand.

"I didn't mean to kill him. I didn't know who he was. Can they hang me if I didn't know who he was?"

"It doesn't make any odds . . ." Then Jem stopped and began again in a different tone. "It doesn't make any odds because you didn't shoot Holy Henry. I did. I recognized him and put a ball through his shrivelled heart as I came down the ladder." He bent and scooped up the pistol. "This yours? You couldn't hit a dead sheep with an old thing like that. Still, I might as well have it." And he slid it into the overcoat pocket.

"You shot . . . ?"

"That's right. Gentleman Jem breaks out of the condemned cell and shoots the nark that put him there. You'll be able to write that in your ballad, won't you?"

"B . . . ballad?"

"On my great escape—and my revenge. It should sell well. Make up for the one you didn't write on my premature decease."

Bark stayed crouched in the darkness, but a great swell of relief swept over him. Jem didn't know. And he hadn't killed his landlord.

"I'm sorry I can't stay to give you the details, but I'm sure you can make something up as usual. Joe and Dandy are waiting on the river with a boat. I shall be wafted along the water singing, like the Lady of Shalott. In due course, you may tell them how I shot the holy dodger and knocked you senseless."

Bark heard a step, the patter of type falling from the printing table. A hand pulled him up by the collar and the world went red, then black.

And as the reverend clergyman lay wallowing in his gore
Jem felled the gallant printer with a mallet to the floor,
Vowing that he would make him rue the night . . .

"Something I don't understand," said the apprentice.

He was checking the proof while Bark read out his ballad from the master copy. Twenty-four hours after the attack his head still ached devilishly, but with such a theme and such interest from the public, he knew "The Audacious Escape of the Convict Gentleman Jem and the Pitiless Murder of the Rev. Henry Hudson" would transform his poor fortunes—especially now there was no Hudson to claim two shillings a gross. After some thought, he'd decided to leave Holy Henry with his more respectable identity. Murdered clergymen were more poetical than dead police informers.

"What don't you understand?"

"How Gentleman Jem shot him."

"But it tells you in the ballad. '*The desperate escaper to the steep ladder clung/And shot the wretched victim right through his heart and lung.*' "

"But you said he had a candle in his hand."

"Of course he did. How could he have seen him otherwise?"

"But if he had a candle in one hand and his pistol in the other, how did he cling to the ladder?"

"How would I know why? I'm not a murderer."

If he cared to think about it, he supposed it was odd. But a lot had happened in a few seconds and the police who questioned him had been too excited by the hunt for Jem and the murder of their friend Holy Henry to worry over details. Already the events of the night before were a nightmare, lurid but unreal. Or nowhere near as real as his headache and the demands of his craft.

"Do you think they'll get him?" asked the apprentice.

On the whole, he hoped not. He frowned at the apprentice to keep him quiet and went on reading.

Jem felled the gallant printer with a mallet to the floor,

Vowing he would make him rue the night
That he tried to frustrate him in his desperate flight.

A little poetic licence perhaps, but safe enough now. Wherever they were going, by land or sea, Gentleman Jem and his friends would be in no position to come back and argue for a very long time.

William F. Wu's work has always related in some way to his interest in Asian American issues and heritages. Wu may be best known for his contemporary fantasy short stories, such as "Wong's Lost and Found Emporium," a multiple award nominee that became an episode of The Twilight Zone *in 1985. The original story was recently reprinted in the 1996 collection* A Century of Fantasy: Best Stories of the Decade, 1980–1989, *edited by Robert Silverberg, from MJF Books.*

Recent short stories include "Kwan Tingui" in the anthology Free Space *from TOR, "Nanoship" in the spring, 1996 issue of* Absolute Magnitude, *and "And Then There Were Some", in STAR WARS: Tales from Jabba's Palace. A 5-time nominee for the Hugo, Nebula, and World Fantasy Awards, Wu is also the author of the six-volume young adult science fiction series titled* Isaac Asimov's Robots in Time, *for Avon (1994–5). His science fiction novel* Hong on the Range *(1989) was a 1990 selection for the American Library Association list of Best Books for Young People.*

Altogether, he has had thirteen novels, one short story collection, one book of literary criticism, and over fifty short stories published. Wu has an A.B. in East Asian Studies and an A.M. and Ph.D. in American Culture. His dissertation was published as The Yellow Peril: Chinese-Americans in American Fiction, 1850–1940.

THE HUNGRY
GHOST OF
PANAMINT

William F. Wu

Panamint, California
August 12, 1872

High in the forested Panamint Mountains rising
from the western side of Death Valley, Hom
Gahgit paused between two of his crewmates chipping
and fitting stones as they built an unmortared retaining
wall. Wearily, he wiped the sweat off his forehead with
the rolled-up sleeve of his black cotton shirt, swaying
the long, black, braided queue down his back. The sun
had fallen behind the western ridge and evening brought
relief from the heat at last.

"All right, boys," Josiah Forrester, the crew boss,
called out as he walked along the Chinese crew lined up
at the wall. "That's it for today. I'll have this week's
pay at the tents." A burly man in a brown, brimmed
hat, sweating through his blue shirt, he passed without
stopping.

Next to Gahgit, Wong Wanli lowered the small steel
hammer in his hand and spoke in See Yup, their native

Chinese dialect. "Have the stinking hungry ghosts bothered you yet? Eh?" He grinned, showing crooked teeth.

"No, I haven't had any bad luck. Is it time?" Gahgit shrugged.

"The seventh month is just beginning."

"Maybe there aren't any hungry ghosts here."

All Chinese spirits roamed the land of the living in the seventh month of the Chinese year. Those with relatives went to visit them and were put to rest by sacrifices of food, wine, and spirit money. Spirits without relatives to make such sacrifices became disruptive and even dangerous to the living, out of resentment. Since most of the Chinese laborers in this land were single men, they rarely had immediate family here. When one died, he was usually buried with the intention that his bones would later be freighted to San Francisco for shipment back home again. However, Gahgit had never worried about ghosts much.

With the other twenty-two members of their crew, Gahgit and Wanli gathered their tools in dirty, sweaty hands and plodded through the small, crowded town toward their tents. All of them wore the long, braided queue down their backs required by the Manchu emperor in China; none of them cut their queues off, because they intended to return home someday. Most still wore the woven, conical Chinese peasant hats they had brought from Chinatown in San Francisco, though some had since lost theirs. Gahgit sported a small black bowler he had bought from a trader.

In the gathering darkness, white miners were hiking and riding into town from their claims in the slopes around Panamint. Mule drivers, prospectors, and drifters also walked up and down the main street, many of them toward the saloon. Lit kerosene lanterns swung over the saloon doors.

Lei Yin, a stocky, muscular man, impatiently brushed past Wanli.

Wanli grinned down at Gahgit and spoke quietly. "I have the cinnabar."

"Keep your voice down!" Startled, Gahgit glanced up as he worked his right hand, stiff from hours of hammering on stone. "Show it to me."

"Not here! After dinner, we'll talk behind the saloon, eh?"

Gahgit nodded. While the Chinese were not welcome inside, the saloonkeeper would sell them full bottles out of the back door. However, they usually left the saloon's drunken white men and returned to their tents.

"It's time to celebrate. We'll share a bottle, eh?" Wanli paused. "I know you're discouraged about our chances here in this country. But you told me how your uncle died unnecessarily because he made a mistake. Without it, he might still be . . . younger than we are now, eh? And I can correct the mistake. A fortune will be coming our way."

Gahgit did not press Wanli, who had watched over him for years like an elder brother. As he followed Wanli to their tent, however, he shook his head doubtfully. Legends of Daoist elixirs for immortality were as common in China as other superstitions were among the white men on the frontier. His uncle had died from one.

In their tent, Gahgit stowed his tools under his bunk. Outside, he drew his pay from Forrester. Then he joined the others at the stream that flowed behind the town. Lei Yin joked loudly with Chun Guan, a tall, skinny, quiet man. Gahgit set his bowler aside and, like them, rinsed his hands and face in the stream beside rocks rounded and smoothed by the water.

Soon the evening cookfire blazed behind the tents. The cook was steaming fish he had caught that day and rice that the crew had brought from San Francisco. In a large wok, he stir-fried greens he had found in the general store. Lei Yin talked raucously. Gahgit squatted among them near the warmth of the fire with his chopsticks and his bowl as the night chill of the mountains came on to replace the day's heat.

The third son in a family of five surviving children,

Gahgit had left his village at the age of twenty-two to reach the Mountain of Gold, as Chinese workers called this land. Hungry and desperate on the docks of Guangzhou, he had been befriended by Wong Wanli. Then twenty-six, Wanli had the name of a man who paid their passage to San Francisco in exchange for payments to be made later; Wanli also had known that two workers would offer the job broker a more attractive deal than one. For four years, they had worked together and paid down their indenture, first grading the roadbed of the Central Pacific Railroad, then of its branch lines.

They had joined Forrester to come south here to Panamint, a silver mine boomtown. The crew's experience had served them well in clearing the narrow road up to Panamint alongside the mountain stream. Now they were building a retaining wall against a loose, rocky slope.

Unlike many men in Panamint, Gahgit did not squander his pay on drink, women, or gambling. Soon he could pay off his first passage and also buy a ticket home to Sunning, a district of Guangdong Province, giving up his dream of finding wealth here. Gahgit missed his mother and father, but not the village life to which he would return. He and Wanli had spoken often of the bitter labor back home in the muddy rice paddies, where the grueling routine would be broken only by monsoons, plague, and famine as they worked in endless cycles for the rest of their lives. Gahgit had hoped to come home wealthy enough to break that cycle, and able to care for his aging mother and father, but now he had given up. Wanli, however, had often declared that he would never return without gold in his pouch.

Gahgit knew his decision would deeply disappoint his friend.

After dinner, most of the crew drifted to the saloon. Gahgit just wanted to get Wanli alone so he could see the cinnabar. However, by the time Gahgit and Wanli arrived behind the small wooden building next to the general store, several of their crewmates blocked the rear door, laughing as they passed a new bottle around.

The door opened. Josiah Forrester came out with Linc Hanford, a mule driver who brought supply wagons up the steep road from Death Valley.

"Evenin', boys," said Forrester. "You know Hanford, here."

"Howdy," Hanford said gruffly. The lamp hanging over the door shone down on his long, unkempt gray hair and beard.

"I'll get right to the point." Forrester shoved his hat back on his head. "Hanford's made a new silver strike south of here."

"That's right," said Hanford. "Fact is, it's rough ground and I'm too old to work it." He held out a few blue-streaked rocks.

"I told him you China boys was a hard-workin' bunch." Forrester frowned. "You know our job here is almost over."

Gahgit adjusted his bowler and glanced at the rocks. He could recognize silver ore now. Of course it could have come from anywhere. He nudged Wanli. "Come on, let's go talk by ourselves," he said in See Yup.

"Not yet." Wanli switched to English. "What you want, Hanford?"

"Here's the deal," said Hanford. "I'll sell the map for fifty dollars."

"Fifty dollar?" Wanli sneered. "Then Chinaboy get there, no silver."

"No silver." Chun Guan grinned, his thin form throwing a long shadow.

"Me, I'm headin' back north ag'in," said Forrester. "I'm no miner. You boys could chip in together, though, for less than two bucks each."

Wanli took the bottle from Lei Yin. He raised it to take a drink, but it inexplicably slipped out of his hand and smashed on a rock at his feet, splashing liquid. "Aiee! Hungry ghost!" Wanli shouted angrily in Chinese.

Gahgit and the other Chinese laughed. Chun Guan shook his head.

Forrester and Hanford glanced at each other and went back inside.

"I'll buy another," said Wanli. "No fifty dollars, no two dollars. I can do better." He banged on the back door of the saloon.

The saloon door opened and the bald, white-bearded barkeeper leaned out, holding a bottle of cheap whiskey by the neck. " 'Nother one, boys?"

"I take one." Under the shining kerosene lamp, Wanli opened a pouch hanging from his waist on a cord. He picked out some coins. "Here, eh?"

"Me too." Lei Yin pushed forward next to Wanli.

Gahgit, watching impatiently, noticed a bit of dull, reddish-brown inside the pouch. Lei Yin stood next to Wanli, looking down as he fumbled with his own coins.

"Here's to the hungry ghosts," Lei Yin called out in Chinese, holding up his bottle. "I hope I never become one!" He took a swallow of whiskey.

Wanli, the lamplight throwing his shadow, laughed derisively. "If you never died, you'd never become a ghost at all!" He drank from his bottle.

Gahgit walked briskly away, eager to see the cinnabar. Wanli followed him to some trees and brush a distance from the saloon and general store. Their crewmates trailed after Lei Yin back to the barracks.

Wanli grinned, his faced flushed. "I have the real strike we need! And I have a map to the spot, drawn on leather."

"I saw the cinnabar in your belt pouch."

Wanli opened his pouch. "You said your uncle's immortality elixir required cinnabar." He pulled the map of folded leather out just enough to show it to Gahgit and tossed the small, red-brown rock to him.

"Yes." Gahgit caught the rock. "But he made a mistake. He ground up calomel into the drink because it looks so similar. The calomel killed him—I think from breathing the heated vapors as much as drinking the elixir.'' Gahgit knew that when red-brown cinnabar lay near the surface of the ground, exposed to the weather, it often had brown calomel with it.

"We know our rocks by now, you and I, don't we?" Wanli laughed and his crooked teeth shone in the faint light from the saloon. "We can mine the cinnabar and sell it for our fortune up north, in all the Chinatowns and Chinese mining camps and railroad camps. We'll pay off our indenture this year. Soon we'll have enough gold to go home as wealthy men—and I won't have to cut off your queue to keep you from returning!" He laughed again. "As I always said, I'll never go home without gold in my pouch.''

Gahgit tossed back the cinnabar, choosing not to tell Wanli yet that he intended to ship home as soon as they returned to San Francisco.

Wanli thumped his back. "Don't worry! I'll always take care of you.''

Dawn woke Gahgit through the canvas tent he shared with Wanli, who had already risen and left. The cook rang his little gong. Gahgit dressed and walked out, heading up the narrow, forested path toward the latrine.

A moment later in the trees, Gahgit stopped, staring at the form of Wanli lying face-down in the path. Blood matted the hair on the back of his head. Gahgit gasped and bent down, trying to turn his friend over.

At the same moment, Chun Guan came up behind Gahgit and he quickly squatted on Wanli's other side.

"He's cold," Chun Guan said gravely, feeling Wanli's face. "He must have slipped in the darkness and fallen. After getting drunk last night, he needed the latrine. Maybe a hungry ghost tripped him.''

Several more of their crewmates came up the path and stopped. They had all seen death frequently in their lives, from the sick and starving infants in their peasant villages to those who fell in accidents while blasting through the Sierra Nevadas for the Central Pacific Railroad. Death could come any time, especially when hungry ghosts walked.

"We will carry him," said Chun Guan.

Gahgit nodded numbly. The others knew Gahgit regarded Wanli as an elder brother. They picked Wanli up and took him back down to the camp.

As Gahgit turned, a smooth rock as large as a man's head caught his eye. He knelt. A dark smear of dried blood and some black hairs told him that this brown rock had killed Wanli. The other rocks here in the trees were rough and sharp-edged. However, this one had been rounded and smoothed in the stream, over sixty paces away. The grass under it was still green; someone had carried the rock to this spot very recently.

Suddenly angry, Gahgit rose and walked down to the tents, where his companions had laid Wanli under a blanket. Several were hiking out to find a burial site. Two more spoke to Forrester in their halting English.

Struggling to hide his anger lest he reveal his intentions, Gahgit went over to Wanli's body. The others politely turned away, allowing him a moment with his friend. However, Gahgit knew that Wanli's spirit no longer remained with his body. He had come to take a closer look.

Gahgit lifted the blanket and saw that Wanli did not have his pouch.

He walked back to their tent, keeping his eyes down as in mourning. Inside, he quickly glanced over Wanli's cot and in the burlap bag holding Wanli's few personal belongings. He did not find the pouch.

Wanli sent most of his pay with Gahgit's every week to the job broker who had paid their passage. He never had much money on him and the entire crew knew it. Someone had killed him for the cinnabar and the map.

The white men in this boomtown cared nothing for cinnabar. Its only use to them was grinding it up to make red paint, and these men had come here for silver. Wanli had been killed by one of their crewmates.

Gahgit took off his bowler for a moment. He knew

that the white men would not waste their time on Wanli's murder. Even his own crewmates might not believe Wanli had been murdered; in their lives of hard labor and risk, maybe they would rather just watch out for hungry ghosts and try to avoid accidents. If he did warn them, the killer would be on guard, too.

No one really cared about Wanli except Gahgit.

His anger rising, Gahgit put his bowler on again. Deciding to keep silent about his suspicions, he left the tent. In the morning light, he got a shovel and joined his companions in digging a grave for his closest friend.

Gahgit and his companions dug the grave and spent part of their pay on food and wine to sacrifice at a brief funeral. They joined in buying a wooden coffin in the town. At home in their villages, the Wong clan would have held a proper funeral and spent time in mourning. Here, in the midday heat, already covered with sweat, the crew merely picked up their tools and walked back to the unfinished retaining wall.

As Gahgit worked, he felt Wanli's absence. They had taken every job together since they had arrived from across the sea. Consumed by grief and anger, Gahgit hammered the stonework hard in a focused fury.

At sunset Forrester walked down the line as usual and called an end to the workday. Gahgit lowered his hammer, still angry but now weary, and turned toward the barracks. His crewmates did the same.

When Gahgit saw Lei Yin's muscular form lifting one last stone onto the wall, he suddenly recalled when he had first seen the cinnabar. Wanli had stood under the kerosene lamp at the rear door of the saloon and Lei Yin had come up next to him. Lei Yin, too, had had a clear chance to see it—and of course he could have lifted that big rock more easily than most.

Gahgit plodded back to the barracks with the others. As he washed his hands and face in the stream, he realized he could not be certain Lei Yin had killed Wanli. Yet he could approach Lei Yin and see how he reacted.

Rising from the bank, he walked to the blazing cook-fire. Right now, Lei Yin thought of him as Wanli's faithful younger brother. Gahgit decided he would have to shake up Lei Yin in order to draw him out.

As the crew took their chopsticks and bowls in the deepening darkness, Gahgit found Lei Yin close to the fire. Lei Yin glanced up warily as he approached. Casually, Gahgit squatted near him.

"Confucius said that if a wise man knew where one corner of a square was, he could find the other three," Gahgit said quietly.

Lei Yin continued to eat, not looking up.

"After dinner, I will sit alone by the stream." Gahgit stood up and strolled away, his heart pounding.

After returning his bowl and chopsticks, Gahgit walked to the stream. Anxiously, he drank with a cupped hand from the stream and sat down on a flat rock by the bank. He had rarely spoken to Lei Yin, whom he had first met working on this crew. Finding the big man loud and brash, Gahgit had avoided him. Now Gahgit waited to see if he had aroused Lei Yin's curiosity.

When Lei Yin's large shadow came toward him against the moonlight, he tensed. He glanced past the approaching silhouette to make sure the others remained by the cookfire. If he shouted for help, they would hear.

Gahgit decided to take the initiative, and spoke gruffly in a low tone. "You probably think the same as all the rest of them."

Lei Yin squatted several paces away, watching the current flow.

"Everyone thinks I loved Wanli like an elder brother." Gahgit hoped Wanli's spirit would not hear him smear their friendship with lies. "We could have been partners, but he wanted to keep everything for himself."

"Maybe a hungry ghost killed him," Lei Yin said casually.

"Hungry ghosts trip you or jostle your hand. They

don't carry big rocks over sixty paces and smash people's heads with them. That takes a strong man." Gahgit felt himself shaking. "I hoped to get a certain small rock from Wanli myself. You see, I know what it must be mixed with."

Lei Yin looked at him sharply.

"My uncle drank a liquid made with minerals. I know the mixture."

"What happened to your uncle?" Lei Yin's eyes remained on Gahgit.

"He never grew a day older." That was true, Gahgit told himself.

"Is it true?" Lei Yin whispered. He watched Gahgit for a long moment. "And you say you were not as close to Wanli as we believed?"

"I hated him," Gahgit said quietly, hating the words as he spoke them. "He would not let me share the drink we could have made, and I will not reveal the mixture unless I can share in it. So we never made it."

Moonlight shone on Lei Yin's face. "Why have you told me?"

Gahgit felt the time had come to tantalize Lei Yin again. "I have given you one corner of the square." He got to his feet, ready to walk away.

"I have it," Lei Yin said quietly.

Surprised, Gahgit stopped; he had not expected such a quick admission.

"I have Wanli's cinnabar." Lei Yin looked over his shoulder; the others had dispersed toward the saloon. "It will bring a good price back up in San Francisco. It would be worth even more with the recipe of the elixir."

"Wait," Gahgit whispered, thinking frantically. "You must have the map, too. We could mine all of it. But first we must drink the elixir."

"Drink it ourselves?" Lei Yin stared up at him, surprised.

"The rest of the crew can go north without us and never know what we have. We will grow no older as we mine all the cinnabar. The *lo fans* won't care if we want to make red paint." He forced a hollow laugh.

"Can we get the other ingredients in this little town?"

"Yes!" Gahgit thought quickly. "The others are common. When our crew finishes the wall and leaves, you and I can mix the elixir."

Lei Yin stood, looming over Gahgit in the darkness. "Get them now."

"Eh? Now?" Gahgit held his breath. "I, uh . . ."

"Now! When the others return, they'll be too drunk to care what we're doing. We shall mix the elixir now and take it!" He grinned excitedly.

Gahgit wanted to protest. He wasn't ready. Yet he could not think of any argument that would not contradict what he had said already.

Lei Yin smiled down at him. "Bring them back here. The cook has gone to the saloon with the others. I'll stir up the fire again."

"I'll see if the general store is open," Gahgit said faintly.

Gahgit walked slowly to the general store, past his drunken crewmates behind the saloon. He had planned to trick Lei Yin, but he needed calomel for his plan. Lei Yin's eagerness had caught him off-guard.

Maybe Gahgit could mix a harmless drink now and persuade Lei Yin to swallow another with calomel later. Yet Lei Yin might not drink two—and Gahgit wanted to ship home soon. This could be his only chance.

At the general store's rear door, the storekeeper was startled by Gahgit's order for small amounts of soda water, salt, pepper, borax, and other routine powders. Gahgit carried his purchases away in a wooden box. Since calomel had no particular value here, the store did not stock it.

Gahgit took an indirect path back toward the barracks. He walked up along the trees away from the stream, desperately trying to think of a new plan. Soon, behind the barracks, he could see Lei Yin's blocky shadow standing by the roaring fire. Gahgit lingered in the shadows, but he could not delay so long that Wanli's killer became suspicious.

Still stalling, he walked up to the modest burial site where Wanli's body now rested. The rocks, dirt, and gravel Gahgit and his companions had dug out of the ground now lay in a long mound over the shallow grave, helping protect the coffin below from wild animals.

Gahgit paused sadly by the grave, looking down at it in the moonlight.

The silvery light glistened on a small reddish-brown rock on the mound. Startled, Gahgit set down his box of ingredients and picked it up. As Wanli had said, they knew their rocks now, after spending so many years digging, blasting, and hammering up and down this land. Dark in color, this rough gray rock had pores partly filled with an earthy substance of a reddish-brown color. That was calomel.

Gahgit's heart raced. Until this moment his plan to avenge Wanli's murder had been abstract, for the future. Now he could carry it out. Remembering Wanli's easy laugh and his unbounded faith that they would find their fortune here, he drew in a deep breath and put the rock in the wooden box.

His anger rising again, Gahgit strode back to the fire behind the barracks, where the flamelight flickered over Lei Yin's heavy torso.

"Did you get everything you need?" Lei Yin whispered in awe.

"Yes," Gahgit whispered back. "Heat water, enough to fill two bowls." He squatted, placing the wooden box on the ground. "You have the cinnabar with you?"

"Of course." Lei Yin hung the cook's metal teakettle over the fire.

Gahgit took one of the rice bowls and carefully poured into it small amounts of all the substances he had bought. Aware that Lei Yin was watching every move, he pretended to measure each amount precisely. Last, Gahgit slipped the rock containing the calomel into the rice bowl of mixed powders and covered it. Then he stood up, holding the bowl.

"Uncover the kettle," Gahgit whispered.

With a cloth, Lei Yin lifted the lid.

"Put the cinnabar in first."

With his other hand, Lei Yin dropped the reddish rock into the kettle.

Gahgit poured all the ingredients in the rice bowl into the kettle after it. "Be prepared. When the vapors grow strong, the elixir is ready."

Gahgit picked up two more rice bowls. "We can drink from these."

Lei Yin took one, nodding, his eyes on the kettle.

Gahgit took a step back, certain that the calomel vapors had helped kill his uncle. When the vapor from the kettle began to grow thicker, he stepped back again. "Look inside. If you see globules of quicksilver, then pour the elixir into your bowl and drink it as fast as you can. It will be very hot." He remembered the quicksilver he had seen in his uncle's drink.

Lei Yin lifted the lid and leaned into the vapor as he looked inside the kettle. He tossed the kettle aside, gasping and coughing, and poured the liquid into the bowl. Then he raised it to his mouth—and stopped.

Instead of drinking, Lei Yin held his bowl out to Gahgit.

Startled, Gahgit shook his head. He bowed and spoke respectfully. "The cinnabar belongs to you. The first drink is yours."

"Drink it," Lei Yin commanded, holding out the steaming bowl.

"The . . . privilege should be yours." Gahgit eyed the vapors in terror.

Lei Yin stepped closer and held out the bowl at arm's length in front of Gahgit's face. "We are partners, are we not? Drink!"

Not daring to breathe, Gahgit tried to think of something to say.

Suddenly, without warning the bowl tipped out of Lei

Yin's hand, spilling its liquid onto the rocky ground at their feet.

Avoiding the vapors, Gahgit gasped for breath and spoke quickly. "That's an entire dose! Only one remains—and I want it!" Bluffing, he dodged around Lei Yin and reached for the kettle.

"No!" Lei Yin smacked him to the ground.

His head throbbing, Gahgit raised himself up on his elbows and watched Lei Yin lift the kettle. Firelight shone on the stocky man as he threw back his head, swaying his queue, and then poured the hot fluid into his mouth.

Lei Yin's eyes grew large and his mouth opened, seeking air; however, he drew in no breath. He staggered and then fell on his back. As the bowl dropped from his hand, his body quivered oddly.

Gahgit picked up his bowler and got to his feet. He looked around for their crewmates. A few were weaving their way back from the saloon. He warily watched the vapors still emanating from the kettle. In the cool mountain night, the vapors dissipated quickly and vanished into the darkness. Lei Yin lay still, the edge of Wanli's folded leather map sticking out of the waistband of his pants.

His head aching and his pulse still pounding, Gahgit let out a long sigh. With a glance back at his approaching crewmates, he slipped the map away from Lei Yin. Then he picked up the kettle and bowl at arm's length and carried them to the rippling stream. He heaved all three into the cold current, where the mountain waters would return any residue of calomel harmlessly back to the soil.

By the time Gahgit returned to the wooden box by the fire, Chun Guan and several of the others had drunkenly stopped to warm themselves.

"What's wrong with him?" Chun Guan pointed to Lei Yin.

"He asked me to bring him this box of items from

the general store. Maybe he had too much to drink while I was gone.'' Gahgit shrugged.

"No one likes him, anyway.'' Anger edged Chun Guan's drunken voice. "Maybe a hungry ghost tripped him, too.''

"Maybe so.'' Relieved yet still shaken, Gahgit walked away.

Alone in the moonlight, standing by the long mound over Wanli, Gahgit considered how he would take Wanli's coffin with him on his way home to Guangdong. Then he remembered how Wanli always said he would not go home without gold. Gahgit had none to send.

Suddenly, his spine tingling, Gahgit realized that Wanli was now a hungry ghost with no relatives here to make sacrifices for him. The small sacrifices at his funeral would not be enough. His spirit could be walking.

Don't worry! I'll always take care of you. Wanli had said to him.

Gahgit abruptly understood that the calomel he had found here had not been a simple accident; the spirit of Wanli, the hungry ghost of Panamint walking in the seventh month, had made sure Gahgit would find it. When Lei Yin had pushed the poisonous vapors up to Gahgit's face, Wanli had knocked the bowl out of his hand. Gahgit knew it.

Wanli had always believed in this land. Gahgit decided to leave Wanli's body here. Maybe if Gahgit remained in this land longer, instead of giving up, he would find his fortune yet. Certainly he would make the annual sacrifices to the spirit of his friend so he would not go hungry.

Gahgit adjusted his bowler and walked back to his tent in the moonlight, certain that Wanli's spirit walked with him.

Sharan Newman is a medieval historian with only a limp grasp on the modern world. Fortunately, she has been able to learn how to type well enough to write nine novels, first an Arthurian fantasy series, now being reprinted by Tor Books, and then her current medieval series featuring Catherine LeVendeur, and her husband, Edgar, who has never felt the need for a last name. The first, Death Comes as Epiphany, *was nominated for the Agatha and Anthony awards and won the Macavity for best first mystery. Others in the series have also received award nominations. Starting in 1138, Sharan has worked the series all the way up to 1146. The most recent book is* Cursed in the Blood, *in which Edgar takes Catherine home to Scotland to show her why he doesn't mind living in Paris.*

Having insisted for years that she can only write about the Middle Ages, Sharan surprised herself by writing a story set on the Kansas prairie in the 1890s. Her only excuse is that all those tales her grandmother told her about growing up in a sod house must have finally percolated to the surface.

THE PROMISED
LAND

Sharan Newman

M ary Kathleen Frances O'Connor knew the exact
moment when she began to plan the death of her
husband, mortal sin though it might be.

It was Independence Day 1891. John Patrick Timothy
O'Connor had invited all the county to a grand celebration at their homestead, uncaring of the fact that she,
who would be doing all the cooking, cleaning and most
of the hauling, was eight months pregnant with their
ninth child. The child was born that night and lived,
thanks be to God and none to John Patrick.

But angry though Mary Kathleen felt as she stirred
and baked and carried trays, even her fury at the cal-
lousness John Patrick showed toward her plight, wasn't
what made up her mind to murder him. If that were
enough, she'd have done it years before. It was what she
heard him say as she passed among the men with her
tray of corn fritters and watermelon slices. It froze her
in horror. It was at that exact moment that she knew that
enough was enough and, even if it cost her own soul, it
was her sacred duty to do the bastard in.

* * *

The seeds of her hatred had been planted long before, so far back that she wasn't aware when they sprouted and began to grow strong and full and ready to blossom, nourished all unknowing by John Patrick himself.

"It'll be a grand, glorious adventure!" John Patrick had insisted, the day he told her that he had sold their shop in Oughterad and proposed to emigrate the family to America.

"But we have so much here!" she had protested.

"We can have more!" he told her. "We're going to the Great State of Kansas, Kate. A broad, beautiful country, suited to our dignity. We'll no more be bowin' and scrapin' to the English. There's land to spare there. A man can have all he can earn. There'll be no limit to our wealth."

Mary Kathleen didn't answer. She gazed out the window of her mother's house in Ballyveane at Lough Mask and the fog curling round the trees, across the green fields and slithering over the stone fences. This was all the wealth she wanted.

"I've already sent in the papers to get the homestead. Your brother Anthony mailed me the forms," John Patrick continued. "Ah, won't it be nice, now, for you to be close to him again? You can drop by his farm in Sacramento every Sunday for tea."

Mary Kathleen had paid attention then and sat mute with shock as her husband rattled on about the glory of life in America.

"Miles of land!" He opened his arms wide, seeing the expanse in his mind. "Belonging to no one. All a man has to do is apply himself. A bit of hard work and a mite of luck and we'll become rich as the lords at Ashford! You'll have silk gowns like the Dublin ladies and our sons will never have to go with cap in hand to the *Sasanaigh* again."

America! Mary Kathleen couldn't imagine it. It was like telling her she was going to die tomorrow. All but one of her brothers had gone before, the family weeping

and praying for their souls as they left and each one of
the travellers setting out with faces so bright you'd have
thought they were off for the Isle of the Blest. The boys
had gone first to Colorado, looking for silver, and then
on to California, where they now had farms and orchards
and grand mansions. Or so their letters said.

But the boys had emigrated only in order that their
oldest brother might have the bit of land the family held,
to farm and raise the sheep and to keep their mother in
her old age. They had known that all the good jobs in
Ireland went to those who had no brogue and no crucifix.

But Mary Kathleen couldn't see why she had to leave,
as well.

"We don't need to emigrate, John Patrick," she had
pleaded. "Don't we have a fine house and shop right
here in town, with a well nearby and food enough for
our children, and a priest who will give us Communion
and preach in the Irish, whatever the English threaten?"

"Don't you see, girl?" John Patrick was so lost in
his vision, he thought it was clear to everyone. "There
are no English in America. We can speak the Irish all
day if we like. We can build our own chapel and hire a
priest. Think of it, on our own ranch. We'll run cattle
and sheep, thousands of them. Oh, Mary Kathleen, don't
you see? We'll no more be prisoners in our own country,
afraid to speak our tongue or make the sign of the cross.
In America, everyone is equal and free."

Mary Kathleen soon realized that there was nothing
for it but to go. John Patrick was her husband, bound to
her for life, and where he went, she must follow.

The shop had been cleaned out, the belongings
packed, the three children washed, dressed and shod for
the trip. On a cold, foggy morning the boat set forth,
with them in second class, as befitted their approaching
wealth, not huddled down below with the other Irish and
the Russians and Italians and Jews. Mary Kathleen
wasn't seasick at all on the boat. She just had morning
sickness from the time they left Limerick to the day they
landed in New York, where all the passengers joined her

at the rail to gape at the skyline with the almost-complete Statue of Liberty welcoming them through her scaffolded face.

Mary Kathleen felt a deep kinship with the immense statue at once. Lady Liberty had been brought across the ocean, too, and was now doomed to stand at the gate to this enormous, raw country, never to go home again. Did she ever dream of the lights of Paris? Kathleen covered her eyes as the ship passed by the sad face.

From New York, the train took them as far as Abilene. At first the green lands they passed through had been pleasant, homelike. The children chattered in excitement, wondering which of the neat, white houses was theirs. Then they had crossed the Missouri River and the prairie began.

Mary Kathleen was sure then that she had sinned dreadfully sometime in her life, for why else was she still breathing and transported to Hell and her poor children with her?

The sky stretched cloudless above her, a great blue bowl trapping her like a bee caught under a glass. The prairie lay beneath it, reaching to the horizon in all directions in a treeless expanse of gold. The town had been raw and wind-beaten, with a few straggly trees at the edge of the Kansas River, more mud than water that summer. The people there had been strangers, all false smiles and loud voices.

John Patrick had arranged for a wagon, oxen and tools, as well as the papers for his claim and his application for American citizenship. He laughed and joked with the men in the shops, telling them he'd be back in the spring to ship out of McCoy's stockyard.

"We'll be sure there's a space just for your herd." The man gave him a broad grin and shook his hand.

Only Mary Kathleen heard the mutter as they left, "Dumb mick won't last the winter. Mackerel-snappers now. What next?"

What next, indeed! she thought as they made the final leg of the journey to their new home.

The neighbors were kind, she had to give them that. They came from all the farms around that first Sunday afternoon, bearing pies and bread and sloe plum preserves. The women all had faces like old leather even though they wore bonnets. The men had weeping-willow whiskers and hands that crushed hers when they introduced themselves. Their voices were as flat as the prairie they lived on.

John Patrick had explained to her about how dear lumber was. They could use it only for the barn, to provide shelter for the animals and to store grain. People lived in solid sod houses that kept out the heat and cold, but not the grime.

"I left a good house in Oughterad to burrow into the earth like a mole!" Mary Kathleen wailed. "I'll not have my children born in a hole in the ground!"

The other women comforted her, mindful of her condition as several of them were in the same. They gave her advice on how to arrange the room and set up the cook stove, to cover the walls and pound down the floor to keep the dust from rising. She soon learned there was no wood, nor turf, to cook over. The children were sent out for a supply of buffalo chips, and Patrick Thomas, the eldest, was taught how to build and keep the fire.

It was over a year before Mary Kathleen finally came to terms with her new life. Not to love it as John Patrick did or to feel it to be home as the children soon did, but at least to accept what she saw no hope of changing, with the dull resignation of the damned. She dreamt of the lough and the rain of Ireland, soft on the skin, not roaring and raging like the Kansas storms. She learned to fill her longing for green in the little space of spring when the shoots first appeared and to comfort herself with the fact that all the children had the Gaelic and spoke it with her at home.

She might never have managed even that much if Daniel and his family hadn't come to the door.

The knock came early on a winter afternoon of their second year on the plains. The wind was cutting across the prairie, making the sod house for once a welcoming place. Clouds threatened snow, but none had fallen. When the knock came, Mary Kathleen opened the door without thinking. When she saw her visitor she slammed it shut, with a stifled scream.

She had known there were savages still on the prairie. The other women had told her stories of the old days, before the American Civil War. It wasn't like that now, they assured her. Indians might be dirty and thieving, but they didn't attack anymore. Not in Kansas. The army had put the fear of the Lord into them.

The knock came again. What should she do? John Patrick and Patrick Thomas had gone south for the winter, to join the cattle drive north. There was no one to run to.

Mary Elizabeth, the oldest girl, had seen the Indians standing there.

"Mam, don't be scared," she said. "They're just hungry. Everyone says so. Give them food and they'll go."

The newest baby, the fifth, began to cry. Mary Kathleen signalled to Mary Elizabeth to see to him. Then she licked her lips and, trying not to remember the horrific pictures in the illustrated papers of maddened savages holding up dripping scalps, she opened the door again.

The man who stood before her did not appear ready to slit her throat. He stared at her with a weary sadness that reminded her of the face of Lady Liberty, lighting the way for the freedom of others with none for herself. He wore a ragged greatcoat that had been mended with bright yarn and feathers. Mary Kathleen looked over his shoulder and saw the woman behind him on a mule, a worn buffalo robe wrapped around her. From beneath the robe, another pair of small legs protruded.

The Indian waited until Mary Kathleen's eyes returned to his face. He closed his own eyes briefly before he spoke.

"My family is in need of food," he said. "You have no man here now. I know they've all gone. I can haul water and chop wood for you, whatever you need."

Mary Kathleen just stared. John Patrick had left them well supplied with food. Part of her was frightened of what the savage might do if she denied his request. Another part looked at them and saw the Flight into Egypt. The thin legs of the child smote her heart. She wished she could ask the priest what to do, but despite John Patrick's promise, there was no Catholic church near them, only Baptists and Presbyterians. Going to them was consorting with the enemy.

"You can warm yourselves in the barn . . ." she began. She shivered. That sounded something like blasphemy, or worse, something the English would do. Hadn't she seen the poor of Ireland turned from the castle gates to starve and freeze in the roads. She couldn't do that.

Mary Kathleen opened the door.

"*Tar isteach*." she said. "Come in and welcome. *Dia's Muire dhuit*. I'm Mary Kathleen O'Connor and these are my children. You'll honor us with your company this evening?"

Now the Indian's eyes narrowed in suspicion. He looked past Mary Kathleen. The house had only one room with an alcove for the bed. The curtain to that was open and the third eldest child, Thomas Edward, and George Washington, the first American-born, sat watching.

"Mam," Thomas Edward asked. "Can the Indian teach me to do a war whoop?"

The man's face didn't change, but he entered the house. Behind him, the woman got off the mule and led it to the barn, the child following her.

"I'll not feed you in the house and them in the barn!" Mary Kathleen told him indignantly.

"They will return presently to eat," the man said. "We prefer to sleep in your outbuilding. I am called Daniel. What would you like me to do first?"

"We get our water down at the creek," Mary Kathleen told him. "I could use some more, but I thought Indians made their women do that sort of chore."

Daniel nodded, as if considering this.

"Times change," he said finally, picking up the bucket.

Although the family stayed with them until nearly spring, Mary Kathleen never got to know Daniel's wife well. She spoke little English and seemed not to wish to. Mary Kathleen understood that. She hadn't wished to learn English, either. But at school they were beaten for using the Irish. She let the woman be. Their little boy was bright and undaunted by whatever calamity had driven his parents to begging. He spent his time with Thomas Edward, the two of them understanding each other in the way children do, without need for words in common.

But Daniel was a different matter. Apart from the newspaper illustrations and comments of the neighbors, Mary Kathleen knew nothing about Indians. One thing she had been told was that they were dirty and stank. But with the odor of burning buffalo chips permeating the sod roof and walls, her nose couldn't take on any more, so she didn't notice any odor. And with the lack of water for bathing, the best she could do was to see that her family's faces, hands and feet were clean. Daniel's wife washed her little boy every time Mary Kathleen wiped a rag across the children. So it appeared that those stories weren't true. As for thieving, what was there to steal? All they had was a missal and the locket with the picture of her mother inside that Mary Kathleen never took off.

At first Daniel said little, but as winter wore on and the snow came to isolate them, he formed the habit of stopping for a few minutes in the evenings to discuss the next day's work. His wife never came with him, but stood outside the barn door, watching until he returned.

"Your wife," Mary Kathleen asked once. "She doesn't like me, does she?"

"She's grateful for your charity, as am I," Daniel answered.

"But she never smiles," Mary Kathleen insisted. "Or don't Indian women believe in smiling?"

Daniel gave her a look almost of amusement. "She asked the same thing of you," he said. "I told her I'd seen many white women laughing, but she didn't believe it. We've never seen you smile. I told her your religion forbade it."

He took the covered dish of corn and salt pork back to the barn, leaving Mary Kathleen to ponder his words.

She sat by the fire that night thinking about it. When had she last laughed, or even smiled? She couldn't remember. She felt her face with her hands. The mirror she had brought to America had broken long ago. Her fingers traced lines she didn't remember from her nostrils to the corners of her mouth and another set pulling from her mouth down her chin. How long had they been there?

It was a stupid question. She knew. The day she had let her feet leave Irish soil the frown lines had begun. What was there to smile at trapped in perdition?

Daniel and his family left when the wild geese flew over, heading north. Mary Kathleen didn't think to ask where they were going, just as she had never wondered how Daniel came by such fine English. All of the New World was a mystery to her.

John Patrick was angry when he learned she had taken Indians into their home.

"Have you no sense, girl?" he shouted. "You all could have been murdered in your beds, or worse! They're wicked, heathen people who would stew baby Mary Margaret for dinner if the Army didn't keep them in line."

His words frightened Mary Kathleen, but not because she believed them.

"They were just poor and hungry," she answered him. "They did us no harm. We ate better thanks to Daniel's hunting."

"Daniel, is it?" John Patrick roared. "He gives you

a Christian name and you think he's just like you? You can be sure they don't call him that at home. It's Chief Cutting-Throat or Bashing-Head to his family, it is. Don't you be lettin' them in again or I'll . . ."

He noticed the children, clustered protectively around their mother's skirts and also how high her apron was tied over her once-again swollen stomach.

"You'll what, John Patrick?" Mary Kathleen asked.

"I'll be wrathful, woman," he answered with satisfaction at finding an unspecific threat. "You don't want to see it."

"That I don't," she said and left him thinking he had won.

Each summer was like the one before, hard work and often another baby. Mary Kathleen loved her children passionately but she couldn't understand how they could take to this cruel landscape and even thrive in it. The next autumn, John Patrick and the oldest boys joined the other men bound for Texas. They took their pay in cattle and the herd grew each year. There was even talk of getting a spur line from the railroad right by their ranch to transport the beef to market in Omaha and Chicago and save the stockyard fees in Abilene. There was money now, to buy a new mirror and a silk dress for Sunday. All John Patrick's promises were coming true. But they were the fulfillment of his dreams, not hers.

Other Indians came to the door sometimes, to beg food or trade for it. They never stayed. Mary Kathleen watched them go and wondered if they were heading for a promised land of their own. She didn't suppose it would welcome her.

Letters came from Ireland. Her mother died and John Patrick sent money for a headstone. He sent more money to his brothers, who wrote asking for support in their struggle to throw off the English yoke.

"If they drive the *Sasanaigh* out of Ireland," she asked him, "will we go home again?"

"Home?" He laughed. "And isn't this our home?

Isn't it all I said it would be? A few more good years and I'll own more land than all the lords in Galway. I'll even buy the boards to make you a real house, with a parlor for weddings, funerals and when the priest comes to call."

The thought of a fine house only grieved her more.

It must be me, she thought. *I'm a wicked, sinful girl to be hating my husband after all the good things he had done for me.*

Nothing could make her love this alien land, but she knew it was her duty to love John Patrick. Nevertheless, she found herself loathing him more each day with each new sign of prosperity he brought her. Why? She wanted to ask the priest, but the new Catholic church only five miles away was staffed by men who were holy enough, she was sure, but who only spoke Czech and Latin.

The winter of 1890 was bleaker than usual, but Mary Kathleen had run out of expectations. There were eight children now and the ninth was beginning to show. Only Mary Elizabeth, Mary Margaret and the youngest two boys, one still in the cradle, kept the homestead until spring.

The knock was soft. At first Mary Kathleen thought it was only something being blown against the door. But the sound was repeated. She sent Mary Elizabeth to see who it was.

Her daughter's gasp made Mary Kathleen leap from her chair and grab the rifle.

"Who is it?" She tried to make her voice gruff.

Even after five years the voice was not one she could mistake.

"I've come to see if you need any wood chopped or water carried," Daniel said.

Mary Kathleen opened the door to him. She peered over his shoulder into the growing blizzard.

"Where is your family?" she asked.

"They aren't with me anymore," he answered.

She didn't ask him then. The grief in his eyes forbade it. She fed him first and gave him his old place to sleep in the barn. But he told her the next day as he cleaned the cow stalls while she milked.

"My wife died of a fever last winter," he said with no sign of emotion. "She said the land killed her. She always hated it here."

The rhythm of Mary Kathleen's milking stuttered.

"But this is your land," she said. "How could she hate it?"

"This isn't our land," Daniel answered, still shovelling manure. "We were driven here, not that long ago. My home is in the woods of the north, near what you white people call the Great Lakes. Soldiers came and told us we had no right to stay. They made us come here, but we didn't know how to live on the prairie and the people already here didn't want us. We should have stayed home and fought. It would have been better to die."

Mary Kathleen pressed her cheek against the cow's warm flank and closed her eyes to stop the tears.

"The English at least let us stay in Ireland, even if it was only to starve," she said.

A bud began to unfold on the tree of her loathing.

Daniel continued. "They took my son this autumn and sent him to the missionary school, the same one that taught me. I told him to learn all he could, but whatever they did to him, not to forget who he was, inside."

Mary Kathleen was ashamed of the tears, for they were as much for herself as for Daniel.

"I should have stayed and died, too, rather than come to a place where such things are done," she cried. "Oh, how I want to go home!"

Daniel stopped his work and looked at her.

"Why don't you, then?" he asked. "White people can go wherever they like."

"I can't," she answered. "My children and I are tied to John Patrick. It says in the Bible that a wife must go with her husband and lodge where he lodges and be buried next to him."

Daniel shook his head. "That was Ruth and Naomi, two women. Not a husband and wife."

She gaped at him.

"Missionary school," he said.

Mary Kathleen shrugged.

"All I know is that when John Patrick and I were married, both my mother and the priest told me my soul would burn forever if I broke my vows."

Daniel nodded. "Then you must remain here." He went back to shovelling manure.

They spoke no more of it. Daniel left a few days later. Mary Kathleen gave him a bag of dried beef and berry jams to take to his son. But his words and the look in his eyes haunted her all winter.

Spring came and with it John Patrick and the boys. The frame for the new house was raised, crops put in. The days grew long with a heat that beat down all day and then rose from the earth after the sun went down. And Independence Day arrived.

John Patrick and his friends were standing where the front drive would be to the new house. They were congratulating each other on their success.

"And to think there were people who wanted to keep us from coming in here," one man said.

"What for?" John Patrick asked.

"Why, you know this all use ta be Indian territory." The neighbor laughed. "Some fool in Washington thought we should leave it to 'em. There was some ruckus about it, but in the end sense prevailed."

"Thank goodness for that." John Patrick laughed, too. "They had their chance and what did they do with it? This place was nothing when we got here. It would be a fool in Washington who'd want to waste prime land like this on a bunch of lazy, dirty savages who never ever put a plow to it. I've seen 'em in Abilene, laying out behind the saloons, dead drunk in the middle of the day. Disgusting!"

The men all expressed agreement and went back to

their discussion of what to plant along the drive.

John Patrick's speech hit Mary Kathleen right between the eyes, and the long-tended plant suddenly burst into full flower.

Mary Kathleen's eyes grew round and her hands trembled with the horror of her discovery. Now she understood why she had grown to hate her husband.

As a good daughter of Galway she had been weaned on resentment of the English overlords. The English were wicked tyrants who had overrun their home and forced the Irish to live according to the English language and English laws. It was the sworn pledge of every good Irishman to resist them.

John Patrick had brought her to a land where all were equal and every man had the opportunity to be whatever he wanted. They had come to escape the tyranny of the invader. But they didn't forget those left behind. John Patrick was proud of being Irish. Didn't he send money home for guns to help in the struggle? Wasn't part of his delight in his success the joy he got from thumbing his nose at the oppressor they had left behind?

With a blinding realization, Mary Kathleen knew then that they hadn't escaped the English; they had *become* the English. They had done in Kansas what the English had done in Galway. And that was the moment when she understood that John Patrick, like all tyrants, had to perish.

It was also the moment when her labor began. She brought forth her last child with murder in her heart.

"I swear," she whispered, when the baby had been taken to be washed and wrapped. "By all the saints of Ireland, John Patrick, as soon as I'm on my feet again, I'll be weeping at your funeral."

Two days later, while Mary Kathleen lay in bed nursing her new son, Patrick Thomas rushed in with the news that his father had been thrown from his horse and killed.

"Something just spooked it, Mother," he told her, tears streaming. "There was nothing there and it just reared up and tossed him off, right onto the rocks. I'm sorry, Mam, I shouldn't a told you like that. Mam? It was quick, I'll say that. He couldn't a felt much. Mam . . . Mam? Don't worry, Mam, we'll take care of you.''

Mary Kathleen stared at the crucifix over the bed, still wearing a dried branch from Palm Sunday. She wasn't worried about how they would survive. Patrick Thomas was nearly eighteen and would keep the ranch and the farm together until his brothers and sisters were old enough to share in it.

She couldn't believe it. Ten years in America and her prayers had never been answered. But one little curse, and God had taken her at her word. She had been spared the trouble of finding a way to kill John Patrick and the shame to her family when they hanged her for doing it. She would have to say a rosary every night in gratitude.

And she would live the rest of her life in Kansas.

Mary Kathleen knew that, without even asking a priest. There was always a penance, a price. Mary Kathleen would pay it, like the Lady in the harbor, with her eyes looking out to the land she was exiled from and her back always to the promised land she could never enter.

She raised her children to be good Irish Catholics. They all married children of Bohemian and German immigrants. Mary Elizabeth's husband was even a Methodist. Twenty years Mary Kathleen served out her penance. Ireland became more of a dream than a memory.

The newfangled horseless carriage raised a cloud of dust as it came up the long drive. Mary Kathleen sat on the porch, fanning herself and wondering if it was some government man wanting to raise the taxes again.

The man who got out of the car was dark, with silver hair and a tailored suit. Government. Had to be.

Then she saw his face.

"Daniel!" she exclaimed. "Where did you come from? What happened to you?"

"I went back," he told her. "I went back home and

fought. My son got some law books and we managed to find a way to buy back what had been stolen from us. We built a settlement way back in the Wisconsin woods, and sell lumber all the way down to Oklahoma. We've down well.''

"I'm glad for you, Daniel," she said. "Then why have you come back here?"

"To thank you," he answered. "It was from you that I understood that we weren't the only ones who had been robbed of our heritage. It gave me the courage to find a way to overcome what the white man wanted me to be.''

Then he smiled at her. "And I came back to bring you this.''

He opened his satchel and brought out a leather portfolio.

"I heard of your husband's death and that you had stayed for your children's sake. But now that they're grown, I thought you might want this, after all.''

He handed her a steamship ticket. One-way to Limerick.

"It's to take you home, Mary Kathleen," he explained.

In wonder, she reached out for the ticket. Who would have thought redemption could come in an envelope?

Mary Kathleen Frances O'Connor looked at Daniel and smiled.

Carole Nelson Douglas seems to be able to write in any genre. She began in the newspaper business and has published fantasy (The Sword and Circlet Trilogy), science fiction (Counterprobe), historical novels (Lady Rogue), romantic suspense (Crystal Nights), and in mysteries, both modern (the Midnight Louis series) and historical. In her Irene Adler series, from Good Night, Mr. Holmes to Irene's Last Waltz, Carole chronicles the life of the only person who ever got the best of Sherlock Holmes. Irene's adventures rival anything that ever happened to the sleuth of Baker Street and are told, not always approvingly, by Penelope Huxleigh, an impoverished parson's daughter not accustomed to the sliding morals of the upper classes.

In the following story, Irene manages to shock Penelope again with a revelation from her past.

MESMERIZING
BERTIE

Carole Nelson Douglas

M y friend Irene Adler Norton was almost super-
stitiously reticent about her past, and especially
so during the first decade of our long association. Even
after the veil had been rent apart by the startling revelations of our American adventure, she remained a life-
long font of sudden, surprising disclosures. At least she
did so to me.

I was never to know when I would be handed one of
these hidden rarities, as if I were an unworthy heiress
being entrusted with the extravagant family jewels piece
by niggardly piece.

Her shocking association with kings had begun even
before she encountered the Crown Prince—later King—
of Bohemia, though I had no idea how early in life she
had begun keeping inappropriate company. Irene had
long been retired from the operatic stage. With her husband, Godfrey Norton, we resided in the village of
Neuilly, then still far outside the pretensions of Paris,
and Edward VII—formerly the inexplicably tolerated
Prince of Wales, dubbed ''Bertie'' even by those who
should never have the opportunity to curtsy to his portly

figure—had finally become King, God rest Good Queen
Victoria.

Forgive my asides. Writing a diary is a scattered sort
of pursuit, and I have been at it far too long to aspire to
organization now.

When I learned the horrid truth about Messrs. Gilbert
and Sullivan, librettist and composer respectively, and
the Prince of Wales, Irene and I were sharing a cup of
good English tea in front of an especially showy French
fire (even the logs of the French cannot burn in a steady,
quiet English manner, but must snap and spark like quar-
reling, ill-tempered poodles). Our dear Godfrey had been
detained in Paris on business, and in his case—if not in
that of most mortal men, apparently—that circumstance
was always true.

Irene almost dozed before the performing flames, a
rare condition for one of her restless temperament.
Twenty years seemed not to have touched her exquisite
features, a fact which made men marvel and women bri-
dle.

"I have not shocked you in ages, Nell," she observed
suddenly, looking up at me.

I was engaged in a useful pursuit and was not about
to be weaned away from my crochet-work.

"Perhaps you no longer notice my pitifully ineffective
remonstrances," I replied. "You never did heed them."

"No, that's not it. The fact is that you have grown
worldly."

"Old, you mean."

"Hardly. I do not hold with the notion of failing powers. Look at Sarah Bernhardt."

"I never cared to do so before and do not see why I
should now."

"You may disapprove of her private life, but her public one is still a triumph. She acts superbly, as ever."

"As you would sing superbly, did you care to keep
it up."

"Oh, I cared to keep it up." Irene sighed and turned

toward the fire again. "Circumstances did not permit."
She smiled. At least the corners of her mouth turned up.
"I was remembering my first vocal assignments after I
arrived in London from New York. My apprenticeship
in those models of a modern major operetta by Gilbert
and Sullivan."

"Extreme nonsense dispensed at an incredible
speed."

"Nicely put. Satire must be speedy, Nell, else it become leaden instead of lethal."

"There was nothing lethal about any Gilbert and Sullivan presentation that I ever heard tell of."

Irene turned to me, what I had pictured as her smile
in profile now revealed in full frontal form as the pred-
atory grin with which a cat might greet a mouse.

"Then let me tell you of my first Gilbert and Sullivan
assignment, which turned lethal indeed."

"Had you and I met yet?"

"Yes, this was the autumn following that fateful year
of 1881. How odd it is to be just past the gate of a new
century, with flying machines and motorcars ahead of
us, with hot-air balloons and horse-buses behind us."

"Apparently ill-behavior is not behind us, or you
would not be resurrecting some sordid incident from
your theatrical past. Why did you not tell me of this
incident at the time?"

"Gilbert and Sullivan are considered the most respectable of impresarios," Irene said with a demureness that
she could still carry off past age forty; perhaps because,
like the Gilbert and Sullivan pieces under discussion,
satire always underlay her amusement. "The Crown
Prince of Bohemia was not my first, you know, Nell."

"First what?" I asked hastily, perhaps paling a bit. I
do so detest late-life confessions of youthful indiscre-
tions.

"First Crown Prince."

"You knew another, earlier? Who?"

"Yours."

"Mine? Unlike you, I count no princes among my admirers. Indeed, I count no admirers."

"Ah, but they count you, Nell. Who? I admit he has grown as large and grizzly as a Wild West bear, but then he was quite the dandy."

"Not . . . the previous Prince of Wales? You met him, Irene, and did not tell me?"

She nodded, settling into her emerald velvet dressing gown.

"I feared you would misunderstand. You were such a sheltered soul in those days. I was performing the obligatory chorus work on the stage of D'Oyly Carte's sparkling new electrically lit Savoy Theatre . . . virtually unknown amidst that bevy of buxom sopranos, virtually unheard amidst all that tremolo and vibrato. Unnoticed, save that when Mr. Gilbert was entertaining the Prince of Wales for dinner he invited all the young-lady cast members he considered sufficiently decorative for an informal state dinner, and he considered me to be of fresh interest. In fact, that was my only reason for attending Mr. Gilbert's dinner: to charm, to bewitch, to beguile, to mesmerize his noble guest of honor. Thus I met my first Crown Prince."

"I never thought of Our Prince that way. I remember shuddering when everyone on the street called him 'Bertie' in that odiously familiar way, as if he were a street vendor or hack driver."

" 'Bertie's popularity is understandable. Ma-*ma* was so boringly formal in her widow's weeds; the people yearned for a gregarious royal."

"The people got a Clown Prince. And his, his amatory escapades. Most unbecoming!"

"That sort of thing runs in royal families, like hemophilia and gout, Nell. Ah, but Bertie's famous failing was why I was fortunate enough to meet him. Mr. Gilbert himself was dedicated to what was called 'feminine pulchritude' then. After dinner, even when the Prince was not in attendance, Mr. Gilbert turned the tables on custom. He would banish the men to the drawing room to smoke their cigars, while the young ladies remained behind with him to sip sherry.''

"A harem! What a detestable image. The man was married, was he not?''

"As Bertie was, and is, so was and is he.'' Irene cuddled her chin in her robe's lavish velvet folds. ''That evening was also my first opportunity to observe another phenomenon of the time: a telephone.''

"The devil's invention.''

Irene glanced at the black instrument dangling its ugly cords from a small round table near the hall. ''Certainly as ugly as the devil, but most useful now, and most amazing then. After dinner, Mr. Gilbert rang up the Savoy, where the new operetta was in rehearsal, and let us all listen to the cast trilling away like high-strung automatons in the background.

"Irene, I fear your memory has deceived you. If that was in 1882, the telephone was not in use yet.''

"Among the privileged, it could be. Gilbert was so proud of his unheard-of link between his handsome house in Kensington and the Savoy Theatre. He handed the earpiece first to the Prince, who listened with mouth agape, growing paler of complexion by the instant.''

"One cannot blame even a prince for being leery of such an unsettling invention. People talking to one from miles away in disembodied voices, as if usurping the right of the angels.''

"You never neglect to take a call when Quentin telephones,'' she returned slyly.

"That is different. He is truly in a foreign quarter of the world and must resort to extravagant means of communication.''

"Extravagant means of communication were what Gilbert and Sullivan were all about. And that early telephone of Mr. Gilbert's was about to play a rather unwanted role in his programme for the evening.''

I knew Irene well enough to know when to prick up my ears.

"Something happened that night? Something untoward? Mysterious? And you never told me until now?''

''How quick you have become.''

Quick as a crumpet! caroled the odious parrot Casanova from the music room, on hearing a favorite cue. Parrots are obscenely long-lived. *Quick as a crumpet*!

I confess that I have often contemplated taking a good length of my sturdy crochet cord and . . .

''Nell! You look so overwrought. I will speed up my narrative like one of Gilbert's patter songs. The call that came a few minutes later announced not a wonder, but a tragedy. One of the peris had died, had been found crumpled before the very phone stand in the wings.''

''One of the Perrys?''

''I should tell you that the operetta in rehearsal was *Iolanthe*; or *The Peer and the Peri*.''

''What is a 'Perry?' ''

''P-e-r-i. A Persian fairy.''

I shook my head. ''Harems again.''

''At any rate, I knew I must see the death scene immediately.''

''You were always morbid to a fault, from an alarmingly early age.''

''So I drew Mr. Gilbert, who seemed quite shocked, to one side. Indeed, the entire room was buzzing and the Prince of Wales, who had been subdued ever since hearing the telephone call of the chorus, was positively pasty-faced. Mr. Gilbert was sick that his gala dinner party for the Prince had taken such a dark turn.''

''What could *you* tell him?''

''That I had worked as a private inquiry agent for the Pinkertons in America and that I must see the dead peri at once. Mr. Gilbert was upset by the social ramifications, but he had never considered . . . murder.''

''Murder? On the stage?''

''Off stage, actually, I discovered when I arrived at the Savoy in Mr. Gilbert's personal equipage. She was found in the wings. Appropriate site for a slain fairy, I suppose. I knew her, Nell. Not well, of course. Her given name was Christine, a pretty girl with a pretty voice, but otherwise unremarkable, except in her manner of death. She lay there in her crumpled gauze, the tiny electric halo in her hair still lit by the device between the 'wings' on her back.''

"Did you know anything more about her, Irene? Her associates perhaps.''

"Hardly. I was new to the company. But the moment I saw her pale, absurdly haloed form on the backstage floor, I knew two things. She had indeed been murdered. Blood had pooled beside her blond head and her crushed halo. A fly-weight—a heavy lead bar, Nell, used to keep the scrims stored high in the above-stage flies—lay not far away. Its surface bore a bit of blood and fairy-dust.''

"Dreadful! Not at all like Gilbert and Sullivan! What else did you know?''

"That the answer to this conundrum was not to be found on this sad site, but back in Kensington at Mr. Gilbert's house.''

"The cast must have been distraught.''

"Indeed. So distraught that they had not thought to use the nearby phone to inform Mr. Gilbert until they had trampled all over the site. That herdlike behavior would have driven our Mr. Holmes mad, had he been called in to consult on the matter, which he was not.''

"In my opinion, he has always been mad.''

"Even in his purported regard for me?'' Irene's smile was wry.

"*Especially* in his purported regard for you. A man of his eccentric habits and meager lifestyle can hardly aspire to one of your talent, beauty and renown.''

"I had no idea I was so highly placed beyond the reach of mere mortals in your opinion.''

"I should have added 'potential' as an adjective. It is a pity that you have not applied your abilities to greater good than meddling in private affairs over the years.''

"I performed a good deed that evening; I relieved two disquieted men's minds.''

"Two? Which two men? One, of course, was Mr. Gilbert, who had heard that his production in rehearsal had been struck by a tragedy that would soon become public, and who else? The murderer?''

"No. The witness."

"But you plainly said that the poor dead fairy-girl had been 'found' in that condition. I presume that the murderer at least had the sense to flee the scene before anyone discovered his deed?''

"Oh, yes. At first, when I saw the . . . depression in the poor girl's skull, I thought that she had been struck by a walking stick . . . something about the angle. But for a walking stick to be lethal, many blows would be required, unless it was a weighted stick. That fact reminded me of the many fly-weights found backstage. When I examined the wing area, I found the lead weight lying on the floor, a weapon far more likely to kill with one furious strike.''

"So there was no witness, unless you could prevail upon this fly-weight to testify. I presume that even in your legendary younger days your charm was not strong enough to coax testimony from solid lead.''

"No. No . . . but I was able to coax testimony from another inanimate object on the scene.''

I frowned. Irene knew how to draw out the point of a story longer than she could prolong a high *C*. Ultimately, either feat became more irritating than entertaining.

"The telephone. So you then—''

"Returned to Mr. Gilbert's carriage and instructed the driver to master to Bolton House in Kensington. First, though, I instructed the stage manager to use the telephone to call Scotland Yard. He was most flustered and said he would have to send someone, as he didn't know how to call the Yard. This shows the extent of utter ignorance about the telephone, and how such a private argument could be carried on in its unnoticed presence.''

"It seems to me you spent most of that evening flying across London in a carriage. Not a very propitious opportunity to meet and charm a Crown Prince.''

"Yes. Crown Princes invariably prove unlucky for

me. No doubt that is why I was wise to settle upon a mere barrister.''

''I will not hear Godfrey described as 'mere,' by anyone, Irene. Not even you.''

''I was speaking in purely comparative terms, as the world recognizes them. At any rate, I was soon hurtled back to Kensington and into Mr. Gilbert's withdrawing room. I reported my conclusions privately, which left the lyricist speechless and nearly as pale and wan as one of his fair maidens in the chorus.'' Irene smiled nostalgically. ''Then I made Mr. Gilbert pale to the roots of his hair. I asked for permission to speak with the Prince privately.''

''Irene! What a scandal!''

''The gentlemen seemed less distressed by the evening's lethal events than by their potential for scandal. Mr. Gilbert was more taken aback than the Prince, and apologized profusely for my forwardness, explaining that when I was not performing, I functioned as a 'sort of professional snoop.'

''The Prince, though, regarded me thoughtfully as well as somewhat lasciviously, then asked that a room be provided. I suggested a small parlor.''

''Did a house as grand as that contain a small parlor?''

''Alas, no, but there was a morning room, and soon Bertie and I were tucked away in it, as cozy as two tea balls on a doily.''

I groaned.

''He really is a charming fellow, though a bit . . . thick. Wanted to do whatever he could to help. I asked him to repeat what he had heard over the telephone from the Savoy.''

''You asked him to sing? To sing Gilbert and Sullivan?''

''That's what I could have evoked, a chorus from *Iolanthe*. Instead, I was rewarded with silence or stutters.''

''From the Prince of Wales?''

She nodded soberly. ''It seems His Highness could

hardly describe what he had heard, he had been so amazed by the mere phenomenon of hearing it from afar, and not a word of it remained in his memory. I told him that a murderer might escape if his memory remained so overawed, and, further, that I doubted some quatrains of Gilbert and Sullivan at their collaborative best could account for the pallor that swept his features the instant he put the telephone receiver to his ear. Besides, I suggested, he surely had tried such a device before; it was not the first such thing in London, and a Royal Personage would be given what passes for *droit de seigneur* these days: first go at a new invention.''

"Irene! I blush for your American effrontery. This was no way to treat a Prince of Wales."

"But it *was* the way to treat a reluctant witness. As soon as I explained the situation, the Prince was only too eager to stammer out his story, on my promise to keep his confession confidential.''

''*His* confession? The Prince killed the peri!''

"No. The Peer killed the peri. But in the course of doing so, he almost gave his future liege-lord a seizure.''

"He was the Heir to the Throne, and you trifled with his health!''

"Not I. 'Twas the unfortunate true-life drama occurring in the wings of the Savoy Theatre that trifled with Bertie's well-being. Neither player noticed the homely instrument set on a table nearby, nor realized that it transmitted their words to His Royal Highness.

"So when the Prince lifted the earpiece to enjoy a bit of musical patter, instead he heard a woman speaking, an angry, tearful woman. 'You have treated me horribly,' she raged in a high, clear singer's voice. 'Do you think that a few paltry jewels allow you to consider me as a mere convenience? I shall tell your wife and family. I shall tell all the world. They shall make a Gilbert and Sullivan opera of it before I am through.' Poor Bertie.''

"Poor Bertie? He had nothing to do with it. For once, he was innocent.''

"Ah, but over all he has never been innocent. He took

the words as meant for him, don't you see, Nell? Instead of a fairyland chorus, he heard a vow of revenge. He relied on none of his mistresses ever betraying what is unspoken common knowledge. Everyone knows, but no one says. Yet, here was this young woman, threatening to break the silence and speak. No doubt the telephone distorted her voice. Did the Prince recognize it? He thought perhaps he should, and, guilty, assumed these threats were directed at him. If the dead girl's words could make a Crown Prince pale, what would they do to the well-born man who had seduced her?''

"So you knew why, and what sort of person had struck her, but no name."

"Of course Scotland Yard could look into her acquaintanceship and perhaps turn up some man. I am sorry to say that in those days hardly a female was on the stage who did not have some wealthy or titled 'protector.' Scotland Yard could not investigate too openly; that would be impolitic. I thought that perhaps the Prince might know, and not know."

"You mean—?"

"He was so unnerved by what he took for a personal threat, that he hardly heard the words, or remembered exactly what she said. That is when I joined him on the settee and took his royal hand—"

"Irene!"

"And then produced a talisman I carried about my person in those days, an item of jewelry on a chain that I seldom wore visibly."

Irene sat up in the armchair to lift the fine gold chain that hung to her waist, weighted down by Godfrey's long-ago engagement gift of a clef-and-key diamond brooch suspended from it. (I choose to think of it as an engagement gift: what else would he have given her it for, since they were not yet wed at the time?) Irene was not speaking of this later trinket, which would not come into her possession for six more years, but now she swung the brooch to and fro before the flames. A fairy

halo of white-hot fire etched itself on the surrounding
darkness.

"Using some bauble like this is a trick I acquired
before I left America," Irene went on. "The Prince was
quite enchanted. And I was there, after all, to charm
him."

"You didn't! You didn't Mesmerize the Prince of
Wales?" I . . . er, wailed.

"He was a most accommodating subject." Her laughter ebbed and flowed like the leaping flames. "His stut-
ter vanished completely. He was able to recall details
omitted in his first recital. The type of jewels, for instance. Not just 'jewels,' but green sapphires."

"Such things do not exist."

"They do, but few know of them, as your remark just
proved. The family who holds them would not be hard
to trace. Besides, the dead woman spat a given name in
her fury. It meant nothing to me, but the Prince knew it
well and, with some further charming, provided a sur-
name and a title. I passed these on to Scotland Yard,
testifying as myself, a peripheral peri, a mere chorus
member who heard the dead girl mention just such
damning things. Whether they ever arrested such a
prominent man or not was up to them. Certainly, everything was done to hush up the matter."

"And the Prince?"

"He seemed distressed by the evening's events. I
played nursemaid and sent him to sleep with a warm
glass of milk and a nanny's kiss. He should have come
fully to himself in the carriage taking him back to his
residence."

"Did you ever hear anything more of the case?"

"Not a word. *Iolanthe* has gone on to recognition as
one of Gilbert and Sullivan's most highly regarded
works; Sullivan soon went on to a knighthood, and Gilbert still waits for his—which shows how the poor
wordsmith is devalued against the note-stringer; the
Prince has gone on to a Kingship. And I . . . have gone
on. A fairly happy ending, would you not say, Nell?"

"I suppose so. Certainly the Peer who struck the peri did so in a rash act of fear and passion. I would guess that your clues were too specific for Scotland Yard to ignore. He must have faced some kind of punishment."

"Discreet punishment. His sins were too reminiscent of those committed by too many in his social circle to earn him prison or death. His peri's sins were too common a story among women of her station to earn her justice. Poor little fairy; it was not such a light opera, after all."

"I wonder if your mesmerizing the Prince of Wales, caused him to forget entirely about meeting you. I mean, later, when we encountered him again. Or you did, rather."

I glanced at Irene. Her head was bent in a pose of deep reminiscence . . . or concealment. When Irene concealed, I recoiled.

"Irene. Surely you did not abuse your privilege of peering into the royal mind by planting any inappropriate suggestions?"

"It depends on what you mean by 'inappropriate,' Nell."

"Irene! You are an American still, and were even more of one then. It would have been unconscionable to use your moments of privacy with the future King of England to advance some agenda of your own."

"Was I really so terribly conscionable in those days? I can't remember."

"I can, and you were not at all conscionable! You were a petty thief and an inveterate meddler."

"Petty? I was petty?"

"Muffins are not a major item of theft, although you have always shown a distressing ability to appropriate what unclaimed valuables you stumble across."

"So has England and most of western Europe. My own nation was acquired in such a manner by the Spanish, the French, the English, and the Dutch. The sun never sets on the British Empire only because it has appropriated so much and so many in such far-flung parts of the globe.''

"I hope you did not instill your opinion on such matters into the King's enchanted ear!''

"His ear was not enchanted, Nell, but his mind was open, shall we say?''

" 'We' shall not say. I had nothing to do with this subversion, with this nebulous nonsense called mesmerism.''

"A pity you have never read Mr. du Maurier's *Trilby*.''

"Svengali! Who has not heard of that monster? He reminds me of a monster we knew far more personally.''

I shuddered then, recalling a past adventure somewhat more recent and far more sinister than the story Irene had related this night.

"His star rises now," she noted grimly, "but I suspect it will fall into the depths of the hell he deserves. In time.''

"Come to think it, *he* had a mesmerizing way about him. I have never met a man of such disturbing presence.''

"Except for your globe-trotting acquaintance Quentin, of course.''

I regret to say that I had finally grown too old to blush.

"And, perhaps, Mr. Sherlock Holmes.''

"There is no comparison, save as of an angel of darkness to one of light," I retorted with hauteur, one habit of the French I had acquired by virtue of long residence among them.

Then I was struck by an even more appalling thought.

"Irene. Is it, er, possible that you have ever practiced the mesmerizing arts on . . . myself?''

"I quite honestly can't recall, Nell. Was there ever a time when I waved a bright object before your face?''

"Dozens. You were always flourishing something under my nose, whether one of your few jewels or some silly object you claimed was the key to a mystery . . . Oh.''

I had recalled our very first night together, when Irene had whisked me from the streets of London to her Saffron Hill lodgings in the city's Italian district. We had shared a supper of ''borrowed'' muffins toasted on the fender, and a glass of what I now recognize as abominably inferior wine. And Irene had held up the gold wedding band just given to her by our strange cab driver, the American Jefferson Hope, a murderer who would soon die at the hand of a greater power.

Irene had lifted this object both homely and (in the Hope case) macabre. The flames had performed a devil's waltz in its contours as in a convex mirror, and after that, I remember . . . nothing.

Irene's remarkably warm amber eyes were regarding me over the delicate lip of her Meissen cup, managing to be both mysterious and enigmatic. Her pupils were darker than undiluted black coffee.

Was it possible?

With Irene, nothing was impossible, except knowing for certain.

*J*an Burke is the author of six novels featuring contemporary newspaper reporter Irene Kelly, including Goodnight, Irene and Hocus. Jan holds a degree in history and once worked as a history researcher before taking up writing. Her short stories—which have earned her the Macavity and the Ellery Queen Mystery Magazine Readers Award—have often been set in other time periods. She usually finds history more chilling than mystery: "A Man of My Stature" was inspired by a true story.

A MAN OF MY STATURE

Jan Burke

You are no doubt surprised to receive word from me, my dear Augustus, but although I have been poorly served by my obedience to impulse, in this case I think it best to give in to my compulsion to communicate with you now. If I have already tried you beyond all patience and forbearance, you cannot be blamed, but I hope that your curiosity—upon receiving a letter from a man you believe to be dead—will be strong enough to lead you to continue.

I have written a letter to Emma, denying, of course, that I had anything at all to do with the death of Louis Fontesque, and telling her that she must not believe what will soon be said of her husband. I will leave that brief note to her here, to be found tomorrow in these rooms I have taken at the Linworth Hotel. But tonight, after darkness falls, I will venture from this establishment one last time; I will make the short journey to the letterbox on the corner, not trusting the desk clerk to mail this to you. He is an honest enough lad, I'm sure, but after all, he now believes me to be Fontesque, and when the hunt for Fontesque's killer inevitably leads law enforcement officers here, the young man's memory may prove too

288

sharp by half. I would not bring trouble to your door, Augustus.

I think it best to give you some explanation of events. There are too many who, out of envy, would be pleased to see a man of my stature in the community fall as far as I have—and in my absence, I fear Emma will become the target of their ridicule. I will have more to say on that score in a moment.

But first, old friend—I hope I may yet count you my friend—let me offer a sincere apology to one who once refused a very different opportunity. Because of your refusal, you alone among my friends are safe from the repercussions of my downfall. You alone never supported my notion of creating a new formula for synthetic silk, you alone thought me bound for failure. I was baffled by your reticence, having been so certain you would be eager to invest in Hardwick Chemical and Supply's latest venture. I knew your objections were not of a technical nature, for although you have great business acumen, you are no chemist. Of course I made no acknowledgment of your professional abilities to our friends, but I was rather quick to point out (in my subtle way) your lack of scientific expertise. I took pains not to be the one who belittled you before them; still I planted seeds of doubt here and there, and made the most of any other man's critical remark. For your wisdom, for your foresight—I punished you. I might now excuse myself by saying that my company had done well for its investors in the past, or that I desperately needed not only their cash but their faith, or that I was myself wounded by your criticism of my dreams.

But even before the formula failed, I saw that I had wronged you, Gussie, and was never more burdened by regret than when I realized that I had done so. In those early days I was heedless, and imperiled not only my own fortune, but that of my family and friends. But as I sit here in a small hotel in an unfamiliar city, possessed of little more than a stranger's traveling case and my own thoughts, I do not miss my standing in the community, or my wealth, or much of anything, save Emma and my friendship with you. And so it is to you, Gussie, that I entrust my final confidence. What happened to me? I seized an opportunity, Augustus, and no serpent ever turned and bit a man more sharply.

My world began to fall apart a few days ago, when my shop foreman—have you met Higgins, Gussie? A good man, Higgins. Trusted me. Just as all one hundred of my employees trusted me. Higgins came into my office that morning and told me that one batch of material had been sent through a partially completed section of the silk manufacturing line, to test the machinery. Rolling the brim of his cap in his hands, he muttered his concerns; there seemed to be some sort of problem with the process.

"Maybe I just ain't seein' it as it oughta be, Mr. Hardwick," he said, "but a'fore we go any farther, you'd best take a look."

I was not yet uneasy. Why should I have been? As I followed him out of the office, I could not help but feel a sense of pride. We walked through the older portion of the factory, where most of the workers were busy with our usual line of products. Men smiled and nodded, or called out greetings as I passed. Higgins was talking to me about the problem, which still had not seemed significant. We reached the new section, the place where several large crates of equipment stood unopened. Higgins was going on, blaming the suppliers, of course, certain the trouble was with the raw ingredients and not the product itself.

I listened to him with half an ear as I studied the machinery and the failed batch and—I saw it then, Gussie, though how I kept my face from betraying the horror I was feeling, I'll never know. The process—my process, useless. A small flaw I could not detect in the laboratory, now magnified on the floor of the factory—after so many thousands of dollars had been spent on the equipment.

Higgins was looking to me for an answer, as were a

dozen or so of the men working near that section of the line. Looking at me, some with anxious hope, others with unwavering faith in my abilities. I kept my features schooled in what I prayed would pass for concentration on the problem.

"Well, Higgins," I said, "this will simply require a minor adjustment in the formulation. I expected that some little changes might be needed—no cause for alarm. You and your men have done a fine job here, it's nothing to do with you. Go on with installing the equipment, and I'll work on a new formula."

I heard audible sighs of relief. I told Higgins that I had some business outside the office that morning, and left the building. I walked aimlessly for several hours, thinking the darkest thoughts imaginable. The humiliation, the financial ruin—if it had only been me, and not so many others who would suffer, I might have borne it. And there was Emma to think of. I am sure that if you place yourself in my shoes, you will understand how terrible it was to contemplate any suffering on Emma's part. If I am not mistaken, you have a special fondness for her, Augustus. I am not suggesting that you have ever behaved in any other than an exemplary fashion, my friend. On the contrary, you have been all that is polite and respectful. But I know your affections for her will let you see what others may not, and hope that you not blame me for contemplating the fact that I was worth more to Emma dead than alive. This was not an original thought—any man with life insurance policies as large as mine will consider such a fact even in better times. The investors had insisted upon this very reasonable precaution, and no one ever questioned my buying additional coverage to protect Emma should I meet with some accident and predecease her. I knew that even if I died by my own hand, the investors would be paid. But while the investors would receive a payment under nearly any circumstances, Emma would be denied the death benefit were I to commit suicide.

Perhaps, I thought, I could disappear at sea, in a boating accident. But would there be some lengthy delay in paying the benefit to Emma if my body were missing?

I had walked some distance by now, and I grew thirsty. Looking for some place to find refreshment, I began to take note of my surroundings. I was in a part of town not wholly familiar to me, a commercial district of some sort. I saw a fellow in neat attire step into a nearby bar. I took out my pocket watch, the one my grandfather gave to me, and saw that it was now just past noon.

As I entered the bar, I was pleased to note that the customers were not by any means loutish. Clean and decently dressed, they were neither as wealthy as those of our own set, nor common laborers. It was not a rowdy group; most were quietly talking to one another as they finished simple lunches of sandwiches and beer. As I moved closer to the bar, one of the patrons standing at it turned to me and said, "Stopping in one last time before your journey, Fontesque?" He soon realized his mistake and quickly said, "Pardon me, sir. I mistook you for another."

"Well, I'll be—" the man next to him said, looking over his shoulder. "You can't be blamed, Bill."

"Don't put the gentleman to the blush, you two," the bartender said, perhaps wary of losing my custom. "What'll it be, sir?"

"Now, Garvey, admit he looks a bit like Fontesque," the second man persisted.

"You've something of his build and coloring, sir," the bartender, Garvey, said, "but you're by no means his twin." Then nodding at the second man, he added, "I'm sure Jim here meant no offense."

"None taken," I said, feeling a desire to camouflage myself among these men. I would, for a few moments, pretend to be one of them, step out of the odious role of being Jenkin Hardwick of Hardwick Chemical and Supply. None of these men would look to me for advice or guidance, none of them had the least dependence upon me.

"Good of you, sir," Garvey was saying. "What's your pleasure then, sir?"

"Same as my eagle-eyed friends, here," I answered, smiling.

The one called Bill smiled back and said, "On me, Garvey."

I extended a hand and said, "Harry Jenson," as naturally as if that were the name my mother gave me. Bill Nicolas and Jim Irving introduced themselves in turn, and we chatted amiably. Bill was an accountant, Jim, a purchasing agent for a manufacturing concern. I easily convinced them I was just returning from Seattle—which I had visited often enough to describe—and vaguely referred to an exporting business there. My appetite returned as I banished Jenkin Hardwick and became Harry Jenson, and Garvey brought me a beef sandwich. I had a nervous moment when Jim, admiring my suit, said that the job must pay well. I took refuge in smiling silence, and Bill, the more circumspect of the two, colored and quickly changed the subject.

My new friends left not long after, wishing Harry Jenson the best of luck, but saying they must get back to their offices. I nearly said that I must do the same, but caught myself in time. The place had emptied out, the lunch rush over, and I was swallowing the last of my beer when I looked up to see the very man I had been mistaken for enter the establishment.

It was an odd moment to be sure, Gussie. Garvey had told the truth when he said Fontesque was not my twin. Fontesque's eyebrows were a little heavier, his mouth a little larger. But he and I were of the same height, of the same build, and our other features were not all together different. His nose was as straight as mine, his eyes as blue, his hair was the same dark brown—only cut a little shorter.

He was as shocked as I, or perhaps more so, because I had the benefit of a warning. Upon seeing me, he nearly dropped the drummer's case he was carrying. An idea which had begun to take seed in my mind caused

me to linger; I wanted the opportunity to study Mr. Fontesque. Garvey smoothed the way, saying, "Louis Fontesque, as I live and breathe! I was hoping you'd come
in before Mr. Jenson left!"

Fontesque brusquely rejected the bartender's theory of
our likely (if perhaps distant) relation to one another. He
said he had no time for foolishness, giving the bartender
some disgust of him. Garvey served his surly customer
in a similar fashion, then was all politeness to me, filling
my glass with his compliments before he withdrew to
clear the tables at the back of the room.

Attempting conversation with my near look-alike, I
remarked that I would not be surprised to learn that we
were distant cousins, or some such. This was met by Mr.
Fontesque with a shrug and a return to the contemplation
of his suds. I was not daunted. Augustus, I ask you—
how many would not see this fellow's entering that establishment at that moment as an opportunity unlikely
to present itself again?

He was wholly uncommunicative until, seeing that he
carried a drummer's case, I expanded on the tale I had
told his fellows, and said I was the buyer for Hardwick
Chemical and Supply, just back from a trip to Seattle.
His attitude underwent an immediate change. He told me
that he sold hardware especially designed for the me-
chanical needs of factories like Hardwick's—pulleys,
cleats, slings, shims and such. I encouraged this line of
talk. After some moments, he blushed to confess that he
had once called at my company but was turned away.

"Why, I regret that I was not on hand to speak to you
then!" I said in tones of outrage. "If you remember the
name of the fellow who refused you, I'll see him rep-
rimanded. Only a fool could fail to see the value of your
merchandise to our company." At this Fontesque puffed
up. While he agreed with me (at length) that the fellow
who had turned him away was a fool, I schooled my
features into an expression of grave consideration.

Recalling that when Bill had mistakenly greeted me
as Fontesque, he had also mentioned something about a

journey, I took a gamble. "Allow me to make it up to you, Mr. Fontesque," I said, in the tone of one hitting upon a grand idea. "You shall see Mr. Hardwick himself! Will you come by our offices in two days' time?"

Fontesque looked so immediately dejected, I nearly laughed. "No, sir. I regret I won't. I'm leaving for San Francisco on the morning train."

My relief was vast, but I dared not show it. I frowned as if in concentration. "Hmm. Mr. Hardwick is out of his office today, but will return this evening. I am scheduled to see him in his office at eight. I know it is rather late, but would you be prepared to come to his office at that time? I feel we have done you a wrong, and would not like you to leave town with such a poor impression of our company. I should very much like Mr. Hardwick to meet you."

"Hardwick himself?" he exclaimed.

"Yes. I wouldn't want others to know I had given you such special treatment, but if you are willing to be discreet about this invitation—"

He readily agreed to it, swearing that no one could keep a secret like Louis Fontesque.

I made one other stop before hurrying back to the factory. As I sat in the barber's chair, watching the beginnings of a transformation, I refined my plans. I ignored the sullen pouting of the barber. Over that good man's objections, I had instructed him to cut my hair in a style identical to Fontesque's; as I left, I assuaged his outraged sensibilities with a tip more handsome than my haircut.

The journey back to the factory was, I knew, a journey that would forever change my fate. I found my courage in this thought: while the task before me was distasteful, it was nothing in comparison to the image of Emma living in shame and deprivation.

At four o'clock, as usual, I called Higgins into my office and asked him to report on the day's work. He remarked upon my haircut, as I had hoped. He then proceeded in his customary fashion and gave the day's production figures without looking at notes. Higgins, I have long known, has a remarkable head for numbers. I found myself thinking that if Higgins were better educated, he might have achieved any position. Perhaps he would have been sitting where I did, owning a factory of his own. Or planning a murder.

My questions to him were nothing out of the ordinary, but I made a show of stacking the coins in my pocket on my desk as he spoke. I lined them up, six twenty-cent pieces, two dimes, two three-cent pieces, three two-cent pieces and a single, worn large cent piece. "One dollar and fifty-three cents," I announced, scooping them off the desk and returning them to my pocket. I pulled out my watch then, and said that I must send a message to Emma, telling her that I would be late. I told Higgins that had thought about the silk process and was fairly sure that I had hit upon the answer to our problems. I would run some experiments in my laboratory that night.

Higgins asked if he might be of any assistance, or if there was anyone else who should be asked to stay and help me. I thanked him, but said no, it would not be necessary. There was nothing remarkable in this. My employees were used to my odd hours and solitary work in the laboratory.

In the hours between four and my appointment with Mr. Fontesque, there were many moments when I nearly abandoned my scheme. On several occasions, I thought of hurrying home to Emma, to see her one last time before I was forever parted from her. Nothing was more difficult than to contemplate leaving her without so much as a last word of goodbye. But I knew I could not hide from her the strong emotion I was feeling then, and all depended upon my remaining calm and presenting a picture of normality.

Just before eight o'clock, I went into the laboratory, and made my simple preparations. I could not bring myself to stay there, though, and began to walk around the building, making sure I was alone. The factory was empty, the machinery still. I recalled the pride I felt when I had walked through it earlier that same day. Would it die with me? Or would Higgins and the others contrive to keep it running? I thought the latter might be the case, and oddly, that made me all the more proud of the place. I turned my back on it and moved to wait in the reception area.

When Fontesque arrived, I had calmed myself. I took his coat and hung it on a hall tree near the front door. I told him that Mr. Hardwick was working in the laboratory. "He's about to conduct a rather fascinating experiment," I said, and offered to take him there. As we walked, I expressed my hope that Mr. Fontesque had not been forced to travel far from his hotel for this appointment.

"No," he said, "I'm staying at the Charles." When I said I did not know of it, he happily supplied its location. Good of him.

I opened the door to the laboratory, and stood slightly behind it as he walked in. The display of beakers and glass tubing enthralled him long enough for me to reach for the short, thick board I had left behind the door, to raise it, and—forcing myself not to shut my eyes as I did so—to deliver the blow which killed him instantly. I felt for his heartbeat to be sure I had not merely stunned him. There was none. Perhaps this is why there was very little bleeding. I exchanged the entire contents of his pockets for my own, even sacrificing my watch. I picked up his drummer's case. I carried it to the front door, setting it near the coat, and walked back to the laboratory. I moved the body to the place where I might have stood working, taking care not to let his heels drag on the floor. I went into my office, to my private safe, used the combination known only to me, and took most of the petty cash I keep on hand there, leaving some cash behind to avoid suspicion should the police break the safe open at some later date. I then had with me

enough money to sustain me in a modest way for a few
weeks.

I returned to the laboratory, started the fire and hurried
out, putting on Fontesque's coat and hat, carrying his
large and battered drummer's case.

The lamplighter had already passed through the streets
by the time I began to make my way toward Fontesque's
hotel. I hurried along the cobblestones, trying to turn my
thoughts from the destruction of all I had built. I could
not look back, Augustus, not even as I heard the cries
of alarm when I was several streets away. No scent of
acrid smoke reached me; only Fontesque's scent. It was
the scent of his cologne and his tobacco and his sweat,
his very body, some part of his skin left to line the coat,
an obscene lining made to fit over my own skin. I was
uncomfortable in it.

I pulled the hat low and averted my face as I passed
into the hotel. It was a modest but clean establishment.
The room key I found in his pocket was stamped with
the number 114, and I used it to open that door.

I had not taken a liking to Fontesque, but I was struck
forcibly with a sense of the monstrousness of my crime
as I stood in his room. The detritus of his daily life—a
lonely life, it seemed—moved me more powerfully to a
sense of shame than had his lifeless body. Scattered
about the desk and dresser were various wooden and
metal objects, small tools and pulleys and gears, the
items by which he earned his living.

His living. The irony was not lost on me.

On the bed were a few more of the objects, and an
open leather satchel with a stained handle. It contained
a pair of dark stockings, one with a hole in the toe; a
set of garters; a nightshirt; two cotton handkerchiefs; un-
dergarments; a pair of black suspenders; two neatly
folded shirts; a pair of trousers and two small wooden
objects not unlike the others on the bed. Near the wash-
stand was a dampened and crumpled towel, a bottle of
hair oil, a simple shaving cup and brush, a rubber comb
(I could not help but miss my ivory comb and its silver

case), a small bottle of inexpensive cologne and a little leather kit. The kit held a razor and strop, and a pair of scissors. There were a few sheets of paper on the desk, among them a carbon copy of a list of his company's wares. He had evidently puzzled over some sums, for one page held crossed out numbers and columns of figures; eventually I saw that he was trying to work out his commission on an order.

Knowing I would not sleep that night—I had no desire to lie where he had lain—I began to study the list of objects, and opened up the drummer's case. The case was much neater, being partitioned off into numbered slots. I began matching the objects to descriptions on the list of wares, and was able to place almost every item strewn about the room back into the case. In this way I occupied the worst hours, those when I most clearly realized what I had done, what I had lost. I concentrated on these objects instead of my sins.

In the end I had replaced everything but the two wooden objects I had found in his satchel. These were stained and worn, and were, I decided, most likely some sort of shim that had been returned by a customer, or which was no longer in use. I looked with pride at the case. I did not recognize all of the various implements, but this was of little concern to me. I had already decided that I would not take up Mr. Fontesque's business. Sooner or later I might meet someone who knew him well enough to reveal me as an impostor. Still, it would be best if Mr. Fontesque was thought to be alive, at least until I was safely out of town.

There was no trouble on that score. I changed into his clothes, packed my own with his belongings, and waited until the last moment before leaving the room to settle his account. The desk clerk was more concerned with the faces on the crisp bills than that of a departing guest, so I escaped undue notice. I did not want to be recognized while waiting at the station, so I timed my appearance on the platform just as the seven o'clock train pulled in with a loud whistle and a squeal of brakes, bellowing cinder-filled smoke from its stack. As the noise of its arrival subsided, I heard a paper boy calling out a headline: "Hardwick Factory Fire Kills Owner!" I kept my head lowered, purchased a paper and tucked it beneath my arm.

I boarded the train, praying that no one who knew me or Fontesque would be riding in the coach cars. The train was not crowded, and I set the cases on the seat next to me to discourage unwanted company. Oh, for a private car as I was used to! But no one molested me.

That no man greeted me as Fontesque could not surprise me. He had been a surly man, and of no importance to our community. I, on the other hand, felt sure that I might be recognized at any moment, even in Fontesque's sorry raiment. Imagine my feelings, then, when I opened the newspaper to hide my face behind it and was greeted with what was meant to be my own likeness on the front page!

It was, to be sure, a rather poor engraving copied from an old photograph. (You remember the one in the small wooden frame which stood above the mantel in the library? Perhaps you would be so kind as to discover if some Johnny Lightfingers from the *Clarion* stole it from my home?) As I calmed myself, I decided that the too-thin lips and enlarged nose in this depiction would be of help; perhaps I would benefit from the artist's lack of attention to detail. I am sure you saw the headline: J. Hardwick Killed In Fire. Aside from my growing dislike of the engraving itself, the two articles on the front page were all I could want them to be. I studied the article on the fire first. Although the pumping crew had arrived in time to douse the fire before much damage was done to the factory itself, the laboratory was destroyed. The fire was thought to have been the result of some experiment gone awry. The body found within the laboratory was burned nearly beyond recognition. (More thoroughly than I had hoped.) My coat had been found in the undamaged entry, still hanging on the hall tree. On the body, an object believed to be my watch was also found. But the prime piece of identifying evidence was supplied by Higgins, who indeed remembered that I had counted out $1.53—exactly the amount of heat-damaged coins found on the deceased.

Blessing Higgins, I moved to the other article, a touching tribute to my achievements that nearly had me weeping over the loss of myself. And so I went on to San Francisco, and booked a room at this establishment, the Linworth Hotel, which is neither mean nor luxurious. For the better part of two days, I slept, exhausted by events and emotions.

Last night I went out to obtain a simple dinner, and as I made my way back to the hotel, I purchased a newspaper. This I took to my room, and feeling much alone, began to read. The article which prompted this letter to you was on page ten.

The story of a fire in a northern city might not have been worthy of the attention of the San Francisco paper, but in this case, there were large insurance premiums which might have been paid upon Jenkin Hardwick's death. Might have been paid, except for one curious problem—the body of Mr. Jenkin Hardwick was two inches shorter than it should be. Two inches shorter? But Fontesque had stood next to me in that saloon, walked next to me, and always at my exact height! Our boots, though of a different quality, did not differ in the size of their heels. What had gone wrong?

I frantically searched my mind for some explanation, and found myself staring at Hardwick's satchel. I opened it and spilled the contents onto the bed. The two strange wooden objects clattered together like castanets. They were easily identified now: lifts. The damnable man wore lifts in his shoes!

To be undone by something so small as a vain man's attempt to hide his lack of stature is more than I can bear at this point, Augustus. Sooner or later, even a man like Fontesque will be missed, and when accusations of fraud are raised and his likeness to me is recalled by the patrons of that saloon, the truth will be known. Emma's nature will not allow her to lie to the police; neither is there any wiliness in her—I cannot hope she will think to mislead them by saying that I, too, wore lifts.

And, Augustus, although others may not believe it, Emma was at the heart of this, as she owns my own heart. Please, I beg of you, do all you can to shield her from what is to come.

I, for my part, will have made better use of my knowledge of chemistry by the time you receive this. In my room, an effective potion awaits me, a strong poison—one which will not allow me to fall short of my current goal.

Farewell, Gussie, from the world's biggest fool.

*B*oth *of Sarah Smith's historical mysteries,* The Vanished Child *and* The Knowledge of Water, *have been named* New York Times *Notable Books of the Year and both have made bestseller lists. In an attempt to break the cycle, she is working on a third mystery. She has been a tour guide, college professor, and manager at several computer firms; she now designs software. She lives in Brookline, Massachusetts, with her husband, two teenagers, her 22-pound Maine coon cat, Vicious, and Gracie, the assistant cat. Her hobbies are writing and brushing cat hair off furniture.*

Sarah's story, "Fearful," takes us back to fin-de-siècle Paris for an atmospheric recreation of life behind the scenes at the cabarets.

FEARFUL

Sarah Smith

❦

L ong ago, when I was just married, I saw a girl die.
I saw it planned, I was there when it happened. I
sat in the audience while she swallowed poison. Now
she haunts me, a pathetic outmoded ghost, a café singer
from the days of Toulouse-Lautrec, with her pleading
eyes and her outstretched hand. I've put her into stories,
I wrote a film script about her, back when I was a little
famous; but no one reads me now, and still she won't
rest. She still comes to visit me at midnight, and she
sings to me.

It's so dark, she quavers. *I'm so afraid . . .*

She of all people should understand why I did what I
did, but she's dead now; the dead never understand.

Read one last story from a forgotten old name, and
maybe you will.

Henry had married me to be seen with a girl a third his
age, so we spent our evenings out. Henry reviewed
everything, books, plays, cafe-concert, opera, even silent
films. We would sit through the first three acts, then rush
to the *Figaro*. Henry would sit in the smoky, sweaty
office with the other reviewers, smoking his cigar, scrib-
bling out his column on long sheets of galley paper, and
swearing at the copy-boy who waited at his elbow. He

had no time for society, or for me, who sat, with less to do than the copy boy, sucking at an end of my hair.

"Write something!" Henry growled. "Make yourself useful! You think like the ordinary woman. Write stories. You'll do well."

I wanted to do well for him. I admired him: his handsome eyes, the way his graying hair shone darkly in gaslight, his beard, his English suits, his name at the top of columns. Henry's name appeared in every newspaper; Henry had the best table at every literary cafe. I wanted him to love me; but I didn't need his love, I didn't know what need was.

Where we went depended on whose desire drove us: to be seen and heard (him) or to look (me). We both liked the café-concerts; Henry could shine as a reviewer and I could see Paris life. At the Ambassadeurs' garden on the Champs-Élysées, I listened with delight to Yvette Guilbert, scandalous scarecrow in black gloves, her dress hanging from the angle of her shoulder. She fascinated me, Yvette Guilbert, who sang like life itself, who could sing what I couldn't yet speak of, murder and suicide and rape, abortion and absinthe, slow mornings at provincial whorehouses, the swaying cabs of afternoon adulteries. Yvette Guilbert was the first real pleasure of my married life.

But almost as fascinating for me as Guilbert were the second-rate café singers. Those ordinary singers, with no talent, spoke to me, who had an admirable lack of talent, whose whole purpose in life was to be shaped by Henry, to be loved by Henry.

The Forbidden Fruits was an unknown café above the Square Perrin, near Montmartre. It was hidden away from the street, in the garden of an old house that had once belonged to one of Napoleon's mistresses. The proprietor had installed an overabundance of gas globes, which singed the leaves of the few trees remaining. The stage, at the bottom of the garden, was the size and height of a dining table; the café's inexperienced singers seemed to be balancing on it, and behind the stage a mirrored screen dazzled us. The audience sat enclosed in the intense public light of a salon or a railroad station. And into this fiery, chalky, Sahara-like desert, which we, the audience, shared with them, stepped one after another of the performers of the Forbidden Fruits.

They all performed under nicknames. The Bunch of Grapes, the Apple, the Carrot (we were not so fussy about what a fruit was!). Occasionally we had the shameful thrill of seeing a performer who had reached the boulevards pause here on her fall downward; less often, a star twinkled briefly on his way up. We liked the tarnished stars, the comic turns, the dog who played a cello. But my favorites were the rivals, the Peach and the Pear.

On stage, the Peach was sweet to look at, blond, straight-haired; she gave the impression that she would be sweet to eat. She was the first to find out that Henry was a reviewer, the first to send us some of the restaurant's bitter champagne and invite us backstage. Up close she was surprisingly hairy, like peaches found in abandoned gardens in the North, covered over with the yellow protective hairs that give them a masculine forbiddenness. There was a small gap between the Peach's front teeth, sign of lust. She flirted with Henry; I watched the down on her cheek and chin, watched him thinking she would need to be peeled before she was eaten, and touched my own, smooth cheek.

The Pear was a baby, younger than me, sixteen or seventeen, with earnestly curled black hair and a dumpy face yellow with powder. Like me, she loved la Guilbert; she wore the same drooping unlaundered dress, the same black gloves; she rolled her *r*'s in the same way, sang the same depraved songs by Paul de Kock; but what a difference! That round, inexperienced shoulder, as helpless as an exposed breast; those eyes of a kitten about to be drowned; that tiny wavering voice, barely making itself heard above the piano.

What she had of her own was desperation.

She had one "success," which she sang constantly.

She was a barmaid in Montmartre, she sang; she was a good girl a good girl, she never did what she shouldn't. But now it was late, the bar was closed, and she had to go home all by herself.

It's so dark
I'm so afraid
Won't you go home with me?

And she was afraid, trembling, begging us—won't you take care of me? Won't you love me? I'll do anything for you, she sang, throwing out her hands in a gesture of despair.

Henry clapped, approving of this desperation, and so did I. She wanted an audience. In Paris, who doesn't? The Pear knew nothing, she had nothing to give but her powder-daubed anonymous face and her little song. But she wanted to be loved, she wanted to be mirrored in our admiring eyes. She needed to be as necessary to us as Yvette Guilbert was, needed to be ours as Guilbert was ours. And we of the Forbidden Fruits, responding to her need, felt our power. We were her addiction, we owed her our applause.

We even gave her a special nickname, Fearful.

No one knew much about her. Henry asked the Peach, who said she was Fearful's best friend; but not even the Peach knew whether Fearful had grown up in an orphanage or a grand house, run away from a farm or a pimp. Fearful responded to every question with a momentary pleading smile and a shake of her head.

Henry would talk with the Peach, I would sit with Fearful. She would sometimes say a few words: "Did you like me? Oh, did you really like me?" and one had to say yes, because, if not, she would burst into tears. The Peach's top lip would draw a little up over her teeth, scornful of these tactics. For her they were tactics; for Fearful, the breath of life.

What is not worth having is most desired: The Peach wanted Fearful's spot on the program. I sat sometimes at one side of the stage, where I could see the Peach waiting to sing after her "friend." The Peach's silhouette was an education: chin high, crossed arms, foot tapping—not in time to the music! The Peach was a better singer; she had a more varied program, more of a figure, more colorful costumes. Poor, quivering little Fearful—what did we see in her?

Mr. Sonny, the English ballad singer, was something not worth having either. He had a big, half-handsome head and a barrel chest, but thin arms and legs; his eyelids were wrinkled and thick, an old man's, but his jacket arms were too short, as if he were still surprised by having grown tall. An *old boy,* as the English say, with long brown teeth, one in front carefully repaired with white wax, and brown hair of a shade that comes out lighter when washed.

One May night, when Henry was taking me on a night tour of Paris by horse-bus—to teach me the city, said he; because there'd been no reviews that week, thought I—we found ourselves in a crowd among two familiar heads, one blond, one a monotonous brown. We were just getting on our bus, but I caught a few words.

"Ah, she likes you," the Peach was saying to Sonny.

"But you know, my dear, I like you best."

"You be nice to her, because she's my friend. No one ever takes her out. Why don't you—" Our bus moved away. I saw her under a gaslight, tapping his hand with a flirtatious finger as he shook his head, laughing.

"The Peach wants to go out with him herself," I said to Henry.

He laughed and shook his head.

Henry was right: Next Sunday afternoon, as he and I were walking in the Bois de Boulogne, arm in arm, being seen, we spied Fearful and Sonny. They were dancing on the splintery little floor of an outdoor dance hall, to the music of an accordion. He looked a little bored, but rather complacent and flattered; she was so young. She was radiant under her hat, she talked constantly, she had an audience, she had meaning to someone at last.

"I want to write about them," I told Henry. "Sonny and Fearful."

"Forget about them. The Peach, she's the interesting one. Such a schemer."

Every day, during the mornings, I sat at the desk Henry had bought for me and wrote words into my notebook. Every afternoon I had a schedule, courtesy of Henry. I was to make myself known: a literary salon on Tuesday, open house at Mme. de Noailles' on Thursday . . . I skipped the literary salons and went to matinees at the Forbidden Fruits.

A café concert matinee was a ghostly thing. The proprietor kept the gaslights on, barely visible in the daytime; the silk flowers wired to the trees were spectral with Parisian dust. The fiddle and piano fought the clink-chock of passing wagons. I hadn't the heart to sit under the trees with my lemonade, pretending to be entertained; I talked myself backstage, I sat on the trampled grass in the shade behind the mirrored screen with the artists, as if I were one of them.

I have forgot to talk about the other distinction of the Forbidden Fruits. They served, as the specialty of the house—of course—"fresh" fruit. Fruit is nothing now, but in the belle Époque, a pear was two days' wages for a weaver. The menu listed a grand procession of mouth-watering delicacies—Indian mangoes! Australian melons!—but, to the waiter's infinite regret, when they were inquired after, they had just been sold, "the last one, madame!" The actual fruits were what one would expect: dried figs, tasteless greenhouse grapes, wizened strawberries, green summer pears clenched like babies' fists; and even those were suspiciously long in coming, as if some fleet-footed boy from the kitchen had been sent to the street market.

At the end of the summer, the first of the apples appeared, and Fearful told me her story.

She had come from a Norman farm, she told me. She had sung while she picked apples, sung in the fields, sung everywhere. (I thought this sounded as if she had read it in some idol's biography.) "Anything's better than a farm," she said. While she talked to me, she was picking at an apple core discarded by some diner, picking out the seeds. Apple seeds are poisonous, she said; so are cherry pits and apricot stones. She had thought if she never got away, she'd roast them and eat them. "It's cyanide. It would have worked quickly; one apple would have been enough." She held the seeds in her palm, black spots of desperation, and then, smiling, she threw them on the grass.

She was happy. Sonny had been kind. When they were—she looked at me, smiled, and blushed—when they were together, with an innocent emphasis on the word, they talked about the future. I could imagine, from my one glimpse of them, how they talked, how *she* talked while he looked a little bored, but complacent and flattered. Sonny was tired of always going from place to place, she said. In my head I married her to Sonny; I turned her into a young woman tending bar at a seaport, Calais perhaps, or Dieppe, where Mr. Sonny sang in the evenings while she listened with an indulgent smile.

She was happy, which lost her her distinction. She did not plead with us as once she had; we had lost our power over her, which was all that had brought us together. We knew it. We read the menu when she sang, chattered with friends, leafed through a newspaper. Her name slid down the program as the Peach's rose.

It was at about that time when, as I came home, I would smell a trace of perfume in the air, find a lace-trimmed handkerchief among the bed linen. My heart would beat hard. And, desperate to please, I would try to find a better phrase than "beat hard"; I would write more furiously, jealous and scornful of Fearful's happiness.

Happy women are all alike. You can tell their stories in two sentences. It's misery that gives them character.

"You know she's nothing to me." One afternoon I was sitting in the shade by the artists' entrance; Mr. Sonny and the Peach had gone around the corner, unseen and unheard by anyone but me.

"Ah, no, *quelle blague*." The Peach laughed. "You're going to marry Fearful, she told me!"

"More than I know," Mr. Sonny drawled.

"What a rose-covered cottage she's building for you, my friend. She thinks you want to settle down, 'now you're getting old' she says—"

"Ah! Old, am I?"

"No! No! Oh, you—Get rid of her, then. Oh, get away, you!" The Peach giggled. I crept away.

Backstage, a few moments later, I saw Mr. Sonny with his mended tooth and evenly colored brown hair, his graying top hat freshened with ink, a spotted handkerchief between his collar and his neck, which would be carefully removed just before he went on. I saw Fearful with her sweet complacent smile, her powdered face, her cow eyes, the look of a woman five years married, tucking the spotted handkerchief in her pocket to keep it safe for him. And I was interested in her again.

At home, that night, Henry wanted to spend the evening alone for once. "We're always going out," he said, looking at me as he had before we were married.

"But we have to go to the Forbidden Fruits tonight." I wanted to see Fearful with her desperation restored, rescued from her thoughtless happiness.

"I'd like to pay attention to you," said Henry.

"Then go with me!"

Fearful was rescued from nothing. She recovered nothing. She cried. On stage! She came on with her handkerchief in her hand—it was his handkerchief, Mr. Sonny's spotted one; she caressed it and smelled it as she wiped her eyes, timidly, with one corner, so as not to spoil it. Fearful's budget had not run to tear-proof mascara (she was an amateur after all); her lampblack ran down her cheeks in black clown tears. She sang her little song

It's so dark
I'm so afraid

Won't you go home with me? . . .

But we were not the "you," of course; and we knew it. We had not been her addiction, we were no more than her first banal romance; she had betrayed us for Sonny. A few of us, young men on the hard benches in front, whistled derisively, picked up bits of gravel and threw them at her. We catcalled, pounded the tables, shouted her name, but with the slow, mocking chant that bites like teeth, "Fear-ful! Fear-ful!"

The catcalls died into a horrible silence. She gave up any pretense of singing and simply stood there, twisting Mr. Sonny's handkerchief in her hands, until someone took her by the elbow and pushed her off stage.

But now we were here, we had to stay here. Henry talked to a friend; he ordered one of the famous house fruits, cut it apart with a little pearl-handled knife. He waved the knife in time with the songs from the stage. He fed me a slice of apple, making me open my mouth and stick out my tongue, feeding me like a bird feeds its fledglings. I swallowed it all at once, dry-mouthed.

"Now she has no one," I said. I wondered what she would do.

"Obviously," Henry said, his mouth full. "Not even herself."

I had not screamed her name, I had not thrown gravel, but in that half hour when I waited for Henry to finish his fruit and his conversations, I did nothing. I wondered what she would do. She had no one, I thought, but me who would write about her.

I did nothing.

And at the end of the half hour, behind the mirrored screens, a woman shrieked.

I ran, darting among the people who were pressing toward the stage. Behind the screens, near the door to the kitchen, was my familiar territory, the grass trampled with the waiters' feet. She twisted on the ground, gurgling, rigid, her back arched. Her heels pushed and scraped against the grass; her mouth was open and brown with vomit. Among the garbage from the kitchen, I smelled roasted apples and the stink of almonds. There was a tiny bottle in her hand, half full of black seeds. After all, she had never lost sight of despair.

"Get back," said someone, "there's nothing to see." I wanted to stay, I wanted to see everything. A policeman touched my arm. I turned on my heel angrily, as though I had a right to be there, and stalked out to the front of the stage. All the gaslights had a white, white dazzle.

The Peach was standing next to me, among the artists.

"I've had worse audiences than that," said one of the singers, laughing nervously.

A bowler-hatted man with a pointed beard, a doctor, hurried behind the screen. The audience was being sent away; I saw Henry hovering at the entrance, looking for me. We stood, listening to her shrieks fade away. The doctor had given her an injection, morphine, a miraculous cure—But what would she be cured for?

"Oh," said someone with a view. "Oh, poor kid." The backs of the men around her relaxed; there was no more urgency. At a nod from one of the men, the policeman left us to go behind the screen. The Peach's lip twitched; she scratched it, then turned the gesture into a dab at both eyes. It was Mr. Sonny's eyes that filled unexpectedly with tears; he wiped his lips with his sleeve, confused by his own emotions.

"She was nicer to me than you!" he said to the Peach.

The Peach let her eyes fill with tears. My husband, seeing her, patted her hand. I watched them; the Peach cried, my husband's hand crept over her wrist, one finger caressing it.

I think of them, Sonny and the Peach and Fearful. A man; a rival; a victim for love. I think of Mr. Sonny surreptitiously touching his front tooth to make sure that emotion had not dislodged it.

I think of Henry and myself. (We divorced a few years later, but here his photo sits on my nightstand by my nitroglycerine pills. I pick it up, an old man's photo cupped in an old woman's hand.) Henry made me a writer. Henry wanted a writer wife; I wanted Henry's attention—someone's attention. I watched her; I think of myself watching her, watching the audience, Henry feeding me, both of us knowing something was going to happen, and waiting. I saw myself that night in the mirrored screen, white-cheeked, shock-eyed, triumphant. I said, I will never forget any of this, not the mirror nor the ragged silk flowers on the trees above her, not the policeman's sagging veined cheeks, nor the smell; I'll be able to use it later, I thought, and I did.

I think of her.

She ought to be a finished little story, Fearful, that born victim, desperate, banal, a long-dead reflection between the stage mirrors and the mirror of our eyes. She did what she ought to have done, according to the best melodrama: She loved, she lost, she died. It was a bad story, the kind I loved. I still do, though such stories are out of fashion.

What I remember, what keeps me awake, is one gesture.

I remember her throwing away the apple seeds, and I remember her continuing the motion after that, flinging her hand up into a gesture almost delighted, not like a woman casting away poison but a girl sowing seed. Fearful is pointing toward something with that hand, that gesture; and that is how I see her, smiling, palm open wide, ready to receive something in return, some satisfaction, some happiness, a way out, neither the bar in Calais nor the pitiful apple seeds in her bottle, something she sensed but never found.

What could I have done? Tried to help her find it?

Listened to her, gone backstage that night, taken the bottle away? Interfered? Befriended her?

But then there would have been no story at all; nothing to write for Henry . . . but it wasn't Henry I ever wrote for, was it?

Read her story; read; try to understand what I did. Listen to me. Pay attention.

Because they are all gone now, and there's no one left but you.

Elizabeth Foxwell, the immediate past chair of MALICE DOMESTIC™ Ltd. is the editor or coeditor of several mystery anthologies, including Malice Domestic 7 *(Avon) and* Murder They Wrote *(Berkley), as well as the editor of* The Armchair Detective. *A fan of historical mysteries since Elizabeth Peters'* Crocodile on the Sandbank *was given to her in her—er—cradle, Elizabeth is also a scholar who has done research on author Vera Brittain and the feminist and antiwar movements at the turn of this century. She believes that "historical mysteries provide us with an entertaining but meaningful window into our past. They enable us to look backward at social issues and assess their impact on our present-day life."*

In the following story Elizabeth draws on her academic research as well as her talent for entering into the minds of the people of the past to present a different view of the final days of the Titanic. *This is her first published short story, but we are sure it won't be the last.*

UNSINKABLE

Elizabeth Foxwell

Sunday, April 14, 1912

Mrs. Simon's dark brows snapped together. "Really, Norah! Forgetting the baby's feeding schedule again! One would think you'd never been a nurse!"

"I'm—I'm sorry, ma'am." I grasped at the squirming Harry as the floor rolled under my feet. He clearly disapproved of the sudden departure of his customary nurse, and the arrival of this stranger in time for sailing. "My . . . my mind was elsewhere."

In the nightmares of the past, and of a tiny boat adrift in a black sea . . .

Did she suspect the truth? I prayed, as I have not prayed since those dark days in prison, that I should be allowed to finish what I was Meant to Do . . .

Mrs. Simon closed her eyes and exhaled, the long-suffering matron. "Very well." With a rustle of silk, she settled at the mahogany desk and reached for the pen. "I shall write it down for you."

"That's very good of you, ma'am."

A shaft of sun from the porthole reflected the rich red highlights in her upswept chestnut hair, and the motion of the ship did not sway the pampered hand with its perfect nails and flashing diamonds. Presently she handed the paper to me. "You *have* managed to remember that Mr. Simon and I have an engagement this evening?"

I bit my tempted tongue. "Yes, Mrs. Simon. I've arranged to have a tray here."

"Good." Her eyes slid away from my face—as most were wont to do—and glanced about the stateroom, as if surprised that her nurse and her maid would have such elaborately carved headboards and oak paneling, and gold light fixtures. But Mr. Simon, gentleman in banking, booked two staterooms on the outside of the ship for us and his family, and two staterooms in second class for his cook, chauffeur, valet, and secretary. His profession seems to suit him—and them—very well.

The maid came in from lunch, and Mrs. Simon, fiddling with her cameo brooch, fastened quickly on her, "Harper, have you mended my black satin for tonight?"

"Yes, ma'am."

"Good. I wondered if you'd ever manage it. Norah," she said to me, "don't *forget*"—she laid a sarcastic emphasis on that word—"to take Harry for his airing."

"No, ma'am."

"I'm going to see Mrs. Ryerson, if Mr. Simon should return."

Harper met my eyes behind Mrs. Simon's back. "I . . . think, ma'am, he's in the gymnasium. Racquetball date with Mr. Wright, no doubt."

"Quite." She turned smartly on her heel and marched next door to retrieve her gloves and hat. Then we heard the stateroom door slam, rattling the letter box on the desk. Harper whistled rudely between her teeth.

"Lady Thunder," observed Harper.

I looked at her. "You have not," I noted, "mended the black."

"Well, I'm going to do it now, so it's much of a muchness, Miss Nosy. No point in settin' her further in a stew." Tossing her head, she strode into the Simons' stateroom and reappeared momentarily with the rich black gown over her arm. "I don't know how she managed to tear this jet beading."

With his mother gone, Harry quieted and nuzzled my collar. I patted the flannel back absently. "Is Mr. Simon really in the gymnasium?"

Harper bit off the length of cotton with pointed teeth. "What do you think? Oh, and don't think you're saddlin' me with that brat tonight. I have a date in second class." She smirked with satisfaction.

"I had no such plans." I set Harry down to change him; as we sailed farther north, the air had become quite cold on the promenade deck. He, divining the approaching treat, gurgled happily, and I smoothed the downy head. Such a little angel, who was not frightened by scars.

"No, I don't suppose so. Not with that face, or washboard chest, or those tired shirtwaists. Pity."

Harper's litany of my lack of attractions grated, and I struck back. "Did you hear that Mr. Williams may be betrothed? A young lady he met during his European tennis tour, I dare say."

Harper's face fell. The wealthy Norris Williams, enroute to Harvard University, was a favorite of first-class mothers. Harper, despite her position, was equally susceptible to his friendly charm. "Idle gossip," she snorted, and I smiled as I bent over Harry and slid the exuberant arms, with a little difficulty, into his coat. Retrieving my own coat, I picked him up and hesitated in the corridor. The perambulator. Had the chauffeur retrieved it from the baggage hold?

"Mrs. Bird." Steward Faulkner appeared before me as if by magic. "How is Master Harry today?" He smiled at the baby, his nice blue eyes crinkling at the corners, and Harry grabbed his fingers.

"Oh, Mr. Faulkner, I'm glad to see you." I explained about the perambulator and he nodded.

"The White Star Line has some wheeled strollers. I shall fetch one for you. Will you be on the enclosed or open promenade deck? It is chilly, but the little one is well wrapped up. Your good care."

Unlike another baby . . .

"Ma'am?" The blue eyes sharpened with concern, as if he'd seen the shadow cross my face.

"Thank you, Mr. Faulkner," I said calmly. "We will be on the open A-deck."

His smile was really very sunny. Perhaps that was the reason I still felt warm even when I reached the cool promenade. Mr. Simon, distinguished in his grey frock coat and ascot, was leaning against the rail—not in the gymnasium—deep in earnest conversation with a rosy, dimpled young woman in a luxuriant fur.

"What is it?" Faulkner reappeared, stroller in tow.

"N-nothing." Courtesy naturally required Mr. Simon to converse with his clients' wives and daughters. Of course. "Nothing," I repeated more firmly, settling Harry in the stroller and walking away from my oblivious employer.

Faulkner fell into step beside me. "For your dinner later, would you care for some chicken? There is some nice fresh fruit as well."

"That sounds delicious."

"I must go," he said. "Shall I reserve a deck chair for you? Surely Master Harry will nap?"

"If he'll consent to it, yes." I smiled, grateful for Faulkner's courtesy. "Thank you for all of your kindness."

"A pleasure." He looked me fully in the face, and there was neither revulsion nor intrusive pity in his eyes, but a kind of—admiration? I looked away, pulse fluttering. Ridiculous. "Until this evening." He bowed and walked away.

I walked up and down the promenade deck with Harry until his eyelids drooped. Tucking the blanket more firmly around him, I settled back in the deck chair Mr. Faulkner had procured, and laid the rug he had thoughtfully provided across my knees.

A few hardy souls strolled the deck, the women with

their hands in plush muffs, the men in heavy overcoats, pausing occasionally for a hot lemonade. Mr. Astor was there, dignified in his dark coat and straw boater, with his young wife leaning trustfully on his arm. I prayed her unborn baby would have a happier fate than mine.

"Excuse me, ma'am." A bewhiskered gentleman raised his hat to me. "Have you seen the second officer? I wish to know our average speed from Southampton." He peered at me, and I quailed. Did he recognize me? Perhaps it was the scar . . .

"No, sir, I have not."

He smiled, a sheepish Father Christmas. "I have a small wager on the matter."

One of Mrs. Simon's lectures had been on the ubiquitous cardsharps who plied their trade on the commercial liners. It seemed that there were all sorts of wagers. "I did hear Mr. Ismay say it was twenty knots, sir."

His smile broadened. "Well, if the director of the White Star Line says it was twenty knots, that should be an unimpeachable source! Thank you, ma'am; I am obliged to you. W. T. Stead."

Mr. Stead, the journalist, once celebrated editor of the *Pall Mall Gazette*. I said my name; elaborate evasions were pointless when a passenger list was easily obtained from the purser. But not a flicker registered in the kindly eyes. He bent over the sleeping Harry.

"What a beautiful child. Yours?"

"No. My employers, the Wallingford Simons of Philadelphia."

He settled on a wood-slatted stool with every appearance of comfort, despite his generous stomach. "Do you have children of your own, Mrs. Bird?"

My throat constricted. "My—my son died in infancy, Mr. Stead." On an impulse, I drew out my locket and showed him the miniature I keep forever close to my heart.

"A great grief." He bowed his head a moment. "Yet I have a very firm conviction, madam, that you will see your boy one day in Paradise."

I blinked back tears, and looked away. "Th-Thank you, sir. It's my fervent prayer that we should not be parted long."

"It's an interest of mine, communication with the next world," he continued tactfully, as I struggled for composure. "You probably have heard of it," said he, with a rueful twist of his lips. "The estimable journalist William T. Stead losing his head and chasing after fairies, like my poor friend Conan Doyle."

I dabbed at my eyes with a handkerchief. "I have some small knowledge of it, sir."

"I am a very elementary student of spiritualism, madam." He leaned forward, his eyes shining, the portrait of the True Believer. "But I can see much more clearly since my contacts with the Other Side, in the séances I have attended and the revelations with which Julia Ames's spirit has privileged me when she speaks through my pen. Indeed, several of my clairvoyant friends told me not to board this ship, having the strongest vibrations of imminent disaster."

The dream again. I cleared my throat. "I too have dreamed of a ship, and a dark sea."

"Indeed. I felt it must be so, Mrs. Bird. You have a sympathetic aura."

"Then why sail?" I asked. "Are you not afraid, sir?"

"The American President, Mr. Taft, has asked me to speak at a peace conference in New York City. It is a summons I cannot ignore. I could ask the same question of you," he added. "But I suspect you are a kindred soul who has seen death, and does not fear it, as I do not. God orders as He chooses, Mrs. Bird, and as I have learned from my otherworldly companions, we are safe in His hands."

Mr. Stead stopped, and drew his watch from his waistcoat pocket with a smothered oath. "I have rattled on too long: I am late for an appointment." He stood and bowed. "You have been very indulgent to an old man, Mrs. Bird, and I am grateful." He beamed. "Especially for the winning of my wager. Your servant, ma'am."

He hurried away, and I pondered the eccentricities of
troubling to collect money when one's fate could be
sealed.

Unless Mr. Stead knew something I did not . . .

Harry yawned and beamed at me. Such an angel, so
like my own one. It was nearly time for his bottle. To
stretch my legs, I decided to take one last turn around
the promenade before we headed for the stateroom.

Harry tossed his blanket repeatedly out of the stroller
as we walked, but the moon face was so gleeful, I could
only join in with his giggles. As I straightened up for
the third time with the wayward cloth, I was surprised
to see Mrs. Simon laughing with Major Archibald Butt,
President Taft's aide, in the white wicker chairs of the
Verandah Cafe. She did not see me as we passed by.
Perhaps Mrs. Ryerson was ill.

I played with Harry for a while and then settled him
in his crib. Harper tripped out, painted and simpering,
to meet her rogue in second class before Mrs. Simon
returned. When Mrs. Simon did come in, flushed, she
did not notice, occupied with kissing Harry and asking
about his afternoon. Harry shied away, and then I
smelled the liquor on her breath. Her eyes widened, and
I followed her gaze. A cigarette case lay on the night
table, and I recognized the initials WS.

She ran next door, and presently I heard the pleasant
timbre of Mr. Simon's voice. "Good afternoon, my
dear."

"You've decided to return, I see. Racquetball games
are lasting much longer than I recall." I heard a sudden
thud, as if a shoe had hit the wall.

"I don't wish to hear it, Lilian."

"You will. I'm not the one who's been having a sordid liaison with my maid."

"Don't be ridiculous."

"Your cigarette case is in the next room. How can
you explain that one away?"

"Oh, isn't that priceless. An affair with the maid." I
heard him sigh, heavily. "I was searching for some writ-

ing paper. I must have set the case down without think-ing.''

''I am not feeble-minded, Wally.''

''Nor am I.'' His voice sharpened to steel. ''You have not lacked male companionship. I suggest you consider your position, my dear.''

''That is intolerable.''

''And I will not tolerate these accusations. I will have order in my household.'' There was a sound, a sharp cry; had she fallen, overcome from the drink?

He appeared quite abruptly in the doorway, tall and grave, and I contrived to look up from my book, as if heedless of previous events. ''Mr. Simon?''

''I understand, Mrs. Bird,'' he said quietly, ''that my case is in here.''

I held it out, and his hand was steady as he accepted it. Except for a little dishevelment of his smooth hair, he was unruffled by Mrs. Simon's outburst, as if by long habit. Perhaps she was subject to unreasonable fancies? He certainly did not conduct himself like a man with a burdened conscience.

He thanked me most civilly, as if I were a lady of his class, and returned to his stateroom. There was another sound, like a bird crying for its mate.

''You must dress for dinner, my dear,'' I heard him say, firmly. ''Harper has laid out your gown. You must make haste; we are to meet the Wideners for drinks first.''

He summoned me a little later, to assist Mrs. Simon with her buttons. Her eyes were red, but she accepted my ministrations and her husband's arm without a mur-mur. Ashamed of her earlier scene, perhaps. They made an elegant couple; he in his immaculate evening clothes, she a silent vision in jetty black and a smart set of grey pearls. Perhaps they would waltz under the glittering lights of the restaurant. I wished them a good night and closed the door.

Andrew Faulkner arrived with my tray and my heart

lifted in spite of myself at the sight of his good-natured face. He glanced at the crib.

"Fast asleep," I whispered. "For the moment."

"No surprise. He's an energetic 'un." He whipped the white cloth off the tray with a flourish. "Sparkling water, consommé, chicken, green peas, French ice cream with peaches."

I shook my head. "You are a wonder, Mr. Faulkner."

"I'm glad to hear you say it." For a moment his eyes held mine, then he bowed and departed.

Angry voices startled me from a semi-doze; I blinked at my little watch fob. After midnight. Mrs. Simon slammed the connecting door, but Harry slept on undisturbed, even when the ship lurched unaccountably.

Harper dashed in, babbling. "The engines—they've stopped. Th-there's ice in second class . . . the stewards are wearing lifebelts . . . we're all going to die!"

I took far more pleasure than befits a Christian woman in slapping the baggage soundly across the face, and Harper ran from the stateroom, shrieking. I heard Mr. Simon snap at his wife, "For God's sake, Lilian, compose yourself! Norah!"

I answered the summons. "Sir?"

"Assist Mrs. Simon. I will go on deck." He threw on his dressing gown and disappeared. I dressed carefully, my stomach knotting, but my hands remained steady and purposeful. What were Mr. Stead's thoughts, I wondered, at this moment? But there was Mrs. Simon to help. Her limbs were stiff with fear, and her dark eyes rolled.

"What could have happened? Oh, where is Wally? I wish he would hurry back."

I could hear a steward's shouts in the corridor, and thumping on doors. Andrew? "Brandy, Mrs. Simon?"

She gulped it, coughing. "Why doesn't he return?"

"He will in a moment, ma'am. I'll see to Harry now."

I roused the baby. As he rubbed his eyes, bewildered

at the abrupt awakening, I dressed him in his warmest clothes. The outside door to the Simons' room creaked— Mr. Simon returning, no doubt—and I slid Harry's shoes, not without difficulty, onto his waving feet. There was a sharp cry, just as abruptly cut off, and I paused in buttoning the shoes.

"Mr. Simon?"

There was no sound from the next room.

"Mr. Simon?" I went to the threshold.

Mr. Simon, leaning over the limp form of his wife, looked up, the eyes like a trapped animal. A dark stain seeped across the pillow, under the heavy chestnut hair. Time slowed, stopped, merged . . .

And Sam snatched the baby from my arms, and dashed him into the lake . . .

His fingers curled around a cudgel . . .

And just my screams, futile in the rushing darkness . . .

The two men's faces merging into one . . .

I think he stepped towards me. *Not again.* My cheek throbbed, and I seized Harry and fled as if the hounds of Hell were after me. They were.

A hard hand grasped my elbow on the staircase; I fought it, shaking.

"Norah!" The voice was younger, less studied than Mr. Simon's. I gazed into Andrew Faulkner's perspiring face, and choked out his name. He took a firmer grip of my arm.

"Come." He pulled me up the staircase—the rushing water was five flights below—and out on deck into the swirling masses around Lifeboat Number 11. He stepped into it. "Give him to me."

I did and hung back. He grabbed on to me, this strange new galvanized Andrew, and pushed Harry at a stewardess, plump as a penguin in her lumpy white lifebelt.

"Mrs. Simon," I mumbled, turning back. "Maybe she isn't—"

"It's too late for them." He yanked me into the boat.

"Let me go!"

"I'm not letting you go. Not ever."

A harried officer told him, "You stay there, mate; we need a sailor in there."

"Right," he answered, and sat next to me. Harry was placed in my arms, but I paid little heed. Tears slid down my cheeks, as the lifeboat began its jerky descent, and Harry's little fists gripped my coat. I hid my face against his bright hair.

Monday, April 15, 1912

I sat in a stupor on the *Carpathia*'s deck somewhere in the North Atlantic, wrapped in blankets that Andrew had scrounged. Dear Harry had come through, thank Heaven, with only a cold from being in the boat all night. I was comforted by the warm little body snuggling into my arms, but set him down hastily in the pram to avoid dropping him.

"Tea, love," said Andrew, appearing from the galley. The cup shook, and his warm hands closed over my cold ones. "Easy, now."

There were many in a far worse condition than I. Widows circled the crowded deck, searching forlornly for lost husbands and children. A few had happy reunions in the first- or second-class galley. A very few. My friend Mr. Stead, with his firm faith in Divine Providence, was not among them.

"Norah—" Andrew gently traced the scar on my cheek. "Forgive my clumsiness; I must ask. You have loved the child so deeply. Is there room for anyone else?"

I avoided the seductive blue of his eyes. "You don't understand."

"We've survived an ordeal together; I understand that. And you're shaking because of our narrow escape—"

"No." I pulled my hands away. "Don't you remember? I tried to go back."

Andrew's face drained at the memory.

"I knew what was going to happen. I'm shaking because I'm not dead. I failed." I covered my face. "That's why I was on the ship. To die."

The world seemed very still, the other conversations around us dropping away. There was only the sound of the waves—and Andrew's strained whisper. "I don't understand."

My hands twisted in the blanket. "My fault. My son's death. They said I did it. But the Home Secretary commuted my sentence. I had no way to atone."

"Why should you? It wasn't you."

The teacup nearly fell from my nerveless fingers. "How—how did you know?"

"You, and Harry. Your good care of him. Did your husband—?"

He read the answer in my eyes, and I bowed my head. "My fault that he died. Mine. He was my child, my responsibility."

As it was to be reunited with my own darling boy, taking my place on the doomed ship of my dream, as I knew I was meant to.

But there had been Mrs. Simon. I couldn't allow her to be branded as the murderess of her son, as I had been.

Perhaps Mr. Simon had seen the ideal way to rid himself quietly of her, as he made a dash for the lifeboats and the rosy young woman. Perhaps I would have died then too, had I not recognized that look, stripped of its moneyed glamour, from my husband's face, and felt the scar on my cheek throb. I heard Harper's voice. *I don't know how she managed to tear this jet beading.*

Perhaps he too had dreamed.

The blankets are very warm on the *Carpathia*, as Harry sucks happily on his bottle, and conversation buzzes among passengers grateful to be alive, and Andrew, dear Andrew, tries to coax me to eat something.

But I still shiver.

Michael Coney has written over forty science-fiction short stories and sixteen science-fiction novels, some of which are mysteries in disguise. His work has won the British Science Fiction Association award for best novel and has been nominated for a number of American and Canadian awards.

Michael grew up in England and emigrated to Canada in the early seventies, after a brief stop to manage a hotel in Antigua. Along with his writing career he has had several jobs, most of which either entailed pushing numbers into order or pushing drinks across a bar. He now does both only informally, and when not writing, spends his time trying to re-create a line of the Great Western Railway in his basement.

This story only just makes it into the category of historical mysteries, as it is loosely based on Michael's own experience as one of the children evacuated to the countryside in England during World War II. In case anyone should worry that it is too autobiographical, he assures us that his younger sister is alive and well in England, but that she did get the larger sugar mouse.

DOROTHY PAST AND PRESENT

Michael Coney

❦

Once she retires, a woman of sixty-two is an in-between thing.

No longer does she earn respect as a career woman; such glory lies in the past. And the glory that attaches to being a wonderful old lady ("You'd never guess she's ninety-two!") lies in the distant future.

So I, Mary Cartwright, am doomed to thirty years of living as a mere nothing, which is probably how I got to be on the books of Crystal, my analyst. I mention Crystal because it's she who got me into this trip to England, specifically to Long Acre in the county of Warwick, to dig into my murky past.

"Suppressed childhood memories are dangerous," she'd said, gazing at me earnestly.

"I've managed to suppress them for fifty-four years without any problems."

"We must bring them out into the open. Okay, let's run through the early years of World War Two again. You were eight, your sister, Dorothy, was six. You lived in Birmingham, England, a large industrial city and a prime target for German bombs. So, like many other children, you were evacuated to a safe place. Long Acre.''

"I was only there a month. I probably have a lifetime of suppressed memories, if only I could remember them.''

"You're avoiding me, Mary. Long Acre is where Dorothy died, and Long Acre is where you had your breakdown.''

"So they told me.''

There had been an element of deception.

We turned through an imposing pair of gates and stopped outside Long Acre lodge. A man and a woman darted out of the lodge as though pursued by flames, and smiled their way toward the car. They'd been watching for us.

"Out you get, kids,'' said Dad.

Suddenly I didn't want to; but Dorothy, ever confident, ever friendly, was opening her door. I followed her out and we stood side by side for inspection.

"These are the two little horrors,'' said Dad. He smiled at us in a false way he never did in real life. All the adults were grinning like crazy, gathered round us eagerly as though we were a barbecue. "And this,'' he told us, "is your uncle Ted and your aunt . . . uh . . .''

"Thelma,'' she said.

Something was strange, here. These relatives were fake.

"Well, now,'' said Uncle Ted, squatting and taking Dorothy's hands in his, "you must be Dorothy.'' His face was pink and countryish.

"So you're Mary,'' said Aunt Thelma to me. "Let's see, you're eight years old, right?'' In contrast to Uncle Ted she was the indoorsy type, probably snatching the apron off just before she'd rushed to greet us, leaving the home-baked bread and scones on the kitchen table.

We went indoors and our parents gave the rooms more than a passing glance; particularly the bedroom.

Dad thumped the double bed with his palm and Mom tested the dresser for dust with her fingertips. It was a dark room with dark wood furniture, just a little bit creepy. There was a big silver dolphin on the dresser, mouth unpleasantly agape.

"You're going to have a super holiday here," Mom said, trying to smile, trying to use the argot of the day.

I asked the obvious question. "How can it be a holiday if we have to go to school here?"

"And you'll meet all kinds of new friends."

"What's wrong with our old friends?"

Dad said, "I don't want you to be difficult about this, Mary. It's very kind of Uncle Ted and Aunt, uh, Thelma to take you in like this. Now stop arguing and kiss us goodbye, and we'll be getting along."

But I felt tears coming. Dorothy seemed happy enough, so I tried to take my cue from her, in case she took hers from me. We went through a tough kissing routine; I could tell Mom was in poor shape and Dad wasn't much better. Then they got into the car and drove off.

"Now, let's get you both settled in," said Aunt, uh, Thelma.

"The bedroom was creepy?" said Crystal. "In what way?"

"I never liked that dolphin; it kind of reared up savagely about a foot tall, on a plinth." I thought about it. "And the board at the foot of the bed was quite high and the door was beyond it. If you were lying in bed with the door ajar, you wouldn't be able to see if anyone—any*thing*—crawled in, until it was too late."

"Did anything crawl in?"

"Not to my recollection."

"You don't recall it, but that doesn't mean it didn't happen. This Uncle Ted. What kind of a man was he?"

"I remember him as much younger than Dad. Maybe mid-twenties. Playful, often noisy. He didn't resent us being billeted with them. Neither did Thelma. I guess they were a nice young couple.''

"But there's something that scares you about the bedroom. Is Uncle Ted connected in any way with this fear?"

I could see what she was getting at; a babe in arms could, these days. I tried to visualize that dingy room with the dark wallpaper. ''I think Ted and Thelma would come and kiss us good-night. I'm sure they did, because I remember Ted used to tickle Dorothy's ribs. She had an infectious laugh. Thelma would make him stop before she got too lively. Then out they'd go, leaving the door ajar, and we'd hear the radio.''

"Ted never came in alone?"

It was at that moment that a cold feeling came over me. Something frightening was clawing at the back of my mind; some ancient memory wanted to break free. Then it was gone.

"I don't remember," I admitted.

So now, fifty-four years older and presumably wiser, I arrived at the great wrought-iron gates of Long Acre. It was raining, of course, and the country road was slippery brown with the dead leaves of autumn. In my memory it always rained at Long Acre. I could make out the square stone lodge and the wide driveway curving away toward the big house. I switched the Avis car off and got out.

Ted and Thelma would be in their eighties if they were alive. "Ted won't represent a threat to you now," Crystal had assured me. Particularly if he was dead. But I'd been intending to visit the Old Country anyhow, and seeing Long Acre lodge might help to lay a few ghosts.

But the gates were padlocked.

Disappointed but reluctant to give up, I walked up the road and arrived at a tree-lined lane passing the back door to the lodge. I was knocking on the door when a heavily raincoated figure approached from out of the trees.

"They're in, ma'am. I saw them less'n an hour ago."
The man nodded and walked slowly on, head down,
about my own age, touching a chord in my memory. I'd
probably known him at the village school.

I knocked again; the door opened and a plump, elderly
woman stood there. She smiled uncertainly.

I said, "I'm Mary Cartwright."

Her expression didn't change much; the smile became
a little more vague. "I'm not—" Then came the recollection and the transformation. The smile became welcoming, the door opened further and she exclaimed,
"Little Mary Cartwright, the evacuee? Is it really you?
I can hardly believe it!"

But just before the smile changed, there had been an
instant of something quite different. Something almost
like fear.

"It's been a long time," I said as she led me through
a scullery, a kitchen, and into a living room. I didn't
recognize any of it, and certainly not the old man who
was struggling out of an easy chair by the fireside.

"It's Mary Cartwright!" cried Thelma. "Our evacuee. You remember little Mary, Ted?"

And I saw that same odd scared expression flash
across his face before he shuffled forward, smooth-faced
and smiling. "Mary. So long ago . . . So good to see
you."

There's no point in detailing the conversation of the
next hour or so; it was exactly what you'd expect. Halting reminiscences and the realization that we were complete strangers to each other. Now I know how
differently children and adults see things. Thelma did
the talking while Ted did the smiling. Nobody used the
word Dorothy, not once. It hung in the room like an
invisible barrier against relaxed conversation. I began to
wonder what I'd hoped to achieve here. Or if there was
anything *to* achieve. Ted shifted in his chair and sighed
during one of the many silences.

"Aye," he said. "The years have gone by. We've all
changed."

Was he referring to himself, specifically? Whatever he'd been in the past, he certainly looked like a harmless old man now. I was wasting my time. I said, ruthlessly, "Maybe we have changed. But you know something? I still miss Dorothy."

A quick glance passed between them. Thelma gave a nervous laugh. "I'm sure you do, the poor little mouse. Such a pretty little thing. Oh, how you two used to quarrel!"

Quarrel? "My recollection is, Dorothy and I got along just fine," I said coldly.

"Well, just little squabbles, you know. I'm sure that underneath it all you loved each other dearly."

"Yes, we did." The conversation had gone way out of kilter for a moment. Her referring to Dorothy as a poor little mouse had touched a nerve, too. I found myself panting as though I'd been running. They'd invited me to lunch but I needed a break from them. I stood. "I think I'll take a walk. The old school's still there, is it? Maybe I'll take a stroll over that way. I won't be long." I glanced at my watch. It was eleven-thirty. I made for the door.

"The old school's all closed down," called Ted.

The lane to the school headed off among tall over-hanging elms, immediately opposite Long Acre's gates. We always called it the lane, but in fact it was little more than a cart track, unpaved and rutted. Even in summer it would be dark with shadows, the kind of place kids nowadays are taught to avoid. On this fall day the ruts were full of rainwater. Huddled in my raincoat, I trod a muddy childhood path to school.

A sudden gust of wind brought down a shower of leaves, and with them came heavy rain. I hurried on, slithering among the puddles, when an unexpected greeting made me jump. It was the man I'd met at Thelma's door. He carried a long-handled gardening fork; the prongs glinted sharply.

"Terrible weather," I stammered. "You live around here?"

"Near enough." He was staring at me. "You were visiting the Snells."

"Yes, I—" It occurred to me to play it cagily; this man could be a useful source. "I needed some information. I'm writing a local history book."

"You're a Yank," he said suspiciously. "What's your interest in Long Acre?"

"I was born in Birmingham. I've lived in the States for thirty years. I guess we pick up accents."

"I guess," he repeated, chuckling and reassured. "I guess we do. You won't get much out of the Snells. They're newcomers. Been here less'n sixty year." He chuckled again and I found myself liking him after all. "Now me, I was born here. Went to school at the end of the lane."

"So . . . I expect you've seen some changes."

"Not much." He jerked a thumb. "Except they're building a bloody motorway right over our heads, right across all the fields. The school closed down twenty year ago. That's about the lot."

"People," I said. "Local history's about people, too."

"People are born here, people die. Most kids go to the city when they grow up. Me, I'm lucky. I work at the big house."

"There must have been some excitement sometimes. You know, scandals . . . accidents . . . the war years . . ."

He hesitated, thinking. "Did Ted Snell tell you about the little evacuee girl drowned in the lake beside the big house, early into the war?" His long face was sad. "I was about ten at the time, yet I remember it like yesterday. Over fifty year ago," he said wonderingly.

A pulse was thumping in my throat. "I expect I'll be able to get details from the archives at the local paper."

"Maybe. Ted Snell's your best bet. He found her." His eyes were faraway, reliving an ancient tragedy. "And I found him, standing there beside the lake with his jacket all muddy and wet, crying his eyes out, and the little kid floating near, face down, poor little mite.''

"Why hadn't Ted pulled her out?"

"Ted couldn't swim. I went out and got her. Towed her to the bank. She was so cold, I've never forgot it.'' He shivered as though to rid himself of the memory, and shouldered the fork. "I'll be getting along. Like I said, ask Ted.''

I watched him go, fork held at the shoulder-arms position but any suggestion of the military belied by his head-down, almost shambling gait.

And I knew him.

"There's Frank Fowler on his way to school,'' said Aunt Thelma. "Time you two were on your way.''

"How do you know it's Frank?'' asked Dorothy as we squinted through the frosty window. The boy was just a shape.

"Frank always walks with his head down.''

It must be a sign of adulthood, I thought, to walk with your head down. Frank strode on down the overhung lane and out of sight. He was a couple of years older than me. I'd first met him on the hillside above the big house, squatting over something.

"What have you got there?''

"Ferret.''

He unsquatted a bit. Fierce little eyes glared at me from his lap.

"What are you doing with it?''

"The other one's down here, see?'' He moved one knee and I saw the entrance to a burrow. "He won't come out. He's got a rabbit down there. Might have to dig him out.''

"Can't you just call him?''

"Independent beggars, ferrets are.'' He sighed, stood; stuffed the ferret in his jacket pocket and picked up a shovel. He'd made a decision based on the evidence, the way grown-ups did. He looked at me for the first time. His eyes were very blue. "Who are you, anyway?''

"Mary Cartwright. I'm staying at the lodge."

"Evacuee?"

"Ye-es." I really didn't want to admit it. There was a stigma attached to evacuees. I'd heard grown-ups talking about us as though we were all exactly alike, and none too clean either.

He said, "I'm Frank," and immediately began to dig.

"Where do you live?"

"In the village."

"Are you allowed to, uh, rabbit here? Uncle Ted says it's private property, all this."

"My dad works for Sir William down at the big house, Long Acre."

"Oh, I see."

He dug on briskly, tossing sandy soil aside. "Uncle Ted, you said? That's Mr. Snell in the lodge?"

"Yes. Aren't you scared of digging into your ferret?"

"He'll shift fast enough when he hears the shovel coming." He threw it aside, lay on his stomach and thrust an arm into the hole. "Come on out, you beggar," he muttered, then grunted in triumph and withdrew another ferret clutched firmly in his hand. He put it in his pocket and lay down again. "Ha!" he exclaimed, and pulled something frightful from the hole.

I suppose it was a rabbit. It had a rabbit's ears pathetically sitting on top of a mangled head. The rest of the thing was mostly red and dripping, with grains of sand sticking to it. I turned away quickly. I'd seen one eye, staring in frozen fear. The other eye had gone. The ground felt very cold through the soles of my shoes.

"Still enough meat for the pot," I heard Frank say. "Look."

"I . . . don't want to look."

"Shouldn't be scared of a bit of blood."

I walked along a further hundred or so yards of muddy lane, and reached the village. Originally the whole village would have belonged to the squire of Long Acre and accommodated his workers. But now the little old cottages, huddled around the village green, would have been updated internally and belong to sales managers and program analysts.

The school lay opposite the church. I'd expected a blinding flash of recollection, but all I saw was an anonymous, olderly single-storey building in local brick with stone trim around windows and doors. It meant nothing to me. I made my way down a short, overgrown path and peered in through a window.

I saw a classroom empty of furniture, although a blackboard attached to the far wall had not been removed. There was something else. In the center of the room stood an ancient cast-iron stove, its chimney rising black and rusty through the ceiling.

And the memories came . . .

The stove had a door in front that gave out tremendous heat when it was opened, but that only happened on very cold days. Otherwise the door was kept closed. Our teacher, Miss Pinchbeck, always hung her brown overcoat on a chair in front of the stove in the afternoons, to warm up ready for wearing home.

Every day she assigned the task of stoking. This was done twice during school hours; once immediately before the first class, and once during lunchtime. You slid a heavy metal bar into a recess on top of the stove and lifted out a circular plate. Then you poured in coke from a tall hod. It was heavy work, only entrusted to children over seven years old. One day it was my turn.

"Not like that! Stupid girl!" shrieked Miss Pinchbeck the first time I lifted the plate. "Don't try to lift it. Lever it! Lever it!"

I wasn't sure what she meant by "lever it." The other kids, all at their desks and waiting for the class to begin, were grinning happily. I was providing an amusing start to the day. I felt my face flush. Miss Pinchbeck, thin, gray-haired, came storming down the aisle. I flinched away. She always carried a flexible wooden ruler and she'd crack you on the head with the edge if you incurred her displeasure.

Dorothy was grinning too. It was unfair, the younger ones being excused this horrid job. Not because of the job itself, but because of the embarrassment, out there exposed to everyone.

Miss Pinchbeck shoved me aside and seized the bar. She tilted it down and the plate tilted up; then she slid the plate aside. "See?" she rasped, triumphant. "Perfectly simple, if you use your head."

As I sat down I heard Dorothy muttering "stupid girl" to herself, practicing for when she told Uncle Ted about it.

Just one good thing happened in relation to that stove.

One lunchtime I was stoking it when Frank came in carrying a can of Heinz baked beans. "Heat up these beans for me, Mary," he said, and laid the can on top of the coke I'd just tipped in through the round hole.

I thought no more of it and, my duty performed, went out to join the other kids, jumping in the puddles in the playground. Later, the afternoon class started. It was arithmetic—never a favorite of mine. Miss Pinchbeck had set two tests, an easy one for the younger kids, a difficult one for the older pupils, and was working through the class demanding answers. It was a terrifying situation. She stood behind each kid as he or she struggled to reply, and her ruler was in constant use. She started down my row, working from the back of the room. I heard someone answer correctly, and glanced around. Miss Pinchbeck's eyes were glittering with spite. She reached my chair. I could feel her standing behind me, ruler at the ready.

"The answer to number eight, Mary?"

I hesitated, doomed.

There came a monstrous explosion and a crash as the circular plate hit the ceiling. Simultaneously the stove's front door burst open and Heinz baked beans blasted through the classroom like buckshot. Fortunately Miss Pinchbeck's overcoat took the worst of it. Smoke began to billow around us, reeking of burned food.

Miss Pinchbeck screamed and screamed.

It was a queer thin sound, like I'd heard from the woods sometimes when Frank was rabbiting, and it wouldn't stop. We all turned to look at her, the first shock over. She stood with legs apart, hands raised like claws, pale eyes rolled up so they were all white. She'd be screaming still if the other teacher, old Mr. Scott, hadn't come hurrying in to see what all the ruckus was about, followed by his class.

"Gladys!" He seized her arms. She struggled, still screaming horribly, and in a moment they seemed to be fighting. She was beating at his chest with her fists. He slapped her across the face. I think he meant to hit her cheek but missed, and caught her nose. She clutched it, looked at her hand and saw blood. It calmed her down. She stopped screaming and began to sob, shuddering violently.

"Go home, children," said Mr. Scott. "School's over for the day."

On the way home Frank walked with me. "You won't tell them, will you?"

"Of course not."

"You're a good girl, Mary. I just forgot all about those bloody beans, that's all."

"Forgot what?" asked Dorothy, walking close by.

"Nothing," I said. "Nothing at all." And Frank patted me on the rump, one friend to another. Now all I had to worry about was talking in my sleep.

We sat around the table eating cold ham and salad. "I met Frank Fowler up the lane," I told them. "It was like seeing a ghost, after all these years."

"Frank?" said Ted thoughtfully. "I'm surprised you remember him. He was older than you, wasn't he?"

"A couple of years or so. He used to walk home with Dorothy and me. I saw the old school this morning; that brought back a few memories. Do you remember the teacher, Miss Pinchbeck? Whatever happened to her?"

"Oh . . ." Thelma hesitated. "She had some kind of a breakdown, didn't she, Ted?" And then she used the old euphemism, "They came and took her away."

"She was too old for the job," Ted said. "Couldn't handle the kids. It was wartime, see? All the able-bodied teachers were in the army or on munitions work. You had to take what teachers you could get."

"Did she ever come back?"

"No," said Thelma. "I don't know what happened to her afterwards. They got a new teacher, Miss Charlesworth. Nice enough girl but not really one of us, if you know what I mean."

Not one of us . . . What she meant, was that Miss Charlesworth was not a member of that tight little Long Acre clan encompassing the village and led by Sir William at the big house. The clan looked after its own, and had done since medieval days. The exigencies of war had knitted people closer than ever, bartering and sharing scarce food and clothing.

And a little girl had died.

She was an outsider. If there was anything unusual about her death, it would have been hushed up. The rest of the world would have been told of an accidental death, and the culprit would have remained free, at large.

"Frank tells me you found Dorothy in the lake, Ted," I remarked.

His knife clattered to the plate. "Frank said that?"

Thelma stared at me, open-mouthed and pale.

"Yes. He said you were crying, with your jacket all muddy and wet."

"Aye," he muttered. "I don't doubt it."

"You tried to pull her out?"

"Aye. I did that. Let's not talk about it, eh? It were all a long time ago."

"But Frank said nothing about your trousers being wet. You'd have been wading, surely?"

"Maybe he didn't notice, not with your little sister floating in the lake." His voice was harsh and angry.

Aunt Thelma said, "Let it go, Mary."

"So you'd been wading in there trying to reach her.

I'm trying to think why Frank mentioned mud on your jacket but not wet trousers."

"Maybe mud from sliding down the bank into the lake."

Or from a struggle of some kind; even a game. He could play quite violently . . . Then suddenly he'd realized she'd gone limp. He'd try to find a pulse, and fail. He'd look up, desperate, to see Frank strolling down the driveway in his direction. Frank hadn't seen him yet. So he'd drag Dorothy to the edge of the lake and roll her in. Then he'd give the body a push, just as one might push a model boat out . . . That's why his pants weren't wet. But it still wasn't quite right. Dorothy had been drowned, not suffocated.

"Frank said you couldn't swim," I said.

He didn't reply. I stood and walked across the room, opened a door, and found myself in the remembered, dark bedroom. On the dresser stood the fearsome dolphin, still there, still gaping. I glanced back into the living room. Ted and Thelma were sitting as I'd left them, staring at each other. I picked up the dolphin and took it over to the window. There was a brass plate on the plinth. It read:

LEAMINGTON SPA S.C.
EDWARD SNELL
100 YARDS BUTTERFLY 1938

The inscription had puzzled me as a child; the butterfly stroke was new, then. Had Uncle Ted in some miraculous way managed to leave the ground, flitting over the rooftops while spectators in the streets of Warwick applauded his feat? I sat on the bed, holding the dolphin in my lap. It was just a trophy. We lose our magic eyes as we grow older.

Ted had risen to his feet. He saw me with the dolphin. He glanced at Thelma, then began to shuffle into the bedroom until he stood at the foot of the bed, raising his hands in a gesture of resignation and despair. The lights were on in the living room; he was in silhouette.

And another memory awakened. . . .

We had a frightening bedtime ritual at Long Acre lodge.

Aunt Thelma would kiss us, cheeks smelling of lavender. But there would be no sign of Uncle Ted. Aunt Thelma would leave the door open when she went. As Dorothy and I lay there we could only see the top half of the doorway because of the tall footboard, and Aunt Thelma bustling about in the living room, the echo of her usual last words in our ears:

"Sleep tight!"

Dorothy would chuckle with expectation. I would freeze with terror.

Then Uncle Ted—who had crept through the door on all fours—would rear up from behind the footboard, roaring, his fingers grasping like talons. Just for a second he was *Tyrannosaurus rex*, then just as suddenly he was Uncle Ted again, red and grinning.

I would be weak and shaking with reaction, but Dorothy would be squealing with delight; then her squeals would dissolve into giggles as Uncle Ted approached her side of the bed—always *her* side—pulled back the covers and tickled her ribs, laughing as she squirmed. Her squeaky giggles reminded me of Shirley Temple. She looked a bit like Shirley Temple, too, curly haired and angelic. Truth was, she was a poisonous little toad who knew how to wind adults around her pinkie. Uncle Ted would kiss us, smelling of beer. And in the morning the window would be all fractured with frost patterns.

Meanwhile the bombs would have fallen on Birmingham and Coventry and missed our house. And because the bombs always missed our house, our stay at Long Acre lodge was pointless, and Dorothy's death was pointless too. Did our parents ever realize that?

Ted watched me from the foot of the bed, face in shadow.

I said, "You used to scare the hell out of me, doing your dinosaur act. I peed myself more than once."

"I'm sorry. I never knew. Dorothy used to pester me to do it, see? I thought you liked it too."

"Dorothy knew damned well it scared me. That's why she pestered you. You were right, we used to squabble all the time. I can't think why I'd forgotten." For reasons unknown, I'd sanctified my sister over the years since her death. Maybe that always happens with those who die young.

"Memory can play funny tricks," he said, waiting.

"What was Dorothy doing at the lake that afternoon?" I asked. "It wasn't on her way home from school. And any normal person, seeing a kid in the water, would swim out and bring her ashore. But instead you told Frank you couldn't swim." I couldn't bring myself to say, *You killed her*; but in my mind's eye I could see him lying on the bank, holding Dorothy's head under the water, then getting to his feet to be found by Frank with a wet and muddy jacket. That had to be it. I didn't know why, and I'm not sure I wanted to. But that would account for water in Dorothy's lungs.

"Let it be, girl." He turned and walked slowly back to his chair. "The inquest said she was drowned, and that's an end to it. Poor little mouse."

Poor little mouse.

"So long ago," said Thelma quietly. "Does it matter now?"

"It matters to me. And maybe it matters to the police."

"You'd best go," said Thelma abruptly. "Before we start saying things we'll be sorry for."

They stood up simultaneously. I wilted before their combined anger. I made my way out of the back door and heard it shut firmly behind me.

What now? Should I go to the police with my suspicions? I walked around to the main gates and got into the car. It was three-fifteen, still raining and miserably gloomy. I started the car up, still undecided, and backed into the school lane to turn around. There was no hurry. This thing had lain dormant for over fifty years; another day or two wouldn't matter. I could spent the night in Warwick and see how I felt in the morning. At the thought of a comfortable hotel and a drink in the bar, my spirits began to rise.

Except that the car didn't seem to be going anywhere.

I floored the gas pedal and heard the wheels spinning. I put the car into reverse; the wheels still spun. I got out. The back wheels were sunk in a deep and muddy rut filled with water. I looked around hopelessly. What did you do in a situation like this? I'd heard of people putting rocks and sticks and stuff under the wheels to give traction. If I was going to do that, I'd have to do it quickly. It would be too dark to see, before long. I began to snap sticks off the undergrowth and force them under the tires.

"Here, Mary!" It was Ted, carrying a pair of long mats. "Many's the time I've helped people out of this lane," he said. He laid a mat on the ground in front of a wheel, then knelt stiffly and began to work it down into the rut.

I knelt beside him, feeling guilty at accepting his help. His head was bowed before me, his hands pushed at the mat, forcing it under the water and jamming it against the wheel . . .

And the final memory came home to roost.

We never got prizes at school like kids do now. I suppose it was because of the war, and things being in short supply. We never got praise either; Miss Pinchbeck didn't believe in it. Once there had been Mars Bars, sweet and sticky, before food rationing came in. They were a thing of the past, like ice cream. It was all part of the wartime rule that you never got anything nice except for birthdays and Christmas.

And except for Frank. I found it difficult to believe, but I got Frank for a friend, and Frank was nice. We'd go for walks around the estate after school, and he never killed any animals while I was with him.

One afternoon while the class was drinking its free

milk, Miss Pinchbeck opened her desk with a strange expression on her face. She'd been acting oddly since the incident of the baked beans—which had never been mentioned since, so I hadn't needed to lie for Frank— and I watched her with alarm. Had someone put a frog in her desk; maybe Bill Collier, the farm worker's son? He often carried a frog in his pocket to frighten us with.

Suddenly I realized: Her expression was a smile.

This was even worse. What vile triumph was she about to enjoy? Was it something to do with the arith- metic test? She brought two flat boxes out of the drawer, placed them on top of the desk and gazed around the room, still smiling. We kept our heads down, sucking Government milk through straws, terrified. By now everyone was aware something was up.

"I have a treat from Sir William for you, children."

Treat? It was an unfamiliar word. We looked up from our milk, bewildered. Was this some dreadful sarcasm? Miss Pinchbeck could be bitingly sarcastic at times.

"I want you to come up to my desk, one at a time. Little ones first."

Doreen Randall was first, and I could see her hands shaking. Miss Pinchbeck held out one of the boxes. Do- reen relaxed visibly, took something from the box and walked back to her desk, smiling. I caught sight of a glint of pink in her hand, and something dangling. Oth- ers followed, and eventually my turn came. Miss Pinch- beck was still smiling. Things hadn't gone sour yet.

The box held rows of pink mice with tails made of string. I took one. It felt hard and rough-skinned. It had no legs; the underside was flat. It took it to my desk and licked it. It was undeniably sugar. This was an incredible situation. We'd got something nice. The rest of the af- ternoon passed in a haze of delight.

But matters took a turn for the worse on the way home. Frank was nowhere to be seen, so Dorothy and I walked home alone. Dorothy glanced at me slyly and said, "Rotten luck you only getting a little mouse."

"What do you mean?"

"Didn't you notice? Us little kids got much bigger mice. There were two sizes, you see. Big for the little kids and little for the big kids. It's fairer that way."

Fair? What did she mean, fair? Bigger kids had bigger appetites, and so should have had bigger mice. What Miss Pinchbeck had done was illogical. Or was Dorothy lying, simply to bait me?

"I don't believe you."

"Well, look, then."

I might have known. Dorothy hadn't eaten her mouse. She pulled it from her pocket, intact and gigantic, mocking me with black eyes. She was going to put it on the dresser in our bedroom and gloat over it. Uncle Ted would say how good she was, to have displayed such self-discipline.

I had an inspiration. "That's the same size as mine," I said calmly.

"It's not. It's not!"

"Of course it is. They were all the same size. Why should they be any different?"

Her lip trembled. "This is bigger than yours!"

"Prove it."

Baffled pause. "Well, anyway, I've still got mine."

"But you haven't enjoyed it. I can still remember the taste of mine. Sugar goes bad, you know. You've probably kept yours too long already. It won't taste as good as mine did. Here, let me have a lick." I made a quick snatch.

"No!" She jerked her hand away, a second too late. I brought my other hand into play, and so did she. We hauled each other to and fro while we both held the mouse in a firm grip. "I'll tell Uncle Ted!" she shouted. We'd reached the end of the school lane. Long Acre lodge was in sight, just over the road.

We slipped and fell together. I swiveled as we went down, so we finished up with Dorothy underneath. I rejoiced at how she'd get into trouble, getting her coat all wet and muddy. And with that thought, all the frustrations and irritations of life as Dorothy's sister came home to me. Her popularity, her goody-goody attitude, her prettiness—all used by people as a yardstick by which to judge me and find me wanting. I rested my weight on her while I twisted the sugar mouse from her fingers. I was blind with rage, thinking only of hurting her and eating that goddamned mouse.

It was a big mouse, made of hard sugar. I gnawed at it, desperate to get it down before anyone came along and found us there. I didn't even hear Uncle Ted's distant shouting. I'd reached the plump hindquarters when I felt hands under my armpits, dragging me off Dorothy and lifting me to my feet.

"Oh, my God," Uncle Ted muttered.

Dorothy lay face down in a deep rut. Muddy water covered her head. Her hair floated up like pale weed.

Ted sensed something, and turned to look up at me. He read my face like the pages of a horror story.

"It wasn't anyone's fault," he said steadily. "You were just kids. I was too late to save her, and I couldn't leave her there for someone else to find. Nobody was going to believe a kid could drown accidentally in a puddle; there'd be all kinds of questions asked. And I couldn't call the police right away, not to put you through all that. So I carried the poor little mouse down to the lake to make it look like an accident. Which it was," he added determinedly. "Frank found me there with her, mud all over me."

"Did . . . Frank know?" It was important.

"I don't think so. Nobody knew except Thelma. We didn't tell your parents. You didn't even know yourself. You'd shut it all out. You lay in bed for days like a dead thing. People said it was shock and grief from losing your sister. We didn't disillusion them."

I heard myself mumble, "Thanks," fifty years too late.

He straightened up, his face set. "Drive off now. You should be all right. Best if you don't come back."

So I climbed into the car, started it up and slipped it

into gear. The mats held and the car rolled smoothly onto the paved road. I glanced in the mirror. Ted was retrieving the mats. He didn't look up.

I drove toward Warwick. Will it be as easy to forget a second time? As I said, I'm sixty-two. Maybe when I'm a wonderful old lady the memory of Dorothy's floating hair will have faded. That'll be in thirty years time.